Seeking Eden

In a world where babies are rarer and more precious than diamonds, Tobin Winter has never even seen a child. When a passing peddler tells him of the rumor that babies are being born in California, Tobin leaves his small town and the only life he's ever known to set off on a quest – and find a new life.

Elanna is a hopemother, one of the few women in her community able to conceive and bear a child -- but never allowed to raise one. When Tobin arrives in her tight-knit world, pregnant Elanna decides to risk everything she has to keep her baby.

Together, Elanna and Tobin escape the city and set out for the fabled land of golden sun. Merely days into their journey, they discover another thriving community where babies are born and raised by their mothers, a place where Elanna and Tobin are welcomed…at first. Their new friends have enemies unlike any Elanna or Tobin have ever experienced, and soon there's no escape from the danger.

For any of them.

SEEKING EDEN

MEGAN HART

SEEKING EDEN

Chaos Publishing

ebook ISBN: 9781465736239

Print ISBN: 978-1-951868-27-7

photo credit: egal

cover: Chaos

Also by Megan Hart

A Night Like This

All Fall Down

All the Lies We Tell

All the Secrets We Keep

A Heart Full of Stars

Always You

Broken

Beg For It

By the Sea of Sand

Castle in the Sand

Clearwater

Dream A Little Dream

Exit Light

Hold Me Close

Hurt the One You Love

Passion Model

Precious and Fragile Things

Ride with the Devil

Stumble into Love

The Favor

Womb

Unforgivable

Pleasure and Purpose

No Greater Pleasure

Selfish Is the Heart

Chapter 1

"There was no apocalypse. Just a slowing down."

The peddler's words rang in Tobin Winter's head as he walked his bike slowly through the rubble. What he knew of the apocalypse he'd gathered from old television shows and movies he'd watched on Old Pa's ancient eTablet before the batteries had finally died, leaving nothing but a frowning icon struck through by a lightning bolt and a blank screen. From reading books he'd found in the library's science-fiction section. From stories Old Pa and Old Ma had told him about how things "used to be."

This expanse of cracked pavement with its rusting hulks of cars and trucks still parked in neat rows, along with the weeds growing up in their wheel-wells, sure looked like an apocalypse to him. Like some giant hand had reached down and taken up all the people, leaving only inanimate objects behind.

This was different than Eastport, which had been as empty as this wide stretch of buckled concrete but had never felt as abandoned. Nor had any of the empty towns he'd passed through along the way. All of them had shown evidence of human occupation at one point or another, even if it was something as simple as a ring of charred wood showing where a fire had burned, or the cleared-out shop windows proving that people had picked them clean.

It was different, too, than the tiny communities through which he'd edged, uncertain enough to be cautious and with Old Pa's warnings about other folks ringing in his memories. People could be conversation, they could be trade, they could be lots of things. They could be danger, too. They must've thought the same about him, because fires winked out and doors closed the few times he'd ventured into a small town, searching for any sort of supplies to supplement what he'd taken with him. He'd taken the hint. If he wanted company, and he did, he wasn't going to find it there.

He'd spent two weeks on the road, one full week picking his way along battered and sometimes completely overgrown local roads before reaching the nearest entrance to the Transcontinental Highway. A full day climbing the crumbling ramp, hauling his bike and gear along with him. Another week since then traveling along the road that had once connected Maine to Delaware.

He'd seen other big buildings from the Transcon, but they'd all been broken down and mostly destroyed, either by time or human interference or both. Nothing to attract him from leaving the high-rising concrete highway that bypassed everything below it. But then he'd spied this place, white walls shining in the late spring sunshine. Curiosity, if nothing else, had made him turn the tape-patched handlebars of his ancient and rusting bike toward it. A convenient exit ramp, curving and full of potholes but still sound enough to take his weight, had led him straight to it. Faded letters on the building's side said WAREHOUSE CLUB. It easily stretched several miles in each direction. The asphalt lot surrounding it looked bigger than Moose Island and all of Eastport's buildings put together. The immense structure looming up in front of him now was definitely abandoned but showed no evidence of destruction other than normal wear and tear from the elements.

Tobin shivered, not from the cool breeze, but in anticipation. He'd been avoiding buildings, wary of what might be inside them or of structural damage that could make them dangerous. He should probably head back up the ramp, get back on the Transcon. Keep going. He had enough food and water to last him another few days, and by then he might find another town or a rest stop that hadn't been fully plundered.

Or, he might not.

Tobin studied the parking lot again. No sign of movement. No sign of life, not human life anyway. The big glass doors in the front were stuck open. Grass grew in their tracks.

He stepped through them and into paradise.

There was more stuff in that building than Tobin had ever seen in his entire life. Furniture, most of it springing stuffing but some of it intact. Glass cases, many still unbroken, filled with jewelry and eyeglasses. Televisions and computers, their monitors forever blank. Batteries still in their plastic wrapping lined shelves reaching all the way to the ceiling.

Skylights let in enough sun for him to see the length of the store, and back there was more of the same. And food! Glorious cans and jars and boxes of it. Some were opened, crumbs and fluids leaking out to stain the concrete floor, but most of it, an incredible amount of it, looked untouched. He ran toward it like a child, incautious.

If he believed in a god, Tobin would've fallen to his knees right there and offered thanks. As it was he fell to his knees and began scooping up armfuls of packages. He checked only haphazardly for signs of spoilage, dents or bulges, mold. Years of lessons about food poisoning flew out of his head, and he gorged himself until he was fuller than he'd ever been. He ate things he'd privately thought to be as much fiction as the stories in which they'd appeared. Things with names like Oreo and Hershey's, cookies and candies of indescribable sweetness. Old Ma had spoken longingly of white sugar, soft white flour, sweet butter and something she called pizza delivery. All things of the past, gone for many years when nobody was left to cross the causeway to Moose Island and bring them to Eastport, or to make them at all.

Tobin ate until sickness forced him to stop. Then, again ignoring every safety rule Old Pa had ever taught him, he passed out in a pile of torn paper and gutted cans. He slept hard and woke, stomach still bulging, teeth and tongue coated with sticky sweetness. After resting for a while, he explored some more. He found an aisle marked "camping goods" and stopped, mouth hanging open. It was only when he tasted salt, the flavor bitter after so much sweetness, that he realized he was crying.

He'd started his journey on a battered bike with a faded quilt rolled up and tied with fishing line on his back, his last pair of socks on his feet, and a loaf of bread and a hunk of smelly goat cheese bound in a square of fabric. Before reaching the Transcon he'd spent hours peddling along roads in various stages of disrepair, some so bad he'd had to get off the bike and walk it around rusting car wrecks and potholes deep enough to break a leg. He'd slept, shivering, in roadside grass and washed his face with water he dipped from puddles.

Now, he stood in front of piles of unused gear, dusty but in perfect condition. It was too much. Tobin sat down on the cold concrete floor and put his hands in his face and cried until he thought he might throw up.

After awhile the tears stopped, leaving him drained. For the first time since the peddler had visited, then left him, Tobin felt as though his journey might succeed. He'd found enough to set him on his way, at least. Plenty of food. New clothes. New gear. It was a far cry from the poverty he'd known in Eastport, though he hadn't thought of himself as poor until he entered this building. He'd simply never known there to be such wealth in the world.

For Tobin, as it had been for Old Ma, Old Pa, Auntie Heather and Auntie Francie, life meant constantly making do. When your socks wore through, you patched them, because there were no more to be had. Not at either of the two small stores, which had been empty since before Tobin's birth. Not in any of the empty houses, either, because anything of use had been stripped from them just as long ago. When Tobin outgrew his clothes, new ones came from old ones, rolled and pinned to fit until he grew into them and then out again.

Food came from the ever-shrinking store of cans in the community storeroom, an old building Old Pa had scornfully referred to as a "church," or it grew in small garden patches. Aunties Heather and Francie had been proud of their gardens, always producing cabbages bigger than Tobin's head and cucumbers as long and thick as his arm. After Auntie Heather fell and broke her hip, dying soon after, Auntie Francie had never been able to make the earth yield such bounty. She said it was because the garden missed Heather too much. After she died of a fever when Tobin was ten, the three who were left tended the plots haphazardly.

Old Ma and Old Pa, who'd been ancient and wrinkled as long as Tobin could remember, kept chickens and a few goats. Old Pa made cheese and leather from the goats, and the chickens provided eggs, feathers and an occasional meal. Old Ma made bread and cake from some of the sea grass and the small crop of potatoes they managed each year. There was always plenty of fish and seafood. They'd never gone hungry, and if sometimes their mouths cried out for something sweet to take away the bitter taste of the sea grass bread, Old Ma doled out a few drops of precious honey to quell their appetites. What couldn't be grown or salvaged from stored goods had to come from one of the rare peddlers who sometimes made their way across the causeway.

The peddlers men and women who usually traveled solo but sometimes in small groups, could be counted on to bring all manner of wonderful things. Kitchen tools. Cans of exotic and interesting delicacies, like "creamed corn" and "frijoles negros." Sometimes clothing, never new but usually in decent shape.

Nothing like what was in this place.

He found a soft, warm sleeping bag that rolled into a ball so small and light it made his faded quilt seem like a boulder. He picked out a lantern, snapping the battery to start the power flowing. These batteries, fully charged, could likely last for the rest of Tobin's life, but he took another set just in case. The lantern itself, small enough to fit into his hand, was more powerful than the ones back home in which the batteries had been fading for years with no replacements available. It, too, folded up compactly so he could carry it in the backpack he found on the next shelf. A small camping stove was next, also powered by the super-charged long-life batteries that had once run everything from televisions to automobiles. Tobin tucked that into the backpack without snapping the batteries into life. Until he did that, they were dormant and would last forever. A small set of collapsible dishes and utensils also went into the backpack. Tobin hefted the weight. He could ride for hours with all this on his back and hardly notice, it was so light. He found a large canteen, which could be battery powered to keep the contents cool or hot, as desired.

The next row of the store outfitted him with new shoes, deliciously unworn, and socks. Greedily, Tobin took a dozen pairs of the soft, cushiony socks and stuffed them in the pack. He'd never worn a pair of socks or shoes that had not first fit the feet of at least a dozen other people before him.

New pants, new shirt. A lightweight coat that would keep the sun, wind and rain from his back. A hat to shield his head. Best and most useful of all, a large book of maps that would guide him on his way. He flipped through them quickly, amazed at the size of the world. California, once just a fairy tale land, became real. And far away, much farther than he'd ever imagined.

The knowledge sobered him. Looking around at the wealth, Tobin faltered. Did he have to go to California? He could live like a king here until he died. He didn't have to risk his life to find a place that might no longer even exist.

But he'd still be alone. The lack of damage inside this building and the abundance of goods made it obvious that few people passed through here. Tobin thought of the babies the peddler had promised and knew he would not stay. An hour later he was back on the road, riding a new bike and carrying new supplies, but with an old purpose.

"New York City," the peddler had said. "That's where you'll find most of the folks left here in the East. Sure, there's some in Boston and Hartford, but New York City's where most people went. Likely you'll find someone to go along with you out to California, if you want someone."

Oh, he wanted someone.

So Tobin packed up all his new gear and got back on the Transcon. According to his new maps, he was maybe a week's ride from New York City. There, he'd find what he was looking for -- and if not, he'd just keep going.

Chapter 2

Elanna loved the rooftop gardens. She loved the smell of the earth and growing things and the feel of young seedlings against her fingers as she plucked out the weeds threatening their growth. Working in the greenhouses and garden beds gave her a sense of peace she usually felt only when nursing one of her babies.

Today she'd spent hours in the honey house, cleaning the hives and tending the flowers forced into the early bloom necessary to keep the bees producing. The constant humming from the hives had hypnotized her into forgetting the passage of time. It felt good to work with her hands and distance her mind.

It wasn't until she glanced up and saw that the morning light had become slanting, late afternoon sun that she realized she'd been there all day. She didn't want to leave, but she did have other duties. Appointments to prepare for and keep.

She rinsed her hands in the basin by the door to the honey house and went out onto the rooftop. She shivered in the cooler air. The cooing, fluttering pigeons scattered out of her way as she passed the dovecote, but she didn't have time to stop and feed them today. She didn't even pause to peek into the small row of cages where the chattering, bushy tailed squirrels romped up and down the special wooden ramps and ladders built to keep them happy in place of the trees they'd normally occupy.

"Not going to help clean out the veal pens today?" Gideon asked as she passed him.

"I'm sorry," Elanna said. "I ran out of time. I have to get back..."

"Deigeh nisht, Elanna. Don't worry about it," the old man replied in Yiddish and flapped his hands at her. "You've done enough today. Gai avek!"

Go away. She could do that. Elanna waved and headed for the heavy metal door that led to the stairwell. She reached for the lantern she'd left waiting for her and twisted the knob. The light flickered slowly into life, barely illuminating the dark stairs. She fiddled with the knob some more, without real hope. The batteries on this lamp were almost dead. She'd have to get another from the storerooms.

She didn't need the light, really. She'd been up and down these stairs so many times she knew exactly which ones were cracked or hazardous. Elanna took the stairs two at a time, thinking of all the things she still needed to do before her first appointment. She hated rushing, but her time spent in the gardens was worth it.

How nice it would be, she thought as she rounded another landing, to simply get in a box, push a button, and ride all the way up and down the way people used to. No use in wishing for what would never be. It was better to concentrate on navigating the old and crumbling stairs without falling.

She made it to the last landing and burst out into the old lobby in less time than she'd expected. Intent on getting back to the Main Hall, she didn't even notice Job until he stepped out of the shadows to confront her.

"Getting your hands dirty again?"

Without stopping or turning, Elanna answered curtly, "Yes."

"C'mon, Elanna." Job caught up to her as she headed for the door to the street. "Don't be like that."

"Like what?" She navigated the series of tall columns dividing the room.

"You know." Job stretched his gait to catch up to her. For a minute, until he reached her, he had to take two steps to every one of hers. "Not so friendly."

"Watch out for the pits," she tossed back to him, stepping around one of the deepest ones. The carpet had long ago rotted away, exposing the buckled concrete that could easily trip the unwary.

"Damn it, Elanna!" Job yelled, sounding really annoyed now. "Wait up!"

She paused just in front of the door. Job caught up to her finally, his handsome mouth pulled into a frown she didn't need a lantern to see. He pushed her up against one of the columns, and she let herself be pushed.

"What?"

He tried to kiss her, and she turned her face away. "You know what."

"Stop it."

Incredibly, he sidled closer to her again, reaching for her hand. The smile she'd always found so charming left her cold this time. When he tried again to kiss her, she ducked away from him.

"It's not allowed, Job."

"You didn't mind before."

She'd been stupid before, and a lot had changed since then. "I care now."

"I won't tell if you won't."

He thought he was flirting, but his casual assumption she'd throw away everything she was for the sake of a three-minute schtup in the shadows turned her stomach. Especially since she'd proven him right in the past. She'd let that handsome face, those sweet words, turn her head, even though she knew it was wrong. More than wrong. Forbidden.

"Get away from me." Even though her voice was low and dangerous, it echoed in the empty lobby until it sounded like a dozen screams. "Don't you ever say such a thing to me again, or I'll go straight to the Beit Din."

This seemed to catch his attention, at least. "You won't. You wouldn't dare. You'd be in as much trouble as me. More, maybe."

"Get off me!"

Only by bursting out into the sunlight at last did Elanna fight away the tears threatening in her eyes. She scrubbed her face hard, willing even that last bit of pain away. She'd made a mistake, one she wouldn't repeat. Job wasn't worth it.

"Elanna?"

"Reb Ephraim." Elanna cursed the scene in the lobby that had forced her to reach the street five minutes later instead of earlier. Perhaps she might've missed the Reb entirely.

"What's the matter?"

"Nothing." Elanna wondered if her hair was in disarray, or her clothes. If he'd see the smear of her mouth where Job had tried to kiss her. There was no way to check discreetly, so instead she shifted uncomfortably from foot to foot.

"I thought I heard shouting." Reb Ephraim stroked his beard thoughtfully.

"I was laughing," Elanna lied. "With Job. In the lobby. It echoed, that's all."

"I see," Reb Ephraim said with another tug at his beard. "I will see you tonight, then, Elanna."

She had three other appointments tonight. She'd have to reschedule all of them. "Yes. All right."

She could deal with another night with Reb Ephraim, closing her eyes while he thrust and grunted above her, his face the color of an autumn sunset only not nearly as pretty. Then later, the trinket or the sweet wrapped in crumpled paper he'd take from his pocket and dole out to her like he was doing her a favor.

Watching him walk away, she allowed herself to close her eyes for one moment, hugging herself in the thin spring sunlight. A baby. She thought of a tender, downy head, and a baby's sweet scent. The weight of child in her arms. A mouth, suckling. Her nipples peaked at the memory, hot fluid leaking out to stain her shirt.

Reb Ephraim wouldn't make an appointment with her if he knew she'd already caught. But then she'd have to explain why she hadn't registered the pregnancy. Why she couldn't pick out the father from her precisely kept and monitored list of appointments.

She'd have to admit to everyone what she'd allowed to happen.

"Elanna!"

What now? It seemed that she spent all day and most of her nights hearing her name called. Everyone knew her, but did that mean everyone had the right to her time?

Instead of replying to the short girl who'd accosted her, Elanna only waved and smiled. It wasn't enough. Chedva plowed toward her, sturdy legs moving her along the dirty pavement with the alacrity and power of one of the Gatherers' trucks.

"Chedva." Elanna knew her lack of enthusiasm sounded in her voice, but she was powerless to stop it. The good mood she'd had from spending the day in the gardens had evaporated from the triple onslaught of Job, Reb Ephraim and now, and probably most horribly, Chedva. "What do you want?"

Part of Chedva's charm, or rather lack of it, was her complete inability to notice when people didn't want to be bothered. Clearly expecting Elanna to stop to talk to her, the other girl frowned when she saw she'd have to keep moving, too. She fell into step beside Elanna with a conscious effort that made Elanna grit her teeth.

"I just wondered how many appointments you had tonight, that's all," Chedva said.

"Three." Elanna spoke before remembering Reb Ephraim had booked with her. She didn't say anything about that. She could tell Chedva wanted desperately to ask who the appointments were with, but Elanna didn't say anything about that, either.

"Oh."

"You?" Elanna asked, though she didn't really care or want to know. She concentrated on putting one foot in front of the other. The pavement here wasn't as cracked and eroded as in other parts of the city, but it still made sense to watch where she was going if she didn't want to end up falling on her face.

"Oh, just one. But it's with Mered. And I'm right in the middle of my cycle, too. So this time I'm sure I'll catch."

Elanna tried a smile. "I'm sure you will."

Chedva, so far, had only caught four times since starting her flow four years before. None of the pregnancies had lasted longer than a few months. Elanna had begun her cycles at age eleven. In the past seventeen years, she'd caught nineteen times. She'd born thirteen children, and eleven had lived. Eleven babies to help the Tribe grow and survive. Suddenly, her irritation with Chedva made her feel awful.

"Mered's very generous," Chedva chattered on as she followed Elanna toward the doors to the Main Hall. "He gives all sorts of neat things. Sometimes clothes and stuff, but mostly candy. I love candy!"

Elanna glanced over at the younger girl, whose round body showed just how much she loved candy. "I'd rather have an extra hour in a hot bath, myself. Or an extra hour of light at night."

Despite the interruptions, Elanna had managed finally to walk the two blocks to the Main Hall. She hated living there, though it was considered by many to be a privilege. She'd have preferred one of the small apartments like those in the buildings surrounding the Hall, or one of the ones located just below the rooftop gardens, high above the city so she could look out her window and see something beyond the buildings next door. Sure, the apartments were dank, dark, without the amenities the Main Hall had, like the bath center. But they were private.

Chedva laughed uncertainly. "But you can have a hot bath or an extra hour at night if you want it, Elanna. You can have anything you want."

Elanna stared at the huge front doors of the Main Hall. Once, when the Hall had been New York's most famous department store, the doors had been made of glass, huge panes of it. Time and the riots had destroyed them. Now the frames were filled with scraps of metal and wood, fabric and plastic, all bound together. It seemed to her that the patchwork effect, created by the Tribe working together, was more useful and beautiful than any simple glass could have been.

She looked at the shorter girl again. "So could you."

Chedva had the grace to flush. "No I couldn't. I'm not like you."

"Like me?" Elanna said rather cruelly, unable to help herself. "You do the same thing I do."

"It's not the same," Chedva said.

"No," Elanna replied, thinking of the babies she'd carried and given away. "I don't suppose it is."

The other girl kept looking at her with a vapid grin, blinking steadily until Elanna wanted to scream. Instead, she forced a smile. It wasn't Chedva's fault she was a pain in the behind.

"Good luck tonight," Elanna said kindly.

"It must be nice," Chedva said wistfully. "Having a baby."

Now Elanna wanted to cry. Hot and surprising tears stung her eyes and her throat was squeezed by a velvet-covered fist. "It's more than nice. It's the best thing in the whole world."

Then she was crying, tears streaking her cheeks, and she fled into the Hall, not caring who saw her as she ran through the lobby and social rooms. She found the narrow escalators that had long ago ceased moving and climbed them, rounding each landing without even a glance to the people and rooms on each floor. At last she'd made it to the top, past the bath center and the latrines until she finally, finally reached the hopemothers' quarters.

Gasping, she flung herself through the open doorway without even pausing to press a kiss from her fingers onto the mezuzah on the doorpost. She passed the other beds and finally reached hers, where she fell into the softness with a cry of relief. Ironically, her tears had stopped with the running. Crying would soothe the dull ache in her throat and chest, but the tears were gone. She'd spent so many years forcing them away that when she needed them they wouldn't come.

Without leaving the bed, she reached into the small table beside her and pulled out a small ledger. Tiny, cramped handwriting filled in every white space. Paper was valuable. Just once, how she longed to write a letter using the lines preprinted on the paper! The luxury of it! But being able to write on anything was a luxury at all, and one she only merited because of her value to the Tribe.

She hadn't asked to be a hopemother. At eleven years she'd woken one morning to cramps and red-stained sheets and thought she might be dying. The realization that she'd only begun her flow had frightened her more than filled her with pride. She'd become a woman before she was ready to leave being a child.

Bracha, the mother who'd raised her, told her what was happening in her body. "Thank Adonai for this blessing. This is a rare and wonderful thing."

The event was marked with celebration and ceremony just as it had been for a hundred years. Elanna was presented to the Tribe in the Main Hall and given gifts to ensure her future fertility: extra rations for dried milk and meat to keep her strong. Later, they took her to the hopemothers' quarters and showed her the bed that was to be hers. They left her there with the other hopemothers, and she'd never slept another night anyplace else. She'd never been her mother's daughter again.

She could still remember the tears she'd cried that first night. The other hopemothers, some only a year or two older, understood. They'd all been through it, too.

Seven nights after her flow ended, she'd had her first appointment. The man had been gentle, but the experience was still awkward and uncomfortable. For both of them. By that time, Elanna had been lauded enough to be excited by what was meant to happen, young enough to think the promise of candy and admiration would be worth everything else. When the Beit Din learned Elanna had caught pregnant from that very first time, she'd been admired as never before. The pregnancy ended in the eighth week. Two months later she was pregnant again.

She flicked her finger down the pages. The first entries were written in a looser, younger hand. The writing grew tighter and more careful as she grew older and the list of names grew longer.

Here, an extra line denoted the man who'd sponsored her first pregnancy. A little further down the page, another line to note that the baby left her womb. Another few pages and another note. Her second pregnancy. And the list stretched on and on. She paused to mark with her finger the name of the man who'd fathered the first child to survive, but passed it quickly by. The child had died before its second day.

Out of all the forty hopemothers, Elanna had caught pregnant the most times. She'd had the most births and the most children surviving. She didn't need her ledger to remind her of those honors. She wanted it to remind her of the children.

She slipped the book back beneath her pillow and found the other item there. She pulled out the tiny nightgown, its pattern of ducks and teddy bears faded into an uneven whiteness. She brought the small garment to her nose, breathing in deep, but the scent no longer clung there. It had been over a year since her last infant had worn it. She rubbed its softness against her cheek, remembering the feeling of her babies' skin.

Elanna forced herself to put the gown back beneath her pillow. "Boaz!"

A little breathless as always, the hopemothers' squire ran into the room. "Yes, Mother?"

Though her heart leaped at the word, Elanna didn't show her emotion. Boaz called all the hopemothers by that name. It was only a title, not a term of affection.

His fine hair was the color of gold, not like her own dark auburn ringlets, but his eyes were the same piercing blue. He had her eyes and her quick tongue, and it got him into just as much trouble as it got her. He was eight years old. Elanna was not allowed to call him her son.

"I need to change my appointments for this evening," she told the boy gruffly. "I need you to run and tell these men I can't see them tonight. Levi, Nachel and Goren. Tell them Reb Ephraim has made an appointment with me."

"I'll go right away!"

She wanted to grab him and kiss the cheeks still so soft and sweet, even at eight. She knew he'd be highly offended should she try. Elanna contented herself with digging a sweet from beneath her pillow and tossing it to him. The boy grinned, his smile as much hers as his eyes. With a flick of his feet, he was gone and down the hall.

Elanna sank back onto the pillows for a few more minutes of respite. She was lucky to have such a soft bed. She ran her fingers over the fresh linens, unstained and smooth. Another privilege. Most people were only allowed to change their sheets once a month. Hot water and detergent was too scarce, as was the energy to run the washing machines, to allow any more often than that. In the hope-mothers' quarters, linens were changed every week.

She didn't have all afternoon to waste in bed, though, no matter how much she would have liked to. Reb Ephraim would expect her immediately after the evening meal. She had to prepare.

She made her way through the maze of halls and stairs to the bath center, which was empty except for the three old women whose job it was to fill and clean the tubs and shower stalls. Elanna nodded at them as she came in, but waved them back to their seats. She didn't have to show a ration tag, and she didn't need any help in the tub.

"Tub three's the cleanest," Raizel, the oldest woman said, probably grateful she didn't have to get up. "Have a nice bath, Elanna."

"Thanks, Raizel. I will."

Elanna went to the tub the old woman had offered, stepping quickly behind the ragged curtain and pulling it shut. It didn't close all the way, as usual, but nothing worked the way it was supposed to. Everything was old and had been repaired a thousand times.

The tub, too, was worn but still sturdy. Once it had been painted white, but years of skin sliding over it had worn most of the tub to a silvery sheen. Tub three was the largest out of the ten in the room, and Elanna's favorite. It was the largest and most private. Even if it had not been the cleanest she'd have chosen it.

Mindful of the time, Elanna opened the spigot until the water flooded out. It hissed and spurted roughly, the pipes knocking. Next she opened the battery panel at the front of the tub. Twiddling with the knobs was a delicate business – too much one way and the batteries would give off too little power. The timer would shut off before the water got hot enough. Turn the knobs too far the other way and the batteries would give off too much power. The water would become scalding, but the power ration would be used up before the tub filled. Sitting in an inch of boiling water was not Elanna's idea of a nice hot bath.

She sighed as she adjusted the knobs just right. The tub would fill with water hot enough to soak in but not hot enough to peel off her skin. Elanna shed her robe and slipped into the tub, enjoying the smooth metal against the curve of her spine. She closed her eyes, letting the water rise up over her legs and belly and breasts, feeling it finally settle around her neck just as the battery panel pinged and the water coming out of the faucet got cold. The stream of water shut off an instant later. Perfect timing.

The water felt delicious, as always. Elanna let herself sink beneath it, feeling her hair fan out and float, tickling her cheeks and nose. It was quiet beneath the water, and warm.

This must be what babies feel like in the womb, she thought drowsily. She let her hands find her belly. As always before an appointment, she thought about the miraculous mess of tubes and eggs and blood that could create and harbor life. No matter how many times it happened to her, she never ceased to be amazed. No matter how many babies she lost, she never ceased to grieve.

If only she could stay here, Elanna thought. Just sleep. Like a baby, protected. Floating.

Her hands rubbed circles onto her belly. Again, Elanna thought of a baby's soft skin and sweetness. She needed to register this pregnancy. Find a way to name a father, figure out to explain away the difference between the DNA of whatever man she'd named and the truth. Pray that even though Job had never been approved to have an appointment with her that nothing went wrong, that the child they'd created by mistake would be healthy. Without blemish or flaw.

Imperfect or not, she'd love her child, even if it could only be hers for a year. An entire year without appointments! A year to nurse and care for her child, watching it grow. A year to love it, and the rest of her life to mourn when they took it away.

Chapter 3

Buildings taller than any Tobin had ever seen towered over him, their blank window spaces like glowering eyes. Many of them were half-destroyed, the upper floors missing or exposed to the elements. Weeds and shrubs grew up there with crazy abandon, and he knew he hadn't imagined the glimmer of eyes watching him from the foliage.

He'd spent four days of hard riding and another two figuring how to get off the Transcon in order to reach the city. Apparently the Transcon had been built to bypass New York City like it did everything else, and though its exit ramps were well-marked most of them had become unnavigable due to damage. A lot of it looked purposeful, as though some time ago someone or some groups of someone had decided to cut off all access from the highway to the city beneath. Tobin had been able, finally, to pick his way down one rubble-strewn ramp, fearing at any moment it might collapse. After that it had been another day's travel across a swinging footbridge that had obviously been newer-built, though it looked as abandoned as everything else.

"So much for finding people here."

The sound of his voice rang through the dirty streets and

echoed in the alleyways. It embarrassed him. In Eastport he hadn't heard any voice but his own for over a year before the peddler came. Here in the city, among the garbage and the buildings, the clear sound of his own words flew back at him as startlingly as a slap in the face.

It wasn't the first time since leaving home that he wondered if he'd been right to follow the advice of a stranger. This city was ugly. Probably dangerous, too.

Tobin pushed his bike a few more feet, picking his way carefully around the detritus that threatened to maim him or the bike if he didn't watch his step. Shards of glass and other junk littered everything. He saw an old tire, charred and sprouting wires from its core. A doll's head, one eye poked out and replaced with a pencil stub. Paper. Unidentifiable pieces of metal.

A gust of wind rattled the garbage and made the hair stand up on Tobin's neck. He pulled his coat closer around his chin against the chill. He strained to look up, up again, wondering if he'd ever get used to the sight. Eastport's tallest building had been the church, and the bell tower had blown off that during a winter squall three years ago. Although he knew logically that they were man-made of mortar, steel, brick and stone, Tobin couldn't help feeling these immense structures had sprung from the earth full-blown, like mountains. Now he knew why they were called skyscrapers.

His stomach goinged. It had been half a day since he'd last eaten. He could stop and open his pack, scrounge around for the last of the bread and cheese he'd brought from home or open a few of the cans he'd brought from the warehouse club, but Tobin thought he'd wait. The sun was dipping too rapidly behind these monoliths for his comfort. Dark would fall in the city sooner than he'd expected. He needed to find shelter.

An empty space yawned at him from the ground floor of the skyscraper closest to him. Apparently it had been a storefront with a big glass showcase window. The glass was long gone. The sign still swung on rusted hinges, creaking.

"Schenk's." Below the letters were some other scribbles, words in a language he didn't recognize. "Kosher delicatessen."

The wind kicked up again, and the sign creaked back and forth with a sound like a kitten crying. It might have been a sad sound, or even a scary sound, but Eastport had many old shops with signs that creaked in the wind. The difference was most of those stores still had glass panes in them, if they hadn't been removed to use in something else. Even if they'd broken, the glass was never left to lie around on the ground.

"It's all we've got," Old Ma had always told him. "You can ask why we care, Tobin, when it's only us here, but that's what I'll tell you. It's all we've got."

When Old Ma and Old Pa had gotten on in years, too old to repair and tidy the town they'd lived in all their lives, Tobin had continued keeping things nice. Old Ma had died in her sleep, peacefully, two years ago. Old Pa had followed not long after, leaving Tobin alone until the peddler came.

He'd been the first in perhaps seven years or more, a wizened old man with hair the color and consistency of summer clouds. Unlike many of the peddlers who had visited Eastport over the years, he pushed no cart. Everything he had to trade came from his pack or from out of his mouth. Canned goods and stories.

Tobin had been happy to give up some eggs and smelly cheese in exchange for the canned goods, but the stories were worth more than anything he had to trade.

"There used to be billions of people," the peddler told him while they sat together at Tobin's scarred kitchen table. "Like the stars in the sky at night."

Tobin wanted to scoff, but couldn't. What the peddler told him sparked a longing he hadn't realized he had. He was lonely. A place filled with people, brimming with different faces and voices, called to him like some sweet but somehow illicit fantasy.

The old man slugged back a shot of Old Pa's liquor, the last in the bottle. "But then something happened. What, I can't rightly say. For a while it must've seemed like the world was full to bursting, and people didn't want to keep having kids. Then time passed and people started seeing that nobody was having babies no more. Even those that wanted them couldn't have 'em."

"Do you remember that?"

The peddler shot him a look of disdain. "I'm old, but I ain't as old as all that. No, son, I just hear stories. Tell the tales. That's all. People stopped having babies, and then there were no children to grow up and take the place of those who died. They had all those batteries to make their cars go and keep their lights on, power their cell phones, but nobody to drive the cars or turn on the lights or answer their calls. Nobody left to do much of anything."

Tobin tried to imagine a world overflowing with people. "That was a long time ago."

The peddler rubbed his eyes. "Not so long as you might think. A couple generations, maybe three, four...There was no storm of fire, like the God-pushers predicted. There was no apocalypse. Just a slowing down. Tell you what, son. Why not come with me? Hit the open road? I can't promise you we'll always have food in our bellies or a roof for our heads, but it'll be a lot more adventure than you're likely to find here. And I'm not bad comp'ny, if I do say so."

Tobin had never left the island, never crossed the causeway. Being alone had been sort of a way of life for him, though for the past year it had been more excessively lonely than it had ever been. He'd mourned his grandparents long enough. Maybe it was time for him to light out.

Before he could answer, the peddler laughed. "You don't have to look so excited. I get it. I'm an old man, and a stranger. You're likely looking for someone a little younger. A little more…feminine, maybe? Can't say as I blame you, son, though I'll say my interest in such things has long passed me by. I can tell you where to go, son. California. I've been up and down this coast a hundred times, Tobin, and I've heard the same stories over and over from travelers who come from the West." The old man leaned forward to whisper conspiratorially. "There are babies being born in California. Lots of babies."

They parted the next morning with Tobin still undecided. It might be one thing to go along with a peddler and another to head for a place Tobin half-believed was just another fairy-tale. The peddler didn't press him, just got back in the patched and leaking rowboat he'd used to cross the sunken causeway.

"Things've changed a mite since I was here last. Been about twenty-nine years or so, I'd say, since I last crossed this water. I recall your mother. She was a pretty thing. Hair just like yours." The peddler had grinned and waved good bye. "Wish I'd come across sooner, but there's no helping it now. Glad to see you've grown up all right."

It was not until that night, tossing and turning on his lumpy mattress, that Tobin realized the old man had been trying to say he was probably Tobin's father. It had been enough of a reason for him to leave the only home he'd known.

He looked back up at the sign. He didn't know what kosher meant, but he thought delicatessen was a sandwich shop. There wouldn't be any food left. He didn't bother with the door, which hung crazily on its hinges and was half blocked by a large metal can. Instead, Tobin stepped carefully through the front window, lifting his bike with a smoothness that came from long practice. Once inside, he propped the bike against the wall and dropped his pack.

Inside, the darkness was nearly complete. Tobin got out his new palm-sized lantern, the one with the fresh batteries, and turned it on. The front room, at least, was empty. If there had been tables and chairs, they'd long been scavenged. The floor was dirty but recognizably of black and white tiles, set on the diagonal. What had once been a glass-fronted case ran the length of the store in the back. The glass glittered on the floor now, and dust and rat droppings covered shelves that once must have held food.

At least the dust was undisturbed, which meant nothing had been here in a long time. Tobin wasn't quite ready for visitors. The lantern threw gargantuan shadows along the walls with every movement. Night had fallen fast and hard, and his stomach protested again, louder this time. He smiled. Old Ma had always allowed she could set a clock by Tobin's stomach.

Tobin didn't want to stay in the front room. The massive window, so innocuous in the daylight, now offered too much invitation to the night. He wasn't afraid of being alone, but in a strange place, he'd feel better if he were hidden.

Behind the empty glass case was another door, and through that, a compact and surprisingly tidy storeroom. The bare shelves lining the walls from floor to ceiling must once have been laden with supplies. Tobin shone the lantern as high as he could reach, not really hoping to find anything.

But wait! What was that, high up on the shelf, tucked so far back in the corner he couldn't be sure it wasn't just a shadow? There was nothing to stand on, but that didn't stop him. The promise of something to eat inspired motivation. Tobin used the shelves as a ladder, climbing to the top and snagging the small shapes he'd spotted.

Cans. Cans usually meant food. He was far from starving, but a find was a find, and he'd been brought up to never waste anything. Tobin pulled three cans and a glass jar back with him to the ground.

"Whitefish in jellied broth," he read on the glass jar. He shook it gently. Several grayish lumps jiggled gently inside a gelatinous mess.

Tobin put the jar inside his backpack. It didn't look like food, but it would be foolish to throw it away when he might be hungry enough to try it later. He'd eaten worse in his life, that was for sure. Maybe he'd have better luck with the cans.

"Manishewitz," he read. "Chicken soup with matzoh balls."

He had no idea matzoh balls might be, or what kind of animal might once have grown them, but chicken broth he knew. Old Ma had kept chickens. He'd scattered plenty of seed for them before leaving, but he knew most of them would be dead by now. Chickens were dumb. No survival instinct.

The other two cans were more of the same. The labels had faded and dust covered the cans, but they weren't bulging or dented. He'd eat one of them for dinner with the bread and the last of the cheese, saving the packages he'd found in the warehouse club for later in the trip.

Tobin made one last trip out to the front of the store to get his knapsack, backpack and bedroll. He felt uneasy about leaving his bike, but there wasn't enough room in the storeroom for it. He'd woken enough mornings already with spoke marks on his cheeks. It could stay out front.

Back in the storeroom, Tobin set the lantern on one of the higher shelves and turned down the glare a little. Unrolling the new sleeping bag, he paused to marvel for a minute at how soft it was. It had no holes, the stitches were still neat and clean, and the zipper worked. And warm! It was luxury, more comfortable almost than his bed had been back in Old Ma's cottage.

He busied himself opening up the stove and activating the batteries. In a few minutes the soup was heating quickly in his small pot, and the last of his bread was toasting on the other burner. He satisfied his thirst with a few quick swigs from the canteen, wishing it would rain so he could collect some fresh water.

He made a spot for his bed and sat cross-legged on it while he ate his soup. It was good and hot, with a sharp tang he recognized as salt. They'd used the last of their table salt to celebrate Tobin's eighteenth birthday, and ten summers had passed since then.

With the dark outside and his stomach full, there wasn't much else to do but go to sleep. He'd finished his last book two nights ago. Now, more than ever, he missed having someone to talk to.

Growing up it had never seemed strange to him that in books cities teemed with people and traffic jammed the highways, while on the island it was only the five of them. There were many things in books that didn't seem possible. Overpopulation seemed just another fiction, like people having babies just by having sex. Sex, he understood…or at least could imagine. Tobin had never seen a baby.

None of his family ever talked about what had happened to empty the world so thoroughly. Maybe they were too old to really remember. More likely, they didn't really know. Old Ma might reminisce about stores stocked with anything you could want, but Old Pa had told him once she couldn't possibly remember that. Their mother had been a young woman when the last stores on the Island were gutted. They'd listened to Mother's stories so many times it seemed as though they'd happened to them, but they didn't.

Tobin knew his mother had died just after he was born, leaving him in the care of Old Ma and Old Pa, and Aunties Heather and Francie. He also knew that the five of them were the only ones living on the island. There might be more folks on the mainland, but they rarely crossed over. For all intents and purposes, the five of them might have been the only people in the world at all.

His stomach full, Tobin got up to stretch. He looked around the small storeroom. Reaching out his arms, side to side, he could just about touch the walls. The accommodations weren't luxurious, but after being on the road for so long, an enclosed space, a safe place, was more than enough to make him happy.

Tobin wiped out his bowl and packed away the stove. Tomorrow he would start all over again, wandering the empty and desecrated streets, looking for the inhabitants the peddler had promised he'd find. The thought depressed him a little and excited him, too. He was setting out on a whole new life.

Tobin rolled himself into the sleeping bag and closed his eyes to sleep. When he opened them, it was because a knife was pressed to his throat.

Chapter 4

When he'd finished his pumping and wheezing, Reb Ephraim left the bed as silently as he had entered it. He started to dress, covering nakedness that only became embarrassing now that they were no longer engaged in the act. Elanna turned her eyes away, not wanting to look at him. Not wanting him to look at her.

It wasn't all bad, being with him. He performed quickly and competently, and always gave her something nice. She relished his speedy efficiency. He didn't waste time in pointless conversation. He didn't pretend he needed to woo her.

Elanna knew other people always had sex solely for the pure pleasure of it. Sometimes she envied those people their sweating and groping and guiltless, unpressured lovemaking. Most times she couldn't imagine what it would be like to make love without the knowledge that she might, this time, be creating life. Sometimes she couldn't believe that was the only time she did it.

"Here," Reb Ephraim said, startling her. She hadn't noticed he'd finished dressing. He handed her a small box that rattled when she shook it.

She forced a smile to her face and opened the box. The contents glittered in the lantern's dim light, and she bit her lip in disappointment. Elanna took the earrings, though she didn't really want them. A new pair of pajamas would've been a more practical and appreciated gift. She could've used a warm coat, too, or a new pair of shoes. Instead, she got jewelry.

"They'll look gorgeous on you, my dear." He sat on the bed to put his shoes back on, hunching to reach.

Quickly, Elanna knelt and slipped the shoes onto his feet, then tied them. "Thank you, Reb. They're beautiful."

He lifted her chin with his finger until she looked into his eyes. "But you don't like them."

Why did such a simple question cause her eyes to fill with tears? Elanna smiled anyway, afraid to wipe her eyes because that would make the tears real. She didn't want him to ask if she were crying. She just wanted to go back to her quarters and go to bed.

"I love them," she said, injecting as much sincerity into her tone as she could.

The Reb looked at her for a long time. Elanna noticed the lines around his eyes and the streaks of gray in his hair and beard. The Reb looked tired. And old.

"I'm an old man," Reb Ephraim said, as if echoing her thoughts.

"No," Elanna began in protest, but he waved her to silence.

"Hush, my dear. I'm an old man, and I know it. I suppose I've forgotten what it is that young girls like." He leaned forward, hands on his knees. "Now, what would you really want?"

She was treading uneven ground. If she told him what she really wanted, he could become insulted that she didn't like the earrings. If she insisted the jewelry was fine, he might get angry at her lies, and she'd get nothing. Elanna swallowed, hating the games she felt forced to play.

"I'd like longer than a year," she ventured. Her words emboldened her. "I'd like to raise a child as my own."

She half-held her breath, waiting for him to strike her. At the very least, to shout. Reb Ephraim was a kind man, but there were limits even for him.

"Elanna," Reb Ephraim sighed and touched her cheek gently. "I wish we all could have what you ask for. But I'm afraid…"

"It's not possible. I understand." She ducked her head to hide her disappointment and anger.

Getting up, she straightened her clothes and began to fix her hair. She held her shoulders straight as she looked into the mirror. She didn't want him to see her agitation.

"Elanna," Reb Ephraim said. "Come here and sit down."

Her first thought was: Again? But she shrugged it away as she did what he ordered. It was unlikely he'd be able to manage again so soon, but if he wanted to try she had to comply. It was her job. Her duty to the Tribe.

"Yes, Reb Ephraim." Her voice shook a little and so did her hands.

"My dear," the Reb said, turning her gently until she looked at him. "We've spent many nights together like this, haven't we?"

She nodded, not trusting herself to speak. The Reb smiled at her. She could not force herself to return the expression.

"You've borne me children, Elanna," the Reb continued. He looked over her shoulder, his gaze far away. "Do you think I don't remember that each time I lay with you?"

"I don't know what you think," she blurted. The Reb had never spoken to her like this before.

He was still looking far away. "You're a beautiful young woman, you know that. But that alone is not enough to bring me to your bed. I'm a married man. I love my wife. I don't come to you out of lust. That would be a violation of the vows I shared with Miriam under the chuppah."

Now he looked at her directly, his face seeming older but his eyes alight with fire. "I know you keep appointments with any who've been deemed an acceptable match, as is required by our law. I know, too, that the motives of some of those men aren't pure. But that doesn't matter, my dear. You're a hopemother. You have a wondrous, precious capacity. You're the future of this tribe, Elanna. Don't ever forget that."

"As if I could," she said more bitterly than she had intended.

Reb Ephraim's eyes grew soft. "Aren't you happy?"

"I don't know." Her honesty stung even her.

He shook his head. "You live a privileged life. You can have what normal women only dream of. You can bear children."

"I can't get married." Elanna got up from the bed. It would make saying what she felt easier, if she didn't have to see his face. "I can't have a family. I can bear children, but I can't keep them."

"How else would a hopemother be able to perform her duties? If she's emotionally and physically taken up with raising a child, how can she be expected to open herself up? How can she expect to start keeping appointments again, or get pregnant again?"

"Women did it." She whirled on him, fists clenched. "Women had lots of children, and they didn't have to give any of them away!"

"Two hundred years ago, perhaps," the Reb said, undaunted by her sudden temper. "But you know that's not possible now. And what of the women who can't have children? Would you deny them the joy of motherhood, simply because you choose to be selfish?"

But they're mine, she thought, even as she knew she could never have raised eleven children herself. Even as she knew she didn't care. "It's not fair."

"Really, Elanna," Reb Ephraim said reproachfully. "I'm surprised at you. This behavior I might have expected from some of the other hopemothers, but not you. You've always been such a good girl."

She had nothing to say. So she swallowed her anger as she'd done so often over the years and stood aside to watch him leave. When he'd gone, Elanna looked down at the bed, at the rumpled sheets and strewn covers that had everything to do with lovemaking and nothing whatsoever to do with love.

She wanted to scream and could not. She wanted to cry and would not. Elanna sank down onto the bed and pressed the heels of her palms hard against her eyes. Her breath felt thick and heavy, and she forced it to calm.

This sudden lack of control over her emotions scared her. She always felt a bit weepy in the first weeks of pregnancy, but this time was different. She'd been walking on eggshells for weeks now, struggling with her temper and fighting tears at the slightest provocation.

Everything and everyone grated on her nerves. Even the things that used to bring her joy -- sharing a meal with friends, gathering in the social hall, visiting the gardens, nothing satisfied her anymore. It was as though she were made of glass, and anything could make her splinter.

She checked the mirror to make sure she looked all right. Aside from a little redness around her eyes, she looked as she always did. Reb Ephraim had called her a beautiful young woman, and Elanna supposed he was right.

Men had told her they loved her blue eyes, or her dark auburn curls. They loved her full red lips, her heavy breasts, her rounded belly. Most of all they loved the womb they hoped might fill with their child. Men loved every piece of her, but not one had ever loved all of her.

She didn't want to stay here any longer. The room was just one of a dozen exactly like it. It was only large enough for a bed, a chair and a washbasin, and it was as bland and featureless as oatmeal. It suddenly disgusted her.

Yanking open the flimsy door, Elanna burst out into the hallway and straight into a solid male body. She hit him so hard he staggered, knocking against the corridor's opposite wall. He coughed, rubbing the elbow that had received the brunt of the blow.

"Job!"

"About today," he began.

She shook her head, shushing him. "Forget it. I was being stupid."

"I'm sorry, Elanna." Job touched her shoulder. "I wish I knew how to make you happy."

"Don't I seem happy?"

"No," he answered. "You don't."

She felt the carefully constructed wall of her expression begin to break. "Let's not talk, okay?"

Job had been determined to be genetically incompatible with her. The risk of a child born with deformities, disease, even something as simple as poor eyesight, was too great. The Tribe desperately needed children but didn't have the resources to care for babies with problems.

Job had been forbidden to her, and maybe that was why she'd let him have her. That small defiance hadn't seemed like such a terrible thing at the time. But now, knowing they'd created life and the consequences both of them would face if she couldn't somehow make this right...All at once she wanted nothing more than to sag into his arms and let him stroke her hair. Let him touch her if he wanted, let him make love to her if he insisted. At least he would be holding her. She wanted to tell him the truth, that she carried his child.

"Come with me," she said, and took him into the dark. The shadows. It wasn't quite love, but it was all she could have.

Chapter 5

"Get up," the man wielding the knife said. He pulled the knife back but didn't sheathe it.

Oddly, Tobin wasn't as afraid as the situation should have warranted. The man in front of him looked about as ancient and withered as Old Pa right before he died. The hand holding the knife shook.

Still, the old guy did look like he could bolt at any time. Slowly, hands out in front of him to show he meant no harm, Tobin wriggled out of his sleeping bag and stood up. The old man squinted at him.

"Toyna round. Alta vay." Only the twirling gesture he made with his knife made the strangely accented words make sense.

Tobin did as ordered, turning slowly with his hands still raised slightly. "I wasn't sure I'd find anyone here…"

"I didden azg to ear yor livez tory," the man said. "Anni fown djew. Vutteryew doyn ear ennyvay?"

It took Tobin a few seconds to decipher the man's words into: "I didn't ask to hear your life's story. And I found you. What are you doing here, anyway?"

Before he could answer, the old guy grew impatient. "Never mind. Pack your things. You come with me."

"Where?" Tobin asked cautiously, as he bent to follow the old man's orders.

"Never mind. You come."

Not a great way of showing hospitality to a stranger. Maybe they got a lot of travelers through here and could afford to be rude. Not like in Eastport, where they treated every new face like visiting royalty. Watching the old man's shifting eyes, Tobin decided things would never be the same as they were in Eastport. The realization caused a sharp pang in his chest just under his heart.

"You alone?"

It sounded like "yewa loan?" But Tobin understood the question this time. "Yeah."

The man looked at him with shifty eyes. "You're not from here."

"No."

"Never mind." The man gestured with the knife around the storeroom. "This your stuff?"

"It's mine." Tobin finished rolling the sleeping bag and secured the ties. Everything else folded or collapsed and went into the backpack.

"Oy, I should have such luck," the man muttered. He gestured with the knife again. "What's your name?"

Tobin hesitated in his answer as he tugged the straps of his backpack more firmly into place. Every movement seemed surreal to him, as though he were moving in a dream. He'd come to New York to find people. He'd never thought about being held at knife-point. His fingers smoothed the tough fabric of the bag, already dusty and no longer so new.

"Tobin Winter," he said, finally, looking up at the man. "What's yours?"

"Asaph."

"I'm on my way to California."

The man began to laugh. He laughed so long and so hard he began to cough violently. A fine spray of spittle left his lips, and his face turned beet-red.

Alarmed, Tobin offered the man his canteen. After a few sips, the coughing stopped. The man wiped tears from his eyes with a ragged handkerchief he pulled from his black coat pocket.

"What are you, meshuggeh? There's no California. California fell off the world a long time ago. Earthquakes. Shook the land so hard even we felt it. Knocked the top right off the Empire State Building. California's gone, boychick. Plop! Into the ocean."

His skepticism offended Tobin more than the knife at his throat had. "I heard there's babies being born there."

The man grew solemn. "This is not to joke about, nu? Babies are precious."

"It's what I heard," Tobin repeated stubbornly. He hefted his belongings. "Now, where did you want me to go?"

The old man put the knife away, squinting at Tobin carefully. He nodded, as if coming to some secret conclusion. His smile showed rotten teeth. The old man laughed again, though not so violently this time. "Where you from?"

Annoyed, Tobin shifted his pack to his other arm. "I'm from Maine."

The old man shook his head. "Main? Where is that? By the stadium? The Bronx, maybe?"

Even though he'd grown accustomed to the man's weird accent, Tobin had no idea what he was talking about. He didn't like this guy, and he didn't like being trapped in this little storeroom. If he could get past him and out into the main store, he'd just make a break for it. The man had a knife, but there was no way he could run as fast as Tobin.

"You a spy? From the other settlement, over there in Queens, mebbe? Brooklyn? You're not a Bridger, I can see that well enough."

"What?" It was Tobin's turn to laugh. He'd read about spies. "You mean like James Bond?"

The man looked at him shrewdly. "I don't know this James Bond."

"He's a spy." Again, Tobin became aware of how surreal this situation had become. "In those books, the 007 books. The library in Eastport had the whole series. And I saw a few of the movies on Old Pa's eTablet before it ran out of batteries."

The old man looked over Tobin's gear with greedy eyes, then back at his face. "You come with me."

Tobin put down his bags with a thunk. More than anything he just wanted to get on his bike and ride away from this city that stank of destruction. He just wanted to find a safe place to sleep, maybe even dream a little. Something pleasant, not like this nightmare he was living now.

"What else you got in your bag?" Asaph whipped out the knife again with hands even more unsteady than before. He gestured with the blade. "Open it."

Tobin looked at the knife and then at Asaph. Finally, he sighed. "Fine. If it will make you feel better."

"Just do it!" Asaph ordered. He kept looking nervously over his shoulder, but refused to step into the room and shut the door when Tobin suggested he might feel safer.

Tobin unlatched the top of his backpack and flipped back the top. The flap made a heavy noise when it hit the back of the pack; he'd filled every compartment. He unzipped the top flap and pulled out his utensils – the knife, fork and spoon that fit together neatly against one another to save space. With them was the collapsible bowl and plate set. Next came the small, flat flashlight and waterproof box he had filled with matches and two short candles.

Asaph's eyes grew wider and wider with every item he saw. His face grew redder and redder, until Tobin began to worry that the old man was about to keel over. He was sympathetic, though. He remembered how he'd felt upon seeing all of these same things on the shelves. Amazed.

"You have more?" Asaph asked hoarsely.

Tobin tugged open the drawstring holding the bag shut. "I have some more stuff, yeah."

"Take it out."

Out came the lantern and the small stove, both collapsed to the size of a paperback novel. Next came the foil blanket, still in its packaging, that was supposed to keep you warm even in "subarctic" temperatures. Whatever that meant. Out came the fleece jacket and pants, the extra underwear and the soft, clean, white socks, all rolled as tightly as possible to conserve space. Underneath those were several flat packages of dried meat and powdered soups, two "snack-pack" bags of cookies and one of cheese curls, three small waxy boxes filled with juice, and a flattened box of tea bags. Also, the jar of whitefish and the cans of chicken broth from the storeroom. Finally, at the bottom of the sack were Tobin's real treasures: the compact book of maps, three well-worn paperback novels, and five packages each of regular, large, and super-size batteries.

At these last items, Asaph let out a low whistle that trailed off and became something like a groan. "Such treasures."

Tobin sat back on his heels and waved his hands over the stuff. "This is it. And I have my sleeping bag, and my bike. And my knapsack..."

"There's more?" Asaph sank to a squat, shaking his head. For a moment he was speechless, his mouth working until the spittle gathered in the corners of his lips and made a froth. Finally he seemed to find his voice again. "Show me."

The knapsack was much smaller than the backpack. Tobin opened it up and pulled out the contents one by one, setting them on the floor by the others. Two bottles of spring water. Two toothbrushes, one still in its package. A super-large tube of toothpaste. A box of dental floss, unopened. A washcloth in a plastic bag. A small bottle each of aspirin, cough medicine and anti-diarrhea medication. A small bottle of shampoo, three-quarters full. A razor and an extra package of blades. An extra pair of shoelaces. A small package of adhesive bandages. Finally, a travel-sized sewing kit.

Asaph stared at all the goods spread out in front of him. Hesitantly, hands shaking even harder, he reached out to run his fingers over the goods laid out on the floor. He touched the clothing reverently and moved his hands over the shiny can opener. The look on his face was something like awe.

"Where did you get this?" His eyes greedily sucked in the sight of Tobin's belongings.

"From a store."

Asaph turned his head and spat. "Liar! All the stores have been rooted clean since before my father's father's day. You must've stolen it."

"I didn't!" Without bothering to ask permission, Tobin began repacking his bags. "I told you, I got it from a store. A big one. I found it on my way here from Eastport. It was filled with stuff like this."

He found himself again with the knife at his throat. He froze, more afraid a slice would come from the shaking of Asaph's hands than a deliberate jab. The old man was sweating, the froth on his lips dried to an unattractive crust. He stank.

"You said you were from the Bronx! Up by the stadium! There's nothing left up there but beggars and thieves!"

"I didn't say --" But Asaph wouldn't let Tobin protest that he hadn't claimed to be from the Bronx at all.

"You stole this from the Tribe! All of this! It's the only place you could've gotten it! You're a gonif, a thief! Thief!"

Swiftly, because he was tired of being held at knifepoint and tired of being accused of things he hadn't done, Tobin reached up and grabbed Asaph's wrist. The knife clattered to the ground. Tobin pushed the old man away, careful not to break the old bones but forcefully enough that Asaph landed on his rear.

"I'm not a liar, and I'm not a thief," Tobin said, his voice low and painful in his throat. "And I'm not from the Bronx. I'm from Eastport. It's in Maine. I don't know who or what the Tribe is, and I don't really care. I've been traveling for more than three weeks. I am on my way to California."

He sat back, watching Asaph warily. The old man made no move toward him, instead just held his wrist and grimaced. Tobin continued to repack his bags.

"I don't have any truck with fighting you, old man," Tobin said, though not disrespectfully. Old Pa had always told him that a man is measured by how he treated those weaker than he is. Tobin was pretty sure that included Asaph. And if that was the sort of people populating this city, he could do without the company. "I just want to be on my way."

Asaph said nothing, even when Tobin stood and hefted his bags, preparing to leave. Tobin watched him for a moment, but the old man didn't move. Tobin stepped over him, watching for any movement that meant Asaph was going to attack him again, but there was none. He left the storeroom, climbed around the empty glass case, and began packing up his bike.

He expected to hear the old man coming after him at any moment, but again was wrong. Tobin thought about checking on him, but decided he hadn't pushed him hard enough to cause permanent damage. Let the old guy go back to whatever it was he'd been doing before Tobin had been unlucky enough to make his acquaintance. He just wanted to get out of here.

It was still dark outside. He wasn't afraid of the night. In Eastport, they'd all gone to bed with the dark. Lantern light was precious and reserved for emergencies.

No, he wasn't afraid of the dark, but he was afraid. Meeting Asaph proved that the city was not as empty as it seemed. If the other residents were anything like the old man, Tobin didn't want to meet up with them in the dark.

He'd have to walk his bike and use the flashlight. If he were lucky, he might find another empty store to camp out in, but he'd get no more sleep this night. In the morning he could be on his way, and forget about this cursed place. It didn't matter what the peddler said. He'd find other people. He didn't need companions like Asaph.

Tobin pulled his flashlight from the backpack and switched it on. It threw only enough light to illuminate the street a few feet around him, but it was enough that he could see where he was going. It also might make him an easy target for anyone hiding in any of the empty buildings. He didn't like that at all, but didn't see any help for it. He squared his shoulders and started walking.

Tobin had hardly gone ten feet when he heard a rustling and a crashing from the store he'd just left. He turned to see Asaph standing in the doorway. The shadows from the flashlight made his grin seem to dance on his face.

"The Tribe doesn't like thieves!" Asaph's quavery old man's

voice echoed through the dark street and sounded more distorted than it was. "Ride fast on that bike!"

Tobin didn't bother replying. Instead he turned back and kept walking. The flashlight bobbed with every step and he gritted his teeth to keep from running like Asaph said he should. He wouldn't show fear. If there were any eyes watching him from the dark, he wouldn't give them the satisfaction.

One foot in front of the other. Step by step. His neck began to ache from straining against whipping around at every small sound. His throat hurt, and when he touched it his fingers came away tinged with pink. Asaph must have sliced him a little, after all.

He stopped and pulled the map he'd torn from the book out of his pocket. He'd marked his route carefully with a bright pink pen, but the markings stopped once entering the city. He didn't have many plans from here. The peddler had said he'd find people in the city. He hadn't said where.

"Or that they'd be crazy," Tobin muttered. Something metal clanged in an alley to his right, but when he shone the light in that direction, he could see nothing.

The buildings, so immense and intimidating by day, were even more hulking by night. If there was one advantage to the dark, it was that he couldn't really see their true bulk. His world had shrunk to a ten-foot circle of light.

He kept walking, if for no other reason than he didn't know what else to do. He was heading further south, into the heart of the city instead of away from it, but he didn't want to backtrack. He'd just plow ahead, follow the streets until he reached something he could find on the map, and go from there.

His eyes were grainy from exhaustion, and his muscles ached and pulled. He concentrated on walking. Step by step. Push the bike. Think about getting out of here alive.

Another clang of metal. This one sounded deliberate. Tobin shone the light, holding it up over his head to make the thin beams stretch as far as they would. He saw nothing, but now every nerve in his body strained to hear or see something.

Tobin realized he'd tensed, as if for flight. Stupid, he told himself, still searching with the flashlight. Stupid to run when you don't know where you're going. That's a good way to get into a trap, or get killed. He'd have to fight, should it come to that, and hope he wouldn't be too badly outnumbered.

"James Bond could do it," he said out loud. Despite the situation, he found a smile. "Hey! Watch out! James Bond is here!"

His voice echoed through the streets and bounced off the empty buildings, making it sound like ten people yelling. When the echoes died away, he thought he heard another sound. A low, steady murmuring whisper. Like people talking, but so low he couldn't hear what they were saying.

He didn't want to run, and if he had to fight, he didn't want to wait. He'd never actually fought, or even hit, another human being before. He'd read plenty of books about sword fights, and fist fights, and wars with guns and tanks and missiles, but when it came to actual experience in hand to hand combat…he had none. No one had ever hit him, not even when he was small and naughty enough to merit a spanking.

"Hey!" He yelled again, recklessly.

If it was going to happen, bring it on, he thought grimly. His ears rang, and his palms moistened. He felt like he was about to jump right out of his skin, but he also felt gloriously alive. He pushed down the bike's kickstand and shrugged off the backpack in one smooth motion that made him feel like James Bond.

"If you're out there, show yourself!" Tobin yelled to the blackness stretching out all around him. "I'm right here! Come and get me, if you're going to!"

Another clang of metal on stone, this time above him. His head snapped up, eyes searching and finding nothing. The light was making him a target. He switched it off, evening his chances. In the few moments it took his eyes to adjust to the dark, an unrelenting panic swelled in him. It constricted his throat and churned his stomach.

He couldn't see. Anything could be out there, waiting, and he wouldn't know about it. It was like when he'd been afraid of something lying in wait for him under the bed. Worse, though, was that now he was certain there were monsters in the dark. They might wear human faces, but beneath that they were full of fangs and scales and claws.

Bit by bit, however, he began to make out differences in the shadows. The buildings blocked most of what moonlight filtered through spring storm clouds, but it was enough for him. Tobin had spent enough dark nights making his way to the outhouse without benefit of a lantern that even the small amount of moonlight helped.

The murmuring whisper came again, a little louder and a little more clear. He could make out two, no, three voices but not what they were saying. What he could not discern was from where the voices came.

"Hey!" He was nearly sick with anticipation. His hands actually shook, clenched into fists so tight his nails cut his palms. If something didn't happen soon, he thought he might just go crazy. "I know you're out there! I can hear you!"

Men dropped like spiders from the sky. Three, four, five of them landed on the pavement in a circle around him, cutting off any chance at escape. They landed lightly, with almost no sound.

Tobin forced himself to breathe. He spread his legs a bit wider and held out his hands. "Who are you?"

The men said nothing, but didn't advance on him. At least, he thought they were men. They had the shapes and limbs of men, but they wore black from head to foot. He couldn't see their faces. If his eyes hadn't adjusted so quickly, he'd only have been able to see them as shadows.

"Don't come any closer!" He yelled, though they hadn't moved.

They all looked at each other. He noticed with some sense of wonder that they wore thick belts around their waists with straps that looped around their legs. Attached to the belts were pouches and loops. He saw some tools. Strangest of all, attached to every belt was a long rope which didn't drop to the ground, but reached up and up in the blackness of the sky and disappeared.

In one unified movement, the men surrounding him gave identical tugs to the ropes. Almost immediately, five identical metal hooks fell through the dark and landed, clanging, on the pavement behind each man. With swift and efficient movements, the men wound up the ropes and tucked the hooks into their belts.

Ears still ringing from the clanging, Tobin turned in a slow circle, trying to watch every figure surrounding him. He couldn't. He stopped, waiting.

"What do you have to say?" A figure asked. This one's voice was light, the figure slimmer and shorter than the others. Maybe a woman?

"I don't have anything to say." Tobin said began to relax a little, his chest hurting from the pounding of his heart. "I'm just trying to get through."

"Through where?" A third man asked. They all looked at each other again.

"Through the city." Tobin's sense of the situation as surreal was coming back. He didn't have much experience with people but surely this wasn't normal.

"Why?"

"I…" he hesitated, remember Asaph's mockery. "I'm going to California."

A low mumble ran through the group.

"There is no California," said one who had not yet spoken. "It fell off the world a long time ago."

"So I've been told," Tobin said dourly. "But I've also heard that there are people there. And that they're having babies."

He'd shocked them. A gasp rippled through the circle. The men looked at each other, quickly, one to the next, and at Tobin. One by one they pulled off their hoods.

"How do you know this?" asked a tall man with dark black hair like coils of wire. His skin was the color of Old Ma's favorite weak tea, his features broad.

"A peddler told me." Tobin looked around the circle at the people now exposed before him.

The shorter one, yes, a woman, laughed. "And you believed him? What would a peddler know?"

"Do you know it isn't true?" Tobin asked.

She looked at her companions and back to him. "California is gone. There's nothing there. Earthquakes shook it off the coast about a hundred years ago. There's nothing past the mountains anymore."

Tobin's stomach sunk. "This peddler…he said he'd heard from someone who'd been there."

Another of the group, a man not as ancient as Asaph but with the same white hair, stepped forward. "Nobody comes from beyond the mountains. We sometimes get people here from the warm lands to the South. But everyone knows California is gone."

"There he is!"

A sudden shriek split the night. Asaph came running down the street as fast as his old legs could bring him. Twenty feet away from Tobin and the circle, he tripped on some rubbish and went flying. Still hollering, Asaph rolled over and over, at last leaping more nimbly to his feet than Tobin would have though possible. Limping, he crossed the last few feet.

"Him!" Asaph hollered. He pointed at Tobin and did a gruesome, gleeful caper on the sidewalk. "I told you he'd be here, didn't I? I said you'd find him here!"

In a burst of white rage that left him shaking, Tobin regretted not slitting the old man's throat when he'd had the chance. The thought sickened him and fled immediately, but nothing could change the fact that he'd had it. This city, he thought. This damned apocalypse of a city! He should never have come here.

"I told you, didn't I? Pushed me down, he did, that bastard. Took what I had found for the Tribe. Look in his pack! Look in his pack! You'll find it!" Asaph stopped his jigging, pointing around the circle. He flashed an evil grin at Tobin. "He's a gonif and a liar! And probably a spy!"

The last word rang out, echoing. One by one those in the circle looked at each other, and then one by one, they advanced upon Tobin.

"James Bond," one repeated. "You have been gathered."

Chapter 6

Ephraim was an old man, as he'd told Elanna Hopemother earlier tonight. And he was tired. But more than that...he'd started to become afraid.

"One more season." Avriham ticked off an imaginary list with his fingers in the air. "The storerooms are full of things we've no real use for. For all practical purposes, trade's been wiped out with the areas beyond the park since most of those settlements have been assimilated by the Bridgers, and the Savage encroachment gets worse every year."

"You'd think they'd simply fade away." Ephraim rubbed at the ache between his eyes.

Avriham made a face. "They multiply like the beasts they run with."

He'd been in charge of the Tribe's supplies for years. Like Ephraim, he was old. Perhaps not so tired, but certainly he might well be as afraid. After all, who knew better than Avriham, keeper of the storerooms, how perilously close the Tribe hovered to running out of…well…everything? Ephraim pushed a mug of hot tea toward the other man, who sipped it and grimaced before pushing it aside.

"It's all we have," Ephraim pointed out.

Avriham shrugged. "Our own grown tea, and it tastes like something we scraped from the bottom of a trash pail. I tell you, Ephraim. The Tribe is..."

"Not failing." Ephraim raised a finger.

The other two members of the Beit Din at last arrived. Livna barely squeezed through the door, and Solomon was close behind her. They nodded at Avriham.

"We need something more. New trade. New ways of growing food. Something," said Ephraim.

Avriham shrugged. "Our resources are limited. The soil in the rooftop gardens is fertilized with manure from the veal pens, but it's not enough. We could have the Gatherers bring more from the park. Maybe enough time's past, maybe the earth has healed. At least enough to grow things."

"You want to take that chance? Have our babies born with extra eyes or, Ha-Shem forbid, not enough limbs? Webbed fingers?" It had happened in the past, Ephraim knew. It was why they were so careful now to keep perfect genetic records, to only allow good matches for conception. Even with those precautions, three out of five pregnancies still ended in the womb.

"No." This came from Livna, who gave the men in the room a shifty eyed glance as she settled her bulk into a chair. "Of course we don't want that. But what about the Gatherers? They're expanding their territory, nu? Moving on beyond our normal borders?"

"Encroaching on Savage territory, yes. Going so far as the Bronx, even. Where other people live," Solomon said. "So we steal from them? Is that better? Is that the way of our fathers?"

"We could trade with them," Avriham put in.

Ephraim shook his head. "What do we have to trade? We make nothing we don't use. We have no extra. We have nothing of value to provide to anyone else, why would what we have left over be of any more use to any of them than to us?"

"They could join us." Livna shrugged. "The offer was extended, long ago. Freshen our DNA pools. Bring in new skills. The Bridgers have no problem."

"The Bridgers force people to join them, or they kill them. They take from others, they don't give. And most importantly…those others are not like us." Ephraim shook his head again.

Solomon snorted lightly. "Why not? Because their ancestors were goyim and ours were not? Do you really think it was keeping the sabbath that let more of us survive when most of them didn't?"

"I do. Tell me you don't," Ephraim told the other man with a glare. "You, a member of the Beit Din, to say such things."

Solomon only shrugged. Livna looked away. Even Avriham wouldn't meet Ephraim's gaze.

"We're the Chosen. It's why we, of all the people in this city, continued having children when the others were no longer blessed. Its why as they died out, we lived on. Yes, we've brought others into our community as time passed. We've always welcomed strangers. Of course. But it's because of our faith. Our ability to adapt without losing our laws and traditions. That's why we are now some two-thousand strong and surviving here in peace when the rest of the world is still empty or battling against each other."

The rest of the room was silent. Ephraim looked at them all, then scrubbed at his face. So weary. "So. Let's talk about what we can do to make things better."

"Maybe you should ask Adonai to send us a miracle," muttered Avriham.

If only that could happen.

Chapter 7

"How many times do I have to tell you?" Tobin snapped. "My name isn't James Bond."

"See? See? I told you he's a liar! And a man who lies will be a thief!"

That was Asaph again. He seemed to be taking a perverse pleasure in trying to aggravate Tobin. After three hours of the old man's gabbing, Tobin now just tuned him out. That only seemed to agitate the old Gatherer so he tried even harder.

"Asaph, for the love of Ha-Shem, shut up!" The woman said. Apparently the old man was succeeding in aggravating somebody, if not Tobin.

"He has a point, Zmorah," a man called Gavish said, though he too looked fed-up with Asaph's blabber.

"Yeah, on the top of his head," Tobin muttered, and stifled a laugh. He was exhausted and getting punchy, as Old Ma would have said. Laughter didn't seem to be the most appropriate reaction to the situation. He could tell it confused them, and that was just fine with him.

The one with the white hair spoke next. "You did tell us your name was James Bond."

Tobin groaned and hung his head. "We've been over this already."

"You were lying," Zmorah said. "He's lying, Levi."

"Yes," Tobin said with an impatient sigh. He rubbed his eyes with the back of his hand and glanced longingly at his bedroll. In another few hours it would be light, and he doubted he'd get any sleep then, either. "But only because...shit."

Raised eyebrows from the lot of them. Apparently cursing went over as well as lying did. Tobin coughed, wishing he'd had more experience with people. Old Pa had cursed like a sailor, Old Ma was fond of saying, but Tobin didn't quite know how a sailor cursed.

He tried again. "I was being sarcastic."

The gatherer with the dark skin was Ari. He seemed to be the leader. Now he looked at Tobin thoughtfully, his black brows knitted over eyes as dark as the night outside.

"If you lie about your name, how can we trust anything else you tell us?"

"I don't know," Tobin said. "But I told you I lied about the name. I mean, that I was being sarcastic about it. Anyway, why would I lie to you about where I got my stuff?"

"Because you're a nasty, dirty liar!" Asaph crowed. A look from the others shushed him, but Tobin could tell the old man wouldn't stay silent for long. He didn't have it in him to be quiet.

They called the quietest and youngest gatherer Dov. "You might lie because you stole these things."

Tobin looked around the dirty, bare room. They'd taken him into another building. The room was vast and dilapidated. Huge stone pillars rose in even rows, and far in the back was a long, high desk. They'd told him it had once been a hotel. Aside from the six Gatherers and Tobin, and his belongings, the room was empty.

"From who? From where?" Tobin pointed around the room. "Places like this?"

Tobin got up and kicked his backpack until it fell over. Everything inside spilled out, clanging on the hard stone floor. Echoes filled the room for several minutes before dying away.

"Do you see stuff like this here?" He glared at his captors. "Huh? Do you see anything?"

"There's lotsa stuff to be gathered in the city." Tall and hugely muscled, the man called Luz had been the one to drag Tobin inside the building.

"New like this?" Tobin knew he was getting in the other man's face and didn't care. "Unused?"

Zmorah and Ari shared a look. "No," she said. "That's why we're confused."

"Well, hot damn," Tobin said, more to see her flinch than because he really wanted to swear. "What do you want me to say? I told you. I found this stuff in a huge warehouse off the Transcon. There were enough goods in there to feed and clothe a thousand people, probably. All of it unused, and all of it good. If I could've taken more of it with me, I would have."

Ari grunted. "We work six days out of seven, eleven months out of twelve, to find food and clothes and necessary items for the Tribe. If this place really exists…"

Dov sighed. "We'd be set for life!"

Zmorah bent to paw through his belongings. The group had been through it all ten times already, but Tobin didn't stop her. He thought she just might want to touch the things again. He knew how she felt.

Tobin couldn't see much of her in the lantern light, but he thought she was about his age. He couldn't tell whether or not she was pretty…hell. What did he know about pretty, anyway? What he'd seen in pictures.

"There are places in the city we haven't covered yet." Zmorah caressed the fleece jacket. Her voice sounded wistful. "Lots of apartments. Lots of offices. Buildings we haven't explored beyond the fifth or sixth floors. And beyond that, we could branch out to the houses on the long island…"

She paused and her voice broke as though she might cry. "But to find it all in one place! And looking like this! I can't believe it!" To Tobin's surprise, she did start to cry.

"It's hard for us," Ari said. "The Tribe is two thousand strong now, James."

"Tobin," he corrected.

The older man stared at him, then smiled. "Tobin. We have two thousand people living here, in a city that once housed millions. And yet, after only a few hundred years, we're struggling to feed and clothe ourselves. We have huge storerooms filled with goods, but they can only last so long with a population our size. We look for more, all the time. We go into these old buildings and we search the places people used to live. Anything we find, we gather. It's how we survive."

Tobin thought of Eastport, and how he'd been alone for so long. They hadn't gone hungry there, but life hadn't been easy. He couldn't imagine living in this city of stone and pavement and rubbish. How could anything survive without sunshine and grass? And water?

"Why don't you leave?"

"Leave!" Gavish said. "And go where? We've lived here for hundreds of years!"

"We have a way of life, Tobin," Ari explained. "We have a government, and schools, and housing. We've adapted our territory to our comfort and well-being. Asking the Tribe to give all that up and start fresh would be like asking a baby to give up its suck."

"Two thousand people." Tobin gave a low whistle. Bending, he stuffed his backpack full again, then rocked back on his heels. "I don't think I've ever seen two thousand of anything before in my life. Damn. Is that even a real number?"

Ari laughed. "Sure it is. You'll see, when you come with us."

Tobin shook his head. "I'm not coming with you."

Another glance all around. "Yes, you are," Ari said firmly. "You have to show us how to get to this place. This warehouse off the...the what."

"The Transcon. The highway. Look," Tobin said, trying to be nice. "Even if I showed you how to get there, it's at least a week's journey away. And once you get there, how are you possibly going to carry enough stuff back with you to make it worth your while?"

They all looked at him blankly, even Asaph. They shared another of those stupid looks again, like they all knew what the other was thinking. Only he didn't know. He felt out of place, and more a stranger than he'd ever thought he could. He didn't like it. It made him feel stupid, and worse, lonely.

"We'd put it in the trucks," Luz said, in a tone that clearly said he, at least, thought Tobin was stupid.

Now it was Tobin's turn to stare blankly. "Trucks?"

"Sure," Luz said. He flexed his arms, something he seemed to enjoy. "Our trucks. The Tribe's got more trucks than any other territory. And they all work."

"I…I didn't think anything like that worked anymore," Tobin said.

He had to sit down. He knew what a truck was, sure. He'd seen the rusted-out hulks at home and on his travels. He'd never believed he'd see one that worked.

"They run on the same batteries that power everything else," Zmorah said. She'd recovered from her spate of tears. As she moved into the lantern light, Tobin saw that she was, indeed, pretty. "They take a lot of power, though."

"But if there are as many batteries in that store as you say," Dov said excitedly, "We could use the power to get there! We'd have enough to do that, at least. And we could gather more there, enough to get us back again."

"Providing the roads are in decent repair," Ari said thoughtfully. "We'd have to take a crew along with us for road clearing. And for breakdowns. We've never taken the trucks out of the city before --"

"But it could work, it really could!" Gavish cried.

Tobin grinned. Their enthusiasm was infectious. He couldn't begrudge them the same excitement he'd felt after stumbling on the treasure trove in that huge store. He just didn't have to be a part of the journey.

He sobered. "The exit ramps were all destroyed. No trucks will be able to get up them."

Ari frowned, looking at the others. "We'd have to leave by the bridge."

The others fell silent.

"We could do it," Ari added. "We have the trucks."

"Yeah, and they have an insane desire to kill anyone who crosses their bridge." Gavish punched one fist lightly into the other.

"How do we know," Asaph piped up in his wheedling old man's voice, "that he's not just lying again to keep us from it? Maybe he's a Bridger! Maybe he's a spy!"

Tobin wanted to punch the old man right in the mouth. He didn't. But he wanted to.

"You don't," Tobin said. He met the gaze of each gatherer in turn. "You'll just have to trust me."

"You'll have to show us where to go once we get beyond the bridge," Ari said.

"I can let you copy my map," Tobin said carefully. At his words, he saw them all exchange looks he couldn't interpret. "But I can't go with you. I told you, I'm going to California."

Luz snorted, flexing his huge arms again. Tobin thought he did it just to show how strong he was. It didn't impress him; he'd seen the Conan the Barberian movie on Old Pa's eTablet.

"There is no California," Luz said, his voice thick with scorn.

Tobin bristled. "Maybe. Maybe not. But there's something West of here, and I'm heading for it."

"Why?" Zmorah asked.

Tobin shrugged. "Why not?"

"You'll show us this place," Ari said calmly, as though arguing with a child. "And then you'll go on to California, or wherever you want."

"No." Tobin shook his head. "I told you, it's back the wrong way. At least a week. Less if you travel by truck, I guess, but still too long for me. Sorry, but I've got to decline your offer."

"It's not an offer," Ari said. "And it isn't an option. You have been gathered, Tobin Winter."

They were on him with the swiftness of cats. Luz bound Tobin's arms behind him before he could even struggle. Though he tried to kick out, the others ducked away from his flailing feet with practiced ease. Zmorah scooped up his backpack and knapsack, slinging them over her slim shoulders. Gavish grabbed his sleeping bag, and Dov took the bike. Asaph just laughed and pointed a bony finger. Tobin worked up enough spittle to send a gob flying the old man's way, but it missed him. Asaph only laughed harder.

They took him out into the street again, their lanterns bobbing until the bouncing light made his head spin. After a moment they turned off the lights. Apparently they not only moved like cats, they could see in the dark too.

Luz grunted, shoving him along. "Hurry up!"

Tobin's toe hit a patch of buckled pavement. Without the use of his arms to break his fall, he landed on his face. White stars flashed in front of his eyes. The pain was nauseating, horrible, all-engulfing. For one bad moment he thought he might pass out.

"Don't kill him," Zmorah said.

Luz only grunted and hauled him to his feet, holding Tobin up when his legs buckled. Hot blood oozed from several places on his face. His nose and jaw throbbed with every step, but he didn't cry out. He might not know about people, but he knew about pride.

"Move it!" Luz said.

Tobin moved, grateful for the muscle man's hands on him only because without them he would have stumbled and fallen again. His eyes might have adjusted to the lack of light before, but now with his face on fire from pain he doubted he'd be able to see straight even when the sun came up.

They'd only gone a block or so when Luz pushed him down an alley to the right. Stumbling again, Tobin managed to go down on one knee instead of falling entirely. Amazingly, the bigger man left him there without tugging him onward.

The rumble of thunder bellowed suddenly in front of him; blazing white light turned night into day. A monster rose up before him, stinking and roaring. Tobin screamed, his voice lost in the roar before him, and fell back.

Chapter 8

It was wrong to want to cry and have no tears. It was wrong to want what any human being wanted – simple, genuine affection, and be denied. It was wrong to love and not be loved in return.

Elanna sat up and scrubbed her face with her palms. Her head ached, but her thinking was clear. From the hall outside came the pounding of feet. The hushed murmur of voices. She sat up, swung her feet out of bed, waited for the room to start spinning. Or to stop.

Before she could, a white-faced Tikva appeared in the doorway. Elanna was in no mood to deal with the other girl, but Tikva didn't seem in the mood to talk to her, either. Instead she went straight to her narrow bed and tossed herself down onto it, face first.

Elanna sighed. "What's the matter?"

Tikva raised her face. "Leah had her baby."

"Oh?" Elanna brightened. Leah was only a few years older than her and had been there all through Elanna's many births. She frowned after a moment, though. "Why didn't anyone tell me? I'd have been there."

"The baby..."

"Oh." Elanna bit the inside of her cheek. "Did it die?"

Tikva shook her head. She shuddered and bit her lower lip, then gasped out a sob. "No!"

"Then what?"

"It's not right," Tikva whispered hoarsely. "It's not...right."

"No." Elanna breathed the word and drew her feet up onto the bed as though a gobbling lay in wait beneath. "No. It couldn't be."

Leah would never have done what Elanna had let herself do. Tikva burst out a sob, burying her face in the pillow again. Elanna swallowed sickness that had nothing to do with the life growing inside her.

"They did the Geneto-Test. It was fine. She caught from Ari, just like she was supposed to, and he was a match. But it was still...not right." Tikva's voice was muffled, but not enough that Elanna couldn't hear it.

She didn't want to ask what was wrong with the child. It didn't matter. Ari had been matched to Leah but had never made a child with her or any other hopemother before. This would've been his first.

"It's because he goes...out," Tikva said. "That's what they're saying. Because he goes into the Blast Zone. And out there."

It could be. It didn't matter. All that mattered was that Leah had given birth to a child that was not right.

It would've been better if it had died.

That thought suddenly sickened and horrified her, even though she knew it was true. Elanna pressed her fingertips to her churning belly. It was true, but it wasn't right. Babies were precious. All babies.

But if Leah and Ari had been matched and still had a child that wasn't right, what chance did she have of bearing a baby without problems when she'd caught with Job who'd been tested and found incompatible? They would do worse than take it from her and give it to another woman to raise. They would take it from her and...

"I have to go." She stood, the floor slipping under her feet.

"Elanna, Tikva, hey!" It was Chedva again. The shorter girl was nearly bursting with excitement, practically wriggling in her eagerness to tell Elanna something. "Did you hear the news?"

"I heard." Elanna knew Chedva was clueless, but couldn't believe she'd take such joy in Leah's misfortune.

"The Gatherers are due back soon," Chedva said, completely ignoring the story of Leah's birth and the child. That was typical. Everyone would pretend it hadn't happened, leaving Leah to mourn in silence. "Zev came on ahead and said the rest would be here in a little while. Oh, Elanna, isn't it exciting?"

"Yes," Elanna answered noncommittally.

"What do you think they'll bring back this time? Oh, I hope they've found some candy! And some new clothes in my size. I'd love a new dress for summer…"

Elanna left Tikva sobbing into her pillow and pushed past Chedva to leave the room. True to form, Chedva followed, rattling on as Elanna made her way to the Main Hall. She wanted to cut through there on her way to the birthing room. She wanted to see Leah, even if nobody else would.

"They'll all be wanting appointments, you know." Chedva nudged Elanna with her elbow. "I hope Luz asks me, though it doesn't really matter. I know. But I'd love to have a baby with Luz, wouldn't you, Elanna?"

Elanna thought of the tall, grossly muscled man and his coarse manners. She'd suffered through several appointments with him before realizing that he'd stop asking for her when she stopped pretending to be impressed with his physique. After she'd laughed when he asked if she thought his arms were getting too muscular, he'd never asked for her again.

"Um…no, not really," Elanna said. "Listen, Chedva, I've really got to go."

Chedva trotted after Elanna. "But guess what else? Something really exciting! I heard him say they found a man!"

By now even more people had crowded into the Main Hall. Elanna could barely move. Even going back the way she came was fruitless.

"Really?" She was only half-listening. "How neat."

Chedva babbled on and Elanna slowly worked her way through the crowd toward the dais. The Beit Din were all there, waiting for the Gatherers to come back. Then she saw Leah, face pale and eyes red-rimmed, her hair damp around her forehead. She caught Elanna's gaze across the room. Elanna moved toward her, but Leah shook her head just slightly.

Then she looked away. In the next moment the crowd had moved, blocking Elanna's view. When it parted again, the other hopemother was gone.

Chapter 9

A cloud stinking of hellfire surrounded him, making him gag. Tobin writhed on the pavement, unable to get up. His eyes bulged from his head, and his ears and nose and mouth filled with the relentless reek and roar.

Luz materialized beside him, yanking him up by the back of the neck with fingers that felt like pincers of iron. The gatherer pulled Tobin along like a rag doll, shoving him to one side. Fresh pain bloomed like some insane flower as his knees scraped the ground, but he forgot it almost immediately when he saw what had created the noise and the stench.

It was a truck, monstrous, like none he'd ever seen or even imagined. Black, with tires as high as his head, it was easily fifteen feet long. It revved and growled, farting huge stinking puffs of crackling air that smelled like lightning.

The windows were glassless and gaping, the cab doors bound with wire and bits of cloth to keep them from flying open. The bed in the back was filled with boxes and packages and all manner of things he couldn't identify, all surrounded by a sagging wall of barbed wire and pieces of wood studded with nails.

Luz grinned at him, showing teeth gone gray. Clearly he enjoyed

Tobin's reaction. The huge man gave Tobin an almost friendly tap on the shoulder that nearly knocked him over again.

"Pretty impressive when you see it in action," Luz said.

Now Tobin saw more black-garbed Gatherers, some in the front of the truck and others in the back among the packages. Five more, if he had counted them all. More people than he'd ever seen in his entire life, Tobin thought, stunned. He had to lock his knees from sagging again. His eyes went from one to the other of them, back and forth, hardly able to take it all in. People! Eleven of them, and they were only a fraction of the population if what Ari had told him was true.

"I didn't really believe it," he whispered, thinking of the peddler.

"Believe it," Zmorah said from beside him. She obviously thought he meant the truck, and he let her think what she wanted.

"You ride in the front," Ari commanded, nodding to Luz who began wrangling Tobin up a short ladder attached to the side of the cab. "If you're tied up you can't fight, and we can't have you getting in the way. Things are likely to get a little hairy on the ride home."

"Fight?" The pain in Tobin's jaw made it hard to talk. "Who?"

"Savages. We'll be going right through their territory."

Tobin's feet were on the bottom rung of the ladder. With his hands bound behind him, he couldn't balance himself. Only Luz's strong hands on his waist kept him from falling. Though he'd only taken one step up the ground seemed very far away. Concentrating suddenly seemed a very good idea.

Luz shoved him up the next step, pushing when Tobin teetered back. Another step and Tobin was able to bend at the waist along the truck's hood. The metal was warm under his cheek, the one that didn't hurt. He didn't see how he'd be able to go any further.

He didn't have to. Two of the Gatherers from inside the cab reached through the empty windshield and grabbed him. Another moment of wriggling and they shoved him over the front seat and into the back. Tobin managed to turn over enough so he was sitting on the seat, facing the front, instead of half-lying on the floor.

Two faces smudged with dirt stared back at him. He'd have thought from the strength they used to pull him in that he'd be looking at a pair of men as big as Luz, but the faces were female. Even through the dirt he could see that. Women had pulled him through the window. He didn't know how to feel about that.

Hell. He didn't know how to feel about anything, did he? Everything that had happened since waking up to Asaph's blade at his throat had been one seamless nightmare. He couldn't wish, wouldn't wish, that he'd stayed home in Eastport, but he did regret not taking another route.

"Whutsya name?"

It took him a second to realize that one of the women had spoken to him. Her accent was the same as the others. From her lips, it sounded somehow perky.

"Tobin," he said.

That, for some reason, elicited a giggle from the two of them. He wouldn't have thought women with arms like that would be gigglers, but then again, he didn't know much about women.

The one who hadn't spoken yet leaned farther over the seat to look him up and down. Tobin didn't know much about sex, but suddenly the cab seemed filled with it. His cheeks grew hot.

Ari had climbed into the cab. "Neta, Liora. Leave him alone. He's been gathered. We've got to keep focused, ladies."

Tobin didn't like the sound of that. Ari's voice had turned grim. Tobin shifted, his bound wrists aching.

"Hey, wait," he said.

Ari turned, one brow raised. "Yeah?"

"Can't you just untie my arms?" Tobin asked. "I can't…do anything…."

"That's the point," Ari said. "We can't trust you not to try and get away. You've proven that."

That was unfair. He hadn't tried to escape, just told them he didn't want to go.

"But if we're going to meet trouble," Tobin said. Damn it! He hated sounding this weak! He forced his voice to firm. "Ari, I can't defend myself."

"You won't have to," Ari said. He nodded toward Neta and Liora. "That's what they're here for."

The truck jerked forward and Tobin nearly fell off the seat. His stomach churned as the vehicle began rolling. Riding a bike was nothing like this. This was like being swallowed by a huge beast.

Any flirtation or silliness vanished. The women sat tensely, heads moving steadily back and forth. Searching. For what, Tobin wasn't sure he wanted to know.

The truck moved along streets beginning to glow with early morning sunlight. The buildings on either side of them didn't look any better than they had yesterday; if anything, many of them looked more dilapidated. In places, parts of them had even fallen down.

Tobin strained to look out the glassless windows, curious to see more of the city. The truck moved unbelievably fast. He glanced at one of the dials in front. The needle hovered at the number fifteen. He felt like he were flying.

"Central Park!" Came a loud voice from above them. One of the Gatherers thumped on the roof. "Heading into Zoo Territory!"

"Now we'll see," Ari muttered. "Damned Savages."

Tobin was surprised to hear the man swear, but even more surprised by what he saw through the windshield. Whatever had happened here, happened a long time ago. And whatever it was had been big and nasty.

The street simply…ended. There was a rough trail ahead, but it obviously had been made in the aftermath of whatever disaster had destroyed the buildings in an area at least ten blocks wide. As far as Tobin could see ahead and on both sides, there was nothing. Everything had been razed to rubble.

Without the tall buildings to block the sun, weeds and foliage had grown wild. Trees, twisted and unlike any he'd ever seen, grew in thick patches interspersed with bushes and tall grasses. A breeze blew through, making the foliage move as though something stood just behind it. And maybe, Tobin thought with a first twinge of unease, something did.

"Blast Zone," Ari said. The truck had stopped, the engine's roar like the sound of some large monster. "This is where they live. Get ready, now."

"We ain't been bothered the past two trips," Neta said. "Maybe..."

She didn't have time to finish her thought because suddenly a howling, gibbering wild thing leaped onto the side of the truck and reached through the window to grab Liora by the hair. Quicker than Tobin could blink, whatever was out there had pulled the woman halfway through the window. Only her knees, caught against the sides, stopped her.

With astonishing calm, Neta grabbed her friend's waist and pulled her inside with a practiced tug. "I tole ya to cut that hair," was all she said. Tobin realized they were grinning.

Then they were surrounded on all sides. Men, and he could only assume they were men, leaped onto the truck. Two jumped on the hood, waving clubs and spears that looked all the more deadly for being homemade. Tobin's innards turned to ice. He could only watch; he couldn't move.

I'm dreaming, he thought finally. Please let me be dreaming.

But he wasn't dreaming. The men, the Savages, were hammering on the truck. They wore furs, not clothes. Their cries were all the more terrifying because they didn't yell with words.

The one jabbing his spear through the windshield wore a tawny fur with a huge ruff pulled up around a burned and oozing face. His partner wore a black and orange striped fur around his waist, and the oozing burns were all over his body. Through his daze, Tobin realized he recognized the furs from a picture book called "My Visit To The Zoo." These men were wearing the skins of a lion and a tiger.

Ari reached up and grabbed the end of lion man's spear. It snapped in half and he flung it out the window. Lion started to dive head first through the windshield, but Neta kicked up one foot and caught him square in the forehead. Screaming, he flew back and off the front of the truck. Tobin felt rather than heard the thud as the vehicle ran over him.

Tiger man wasn't as bold. Liora leaned out the windshield toward him and butted him head to head. The crack was loud enough to hurt Tobin's ears, even above the rest of the cacophony, but Liora didn't even flinch. Tiger did, though. With a scream that echoed Lion's, he tumbled off the truck too.

In minutes, there was no more yelling. All the Savages had been pushed off or away, and had disappeared back into the brush. Neta helped Liora fix her hair, and Ari kept driving as if nothing at all had happened.

"Damage?" Ari yelled out the window.

Luz appeared, upside down. He'd been cut on his cheek and the blood flowed up into his hair. He grinned like a mad man.

"They got Brosh in the side, but nothing else serious!"

Ari nodded. "We'll go another mile and then drop the package."

They drove in silence for a few minutes, until Tobin could find his voice. "What the hell!"

Ari turned around. "You weren't worried, were you, Tobin?"

"Back during the riots, someone dropped a bomb on the Blast Zone," Liora said, turning to look at him. "Whatever was in it made them the way they are. Crazy. They live in the forest, hunting animals for their food and clothes. There's something in the water here that makes them look that way, too. If you stayed here long enough, it would happen to you, too."

"Where'd they get the skins?" Tobin asked hoarsely.

"From the animals," Neta said matter-of-factly. "Where else?"

"But a lion? A tiger?"

She smiled at him, and he saw she'd never flirt with him again. The earlier interest in her eyes had turned to pity. She thought he was a moron, and he felt like one.

"There was lots of animals living in the zoo," she said.

"I seen a giraffe once, through the trees," Liora said. "Only once, though."

Tobin shook his head. "This is too much."

Ari laughed, but not meanly. "You've lived too long by yourself, Tobin."

"Maybe it was better by myself."

A moment later Ari stopped the truck. One, two, three, packages were tossed off the back of the truck into the underbrush. Immediately, Savages appeared from the weeds and grabbed the packages, then disappeared again.

"I'm not going to ask," Tobin said.

"We have to give them something," Ari said. "They're no better than beggars. If we don't give them something, they'll just try to steal it from us and we'd have to kill them. They can't help how they are. We're just trying to do a mitzvah. A good deed."

"But why do they attack you, then?" Tobin demanded, head spinning.

"Well, because they're Savages," Liora said, and he knew she wouldn't be flirting with him again.

"We'll be all right from here on out," Ari said as the truck moved slowly along through the undergrowth. "Just a few more miles and we'll be in Tribe territory. Home."

Home, Tobin thought. Would he ever find it again? Without thinking he slumped down along the seat, his bound wrists making even laying uncomfortable. Shock and exhaustion won out, though, because before he could even try to fight it he'd fallen asleep.

He woke when the truck stopped. They were out of the jungle and back into the city. The buildings here were, if it were possible, even taller. Neta and Liora helped him slide out through the windshield again, and Luz helped him down the ladder. When he reached the pavement, Ari slipped the ropes off his arms.

"You can't run from us here, so don't try," Ari warned, and Tobin was so glad to have the use of his hands that he couldn't even be insulted.

Rubbing his wrists to get the feeling back, Tobin stopped, not caring that the hulking gatherer was pulling on him. Up, up, impossibly high, stretched a building unlike the others. Only by craning his neck could he see the top at all. It ended in a tall triangle. Just feet away from the building's foot, buried in the pavement, was an enormous metal spike bigger than his entire body. It must've fallen from an enormous height to have been buried so far into the concrete.

"This way," Luz said, pushing him.

They led him into another big building, pushing him through

doors covered in a patchwork of glass and metal and wood. Once inside, Tobin could only gasp. It was easily as large as the warehouse store, but this was filled with people.

Everywhere he looked there were people. Men and women. Old and young. Laughing, frowning, talking, kissing, hugging, smiling and shouting. More people than he'd ever imagined could exist.

Chapter 10

"The Gatherers!"

"They're back!"

The cries sprang up all around the vast room, from one person to another. Luz pushed Tobin again, toward the back of the room and another set of doors. Tobin stumbled in that direction, too preoccupied to resist. He heard a buzz of excited mumbling spread out from all around him, and he realized that people were pointing at him. Talking about him.

"We're taking you to the Beit Din," Luz told him. "You can tell your story there."

Tobin didn't really care about the Beit Din, or telling a story, or anything else. He was too enthralled with the sights before him. He'd never imagined anything like this. He was overwhelmed.

Just outside the doors they passed a smaller area marked off by a serious of soft chairs and couches set up in small groups around a large fireplace. Lots of people sat on the chairs. Some played chess, a game he recognized. Others talked or worked on mending, something he was also greatly familiar with.

Luz pushed Tobin in front of one of the couches set up along the wall next to the door they were heading toward. A young woman sat on the couch, holding something wrapped in a blanket. She was talking to it, cooing and smiling, and as Tobin watched she bent to kiss it.

Just as Tobin passed her, he saw inside the blanket. A baby. Everything stopped for him in that moment. Luz's insistent shoves did no more than shake him, for Tobin's feet had become like stones attached to the floor. It was a baby.

The baby giggled and kicked its tiny feet in the blanket. The mother stared at Tobin curiously, watching him as he reached out to brush his finger along the baby's impossibly tiny, downy head. It was soft.

"His name is Daniel," the mother said.

Then they were dragging him away, but they couldn't take the feeling of the baby's head away from his hand. A baby. He'd never dreamed…

"Welcome back!" Spoke an older man with a long beard, dressed all in black. "Ari, tell me what you've gathered for us this time!"

Ari outlined Tobin's story, leaving out the part where Tobin refused to go along to show them where to find the store. Tobin stayed quiet, still wrapped in the dream of the child. The Beit Din, two men and an enormous woman, all in black, listened carefully.

"This is cause for celebration! We're honored to have you as our guest, Tobin Winter. You've brought us joyous news," the man with the beard said. He clapped Tobin on the shoulder, making Tobin wince as pain flared from his many wounds. The man's eyes met something in the crowd, and he smiled. "Adonai has surely listened to our pleas."

An enormous woman standing next to the bearded man let out a low, scoffing laugh. "You were right, Ephraim."

"Come," said the man she'd called Reb, holding out his hand to Tobin, "let's make sure you're taken care of."

. . .

LEAH HAD STARTED CRYING and been unable to stop; they'd taken her away "to rest." Everyone knew what that meant. She wouldn't be back for a long time, perhaps ever. Elanna knew she needed to put this away from her head and stop thinking about her own child, but she couldn't.

What she hated was that nobody would talk about Leah's child, nor Leah herself. There was plenty of talk, all right, but all of it centered around the man the Gatherers had brought back with them. She couldn't walk down the hall without hearing the whispering. Who was he? What was he like? And most of all, was what he said true? Was there a place filled with new clothes, food and batteries still in their packs?

"I don't know," Elanna snapped at last to the impatiently wriggling Chedva. "I haven't talked to him. You know the Beit Din's taken him away until they can make sure he's all right. Not sick."

"Tamar says he's from uptown," Chedva said conspiratorially, inching closer.

Elanna sighed, but she couldn't escape. It was her shift to work in the kitchen, something even hopemothers couldn't get out of. Two thousand people ate a lot of food and used a lot of dishes. She continued scraping plates and scrubbing platters. Maybe Chedva would be called away to do something else. Eventually.

No such luck. The kitchen bustled, as it always did, with several of the ovens always going and the stovetops covered with bubbling and steaming pots. Meals were served three times a day in the main dining hall, but not everyone could fit in there at once. Each meal period had three sittings, and everyone rotated their sitting time from week to week. It made seating easier, but meant the kitchen never closed.

Chedva had switched with another girl solely for the purpose of working with Elanna. She was a good partner, too, keeping up despite all her chatter. Dish duty was Elanna's least favorite of all, except perhaps for privy duty. Having a swift moving partner was a blessing, and almost worth the chatter. Almost.

"Tamar says the Gatherers found him there!"

"Don't be silly, Chedva," Elanna broke in, unable to stand any more. "He's not from uptown."

"How do you know?" Chedva asked, scrubbing furiously until her plump cheeks turned pink.

"He was wearing clothes," Elanna said.

"Oh. Yeah. Maybe he's a Bridger."

Elanna sighed, scrubbing. "I don't think so. They hardly ever leave the bridge by themselves."

"Well, wherever he's from, I think he's awfully cute," Chedva said dreamily.

Elanna turned to look at her, amused. "Do you?"

"Oh, definitely," Chedva said a trifle defensively. "He looks so…exotic."

"Maybe you'd like him better if he were from uptown," Elanna said and laughed. She blew a puff of suds at the other girl. "You know, that savage attraction."

"Wouldn't it be wonderful," Chedva said earnestly, "if what they say is true?"

Elanna thought of a new coat and not having to worry about whether the Gatherers would bring enough food to last another winter. Not worrying if they'd be able to get another season's growth out of the roof top gardens. Having bright lights again, at least for awhile. Maybe even some pretty things, like scented soap and soft sponges.

"Yes," Elanna said. "It would."

"I TOLD you Ha-Shem would send someone to help us." Ephraim tried and failed to keep the smug tone from his voice. It was a failing, he knew it. Miriam had often told him so. But just now he had reason to be smug.

"So you said. But who's to say this outsider is what he claims to be?" Solomon asked.

Livna raised both brows. "So far as I can see, he hasn't claimed to be anything."

Ephraim passed a hand over the items laid out on his desk, all of them taken from the man Tobin Winter's backpack. Everything new, fresh, unused. Unlike anything they'd seen in years. "This doesn't lie, does it? And he says there's more. An entire building greater than the size of the Main Hall, stocked with everything we could need for years."

"He also says he doesn't want to stay here. That he wants to move on. To California." Livna snorted laughter, shaking her head. "Of all the stories..."

"First, he needs to show us where to go to get to the supplies. That's all. After that, he can go wherever he likes," Ephraim said.

"He says he'll draw us a map," Livna said.

Ephraim shook his head. "Not good enough. I'd like to believe his good intentions in sending us toward the warehouse, but our Gatherers haven't been beyond the city limits since before my father's time. Without the trucks, we'll need as many of them to make the journey as possible. He can lead them there and back. Then he can move on to wherever he wants."

"Without the trucks? You mean you'll send them on their own?" Livna said.

Ephraim looked at the other two members of his council. "You know the bridge people would have issue with us crossing. That's even if the bridge would hold the weight of the trucks. It's too dangerous. Tobin made it here himself on a bike, with a backpack. Surely our Gatherers can do the same. Probably more efficiently too."

Solomon nodded. "See if he can't contribute to a few of our hopemothers too, while he's here. He looks strong. Healthy. We could use some diversity."

All were silent, perhaps thinking, as Ephraim was, about the child born to the hopemother Leah. Fathered by Ari, one of their most honored Gatherers, and yet still not born healthy despite the careful testing that had gone on beforehand. It happened, sometimes.

Livna shifted in her seat. "And if he doesn't want to lead them? What if he's not interested in making babies for us, either? He's not one of us, Ephraim, and you wanting him to be isn't going to make it so."

"We'll have to convince him, that's all," Ephraim said.

"And if we can't?" asked Solomon.

Ephraim looked at them all, grimly. "We'll have to."

Chapter 11

Tobin's body still screamed in a hundred different places. His head throbbed like someone was banged on it with a stick. Which made sense, since that was pretty much what had happened.

The woman in front of him wore flowing rags of every vivid color he'd ever seen. Purple, orange, red, blue and colors he had never seen too, greens that shimmered in the lamplight like the sea on bright days and golds that gleamed like sunshine itself. Her face was wizened but kindly, and her iron gray hair piled on top of her head in a myriad of tiny braids. Her name was Frieda, and she'd told him she was a healer.

The old woman passed him a cup filled with clear, cold water. It tasted a little metallic but he drank it down anyway. The room they'd brought him to that first night was small and painted stark white, as were the furnishings within. He was in a narrow bed, propped on pillows that were comfortable but smelled slightly of mold and had a few lumps. The linens, white too, had been patched so many times it was impossible to tell which parts had belonged to the original sheets. The comforter was just as patched and faded, though it was nice and heavy. The only other items in the room were a small metal-backed chair and an equally small table. On the table were a basin and a pitcher draped with a rather threadbare towel. He set his glass on the table.

"How long are you going to keep me in here?"

"Logical question," Frieda said. "You're in one of the healing rooms. It's where we bring people when they're sick, or if they've had an accident. Like you."

"I wasn't sick," Tobin said gruffly. He touched his face, wincing. "And what happened to me was no accident."

Frieda bent to pick up the damp cloth from the floor where it had fallen when he sat up. She wrung it out into the basin and used the pitcher to freshen it. She handed it to Tobin.

"Put that back on your head. It will help."

"I need to get out of here," Tobin said, but he did as she asked. He knew better than to disobey an old lady bent on fixing him.

"You need to sit and rest so I can look at you. You've had some nasty bumps on that keppy of yours."

"Do your people treat all travelers with such hospitality?"

Frieda ignored the acid in his tone. "No, of course not. But I understand that you're not just a normal passer-through, Tobin."

He sighed heavily. "I guess not."

"You bring wonderful news," Frieda continued, taking down the covers and exposing his legs. They'd insisted on taking his clothes the night before, giving him instead a long gown of thin material that left him feeling worse than naked. She lifted the hem and pressed nimble fingers to several of the sore spots. "If it's true, that is."

"It's true."

"Ha-Shem must truly have been watching over you, to send you here to us." She pressed some lengths of cloth onto the worst wounds and tied them with strips of clean towel. "To have found what you did…"

The door opened and a bearded man came in. Tobin recognized him as the man who'd welcomed him in the great big meeting hall. He was still smiling, but the grin didn't make Tobin feel any more comfortable. There was steel behind that man's grin, and possibly razor blades, too.

"And how are you feeling, Tobin?"

"Reb Ephraim," Frieda greeted, giving a sort of little head bob that made Tobin think the man was even more important than she was. "He's feeling much better, I think. Aren't you?"

Tobin nodded, not quite trusting himself to speak. Reb Ephraim didn't seem to mind. He sat on the edge of Tobin's bed, folding his hands across his middle and still grinning.

"I'm glad to hear it," Reb Ephraim said.

There was an interminably long silence in which Tobin felt he was being expected to speak. He didn't. The silence stretched on with Tobin stone-faced and the bearded man grinning and waiting. Frieda looked from Tobin to Reb Ephraim, holding her tongue, but at last it seemed she couldn't keep quiet any longer.

"His injuries are rather minor," she said briskly. "He should recover in a few days. He won't be left with any permanent damage. I can give him some aspirin for the pain if you allow it, Reb Ephraim."

"I suppose that depends on what Tobin has to tell us," the Reb said, and though he was grinning his eyes were hard.

Tobin shrugged. He knew what aspirin was. He also thought that if he had the choice between living with the various pains in his body or agreeing to do anything this man said, he'd clamp his mouth shut and refuse to take anything.

"He says it's true," Frieda whispered. She cast one incredulous look at Tobin, and he saw tears in the old woman's eyes. "He says it's true!"

"I don't doubt him," Reb Ephraim said.

Ah, Tobin thought. Now it comes. The interrogation.

"It is true. I told Ari and the others what I found and where to go. It's pretty far from here, but I have maps. You can have them. Then you can let me go."

At first he thought the Reb was going to turn mean on him, but instead the old man grinned again. The smile still didn't quite reach his eyes, but it was close enough for government work as Old Pa would have said. Someone less wary might have been fooled, but not someone whose head still ached like a son of a bitch.

"Tobin, Tobin!" Reb Ephraim said. "I'm so sorry you feel you've been treated without the appropriate hospitality. That's not our way, I promise you. I know that Luz can be a little…overenthusiastic. I've spoken to him about it."

"Huh."

The one syllable expression didn't do much to make Reb Ephraim happy, Tobin was pleased to note. It didn't stop him grinning, but the smile did falter. Just a little bit, and just for a moment, but enough to show it wasn't real.

The Reb apparently decided to change tactics. Leaning forward he met Tobin's eyes directly. His smile softened, became more serious and less jovial.

"Frieda, would you leave us alone for a few minutes?"

"Of course." Frieda bustled out of the room in a blur of color.

Reb Ephraim scrubbed his face with his palms, looking weary. When he looked at Tobin again, the hard bright grin was gone and so was the glint. Instead of looking like a man who always got his way, he just looked tired. Tobin didn't trust the change. It might be a trick.

When, he thought with some sad surprise, did he get so suspicious of people?

"The Tribe is the strongest community anywhere, and our territory is the largest and the richest. The most well-organized. Such a community does not grow without a price, Tobin. Without costs. We have mouths to feed and backs to clothe. We have people who need shelter, and health care, and education if we want to stay a civilization and not revert to a dark age. We've done all this for over a hundred years now, but our resources are becoming depleted. Rapidly and thoroughly."

The old man turned to look at Tobin, and his eyes were naked helplessness. "If we can't provide for our people, they will leave. And if they leave…" his voice rasped. "We can not survive."

Tobin felt a stirring of pity for the old man before him, but he fought it. "I do understand, Reb Ephraim. I can't even imagine what two thousand people must be like. I grew up in a tiny town. There was only me, Old Ma and Old Pa and my aunts Heather and

Francie. They were all really old, even when I was young. And they all died, one by one."

Tobin was embarrassed to hear his own voice turn raspy with emotion. "I was alone for almost a year before a peddler came to Eastport. He told me about California. He said there were babies being born there. I didn't want to be alone anymore. I wanted to find…someone. Anyone, really, but I also wanted to find someone for me. I want to have a family. I want to see babies. I want to have children, if I can."

"But Tobin," Reb Ephraim said with the first genuine smile Tobin had seen from him. "You can have that here."

Chapter 12

This was the man Chedva had thought was so cute, Elanna thought. She looked carefully at him sleeping, his dark lashes casting sooty shadows on golden cheeks. He'd been in the sun. Not many people in the Tribe had that glow, unless they worked on the rooftops, in the gardens. Even those whose ancestors had been brown-skinned were dark from heritage, not time in the sun.

Purple bruises, some already fading to yellow and green, marred the smoothness of his skin in many places. His right cheek was heavily scratched, the wound scabbed and ugly. She found herself hoping it wouldn't leave a scar.

His hair was dark, too, and sleek against his head. A little longish, perhaps, falling over his eyes, but that could be cut. His brows were fine and dark, his cheeks high, and his nose was not too thin or too broad. He was cute. She wished she knew what color his eyes were.

She'd know as soon as he woke up, but Elanna didn't want to shake him just yet. For now it was enough to watch him sleep, his chest rising and falling regularly, his lips parted slightly. He was handsome, and she would have to have his hands on her soon, but she just wasn't ready.

She'd never minded having appointments with travelers before. Even the ugliest ones served a purpose, and most were so grateful to be allowed access to her bed they treated her like a queen. They gave good gifts, too, items that were scarce around here. It was a good bargain; her body for a few minutes of disinterested grappling in return for a new pair of socks or even something special like a candy bar. Some of the peddlers and passers-through were handsome and talented lovers and so she got even more out of the deal.

Something had changed within herself, she thought, preparing the needle and syringe by rubbing them thoroughly with alcohol. She laid them on the clean white cloth still smelling of bleach and picked up the Geneto-Tester, its casing so worn she could no longer see the numbers on the dials. It didn't matter. She'd used it often enough that she could tell by feel what settings to use.

Her thoughts of running away had faded with the past two days. Replacing them was a subtle sort of despair that left her tired and disinterested in everything. She didn't know what she was going to do, and she felt more on edge than ever.

For now, though, she'd been ordered to keep an appointment with this newcomer. It was the Reb's way of rewarding him and convincing him to help the Tribe. It was also just a standard procedure to try and get fresh bloodlines started within the Tribe.

She finished with the Geneto-Tester and readied the Communicable Diseases Monitor. She didn't need the first one, since she was already pregnant, but she still had to test him for the records. If she didn't, someone would ask why. Both machines were worn and worked only erratically, but she tapped the CDM lightly with one finger until the LED screen flickered. Someday it would stop working all together, just like everything else. And there would be no more. What would they do then?

"What are you doing?"

Startled, she nearly dropped the palm-sized machine. It clattered against the side of the table, the screen going black. Elanna mumbled a curse, aware that her hands were shaking.

"You're awake!" She let the CDM rest alongside her other tools.

"Yeah, I guess I am." He stretched, revealing bare arms finely etched with muscle. He scratched his fingers through his hair, rumpling it.

"Did you sleep well?" Elanna asked. His eyes were dark, like his hair. When they met hers, the hair on the back of her neck rose, making her shiver. Feigning disinterest, she fussed with the tray.

"Better. The aspirin helped."

She looked at him again, her eyebrows raised. "They gave you aspirin?"

He smiled, a slow grin that lit his eyes and gave them a glow like sun through honey. Her mouth dried. Elanna took an inadvertent step back, as though his smile could burn her.

"I must be special, huh?"

"We don't have much aspirin left. Your injuries must have been severe."

He touched his face. "They're not so bad."

They just looked at each other, him with a puzzled look in his eyes. She couldn't imagine her expression. She could only hope it didn't look as hungry as she suddenly felt.

Heart pounding, she turned back to her tray. She'd had hundreds of appointments with men handsomer than this one. What was so special about him?

Was it because of what he knew? What he could do for the Tribe? She forced her fingers to stay steady as she prepared the alcohol swab she'd need to clean the needle when she was done. Reb Ephraim had told her Tobin knew nothing of their customs. That he came from someplace far away, and that he'd been alone for a long time. Was it because he seemed so…innocent?

"What's your name?" Tobin asked.

"Elanna."

"That's pretty."

She surprised herself by smiling. "Thank you."

"What are you doing, Elanna?"

Of course, she thought. He didn't know.

"I'm preparing the Geneto-Tester and the CDM – The Communicable Diseases Monitor."

She showed him the tray and the white cloth, the needle and

syringe, the shot glass of alcohol and the two small machines. His brow furrowed, creasing some of the small scratches there. He frowned, looking at the tray and then back to her with a wariness that hadn't been there before. She couldn't pretend that seeing it didn't make her uncomfortable, but why should it bother him? Even if he was unused to the Tribe's ways, certainly he couldn't argue with the tests' necessity?

"You'll need to be tested," she said. "Before we have our appointment, I mean. I need to make sure you're clean and that we're compatible."

His mouth worked for a moment before he spoke. "Clean, how? What do you mean, compatible?"

She shook her head uncertainly. How could he not know? Even the most widely traveled peddlers knew about the tests. Where had he come from that people didn't need to worry about such things?

"Your blood," she said, and watched his expression slam further shut. He looked like he was going to start yelling, or bolt from the bed, so she talked faster to soothe him. "I have to test it for disease, make sure you don't have anything that could be passed along. And the same with the Geneto-Tester – it types you out. To see if you have any genetic defects that could be inherited, or any anomalies that might cause problems when matched with my geno-makeup…"

"Wait, wait, wait." He shook his head and glared at her. She took another step back. "For what? Why do you need to know this stuff?"

She looked at him blankly. "There's no sense in having an appointment if the baby will inherit a faulty geno-structure, or if you give me some disease…"

"Stop." He held up his hands as if warding off a blow, and then looked at her intensely. Though his gaze was no longer warm, it still made her tingle. Uncomfortably, but unavoidably. "Go back. What did you just say?"

Was he hard of hearing? Deafness would only be a problem if it were genetic and not resulting from an accident or disease. "We don't need to waste an appointment if the baby would inherit…"

"Baby?" He broke in. A light of understanding glimmered in

the dark eyes that were mesmerizing her. "You mean…an appointment is…?"

She waited for him to finished, but he didn't. "I'm a hopemother, Tobin."

Now it was his turn to stare at her blankly. Could he really not know? She felt a warmth in her belly that she couldn't explain and didn't want to. He didn't know. He didn't know anything. And why did that make this seem so much more special?

"A hopemother can have babies. It's my job to have babies," she told him proudly. "I'm the best here."

The change in his eyes was subtle, but she saw it. She couldn't quite identify it, though. He looked away before she had the chance to figure it out.

"You mean you want to…to have sex with me?" His voice cracked. She thought she saw his hands shaking before he slipped them back beneath the sheet.

"Well, yes," Elanna said matter of factly. "How else do you expect me to get pregnant?"

"But I don't even know you," Tobin whispered as though he meant to speak louder but wasn't able to.

Before she could stop it, the laugh burst out. She didn't mean to make fun of him, she really didn't. She just had never heard such an absurd statement before.

"What difference does that make?"

"It makes a difference to me," Tobin muttered, and she instantly felt sorry she had laughed at him.

"Well, it doesn't have to," she said, trying to make him feel better. "I'll take care of you, Tobin. I know what I'm doing."

He looked as though she'd poked him in the eye unexpectedly. Blinking, Tobin shook his head as though in disbelief. Uncertainly, still wanting to reassure him, Elanna continued.

"I really am the best. I've caught pregnant twenty times." Elanna couldn't keep the pride from her voice. "I've had thirteen children. Eleven lived. That's some kind of record, you know. I --"

"Get out."

She wasn't sure she'd heard him right. "What?"

"I said," Tobin repeated deliberately, "get out."

"What?" Elanna repeated, knowing she sounded stupid but completely confused. She took a step toward him, but the look on his face forced her to stop. He stared at her like he was looking at something that had died and been left to rot in the sun. He was looking at her with disgust.

"Get out!"

The shout followed her as she fled the room, echoing even after she'd slammed the door behind her. Tears scalded her eyes, and she thought for one crazy moment she might vomit. She sagged against the wall, trying to catch her breath and calm herself down.

Nobody had ever rejected her before. No one.

Chapter 13

In the three days since he'd ordered the girl from his room, Tobin had been lost about a dozen times. And he hadn't yet ventured out of the main complex! It was huge, a veritable warren of rooms for washing, eating and eliminating, other rooms for sleeping and gathering and entertaining, more rooms for functions he didn't even know. All of this on merely the first two floors of a building Reb Ephraim had told him once housed the city's largest department store.

The Tribe had additional holdings outside the main complex, places for people to live and work and go to school, but most of the main living was done inside. Even those people who made their homes in apartments around the Main Hall came there for most meals, and to visit with friends.

Now Tobin needed to find Reb Ephraim and the Beit Din's office. It was supposed to be down this hall and to the left, past the kitchen. There were at least five doors, though, none of them marked. He'd knocked on one and interrupted an appointment. He didn't want to knock again until he was sure he had the right place.

He still wasn't used to seeing so many people, though he'd gotten better at hiding his astonishment. He didn't want to keep walking around all the time with his mouth hanging open like an idiot. He stood out enough as it was. He couldn't walk into a room without a dozen voices calling out greetings to him, and he was lucky if he'd even met half of the people saying hello. Luckier if he could remember their names.

He didn't have trouble remembering the girl's name. Elanna. He'd seen her around, mostly from across the room, but she'd never come over to him. He supposed he couldn't blame her. He'd only been with the Tribe for a week, but he'd learned enough of their ways to know he'd badly insulted her.

He winced inwardly, even now, thinking about it. He'd been an imbecile to react the way he'd had, but just hearing her rattle off the statistics as though she had something to brag about had turned his stomach. Except now, knowing how the Tribe lived, he knew Elanna did have something to brag about.

"Tobin! Come on in. I've been waiting for you." The door at the end of the hall opened, and Reb Ephraim peered out.

Once inside, Tobin refused the Reb's offer of a seat. The room was small but clean, lit only by one dim lantern and a series of flickering candles that smelled like cooking oil. It was dominated by a large desk and chair, with several smaller chairs arranged in a semicircle around the front of the desk.

"Books," Tobin said, ignoring everything else in favor of the floor-to ceiling shelves that lined the back wall. They were filled with rows of books.

Reb Ephraim looked over his shoulder as he sat down behind the desk. "Yes."

Tobin hadn't seen anyone with books since he'd been here. He hadn't been allowed access to his pack, so he hadn't even been able to read the ones he'd brought from home. He didn't realize how much he'd missed them.

"I haven't seen any other books around here."

The Reb looked at the wall. "That's because we don't have many books. They're special and precious."

Tobin didn't disagree. "But people can read. Can't they?"

The Reb laughed heartily. "Of course we can read, Tobin.

We're not Savages or Bridgers. We have textbooks. We have our Torah, our Tanach, our holy books. What you see here are the last books, anyway, unless the Gatherers bring in more. And those are immediately used in ways that better benefit the Tribe."

"What can you do with a book besides read it?"

"The Tribe has been through some dark times," Reb Ephraim said. "Before we managed to find a way to hold ourselves together, lots of things were destroyed. When winter came and people had no heat, or any way to cook their food, what did they use? Anything they could burn. Books are scarce around here, and if there are any found, they're usually broken down and used to make paper. We have a wonderful recycling program. We need to."

Tobin thought about the hours he'd spent with a book as his only companion. After Old Pa's eTablet had run out of batteries with none to replace them, books were all that was left. He'd made friends with Huckleberry Finn and Harry Potter. He'd fallen in love with Scarlett O'Hara and Clarice Starling. Even in the coldest Maine winters, it would never have occurred to any of them to burn books.

Reb steepled his fingers on the desk, looking grave. "Tobin, I know that your greeting wasn't the best representation of life here, but you've been here for a week now. Our Gatherers have been preparing to make the trip to the warehouse. Have you changed your mind about staying?"

Tobin hadn't actually made up his mind. He liked the meals. He liked the soft bed. He liked the company...and the babies. Of course, there were babies here. He just didn't really like how they were made.

"We're a thriving community, Tobin. We have limited resources. Each and every person in the Tribe performs a function valid and necessary for the survival of the whole tribe. Can we expect you to contribute?"

"If life's so tough here -- " And he knew it was, for despite the many luxuries he'd lacked in Eastport they at least hadn't been forced to live in darkness, piled on top of each other, "why don't people ever just light out on their own? Don't people ever just want to leave? Or don't they ask questions from people who are passing through? Don't any of you people wonder what's out there besides this place?"

Reb Ephraim looked hesitant. "We don't force them to stay if they want to go, but very few people want to leave. Certainly, some of them ask questions of the few peddlers we get through here, but Tobin, you have to remember something. Even those peddlers are from no farther away than perhaps a week's travel. As far as I know, we've never had anyone from as far away as you've come. Our people don't ask questions simply because they're not aware that there are any questions to ask."

"But they know about California," Tobin said. "At least Ari does, and Asaph."

Reb Ephraim chuckled. He reached into his desk drawer and pulled out a thickly folded sheet of paper. With practiced motions he unfolded about one third of it, laying it out on the desk for Tobin to see.

"To them," he said with another laugh, pointing, "this is California."

Tobin looked at the paper and the professionally drawn map on it. It looked like his maps, but where his Atlas of The United States showed an entire continent, the Reb's paper showed only what Tobin recognized as New York City. The areas all around were marked, but not in detail, and where Colorado began on Tobin's map, the Reb's showed only the edge of land, the beginning of the sea.

"You've erased nearly an entire country!"

The Reb shrugged, refolding the map. "And what difference does that make? There might as well be nothing there, Tobin. If there are settlements, we'll never meet them. Never have contact with them. All of that is lost to us, so why offer it to people who would be better off just staying here, with the Tribe?"

"They should be able to make that choice," Tobin said stubbornly. "It should be up to them."

"Really," said Reb Ephraim somewhat condescendingly. "Why would anyone want to leave a comfortable life here and risk their lives to maybe, only maybe, find something else? Because despite our hardships, Tobin, we do have a comfortable life here. It's not a luxurious life, not like it was in the days when this city was overflowing with people. No. But we have food and shelter and each other. Why would anyone want to leave?"

"I want to leave."

Reb Ephraim sighed as though he were talking to a very tiresome child. "I don't understand. I explained to you that all the things you claimed you wanted to find in California, you could find here."

Tobin frowned. "No. Not exactly."

"You said you wanted to have children," Reb Ephraim said finally. "Why do you think I sent you Elanna?"

At the sound of her name, Tobin's stomach flip-flopped. She was so beautiful, that girl, the most beautiful he'd ever dreamed of. And he'd turned her away.

Tobin thought of all the books he'd read. Mother. Father. Husband. Wife. Son. Daughter. Family. Those were words he knew. He'd had Old Ma and Old Pa to learn from, and books, and that was all. Descriptions of how families were long ago, and maybe they had nothing to do with the way things were now.

"I'm sorry," Tobin said finally.

He thought of Elanna again, her smooth perfect features and smoky blue eyes. The curls, the same color as an ocean sunset, tumbling over her shoulders. How she had smelled like nothing he'd ever smelled before, but he knew all the same it was the scent of a woman. How he'd ached for her to touch him as he'd read of and dreamed about. He thought about her making love to him only because it was her job, and he shuddered. Impossible. He couldn't do it.

Reb Ephraim seemed barely appeased. "We honored you by giving you an appointment with Elanna."

Tobin thought of the stricken look on Elanna's face as she'd fled the room. He'd insulted and embarrassed her. "I told her to leave. I didn't sleep with her."

Reb Ephraim shook his head slowly. "Why not?

"When I said I wanted to find a woman, I meant one just for me," Tobin said. Only after he spoke did he realize how foolish and selfish that sounded.

"A wife," Reb Ephraim said.

"Well, yeah."

The Reb tapped his fingers together. "I can't give you that. Love can't be given by someone else. If you find love with one of our women and she agrees to stand beneath the chuppah as your bride, then we'll all rejoice. But I can't make that happen. I can, however, almost guarantee that you can father a child. And with a child, almost any of the women here would be eager to wed you."

It still didn't sound like what Tobin had dreamed about back in Eastport, but he didn't have time to protest. Reb Ephraim got up and went around the desk past Tobin, jerking open the door to the hall. "Yavin!"

A small boy, about seven years old, appeared as if by magic. "Yes, Reb Ephraim?"

"Go and find Elanna. Bring her to me immediately."

The boy nodded and then grinned, showing an endearingly gap-toothed smile. He held out a hand for the candy Reb Ephraim was already pulling from his pocket before tearing off down the hall. The clatter of his shoes against the concrete floor was very loud.

"Don't," Tobin said as the Reb passed by him to sit back at the desk. "Don't embarrass her."

"More than you've embarrassed her already, you mean?" Reb Ephraim said gruffly. He looked around as though he wanted something to occupy his hands, but found nothing. Instead, he reached into his coat pocket and pulled out another candy. He offered one to Tobin.

It was sweeter than anything he'd ever tasted, and more sour, fruitier, tangier, all at once. It puckered his mouth and blasted his tongue with sensation. His eyes watered.

Reb Ephraim popped one into his own mouth. "Starburst. Last month the Gatherers found an entire case in the back bedroom closet of a twelfth-floor apartment in Queens. One of them was nearly killed when his rappelling rope broke. Is it worth it, Tobin?"

Tobin swallowed the candy square. "I don't know what you mean."

"Is it worth the lives of our people to have something like this?" the Reb asked, leaning forward. "Is it worth that risk, when if the place you told us of exists, we can supply ourselves with better, more worthy items at half the danger?"

"I don't know."

"What I'm asking you, Tobin, is if you'd consider becoming a gatherer."

Tobin eyed the other man, saying nothing for a long moment. "Why me?"

"You're fit. You're young. And you seem to have a knack for finding things. You're...bold, Tobin. Bolder than we are. And if we're going to grow, survive, continue, we need fresh and bold young men to join us. And we need you to lead us to the warehouse. You know where it is."

"I said I'd draw a map --"

The Reb looked down at the map on his desk, then back at Tobin. "You would have us trust a map?"

The man had a point. Tobin's maps were accurate, so far as he could tell. But they *were* outdated.

Tobin looked around the Reb's office. Just a few weeks ago he'd have given anything just to find a community as big as this one, as well-established. A chance to find friends, make a family. Work at something important.

"I don't think so," Tobin said.

"I'll change your mind," Reb Ephraim replied.

Chapter 14

“Ah, Elanna,” Reb Ephraim said, and sent the child out of the room with two sweets for his troubles.

“You wanted to see me?”

Elanna looked at the young man who’d refused her so rudely. Did she imagine that his face was nearly as red as her own? She met his eyes, wanting to challenge him. Didn’t he know what he’d passed up?

But of course he did, she thought, only half-hearing the Reb as he scolded Tobin for not keeping the appointment. She could see the way he looked at her; it was a look she’d seen dozens of times before. So why had he sent her away?

The Reb was saying something to her now, but Elanna hadn’t been paying attention. “I’m sorry?”

The Reb sighed. “I told you to take Tobin and show him around. You are to be his constant companion. You’re excused from making other appointments, and cancel the ones you’ve made for the next few days.”

“But why?” Elanna asked, stunned. She’d never been ordered to stop keeping appointments, unless she was carrying or nursing. Never. Others had been restricted for one reason or another, but never her. Not even when she'd miscarried for the third time in as many months!

"Because," Reb Ephraim said, "That is how I want it."

"For how long?"

"Until he," the Reb said, pointing to Tobin, "agrees to keep an appointment with you."

"What?" Tobin yelled. "Why?"

Faintness overcame her. Elanna sunk into the chair next to Tobin's, intensely aware of the warmth of his skin as her leg brushed his. Equally aware of the way he jerked away from her as though she smelled bad.

"Because we want you to be happy here," Reb Ephraim said to Tobin patiently. "Because you said you wanted children, and chances are excellent, if you have no problems, that Elanna can give them to you. Because you seem to have an aversion to sharing your woman with other men. Because we need what you can give us, Tobin, and it's worth it to us to give you something you want in return."

The older man turned to Elanna. "You're not carrying now, are you?"

Still stunned by his order, Elanna shook her head, though of course it was a lie. "I...I don't think so. I won't know for sure for another week..."

"Good. Then you'll only be with Tobin until you catch."

Numb, Elanna nodded her assent. It was unheard of to restrict a hopemother to one man just to guarantee a child by him. Was she being punished or privileged?

"No." Tobin stood. His entire body shook. She'd thought he looked timid before, when the Gatherers brought him in, but not now. He looked as though he could strike out at any minute. "You can't use her to buy me."

The Reb looked at Elanna kindly. "You don't know even realize the price she's worth."

They were talking about her like she was something the Gatherers had found, not like she was a person. And a hopemother, the best among them! But Elanna dared not say anything. She didn't know why the Reb was doing what he was, but she knew she had no way of fighting it. If the Reb said it was going to be, it was so.

"You're a bastard," Tobin said through gritted teeth.

No one talked to Reb Ephraim like that. Elanna looked at the man who kept the Tribe together, not certain what to expect. She'd never seen him show rage, but she'd seen the results of what had happened when people made him angry.

"I don't understand your anger. We offer everything you could want, and ask for so little in return. Why would you refuse? If you do what we want, in the end we'll all be happy."

What about me? Elanna thought, burning inside. Will I be happy? She looked at Tobin, the man who'd rejected her. And she had to spend time with him? Beyond just having sex with him, she had to be his…his companion?

"You don't mind, do you Elanna?" Reb Ephraim asked her suddenly.

Tobin turned to gaze at her, his eyes searching hers as though he were trying to read her thoughts. "No, of course not," Elanna lied. "It's an honor, Reb."

To her surprise, Tobin reached out and took her hand. "I'm sorry for hurting your feelings, Elanna. I didn't understand."

She felt his fingers warm around hers, felt them squeeze. It felt good. Like a friend.

"It's all right," she said.

"I would be happy for you to teach me about the Tribe," Tobin continued. He didn't let go of her hand until she tugged it gently away. His eyes didn't leave hers. "And as for the other…"

"Yes?" She didn't want to sound eager, damn it! Because she wasn't.

He shrugged, finally looking away. "I just want you to know that I don't…I can't…"

He looked helplessly at Reb Ephraim. "I can't. Not like that."

Elanna still didn't understand, but she remembered his reaction the last time she'd tried to make him feel more comfortable about it. She didn't want to go through that again, especially not with a witness. She looked to the Reb for guidance.

"Tobin…isn't used to our ways," Reb Ephraim said. That was an understatement if she'd ever heard one. "He's uncomfortable with the idea that you've been with other men."

She still didn't understand. "Oh."

Tobin met her eyes again. "I'll help you, Reb Ephraim, but not so that I can…be with Elanna."

"I don't care if you do it," Reb Ephraim said. "Only that you understand that you can." To someone who didn't know him, the relief in his voice was well-hidden. But Elanna heard it, and she understood it.

"Come on, Tobin," she said. "I'll give you a tour."

When she passed Yavin standing outside Reb Ephraim's door, she bent to hug and kiss him. The little boy returned her affection but quickly wriggled away to continue playing with the small wooden top he spun on the concrete floor. Elanna stole another quick kiss, grateful that Yavin, unlike Boaz, was still young enough for kisses.

As they were walking away, Tobin spoke. "He's yours, isn't he?"

"If you mean did I birth him," Elanna said, "Yes. But he's not mine. His parents are Nedira and Doran."

"He looks like you."

"You think so? I always thought he looked like his father."

"You mean you know who his father is?"

She glanced at him as they walked, taken aback by the question. "Well…of course I know who fathered him."

"I just thought…" Tobin paused, clearly struggling with what he wanted to say. "I mean, if you keep so many appointments, how do you know?"

Elanna stopped, glad they were in an unfrequented part of the complex. She didn't feel like running into anyone right now. "I keep records."

"Look, I know about the birds and the bees. If you've…been with…a number of men in one…cycle…how do you know for sure which one…?"

It was almost funny watching him struggle. The blush looked

good on him. She thought about the squeeze of his fingers against hers and felt more kindly to him.

"We don't know until the baby is born," Elanna said, remembering how he'd lived.

He hadn't known about the Geneto-Tester or the CDM, two things she knew had once been widely available to even average people, at least in the city. Maybe in the country people hadn't needed machines to test for disease, and so he'd never heard of them. It would stand to reason then that he'd never heard of the Paternitester, either.

"We have a machine that takes a blood sample from the baby and can match it with the DNA of the father. Everyone's DNA is on record here. It's easy to keep track."

Tobin sighed. "Sometimes I think I never should have left Eastport."

Elanna started walking again, taking him toward the social hall. "Are we really so bad?"

He laughed, surprising her. It was a nice laugh, and she found herself returning it. "I don't know, Elanna. I don't have much to compare you to."

They'd entered a busier corridor. Elanna ignored the curious looks, noticing that Tobin seemed ultra-aware of them. She smiled and nodded at a few people but kept the pace steady, not stopping to invite talk.

"Rumor is that you only had seven people in your town."

"Five," Tobin corrected.

They pushed through a set of swinging doors and down another hall. She walked without thinking, realizing too late that it must be a maze to him. She'd have to take more time to show him how to get around.

"Five," she repeated. "I can't imagine it."

"Believe me," Tobin said with a rueful chuckle. "I couldn't imagine two thousand, either."

She stopped in front of the doors that opened onto the social hall. "Why did you come here?"

He took her hand again, gave it another squeeze that shot

warmth down to her toes. She wanted to pull away, if only because the touch made her feel closer to him than she wanted to. She couldn't without effort, so she just let him hold it.

"I came here," Tobin said with a small smile that made her feel more sad than anything else, "because I didn't want to be alone anymore."

"I've never been really alone," Elanna said without thinking. "I think I would like it."

"You are so beautiful," Tobin said and dropped her hand.

Supremely conscious that at least half a dozen other people were close enough to hear him, Elanna unsuccessfully fought a blush. "I can't be that beautiful. You wouldn't even keep your appointment with me."

"I think you have a lot of men who'll do that," Tobin said. "How many of them would like to be your friend?"

"Not enough," Elanna said.

"I'd like to be."

"I'd like that," she replied, and took him into the social hall.

Chapter 15

The small fire burned low, and there'd be no more fuel allowed until Shabbat ended the next evening. The lanterns had been dimmed to next to nothing. The social hall was nearly empty. They were the last two in the leisure room. Even the teeners had given up their silly flirtations and gone to bed.

"Tired?" Elanna asked when she caught Tobin yawning.

He grinned at her. "Yeah. And my legs hurt from all that climbing."

She'd taken him to the rooftop gardens today. If he'd been anyone else, particularly someone she wanted an appointment with, she'd have offered to rub his legs. But she couldn't offer him that. He'd think she was trying to seduce him.

"The climb down wasn't so bad, was it?" She leaned back into the softness of the sofa cushions. She wasn't tired at all. Being around Tobin made her skin feel like it was crawling with ants.

They'd spent nearly every waking moment together for the past four days. She'd never spent so much time with one man in her life. She'd thought he would bore her. He didn't. Or worse, irritate her and make her angry. He didn't do that, either. Tobin had a gentle sense of humor she wasn't used to with the men she'd known. He made her laugh. And he listened to her.

"It wasn't so bad," he agreed. He yawned again, stretched.

"Can you find your way back to your room?" she asked finally. "It's easy to get lost when the lights are dimmed. If you don't know where you're going, I mean."

He stretched again, reaching his long arms up behind his head until his shirt pulled up and exposed the tautness of his stomach. Elanna looked away as though she'd never seen a male torso before, and cursed herself silently for being ridiculous.

"Maybe you can walk me there," Tobin said, but made no move to get off the sofa.

They'd commandeered one of the more comfortable ones from the teeners, who grumbled but got up when Elanna ordered them to. Orna had been one of the grumblers. At eleven, she was one of the youngest in the group. Soon they'd know if she was going to be a hopemother like Elanna. Though Orna hadn't been hers for ten years, Elanna found herself squeezing the girl's hand as she went by.

She thought of that touch now, sad because Orna had twisted away from it. Politely, but firmly. Elanna knew that was part of growing up, part of changing from child to teener and then adult. It didn't stop the sting.

Now she watched Tobin relax against the cushions not so recently vacated by her first-born daughter. What would a child of his be like? Dark haired and dark eyed? She'd likely never know.

"When are you going to leave?" she asked.

The question seemed to surprise him, but he recovered quickly. "You mean with the Gatherers?"

"Sure," Elanna said. She realized something quickly, something he thought she didn't catch. He was thinking of leaving, all right, and not with the Gatherers.

Tobin shifted in his seat, stretching out his impossibly long legs as though looking for a way to answer her. "I don't know when they're going to be ready. Soon, I guess. They must have some work to do on the trucks. I hear they're going to take them as far as the edge of the city, then they'll go forward on bikes after that."

"I guess so." Elanna watched the firelight, golden and red, reflected in his eyes. Why couldn't she forget the revulsion she'd seen there before?

She'd never been afraid before, to ask a man to her bed. If she'd had to do the asking at all. Until Tobin, she'd never been rejected.

"Thanks for taking me up there today. Tobin looked around the room, empty now. "I feel like…I mean, do you want to…"

"What?" She sounded too eager, but he didn't seem to notice.

"Go for a walk."

"Now? Outside? It's dark."

"Oh, sorry. Is it because it's your Shabbat? I know you can't light the lights but I thought that's why it would be good to take a walk instead of you know, just sitting here in the dark."

She shook her head, confused. "No. It's not that. But you don't want to take a walk now. Not at night. It's dangerous."

"I thought there wasn't any crime here. The Bridgers and the Savages stay far away."

"Not from them," Elanna said. "From the trolls and gobblings."

Tobin stared at her for a long, silent moment. "The what?"

"Trolls. Gobblings. They hunt at night. They eat people."

Tobin shook his head. "You're kidding, right? I mean, is this a joke? It has to be. Right?"

"Why would it be a joke?" She studied him, not understanding. "Surely you've seen them."

"We didn't have them where I came from."

She shivered. "You're lucky."

Tobin gave her an odd look. "Yeah. I guess so. What do they look like? These…trolls. And gobblings."

"I've never seen one. And I don't want to," she added hastily. "When one's spotted, we all have to go inside. They bar the doors. For our protection. We haven't had any attacks in years. But they're still out there."

"How do you know?"

"The Gatherers find signs of them," she said.

"And you trust them? You trust the Beit Din." He said the second not like a question.

Elanna gave him another curious look. "Of course. We have to. The Tribe couldn't survive very well if we didn't trust the Beit Din."

"I didn't have a council to help me," Tobin said after a pause. "And I turned out all right."

"It's what we know, Tobin."

"Is that why none of you leave your territory? Why you all stay here?"

"Where would we go?" She said this as though the idea of running away had never crossed her mind.

"Anywhere you wanted?" Tobin gave a small laugh. "Where nobody told you who you had to love."

At this, she frowned. "You're talking about this. Us. About what Reb Ephraim said I have to do."

He wouldn't look at her.

Elanna was tired of biting her tongue and holding her temper. She'd spent years doing it with the Tribe, but Tobin wasn't from the Tribe. She owed him nothing. "What are afraid of? Do you think I'm going to try to force you into bed with me? Is that it?"

"Yes, maybe," he said. "Yes."

He rubbed his hands up and down along his thighs. The motion annoyed her; she grabbed his hands until he stopped. She forced him to look at her.

"What's the matter with you, Tobin? I thought…I thought you wanted to be my friend."

"I do." He didn't pull his hands away from hers.

"Then what?" Elanna asked, dismayed to hear the sound of tears in her voice. She didn't want to cry. She didn't want this to matter. She didn't know why it did.

"I don't know much about women," Tobin began.

"Obviously," Elanna said, but not as bitterly as she might have a few moments before.

That earned a hint of a smile. It made her bite her lip, that smile. In the firelight, with the light gleaming red in his dark hair, Tobin's smile made a flame curl in her belly.

"Elanna," Tobin said.

She waited for him to say more, but he seemed to be at a loss for words. The fire crackled and popped, growing dimmer. Soon they'd be sitting in the dark.

"Elanna," he tried again. "I used to dream about a woman like you."

"You did?" She was confused, didn't quite know what to say.

"It's why I left Eastport, and came here," he continued softly. He still hadn't let go of her hands. "The peddler said I'd find people here. And I did. I met you. I just…I just didn't know that people…"

"Yes?"

She had no idea what he was trying to tell her. For all the time they'd spent together, he was a complete mystery. They didn't have the same frames of reference; he didn't understand life in the Tribe and she didn't understand how he'd lived before coming here.

"I always thought about finding one woman, that's all. Getting...married."

She laughed, wishing she could call it back once it was out of her mouth but knowing it was too late. The laugh was harsh. "Hopemothers don't get married, Tobin. We have to be available to any man who could get a child on us."

And yet, didn't she feel as wistful as he sounded? Hadn't she too dreamed of finding one person to be with? It was an impossible dream, but he didn't know that. How could he? He hadn't lived here all his life, as she had. He didn't know that there was no defying the rules of the Tribe.

The fire was even lower now. The lanterns were too high up on the walls to shed any light. Even in the pitch black she would have known he was there.

"I know it's your duty," Tobin's voice thickened. "To be with all the men, I mean. I know that. And I know why. I know that to you, there's nothing wrong about it…"

"There *is* nothing wrong with it," Elanna said.

"I know I should be honored that Reb Ephraim tied you to me," Tobin said. "I know that there are men here who would pay a high price to be in my position."

"Yes, that's true." What was his point?

"But Elanna..." He sighed again. "I can't make love to you. Not knowing that it's only a duty for you. I want more than that."

Now she really didn't understand. She'd never heard a man say anything like that. They made appointments with her and she kept them, simple as that.

"You mean like a child?" she asked.

"Yes, I'd like to have a child," Tobin said. "It's why I want to go to California. But that's not what I meant."

Now it was her turn to sigh. "I don't understand."

"I don't want to be just one more appointment, Elanna. Without feelings, it wouldn't be any good for me."

She turned this over in her mind. "You mean you don't want to make love with me because..." and now came the stretch, the leap of faith to a concept she'd never considered, "because you don't love me?"

"Elanna, no! I don't want to make love to you because *you* don't love *me*."

"Love?" The laugh came out before she could stop it. "I don't think I'd know how."

She didn't need a light to know when he got up and left.

Chapter 16

Elanna hadn't looked at him, really at him, since two nights before when he'd left her. She hadn't said anything to him about that night. She hadn't avoided his company. She'd only stopped looking at him, not stopped talking to him; but although she did everything she was supposed to, it was different. Tobin wanted to apologize but thought that would probably only make matters worse. He'd only known her for two weeks, and he'd hurt her twice. Badly.

He needed to leave this place. Soon, before the Gatherers finished their preparations and he could no longer put off the invitation to join them. But not before he'd made things right with her.

Why did he have to keep dreaming of California, when he could find everything he'd dreamed of right here? Because he didn't want to live in a place where stories about trolls and goblins were used to keep people from leaving, he thought fiercely.

"Thanks for meeting me," he said when Elanna pushed through the front doors to the Main Hall and onto the street.

She shrugged, still looking through and not at him. Tobin tugged Elanna's elbow, leading onto the street. She followed without eagerness, but she didn't balk, either. He was aware of the looks and the whispers that surrounded them as people went about their business, but he ignored them.

He wanted to find a place where they could be alone. No easy task, since even the buildings were still teeming with people who'd come out to see the parade. They'd have to go further.

"Where are we going?" Elanna hesitated when they reached the end of the block and Tobin showed no sign of stopping.

"C'mon," he said, glancing over his shoulder. Nobody seemed inclined to follow them. "Let's just go a little further."

Her face was a mask of stone, but she did as he requested. Even unsmiling she was so lovely, Tobin thought as he scanned the street and buildings for a spot to stop and talk to her. Just ahead and around the corner was a cluster of tall buildings around a sunken spot. Stairs led down to a sheltered concrete patio, with plenty of benches to sit on. Weeds and impoverished looking grass grew in patches among the ruins.

Magnificently, the sunken area had an even lower pit filled with water. A huge statue of a reclining man, once golden but now faded a motley green and gray, watched over the huge fish swimming lazily in the artificial pond. Tobin led Elanna down the steps to sit next to the water.

"Here," he said. "Sit down. Please."

She did as he asked with stiff dignity. The late afternoon sun, broken up by the taller buildings, fell in dappled patterns across her face. She smoothed her fingers over the rough concrete, pulling away her hand when it became dark with grit.

"What do you want, Tobin?"

He sat beside her, not touching her but close enough that he could if he wanted to. "Will you look at me, please?"

Her lower lip trembled, and with shame he realized she was close to tears. He had done that, made her cry. He was the monster, not some made-up troll or gobbling.

"Elanna, I'm sorry."

She looked at him then with tear-bright eyes. She lifted her chin almost defiantly, as though daring him to notice the wetness. Her gaze was steady, and it pierced him.

"It's easy to say you're sorry, isn't it? Wouldn't it be better and easier just not to hurt people?"

"Yes," he answered. "But I did hurt you, and I'm sorry."

She waved her hand back and forth. "Never mind. It doesn't matter."

"It does matter," he contradicted. "I'm an idiot."

She let the barest hint of a smile tug at her lips. "Yes, you are."

"I shouldn't have left like I did."

She sighed. "I know what I said must have been…abrupt. And I'm sorry."

He smiled at her. "It's easy to say, isn't it?"

She played with the gravel some more, watching her fingers make patterns in the dirt. When she looked at him again, her eyes were dry. "You don't know anything about people. I don't know anything about love. I don't know what you want, Tobin. I only know how to be the way I am. I'm sorry it isn't enough for you."

She could have been stabbing him, so sharp was the pain he felt at her words. "I never said --"

She waved him to silence. "You didn't have to. I offered you my body because that's all I know how to give. You didn't want it. Did you bring me here to talk about this?"

"No," Tobin replied, though he wanted to talk about it now. He just didn't know what to say.

"Then what?"

He gathered his thoughts quickly. "I wanted to talk to you about monsters."

That seemed to startle her. "What about them?"

"How do you think I got here, Elanna?"

"The Gatherers brought you." Her brow creased. "Right?"

"But how did they find me?" Tobin asked. "How did I get into the city?"

"I don't know," Elanna said. "I never thought about it."

"I rode a bicycle," Tobin said, remembering he hadn't seen the bike since he'd been here. Or his pack. "From Eastport, Maine."

Now she frowned. "Maine?"

"It's a state," Tobin told her.

"State?"

He thought about the maps that showed the city and little else. "It's part of the whole country. Like New York or California. It took me six weeks to get here from there. It's where I lived my whole life. And I didn't see any monsters along the way, Elanna. Not one."

She sat back, still frowning. "I don't understand."

"There aren't any trolls or gobblings," Tobin said gently. "At least, I didn't see any. If there were such things out there, don't you think they would have tried to get me? How did you think I got here without getting caught by them?"

She stood up agitatedly and began pacing along the edge of the pond. It made him nervous to see her so close to the water's edge, but he knew better than to try and pull her back.

"I just thought…you must be a great fighter…or a good hider," she said in a low voice as she walked. "And when you said you found the storehouse with all that stuff in it…I thought you just must be very clever. And brave. I…I just never thought much about it, Tobin. I didn't think of how long it took you to get here or anything."

"Because Reb Ephraim and the council told you what you needed to know, right?"

"They always do," Elanna said, finally standing still. "Don't they?"

"There's a world out there you've never heard about. It's huge. There's more to the world than just New York City, or the Tribe. More beyond even than the Park and the Savages, Elanna. California might have fallen off the edge of the world like you were taught, I don't know. But if it did, it was an edge much, much farther away than you could imagine. There are other people living in this world, maybe even more than two thousand. There are places you've never heard of. Places I've never heard of. The stories that Reb Ephraim's told you all…some of them just aren't true. Do you believe me?

She crossed over to him and sat. "I believe you. I don't know why, but I do."

A brief puff of breeze brought the fresh scent of her to him, and Tobin's heart double thumped. Suddenly, he didn't care any more about her past. Pulling her toward him, he pressed his mouth against hers. All that mattered was the future.

Chapter 17

She couldn't stop smiling. She'd been kissed what? A thousand times maybe? More than that? But none of those kisses had ever stayed on her lips like Tobin's had. She wanted to laugh out loud, and she didn't really know why.

Something had passed between them among the rubble and the weeds. She didn't quite know what it was, but it had turned her entire world upside down. She didn't know if her stomach churned from excitement or terror. Maybe both.

"I'm leaving tonight," he said.

Her stomach twisted again, but this time she recognized the feeling as disappointment. She didn't want him to go. She couldn't bear for him to go. Not now, when his kisses had held the promise of something for which she'd yearned but never dared dream.

"Do…do you have to?" The words came out sounding weak and silly, and she hated them. Her heart had leaped at his words, her dream of finding a place to go where she could live as a woman renewed. Yet now, when the chance arose before her, she feared taking it.

"After what I told you, do you have to ask?"

She thought of the years of lies. The stories. The things she had always, in some deep corner of her mind, suspected were not true but had never questioned.

"The Tribe is my family," she said helplessly. She turned back to him, feeling the tears hot in her eyes but not willing to brush them away. Ashamed not because what she said was true, but because she'd already thought of running away but had never found the courage. She had a reason, though. "My babies are here, Toby."

He looked startled. "Nobody's ever called me that before."

"If you don't like it --"

"I do."

She thought, hoped, that he might kiss her again, but instead he merely smoothed the hair away from her forehead.

"I have to go," he said. "I don't expect you to go with me."

That set her teeth on edge, and her mouth turned down in a frown so tight it hurt. "You don't?"

"I couldn't ask you to do that."

He shook his head. Nervously he rubbed his hands together, cracking the knuckles until she thought she might scream.

She wouldn't ask him why. She wouldn't let the words come out of her mouth. She'd bite her tongue until it squirted blood before she'd open herself up to hurt again.

"Why not?" she asked anyway, powerless to stop the question.

"This is my journey, my quest." Tobin bent and put his face in his hands, rubbing his cheeks and then running his hands through his dark hair again and again until it stood wildly on end. "My danger. I don't know what's out there, Elanna. I don't know if I'll find anything at all, much less what I'm looking for. I can't ask you to give up the life you have here just to follow a stranger."

"I didn't think," Elanna replied stiffly, "that we were strangers anymore."

He sighed, and when he looked up at her she was alarmed to see that red rimmed his eyes. He looked haggard. The scruff of a beard she hadn't paid attention to before stood out on his cheeks.

"You have so much here," he said. "You don't even know. Everyone's talking about how much better it will be when the Gatherers bring back the goods from the warehouse, and that's probably true.

But the Tribe is living pretty good. You have things here I've never even seen. Candy. Food. Clothes. Lanterns." He laughed hollowly. "Indoor plumbing, for god's sake. Compared to how I lived in Maine…in some ways this is like a paradise."

"Then why leave?"

"Because it's only *like* a paradise." Tobin touched her hair again, her cheek. "I can't stay here and be silent about the truth I know. It's fine to want to stay somewhere, but to be told lies to prevent you from even wanting to leave, or being afraid of leaving, I can't stomach that."

"You said you wanted children," Elanna said, hating the desperation in her voice. "I can give you children, Toby!"

He held her face in his hands. "But you can't give me you."

Hopemothers did not marry, nor did they keep themselves only for one man. It was a truth she'd railed against but couldn't imagine differently. She put her hands on her belly, where she kept the secret she'd be unable to keep much longer.

"Then take me with you," she said quietly. "I'll go."

He smiled at her condescendingly, and she frowned again. "I need to travel quickly. I need to go a long way."

"And what? You're afraid I'll hold you back?"

"I didn't say that."

"Then what?" she demanded.

"Elanna." Tobin sighed. "You have no idea what it's like beyond the city. You'll have to walk a lot. Scrounge for food. There won't be any privileges like you're used to. You have to be tough."

She shoved herself away from him and stood. Her fists clenched so she wouldn't give in to the urge to throttle him. She bit her lip for a moment until she was certain she could talk without screaming.

"I've given birth thirteen times. I've labored for three days in a row, without pain relief, with nothing but a piece of leather to chew on to stop myself from passing out, Tobin. I've had babies torn out of me because they couldn't get out on their own. I think I'm pretty tough."

His face grew white at her speech, and he swallowed heavily. "Think of what you'd be leaving behind."

She thought about it. Babies she carried in her womb and nurtured, only to have them taken from her before they could even call her mama. Men who touched her body but didn't even think about her heart. Privileges and honors that did nothing to combat a life of loneliness. And despair so deep, so keen that she had once thought about taking her own life. She thought too of the secret she carried in her womb, the one even Reb Ephraim didn't know about.

"Isn't that my choice to make?"

Chapter 18

Chedva caught up with them just inside the main doors. "It's almost time for the banquet! They're serving veal."

"Veal?" Tobin asked. Where did they keep the cows?

"A real treat," Elanna said. "The Reb and the Beit Din must really be pulling out all the stops for you."

"For me?"

"The banquet is to honor you, silly," Chedva said. "There'll be veal, and challah, and matzoh ball soup…." She clapped a hand to her mouth and hiccupped.

"You look a little green," Tobin told her. "Do you feel all right?"

Chedva grinned and wiggled, though her normally rosy cheeks were still pale. "I feel terrible, but I'm fantastic!"

Tobin didn't have a clue what she meant, but Elanna must have. With a cry of delight, she hugged the other girl.

"Mazel tov, Chedva! At last! I'm so happy for you!"

Chedva grinned shyly, rubbing her stomach. "I can't believe it."

"Believe it," Elanna told her and gave her another squeeze. "When does the baby come?"

Chedva beamed. "Not until the start of January, I think."

Baby? Chedva was a hopemother too? Tobin looked at the

short, plump girl. She looked even shorter and fatter standing next to Elanna. As he looked at them closely, though, he noticed something he never had before.

When Chedva moved away through the ever-present crowd, he mentioned what he'd seen. "You two look alike."

Elanna looked surprised. "You think so?"

He'd thought she might be offended at his comparison. "Yeah. You have the same eyes. The same shape of the face, except Chedva's is fatter."

"Fuller," Elanna corrected absently. She stroked her cheek, looking after the other girl. "I never thought about it, but I guess it does make sense. The same woman birthed us both."

"You mean you have the same mother," Tobin said.

She looked at him, a faint smile on her face. "No, Tobin. We had different mothers. The same woman birthed both of us, but she wasn't our mother. Just as I'm not the mother of any of my babies."

For the first time he really understood her role in the Tribe, and why she wanted to leave with him. "But you two are sisters."

She shook her head. "No. My parents didn't raise any other children. But I think Chedva had a brother."

"What happened to your parents?"

She made a gesture with her hands that could have meant anything. "My mother died a number of years ago. I believe my father remarried since then."

"You don't know?"

She blinked. "Once I became a hopemother, Tobin, I didn't live with them anymore. It's been a long time since I was part of their family."

"You mean they just send you away?" he cried, aghast.

She shrugged. "Nobody ever really goes away."

"I'm glad I'm leaving," he muttered, taking her hand. "Your people have a lot of crazy ideas."

She frowned, looking around. "Shh. Someone might hear you."

She didn't contradict him, he noticed. More and more people were streaming toward the dining hall. Tobin didn't really feel like eating. His mind was on tonight and how'd they'd make their escape.

Elanna seemed to sense his thoughts. She leaned in to brush a kiss along his cheek. "I have to go get some things ready. You go on ahead."

He tried to protest, but she shushed him again. "Go. We aren't going to sit together, anyway. I'm sure the Reb has you up at the Beit Din's table, since he's going to announce you as a gatherer."

"I don't want to be one any more," Tobin said.

"Well, don't tell him that. Go. I'll see you later."

He didn't have time to kiss her again, or even to ask her how he'd find her. Him, a gatherer? It was an honor he didn't want. Tobin joined the crowd and went into the dining hall.

He wouldn't have thought the large room could hold more than a few hundred people. Now every table had extra chairs, stools and benches squeezed around it, and extra tables had been maneuvered into every spare space. Not enough to seat two thousand people, but enough to seat many of them.

The lanterns fixed into niches along the walls glowed brighter than he'd ever seen them, and hundreds of burning candles on every table supplemented the light. Fine linens, dishes and silverware were at every place; though few of them matched, the effect was nice. The large head table on its raised dais on the room's far end, normally set with food and beverage during regular meal times, now held place settings as well. One for each of the three members of the Beit Din and eleven more. Ten, Tobin guessed, for the top ranking Gatherers, and one more. For him.

His skin itched uncomfortably under the coarse shirt he wore. Not for the first time, he longed for the soft shirt and pants he'd found at the warehouse. The clothes the old man from the storeroom had provided were the right size, but they didn't feel half as nice.

Now, scratching at his neck and tugging at his collar, he stood awkwardly in the main doorway. The room was filling quickly. Delicious smells wafted through the air, making his stomach rumble.

"Tobin, up here," the woman from the Beit Din said, tugging his elbow.

He couldn't remember her name. Cosmetics covered her puffy face. Since so few of the women in the Tribe used any sort of makeup, the effect was doubly ludicrous.

"I don't need to sit up there," Tobin protested, knowing it was useless. The woman propelled him with surprising strength past the other tables and up to the dais.

"Don't be silly," she said, clucking her tongue. "You're the man of honor tonight."

Looking around the room at the excited faces, and the way the Tribe members pointed and whispered as he passed, he felt a pang of guilt. It wasn't their fault he had plans that didn't include their welfare. To them he was some sort of hero.

"I don't want to be a hero," Tobin said aloud as the woman pushed him up onto the dais.

She stopped to chuckle before nudging him to the end of the table. "You can't help what you are. Nobody can."

Livna. That was her name. He let her force him into a chair, the last one at the long table. He didn't care that he wasn't in the middle, even though he was supposed to be the man of honor.

One by one the places at the table filled. Beaming, Reb Ephraim waved at Tobin. Tobin raised his hand in return. He nodded at Ari and exchanged a scowl with Luz. Asaph, to no great surprise, was not seated at the head table.

The large room droned with conversation. Livna kept up a steady stream of observations and gossip, not hesitating to point out whom she was mentioning with her fork or her knife. To his relief, Tobin found that a simple grunt sufficed as a response. Livna just liked to talk. She didn't like to listen.

"Mmmm. Salad," she murmured as several of the younger tribe members, the teeners, served plates of lettuce and onions. "Nothing better than fresh salad."

Knowing it might be the last decent food he'd have for a long time, Tobin enjoyed the meal. Leaving the Tribe meant leaving comforts he'd only just begun to appreciate.

He would have liked to be sitting with Elanna. He scanned the room, nodding and grunting in reply to Livna's commentary, but he didn't see her. He saw Chedva and several of the men he shared a room with. He saw a young woman chasing after a frisky toddler who tripped and fell, bursting into tears. But no Elanna.

After the salad came bread, fresh and hot from the oven, and tiny vials of olive oil with garlic cloves swimming inside. He nearly moaned aloud as the flavors burst open on his tongue. Food like this was paradise. Tobin tried to chew slowly, to prolong the bliss. Even the sight of Livna picking apart the loaf they shared with her fingernails couldn't deter him.

"Oy! White bread! Baruch Ha-Shem, where'd they find the flour? And matzoh ball soup!" Livna cried, wiggling against him in an ecstasy he found a little embarrassing. Olive oil glistened on her lips and dripped down her chin. "We haven't had that in years! Years, Tobin!"

The woman was nearly crying, her artificially thickened eyelashes clumping with tears. She grabbed him by the shoulders, leaning close so he could smell the garlic on her breath. Guilt stabbed him again at Livna's obvious gratitude.

He shoved it away again to concentrate on the soup. Yellow broth, steaming, with fat dumplings floating in it. Salty. He slurped it up, sorry he didn't have more room in his stomach.

Voices grew louder, more boisterous with each course. Some people called out toasts, many of them praising Tobin and what he would bring them. Reb Ephraim gave a brief speech about giving thanks for the bounty before them. Children laughed and cried, and people ate noisily. None of it changed his mind about leaving, but the guilt worsened.

"Here it comes!" Livna said, elbowing him in the side. She grinned. "Veal. What a treat!"

Meat in Eastport had been scarcer than hen's teeth. They'd slaughtered chickens when they became too old to lay and sometimes a goat or a kid. Once, he'd had a strip of beef jerky brought by a peddler. It was a treat for his birthday, and Old Ma had traded an entire bolt of cloth for the tiny shreds of meat. Sometimes they had potted meat, but it was never very good. Fish was plenty, but not meat.

The teeners brought out platter after steaming platter of meat piled high in slices and swimming in gravy. Tobin realized he was drooling. Looking around, he saw he wasn't alone. Everyone in the dining hall stared at the platters with ecstatic looks, and more than one person clapped.

"Dig in," Livna said, slapping a thick slice onto his plate. "Oy, will we fress tonight! Why not? In another few months, with what you'll bring back, we'll be drowning in good stuff!"

The first bite was unlike anything he'd ever eaten. The meat was so tender it fell apart in his mouth; he barely needed to chew. The gravy was redolent with spices and flavors he couldn't identify and didn't care to. It was delicious. He could barely stop himself from gobbling the whole slice in two or three bites.

But that wasn't all. Next came more platters of food, and Livna told him the names of everything he didn't know. Mashed potatoes with their own gravy. Jellied cranberry sauce, such a beautiful, shimmering red that it seemed almost a shame to eat it. Small bows of what she called macaroni. He declined the small dishes of gefilte fish, the gelatinous goop he'd found in the storeroom his first night in the city. Livna ate his share, smacking her lips and holding her stomach, rolling her eyes in rapture.

More plates of veal came out of the kitchen, served several different ways. Tobin ate. And ate. And ate some more. Breaded veal in thin strips, served with a sauce of crushed tomatoes and more olive oil. Small chunks of it speared on long rods, interspersed with hunks of bread, onion, and the first new carrots. Shredded veal with more gravy. More and more and more!

There were other things, too, tuna cakes and pasta, things he didn't know, but mostly what he ate was the meat. He didn't think he'd ever get enough. It was as though he'd been starving his entire life, and had never realized it until now.

"Ah! The piece de resistance!" Livna said, stifling a burp with one gravy-spotted hand. Nobody's manners were very good tonight. She pointed toward the kitchen door, where the main cook, Amnon, and his assistant Balfour stood, holding yet another platter. "This is their trademark, honey. Veal Mazeltov! Now that's something I haven't seen since Reb Ephraim married his first wife. And that's a long time ago."

His stomach was full to bursting, but he couldn't stop eating. Every flavor was too good, too rich, too sweet. Too rare. He was on overload and didn't care. He'd have a piece of Veal Mazeltov, whatever that was. It looked good.

The two cooks, with great pomp and ceremony, carried the platter up through the rows of tables, toward the head table. Tobin couldn't quite see what was on it. Something large and brown, with something red in front of it. Greens and garnish hid most of it, and the cooks were holding it too high. He strained his neck, trying to see what had everyone oohing and ahing.

Livna refilled his glass with water. "Clean your palate, sweetie. You're going to want to taste this, all right."

He did as she said, swallowing the slightly bitter water and wiping his mouth with a napkin that had only a few clear spots left on it. The cooks were closer now, their faces proud as they brought their masterpiece toward the table. They were going to present it to him, Tobin realized as they turned to walk down the head table's length.

"One thing I don't understand, though," he said to Livna as she craned her neck to see the platter too.

"What's that, honey?"

He'd read about feasts and meats and veal. "Where do you keep the cows?"

She turned to look at him in confusion. "Cows?"

"Yeah," Tobin said. "You know. Cows. Veal?"

Livna laughed, shaking her head. "Oh, honey. I've never even seen a cow, much less eaten one."

"Then what…?"

As he spoke, Amnon and Balfour, with many flourishes and great presentation, set the platter of Veal Mazeltov in front of him.

Tobin had seen rats before. Big ones, even, in the rocks by the shore. He'd thrown rocks at them to chase them away. The one on the platter was the size of a small dog.

It had been skinned so expertly that the head, tail and legs still remained attached. The skin of the body was crisp and glistening with fat. The rat's mouth gaped wide, its sharp teeth sunk into a ripe tomato. The eye sockets held sprigs of green.

"To honor the man who'll bring us prosperity!" Amnon announced proudly.

Only the thought that he didn't want to call attention to himself kept Tobin's dinner in his stomach. He couldn't get sick. He had to leave tonight. Secretly. If he got sick he'd be watched. They'd send him back to Frieda and he'd be forced to leave with the Gatherers tomorrow morning. He couldn't. Get. Sick.

"Excuse me," Tobin said and was amazed at how calm he actually sounded. "I'll be back in a few minutes."

The halls were so damned long, and so confusing! He took a wrong turn and another, and still hadn't found the lavatory before his stomach actually stopped churning. Leaning against the wall, he burped loudly, covering his mouth, but that was all. His stomach gurgled a few times and subsided.

"Damn," he said aloud. "Veal."

Chapter 19

The bag on Elanna's shoulder was small and it didn't hold much. She didn't have much. The baubles and candies she could claim as her own meant nothing and would be no help on a trip.

The only thing she had that mattered, really mattered, was the tiny dress she wore tucked inside her shirt. The dress her first child had worn for the few short hours of its life. The material was thin and faded now, so worn the pattern of ducks and bunnies had nearly disappeared. Elanna felt it against her skin, and it calmed her. It always did.

In the shadows, she waited with her bundles at her feet. While everyone else was feasting at the banquet, she'd made a trip to the storerooms. She'd probably taken too much, but she wouldn't be carrying it all alone. Tobin would help her.

She had a lantern and a package of batteries. Some matches. Some cans of food and a jug of water. She'd even managed to find some extra clothes, too large for either one of them, but better than nothing. Everything was rolled inside some heavy blankets and tied with some thick cord. The bundles weren't light, and they were a little awkward, but overall she was proud of what she had done.

She heard him before she saw him. He was trying to be quiet, but he hadn't had much practice at it. He was lucky to have gotten this far without being heard.

"You were going to leave without me," she said from the darkness as Tobin passed by her.

She frightened him. His breath hissed out in a great whoosh, and he fell back against the wall, face white and strained. She tried not to let his harsh tone sting her.

"What are you doing here?"

"Waiting for you," she said calmly. "Be quiet, unless you want to wake the everyone."

"Elanna," Tobin said warningly. "Go back to your room."

"No."

He sighed, running his hands through his hair in the distracted way he had. "I thought we already decided this."

"Apparently we didn't decide the same thing," she said, hoisting the bag over her shoulder. She tossed him one of the bundles and wrapped the cord of the second one around her fingers. "Let's go. It will be light in a few hours. If we want to get a head start we'd better hurry."

"I can't ask you to take on my quest," Tobin said, holding the bundle awkwardly with both hands.

"Who says I'm asking? Come on."

Without waiting for him, she slipped down the hall and into the main entryway. She pushed open the heavy front door and went into the night outside. The moon was full, its silver light making even the dirt of the streets look somehow prettier. Tobin trailed behind her.

"Elanna!"

She stopped, turned. "Argue with me later, Tobin."

He'd managed to sling the blanket roll over one shoulder. He put his hand to her and she took it. "Are you sure this is what you want to do?"

She squeezed his hand and let it drop. Nodded. "Yes. I'm sure."

"But you'll be leaving everything behind…"

"I don't care."

"I don't believe you."

She felt a brief sting of tears in her throat but she forced them away. "I know what I'm doing."

He lifted his face to the night air and took a deep breath. "Things smell better already."

She took a breath and smiled. "I think you're right."

He turned around in a slow circle, pointing. "Which way do we go?"

Elanna laughed softly and pointed. "This way. See? It's a good thing you do have me. You'd never get out of here. You'd be on one of the gatherer's trucks in a few hours."

"I'd manage," he said stubbornly, but he followed her lead. "I was doing all right before."

"That's a relief. I'm counting on you to take over from here."

Bantering with him felt good. They walked easily and quickly along the sidewalk, passing through patches of moonlight broken by shadows from the tall buildings.

"How do you know this is the right direction?" he asked after a few minutes.

She stopped to shift the bag and blanket roll. "I've never been beyond 39th street. But Ari told me once that if you keep going past the old bus station, you can reach the tunnel."

"Tunnel?"

She nodded, starting to move again. The night was waning. When the Gatherers grouped to leave, they'd notice Tobin's disappearance right away. She hoped they'd waste time searching the Main Hall before branching out to the streets.

"It's collapsed now. You can't really get through it. But the rubble has been built up enough that you can cross the water. It's one of the old ways out of the city. Sometimes, when we get peddlers through, they talk about it. It's not a nice place. I haven't seen it, but…." She stopped. "They say there are trolls there. But they…they're wrong, aren't they?"

Tobin grimaced. "I hope so."

The answer did not reassure her. "You said there were no monsters, Tobin!"

He shifted his bundles and kept walking. His legs were longer than hers, and he was moving fast. She had to take two steps for every one of his, like she was running.

"Tobin?"

He looked at her but didn't stop walking. "I don't know for sure. I know what I saw, or didn't see on the way here from Maine, but I've never been here before."

She stopped, glad for the chance to rest but unwilling to say so. "You mean there really could be things out there?"

"I don't know," he repeated, and she wanted to pinch him. "C'mon. Let's keep walking. It's going to be daylight soon."

Elanna took a deep breath, trying not to think about it. "You told me there are no trolls or gobblings, Tobin. I trusted you."

"I told you this wouldn't be easy. I didn't ask you to come!"

His words hurt, but she couldn't deny them. "No, I guess you didn't. Do you want me to turn back? I'm sure you can find your way on your own. You don't need me."

But she wanted him to need her, didn't she? The sarcasm in her voice was forced. She wanted him to ask her to come with him. She wanted him to want her. It was stupid and unfamiliar. She hated it.

"Do you want to go back?"

"No."

"Then let's keep walking. Come on. I don't trust Reb Ephraim not to send Luz after us."

Ignoring the stitch in her side, Elanna hitched up her baggage and began walking again. "Of course he will. We've stolen from the Tribe. Not just things…but me."

Tobin stopped. "You're not something that can be stolen."

In that moment, she thought she might understood what love was, after all. "They'll send someone after us. And the punishment…for me it would be bad. But for you…worse."

Tobin frowned and started walking when she did. "He knows I want to head West. I'd imagine if you know about the tunnel, the Reb does too. It wouldn't be hard to figure out where I'm going. I guess it depends on how badly he wants me."

She thought about the Gatherers and the trip planned. "He seemed to think he needed you."

Tobin smiled. "He doesn't. I told him that. Before I left I drew a map for them and left it in his office. If he wants to send them, they can find it all right."

"You left a map?"

"Sure," Tobin said. She was surprised to see that he looked bashful. "I felt bad. I didn't want the Tribe to suffer just because I'm searching for an ideal. I left the map, and it will show them where to go. It's up to Reb Ephraim and the Beit Din now."

"They'll do what's best for the Tribe," Elanna said.

"I hope you're right," Tobin said with a shrug. "But it's out of my hands now."

"Let's go," she said grimly, matching his pace.

Her legs were starting to get tired, and they'd only reached 37th street. Another few blocks to the bus station. The bundles were getting heavy. Elanna tried to ignore the ache in her legs and arms, and the uncomfortable way the breath hitched in her lungs. She didn't want to be a burden on Tobin. She didn't want to prove him right.

"Do you need to take a break?" Tobin asked, and she burned at the concern in his voice.

"I'm fine," she said through gritted teeth.

They walked in silence a few blocks more, until at last she had to stop. Bitter tears of anger coursed down her cheeks as she tossed her baggage to the street and kicked it spitefully. She was a failure.

"Hey, hey," Tobin said, trying to soothe her. "Calm down. It's all right."

"It's not all right!" She sobbed. "I'm pitiful!"

He patted her shoulder. "No."

"I am! I can't even walk a mile without getting tired! How am I going to get to California?"

"You've never had to do anything like this before," Tobin said. He pushed her gently until she sat on the blanket roll. With one finger he wiped her cheeks. "It's not easy."

"But I told you I was tough!" She cried miserably, rubbing her legs to ease the cramping ache.

"And I believe you." Tobin sat next to her. "We can do this."

"No." She shook her head. "Just go. Go on without me."

"I can't do that," he said.

He looked around them, at the fading darkness that meant the day would soon be upon them. "I won't just leave you here. Especially knowing they'll do something to you for trying to leave."

It wasn't just being tired. She had to admit it. She was afraid. She looked up at him, knowing her eyes were red and her nose runny. She probably looked pathetic.

"I'm scared," she said simply.

"It's going to be all right," Tobin said.

He didn't say "I told you so." He didn't frown or scoff at her. He didn't make her feel like an idiot.

Elanna stood, hefting the bundles back over her shoulders. "Let's go."

"Are you sure?"

He tried to take her bag from her, leaving only the blanket roll, but she didn't let him. It was her bag to carry. She could do it.

She nodded. "I'm not going to be a wimp about this. You're right. You didn't ask me to come with you. You don't want me. I forced myself on you. I made the choice, and I'll live with it."

He didn't start walking. "Is that what you think? That I don't want you?"

Her heart skipped a beat. "Isn't that true?"

He shook his head slowly. "No. Nothing could be farther from the truth."

"I don't understand."

Tobin put down his blanket roll. He took hers from her hands and set that down too, then tugged the bag from her shoulder and placed it beside the others. Gently, he put his hands on her shoulders and stared into her face.

"I want you," he said clearly.

Her heart jumped again. Her cheeks burned. Her eyes searched his, trying to find the joke, but there was none.

"Why?" she asked finally.

"Because you're kind," Tobin said. He pushed her hair back from her forehead. "And you're beautiful. And you make me laugh.

Because…hell, Elanna, I don't know. I don't know anything about women."

He bent to kiss her, a light touch of his lips on hers that promised greater passion. When he pulled away, her fingers went to her mouth, as though to hold the kiss there.

Tobin looked to the sky, which had lightened dramatically. "We'd better go. Reb Ephraim will have found the map by now and noticed I'm gone. Maybe they'll have seen you're gone, too. We'd better keep moving."

"There's the bus station," she said, pointing to the large building straight in front of them. We can get to the tunnel from there."

"Then let's do it." Tobin shot her another grin.

Laughing, she took his hand and they ran toward the building. The bus station was long, with many doors that had once been glass but now only held darkness. It didn't look inviting. They were almost there when the troll reared up from its hole in the street.

Chapter 20

Tobin didn't hesitate. He shoved Elanna behind him and held out the blanket roll. It was a poor weapon, but the only one they had. Elanna let out a small cry and stumbled against him.

"What's it got?" shouted the thing emerging from the hole in the middle of the street. "What's it got, now? What, what?"

Tobin thought about Golem, the creature from Tolkien's The Hobbit. A shrill giggle escaped him, and he bit it off. This was no time for laughter.

"A troll!" Elanna moaned in his ear.

The troll climbed out of its hole and stood. Although it looked as though it only stood as tall as Tobin's chest, it was at least twice as wide. A flat head covered with sparse wisps of gray hair topped lumpy shoulders that ended in dangling arms and wide, flat hands. It wore clothes, or at least what once had been clothes but now had disintegrated into rags. More wisps of the same gray hair covered its chest, and spots mottled its skin.

Still, it had the shape of a man and the voice of one, too. It hadn't moved any closer to them, just stood beside the hole and rocked back and forth. Once in awhile it scratched itself under the arms or on the head. It was ugly, yes, but a monster? Tobin didn't think so.

"It's just a man." Tobin didn't put down the blanket roll.

"What's it got, now? What, what?" shrieked the thing in the street, scratching. It still made no move toward them.

"It's not like any man I've ever seen," Elanna said doubtfully. She grimaced. "I saw a Savage once that had wandered down into Tribe territory. He didn't even look as bad as that."

"Maybe it's because they live down in those holes," Tobin said, still watching the thing. It shifted back and forth on dirty feet, mindless of the rubble and debris on the pavement. "What's down there?"

Elanna shrugged. "Old sewers, I guess. There are lots of tunnels under the city. Sewers and subway tunnels. The holes and entrances in the Tribe's territory were sealed off a long time ago. I think there used to be people that lived down there, who used to come up sometimes and steal from us. But not in years. Not ever since I can remember."

"We're not in Tribe territory anymore?" Tobin relaxed a little bit, but kept his eyes on the shaking and scratching troll. At least it had stopped its shrieking.

"We're at the very edge. I think this part of the city has been pretty well gathered already. Not much left. Oy vey, that thing is ugly!"

From the hole emerged another thing just like the first. This one stood a little taller, and a little wider, too. Its clothes were in even worse shape than the first one's. Its legs showed through the tears in its pants; lumpy and gnarled, they were the same mottled brown, and covered with hair.

"What's it got, what? What's it got?" The second troll cried in a higher voice. It pulled itself out of the hole and stood by the first, making the same rocking motion.

"I don't think they're going to attack us." Tobin let the blanket roll drop in front of him, but he kept a good grip on it. Just in case.

The pair of weird things in front of them rocked and scratched.

Every few minutes one would spit or sneeze, then the other. It was pretty disgusting to watch, but really not that scary.

"What's it got?" shrieked the pair in unison. "What's it got, now? What! What! What?"

"Nothing for you," Tobin shouted back, not sure what to say.

The two ugly things stopped rocking and scratching. They looked at each other, misshapen jaws dropping. The taller one turned back toward Tobin and Elanna.

"Nutting?"

"No!" Elanna cried bravely from Tobin's side.

"Nutting?"

Now the two began rocking again. "Nutting?"

"Nutting?"

"What's it got, now?"

"Nutting?"

"What, what?"

"Nutting?"

"No, nothing!" Tobin shouted, just to shut them up. They were getting on his nerves.

The taller, thinner thing began to cry. Now it rocked, scratched and cried. The shorter, heavier one just grunted.

"What's wrong with them?" Elanna asked.

"When people talked about trolls," Tobin asked, "did they say they looked like that?"

"They never said they cried," Elanna said. "And I'm not sure what they were supposed to look like. Ugly, I guess."

"Well that fits those two for sure." The trolls weren't moving from their place in the street, but they blocked the way to the bus station. "Is there another way to get to the tunnel?"

Elanna shook her head. "I don't really know. Ari said to go through the bus station, and the tunnel entrance was in there."

"How fast can you run?"

She laughed shortly. "I don't know. I don't think I've ever tried."

Tobin sighed, looking back at the pair of rocking, wailing things that stood between them and the bus station. "I don't know if they'll attack or not. They seem pretty pathetic, but it could be an act."

"Nutting!" shrilled the taller troll. Tears streamed down its mottled cheeks. Snot dripped from its nose in thick curds. Disgusting.

"What, what?" answered its companion.

Elanna shook her head. "It's a pretty good act."

"We can try to go around them," Tobin said. "We may have to run, though. Or fight."

Elanna looked up at the sky. "It's daylight now. I'll feel safer when we're crossing the tunnel. Let's try it."

He looked at her in admiration. She really was pulling through. He was glad she'd decided to come with him. More than glad, really. Near to ecstatic. The feeling gave him courage he might not have had if he'd been alone.

"Yeah, let's." Tobin hefted his bundle and took her bag from her. When she protested he stopped her with a look. "If you need to run, you don't want to be carrying extra weight. I'm stronger than you. I'll do it."

She let him take the bag. Tobin wanted to take her hand but didn't. He'd need to be ready, in case the things started after them. He tensed, judging the distance to the doors of the bus station and hoping he was right.

"I feel bad for them," Elanna said quietly. "Look at them!"

Now both trolls were sobbing and groaning. The shorter one stomped its feet up and down in grief. The taller one pounded its chest. Tears and snot flew as they shook from side to side.

"If nothing else, let's run fast enough so we don't get hit with any of that," Tobin said. "Damn, that's nasty."

"I'm ready," Elanna said.

"Go!"

Tobin ran, aware that she was beside him, keeping up. Not bad for a girl who'd probably never had to run more than a block in her life. The bags slapped against his legs as he ran. They were nearing the farthest point of the trolls' reach.

With a strangled cry, Elanna tripped and fell. The string holding her blanket roll had come undone, tangling her legs. She landed hard on the street, shredding away the leg of her pants. Bright blood spilled from the gash in her calf.

What's it got, now!" shrieked the taller troll, whirling on Elanna as though it had been pulled by a string.

"What, what?" yelled the shorter one, already moving toward her with jerky, scrabbling movements.

They were drawn by the blood, Tobin realized in alarm as he bent to help Elanna. The wound didn't look too serious, more of a scrape than a cut, really, but it was bleeding fairly heavily. In a minute, the things would be upon them.

Elanna held her leg, trying to stanch the flow with her fingers. "Leave me," she said through tensed jaws. "Get them!"

Tobin stood, feet apart and hands gripping the rope that had come loose from her blanket roll. He had no idea what he was going to do with it, but it was his only weapon. His heart pounded, thud, thud, like the banging of a drum. His breath burned in his chest. He was, he thought as though from far away, terrified. But exhilarated.

The pair of trolls came at him in unison with their arms outstretched, still gabbling their freakish refrain. They didn't have claws, exactly, just filthy fingernails which had grown long. They still looked like they could do some damage.

Just as they came within grabbing distance, Tobin was surprised to see the second blanket roll shoot from behind him. It connected solidly with both trolls' legs. The things stumbled, one at a time, the taller one going down first and taking the shorter one with it. They both went down on their knees, the sound like ice cracking as they hit the street.

Their howls of pain and anger were terrible, low growls that rose to a crescendo that hurt Tobin's ears. He didn't have time to worry about that. While the things were down, he swung the ends of the rope around their necks and pulled tight. The trolls' heads came together with a loud clunk, sending out another round of shrieks and wails.

Now they were struggling to their feet, bound together at the neck. It didn't seem to stop them. Contorted with rage, their ugly faces were even uglier. Blood oozed from their knees, and Tobin had time to notice that it was red before the pair lunged at him again.

Jerking out of the way, Tobin saw Elanna get to her feet. With a triumphant yell, she swung her shoulder bag over her head by its strap. Once, twice and again she swung it, building up speed and force. With a sharp grunt, she swung it into the trolls' faces.

Noses cracked. More blood flew. Tobin saw a few teeth go rattling down to the pavement. The trolls fell face forward onto the ground and lay there, silent. Blood began to stream from beneath them, puddling on the pavement.

"Are they dead?" Elanna was breathing hard, her cheeks flushed. She stood stiffly, her unwounded leg holding her weight. "Did I kill them?"

"They don't die that quick," said a familiar voice from behind Tobin. "They'll be out for a while, maybe, but that's it."

It was Luz. Dressed in black, his Gatherer's uniform. He was grinning, and not pleasantly.

Chapter 21

"Good work, Elanna." Luz sneered at Tobin. "Nothing like letting a lady save your ass."

"How long have you been there?" Tobin asked.

"I've been following you two since you left.Wondering how far you'd get."

"Why didn't you help us?" Elanna said, outraged but not scared.

"I thought maybe if I let you go, the trollies would do my work for me," Luz said with a grin. It was a nasty smile, like something a spider would have on its face before it ate the dinner caught in its the web.

"If you came to take us back, you're wasting your time," Elanna said.

She moved away from the puddle of blood and sat down. Quickly she tore the useless shreds of her pant leg into useable strips, then wrapped them around her leg. It stung, but it stopped the blood from oozing out.

She'd have to clean it, so it wouldn't get infected. That was the first thing Frieda taught them all. Clean wounds meant clean healing. There was no medication for infections. A person could die from a dirty wound faster than from anything else.

She looked up at Luz, that arrogant jerk. It figured he'd be the one to come after them. He was always trying to throw his weight around, just because he was Ari's right hand man. Elanna didn't like him, but she wasn't scared of him.

"I didn't come to take him back." Luz cracked the knuckles of one hand in the opposite palm, and then did it again in reverse. "Just you."

"And what about Tobin?"

Luz shrugged. "I can kill him if I want to, or just let him go."

"Kill him!" Elanna said, stunned. To cause deliberate harm to another was an inviolable rule of the Tribe.

"If I want to," Luz said with a sneer. "But I don't think I'll waste my time. Reb Ephraim found the map. We don't need this waste of space to help us."

She couldn't believe that Reb Ephraim had ordered Luz to kill Tobin. To track them down, sure, and bring them back, yes, she could see that. Punish them, certainly. But kill?

She stood, testing the pain in her leg. With the bandages it would be okay. She smoothed her hair and straightened her clothes. She knew how to deal with men like Luz.

"You're still wasting your time," she said, the sweetness of her tone contradicting the bitterness in her thoughts. "I'm going with Tobin."

"You're betraying the Tribe," Luz said, his mouth twisted with disgust. "For what? Him? That puny excuse for a man?"

Elanna expected Tobin to rise to the bait, but he stayed quiet. He was busy rerolling her blanket, tucking all the odds and ends inside. He almost seemed to be ignoring Luz.

"I'm not betraying anybody," she said.

"You're a hopemother," Luz said. "You belong to the Tribe."

"If you're trying to convince me to stay you're doing it the wrong way," Elanna said, more than annoyed now. Now she was angry. Not just at Luz, for being such a pain, but also at Tobin for saying nothing.

Tobin launched himself at the much larger man. Clutched in

one hand was a sharp chunk of concrete. He must have picked it up while he fixed the blanket roll.

She never would have expected him to land a blow on Luz, but he did. Right to the temple. Blood flowed rapidly, running into the Gatherer's eyes and down his face. With a grunt, Luz slumped to his hands and knees, head hanging low.

Without stopping for pity, Tobin struck the man again. More blood squirted, and Elanna had to look away. Feeling faint, she bit her lip until the pain sharpened her mind again. From behind her she heard thuds and grunts, but she didn't turn to see what was happening. She didn't want to know.

"Let's go," Tobin said quietly. He wasn't holding the stone anymore. His hands were covered in blood.

Numb, Elanna picked up her bundle. Wordlessly she followed Tobin past the trolls, who were beginning to stir. The bus station loomed ahead. She put one foot in front of the other, just walking, not thinking. She couldn't think. Didn't want to think.

"Wait a minute."

Tobin paused by a shallow groove along the curb. Dirty water had accumulated there, and he bent to wipe his hands in it. They came away gray, but that was better than red. At that thought, Elanna bit back a cry.

He had caused harm. More than harm, he'd severely wounded a man, perhaps even killed him. She felt sick. Luz would have done the same to Tobin, she told herself fiercely, following Tobin to the front doors. That didn't make it all right, just easier to bear.

Several of the doors were hanging off their hinges. Tobin stepped through, then waited for her. The station was dark inside. Their footsteps echoed menacingly as they moved in the few feet of light just inside the doors.

"Elanna, are you all right?"

She nodded, but the tears came anyway. Then he was holding her in his arms, touching her face with his hands, the hands that had killed. And she pulled away, shuddering.

"I'm sorry," Tobin said. "But I had to do it."

"I know," she said, furiously wiping her face. "I know, Tobin, but…"

Tobin reached out and held her shoulders, turning her until she looked at him. "I think I killed him."

His voice broke, and his face crumpled. She realized that he was shivering. Without thinking she pulled him to her, cradling him against her. She smoothed her fingers through his hair over and over, the rhythm soothing them both.

"It's all right," she whispered, feeling his cheek hot against hers. "Toby, it's ok. I understand."

"I never even punched a man before!" Tobin said, his voice agonized. He clutched her with a desperation that frightened her a little. "Oh, God, Elanna! I had his blood on my hands!"

She rocked him against her, humming the song she sang to her babies when they fussed. It worked as well for him as it did for them. Within moments his shivering had stopped. They held each other tightly, and then he pulled away.

"Luz was right," Tobin said. "I'm a puny excuse for a man."

"No," she said. "No, you're not."

He looked out through the door and she followed his gaze. The trolls had awakened and torn away the rope holding them together. She had no fear they'd come after Tobin and herself. They were occupied with what had, until a few moments before, been Luz.

"Don't look," she said, forcing him to turn away. "Let's go."

They stopped to get out the lanterns she'd packed. She showed him how to set the switch to keep the battery steady, but the light was still dim.

"Which way?" Tobin held the light up high.

Elanna searched for a clue. "Up the stairs. See the sign?"

The letters were faded but legible. Some peddlers or other travelers had left handwritten arrows too, though most of them were nearly as worn. Still, they had no choice.

"The worst that could happen is we'll wander around until we reach the other side," she said more brightly than she felt. "It's a big building but it's got to have an end somewhere."

Tobin grabbed her hand. "Lead the way."

They climbed the ridged metal stairs and found some more signs pointing the way. Maybe this wouldn't be so difficult, after all. The corridors were long and confusing, especially since everything was dark. She found herself jumping at shadows.

"This would be easier in the light." Tobin's voice echoed.

She was thinking about the trolls. If they were real, what about the gobblings? Suddenly her palms began to sweat. A chill trickle ran down her back. She wanted to run, but didn't know where to run to.

They came upon a row of small booths to their right. Once, long ago, they had probably sold gum, candy, cigarettes and magazines. They were empty now, stripped of anything worthy long ago by other generations of Gatherers. They would be perfect places for something to hide.

"There!"

The sign, most of its letters worn away, read "Hnd unnel."

"That's it!" Elanna said.

They began to run, their lanterns bouncing and throwing up shadows. They pushed open the door and ran out onto the vast parking lot. Many of the busses were still there, looking like huge sleeping beasts.

"Busses only. No through traffic. Have toll ready," Tobin read. "This way!"

They ran up the long ramp, finally emerging into the morning sun. Fresh air had never smelled so sweet, and sunlight had never seemed so bright. Elanna smiled, meeting Tobin's eyes.

"Almost there," she said and pointed. "Look."

From where they stood they could see the water. It rippled in the morning sun. It was lovely.

The tunnel no longer went beneath the water. Time and long-ago riots had collapsed it. Now, huge chunks of metal and concrete wide enough to carry one of the Gatherer's trucks stuck out of the water in irregular intervals. Smaller piles of debris filled in the spaces between the chunks, but water glimmered there, too. Walking wouldn't be easy.

"I can see land on the other side." Tobin turned and looked at her seriously. "Are you sure you want to do this?"

She thought of Luz and knew that even if she'd changed her mind, she could never go back. She didn't want to go back. That was the past. Her future lay with Tobin and whatever lay ahead.

"I'm sure," she said.

The crossing took a long time. Both of them got their feet wet more than once. At one spot, way out in the middle, they even had to swim, a skill she hadn't realized she had until it was swim or drown. Then they were across and the sun was high overhead. They were tired, hungry and soaking wet, but they were out of New York.

"Welcome to New Jersey," Tobin said with a grin that took away all her aches and rinsed her clean.

She kissed him then, just because she wanted to. His arms were strong around her back as he returned the kiss. His mouth was sweet with promise against hers. The promise of a new beginning.

Chapter 22

It took them two weeks to walk across the blasted remains of what had been Northern New Jersey. Whatever had happened there had been big, and it had been bad. Nothing remained: no roads, no houses, no trees. No life. Their footsteps left crumbling indentations behind them when they walked. Ditches filled with water that was brackish and undrinkable. The only vegetation was stunted and evil-looking weeds that oozed nasty sap when broken.

After three days of walking, Elanna's shoes fell apart. Her feet blistered, at first just one or two sores but then so many she could no longer walk without crying out. Tobin could tell she was trying to be brave, but at last he forced her to show him her feet.

Tobin tore the soles and the laces, the only salvageable parts, from her shoes and threw the rest away. He wrapped her feet in strips torn from one of the blankets. They kept walking. They had no other choice. Eventually the blisters scabbed over and began to heal. Elanna never complained, and Tobin's respect for her grew with every step she took.

They followed the sun. Since there were no roads, it was the only way to tell direction. Every day they walked until the sun grew high overhead, when they sat to share a few bites of food. Then they walked some more, until the day faded into chilly night, and they slept huddled together for warmth under the single remaining blanket.

At last they reached a river, far below them, rushing blue and green and clean. Tobin didn't know what river it was, only that beyond it the land was green and growing. He stared at it, afraid to blink in case it was just a dream. He held Elanna's hand tightly. She began to cry.

"I thought…" she sobbed, leaning on him. "I thought it was all like this! All dead!"

"But it's not all dead." Tobin pressed his lips to her hair. He didn't tell her he'd been afraid of the same thing. Tears stung his eyes, too, but he didn't let them fall.

Crossing the river wasn't as easy as crossing the tunnel had been, but they did it. If for no other reason than getting out of New Jersey, he and Elanna both managed to swim when they needed to. Once on the other side, he spared a look back.

"What do you think happened there?" He asked.

"The Blast Zone happened when a plane accidentally dropped a bomb," Elanna said. "But that doesn't look like an accident. It looks like someone did that on purpose."

"I don't suppose we'll ever know."

"No," Elanna said, and she set herself firmly in the opposite direction. "And I hope I never see anything like it again."

Several miles beyond the river, they found the first signs of civilization. Old buildings, crumbling and unused, with a service station among them. The pumps in front, which ages ago had dispensed fuel, still stood tall though their tanks had gone dry hundreds of years before. The battery charging panels for the cars that had replaced fuel-driven vehicles were still set into the concrete, but all were dark, most of the glass broken. Inside the station there wasn't much left to take along, but what they did find was worth stopping for.

Maps, racks of them. New Jersey and Pennsylvania. The United States. Road maps and atlases. The sun had faded some, turning the pages to a brown and crumbled ruined mess. Others though, on the rack's far side, were fine. A little brittle with age, maybe, but clear and easy to read.

"It's so big!" Elanna said when he unfolded the map of the entire country. "I never believed...I never thought...."

She looked at him with eyes full of wonder. Her smile made him want to kiss her. So he did.

"I don't know what we're going to find," Tobin said a moment later, the taste of her still on his lips. "California may be gone, just like Ari said. The rest of these places – I just don't know. But we got this far. There has to be more."

Elanna looked around the store, at the glass-front case that had once displayed meats and cheese. She ran her fingers along the top of the case, bringing it away coated in grime. Grimacing, she moved toward the back of the store, weaving through empty shelves and racks.

She glanced up at the sign over the counter. "*Boar's Head Brand. Convenience Store.* It would be a lot more convenient if there was something to eat in here!"

"People in cars used to stop at these places to refuel or recharge," Tobin said, following her. The back of the shop was still pretty bright. Glass cases that had once held beverages lined the back wall. "I guess they also stopped to buy food and stuff."

"Refuel their bodies instead," Elanna said with a chuckle. She poked a rack stacked with several small blue boxes. "Buy tampons and chewing gum."

That made him think of something. "Do you need some of those?"

"What?" she asked, smiling. "Chewing gum?"

Tobin pointed at the boxes. "No. The other."

With furrowed brow she looked to where he pointed. "Tampons?"

"Yeah." He'd never said the word aloud, though he knew perfectly well what they were for. He wasn't embarrassed exactly. He'd been raised by three women, after all. He didn't want Elanna to become uncomfortable on the journey, if she needed something she didn't have.

She looked at him strangely. Even though they weren't in the full bright of sunshine, he thought she blushed. Curiously, Tobin moved toward her, trying to get her to meet his eyes.

"I might need them, some time," Elanna said. "But…I don't think I'll need them for awhile. At least, not if everything is all right."

"I don't understand," Tobin said awkwardly. "I mean, I don't know much about that. I just thought you might need something…"

"You're very sweet," Elanna said and touched his cheek. "But there's something I probably should tell you, before we go on."

He didn't like the sound of that. Yet, her face wasn't solemn. Maybe it wasn't bad news.

"Go ahead," he said. "Tell me."

She hugged herself, seemingly unable to fight the grin. "I'm pregnant, Tobin."

Chapter 23

He just stared at her like she'd gone crazy. Elanna's smile began to fade. She'd never had such a lack of reaction before. Catching pregnant was a reason for celebration in the Tribe. Her elation was even greater now because this baby, this time, she would keep for herself. It was why she'd left with him. Wasn't he happy?

"But I thought you told Reb Ephraim you weren't." His voice sounded strained. His face didn't look so great, either. "He said you weren't supposed to have any other appointments."

Her joy disintegrated, replaced with a crushing disappointment. He wasn't happy about the baby. She couldn't imagine why not, but he wasn't.

"The baby didn't happen during an appointment. I didn't register it because..." Her shoulders slumped. "I don't know why. Because I'd have face discipline. Chastisement, at least. Because I didn't want to."

"They'd punish you for getting pregnant? I thought that was your purpose."

She didn't like the way he made that sound. "Hopemothers don't take lovers, Tobin. Our partners must all be tested and approved. Genetically matched. With such a small pool of DNA to pull from, we have to be careful not to --"

"Wait a minute. What?" His brow furrowed, mouth thinning. "You mean...you slept with someone who wasn't an appointment?"

She lifted her chin. "Yes."

His mouth twisted. "He was your lover?"

She thought of Job. The taste of his mouth, the sound of her name in his voice. She thought of secrecy and shadows. "Yes. But I didn't love him."

Tobin studied the dusty wire shelves, running his fingers over the crumpled and faded packages that still remained. He didn't say anything. Neither did she. Silence stretched out between them.

"How do you know?" he asked her finally, and she lost her patience.

"I've been pregnant enough times," Elanna said frostily. "I think I know."

She pushed by him to the front of the store. As she thrust open the door, she knocked into the rack of maps, sending it flying. The impact stung her shoulder, but she kept going.

The parking lot was empty and the sun getting high. Elanna stood in front of the ancient pumps, reading the time-weathered signs. "Electro-Juice lasts up to 10 times longer than the other leading battery!" "Dispose of batteries properly!" And most strangely, "Give a hoot, don't pollute!"

She heard the door open behind her. She felt Tobin rather than heard him; he stood behind her without speaking. She spoke to him without turning.

"I thought you'd be happy," she said. "It's a baby."

"It's not *my* baby."

She spun on him, fists clenched so that she wouldn't reach up to slap. "Does it matter?"

He recoiled just a bit. She softened, relaxing. She had to remember he didn't understand.

"The men of the Tribe fathered children they didn't necessarily create. For that matter, so did all of the women. A child's mother and father are the ones who raise it, not the ones whose bodies made it. Does it matter, Tobin?"

He sighed, his mouth turning down in a look so sad she wanted to cry herself. "Am I an idiot for thinking that it does?"

Elanna touched the tightness of her belly. "Yes. A baby is a baby. And you don't know, you might not even..."

She trailed off, not wanting to insult him, though everyone knew being sterile was no shame. More people couldn't make babies than could. Elanna shook her head. "Not by your seed, Tobin. But this baby will need a father. Can't you be a father to this child?"

To her astonishment, Tobin went to his knees before her, pressing his face to her stomach. Alarmed, she bent to lift him up, but found herself kneeling with him instead. "Tobin, what's wrong? What is it?"

"I made you walk this whole way! I should have left you behind…"

"In the name of Adonai, why?" She cried, pushing him back until he looked at her.

"To keep you safe!" He said. "And the baby safe. This is no place for you to be."

She looked around the empty parking lot and the equally empty road beyond. "This doesn't look so bad to me."

He wouldn't be placated. "Walking like this, the blisters on your feet…"

She shushed him. "My feet are healing. And walking is good exercise. Tobin, I'm pregnant. I'm not sick. I've been pregnant lots of times."

"And sometimes you lost the babies," he said, more calmly now.

"Yes. Sometimes I lost the babies. But it had nothing to do with what I did or didn't do. It just happened."

"What if it happens now?"

She didn't want to think about that. Her heart tightened and her throat closed. Instead of speaking for a moment, she just touched his cheek.

"It's up to Ha-Shem if He wants to take this child," she said finally. "Nothing we do or say can change that. I came with you because I wanted to, Tobin. Because I want to be my baby's mother for its whole life and not just a year. And I want you to be its father. And when this one is old enough, I want us to try to have another. I want this with you."

He kissed her with an intensity that took her breath away. Tobin's fingers found her hair, tugging on the tangled lengths of it, and she wanted to push him away. She was dirty, her hair was dirty and greasy and matted. She didn't have the strength, though, to deny him access to her mouth. His kiss was too sweet.

"Elanna," he whispered, holding her tightly. "Forgive me."

"I do."

He clung to her so fiercely she wondered if he were ever going to let go. "I think we should see if there's anything worth salvaging in the store, then check out these other places. And it's getting late. Maybe we should plan to stay here tonight. Get a fresh start tomorrow."

"Sounds good." She stood, dusting off the knees of her pants. "I'd like to be able to find some new clothes. New shoes. Think there's any chance?"

He looked around at the cluster of decrepit houses set back on the road. "You never know until you try, I guess."

She smiled. "No. I guess you don't."

The convenience store yielded several dusty bottles of water from one of the cases along the back. Elanna scooped up the packs of gum, the sticks as hard as concrete until she softened them in her mouth for several seconds. The flavor was brief but intense. She propped open the doors to the restrooms while Tobin scouted inside, but the paper on the rolls was mouse-eaten and worthless. The soap had congealed into sludge.

The magazine racks were full, and Tobin packed a few to use for starting fires. Behind the counter Elanna found a few packs of matches that to her delight still lit.

The first house in the row had no front door. Or rather, the front door had fallen off its hinges and was now half-hidden in the brown grass by the front stoop. The stoop itself was made of concrete and had weathered the years well. In the living room, furniture still sat grouped around the television set, though the screen on the set had shattered.

"Amazing, isn't it?" Tobin asked her as she followed him inside. "It's like nothing's been touched, in all these years. It's like a time capsule."

"I wouldn't say nothing's been touched," Elanna said, pointing to a tuft of stuffing that had sprung from a hole chewed in one arm of the sofa.

She looked around the room, at the furniture, the rugs, the pictures on the walls. People had lived here once. They'd married and had children here, maybe even died here. She felt melancholy.

"Are you all right?"

She smiled. "Yeah. Just thinking about how different life was when people lived here. How different it all used to be."

Tobin moved behind her and hugged her. She leaned into his embrace, grateful for it. They rocked together for a moment before she moved away, determined not to let herself feel sad for things she couldn't change.

"I've never seen a house like this. I feel so naïve. I've never seen so many things."

He laughed. "And you, the big city girl. I lived my whole life on an island!"

"But you saw houses. You saw the way people really lived. You *lived* the way people really lived."

"You had hot water for baths and toilets that flushed," Tobin countered. "You had candy!"

She shook her head. "Not any more. Let's check out the kitchen."

Everything seemed so small compared to the Tribe's kitchen. A stove with only four burners. A table with only four chairs. Cabinets that had only three or four shelves, not ten or twelve.

"Not much left in here," Tobin said, peering in one of the cabinets. "Let's get the lanterns out."

"I hope we can find some new batteries," Elanna said as she lit the lanterns. "These are almost finished."

Tobin pulled open a drawer, loosing a flood of paper and pencils. "Junk drawer."

"What?" She wasn't sure she'd heard him right.

"Junk drawer," he said again. "Old Ma used to say that every kitchen needed one. We might find some good stuff in here."

A flashlight and some more matches. Some heavy twine. A few tiny, skinny candles in pastel colors that Elanna couldn't begin to imagine a use for. As Tobin emptied the drawer, she sifted through its contents, laid out on the kitchen table. Rubber bands, most crumbling with age. Some keys.

"No batteries," Tobin said. "Let's check if there's any food!"

The pantry, a small closet just off the kitchen, proved to be a treasure trove. Cans lined the dusty wire shelves, and plastic wrapped containers of flour, rice and beans were stacked on the floor. Jars and bottles, some cracked and empty, also filled the shelves.

"Someone liked to stock up," Tobin said. He touched a few of the cans. "Some of this stuff might still be good."

Elanna's stomach rumbled, and she clutched it, groaning. "Baruch Ha-Shem for that. I'm starving."

"You have to keep up your strength," Tobin told her, tossing a can at her.

She caught it and checked the label. Potted meat. She knew without searching that she wouldn't find the tiny symbol that marked it kosher. She tossed it back at him. "Sorry. This won't do."

Tobin laughed. "Beggars can't be choosers."

He must think she was kidding. She edged past him and began checking the other labels. "No, I guess not. But I can't eat that."

She picked up a can of corn, but the label had none of the symbols she recognized. No OU, no circle k. She scanned the ingredients to be certain the can contained no meat, which would render even the vegetables treif. "This one's ok."

He was staring. "You're serious?"

"Of course I am." She picked up another can. Pork and beans. She shuddered. "This definitely won't do."

He took the can from her and studied it. "What's wrong with this one?"

"Tobin," she said, realizing this was another of those areas she took for granted and he didn't know. "There's pig in there."

"So? You guys ate rats."

"I don't eat pig," she said flatly. "The Tribe made some compensations over the years, but that isn't one of them."

He looked completely confused. She tried again.

"Certain foods are forbidden," she said, and took the can of pork and beans away from him, setting it far back on the shelf. "Pig. Shellfish. Not that we actually ever saw either of those, of course, except in canned goods."

"But...but why?"

"Because Adonai said don't eat it," she said.

Tobin gestured around the pantry. "Elanna, with all respect, do you think we have much choice?"

She picked up a can of green beans, and pointed to the tiny letter "u" encircled on it. "As long as we have things like this, we have a choice."

"Okay," he said with a sigh, and she could tell he still didn't understand. "I'll find something else."

There proved to be plenty. They found the pump over the sink to be rusty but workable, and though the water that gushed from it was dirty red at first, it cleared up nicely. The oven's guts had been hollowed out, leaving ample space to line the interior with wood and paper; the heat from the fire warmed the burners on top to cook the food. She and Tobin managed to put together a decent meal by the time the sun began to set. She only burned her fingers twice.

After they'd both eaten until they thought they might burst, Elanna caught Tobin yawning. As he stretched, she watched his face in the flickering firelight. Could this be love, this overwhelming comfort that came just from watching him? She knew desire, and she knew love for her babies, but this was different.

"It's late," Tobin said. "We've had a long day. I think we should go to sleep."

"In comfort tonight." Elanna pointed to the ceiling. "Think we could look around upstairs?"

At first he didn't say anything, just stared at her with an intensity that made her blush. His eyes were so dark, so penetrating. She thought he might be able to see right inside her.

"Sure." He cleared his throat. "I'll take the lantern. You take the candle."

She did, lifting the fat white candle in its holder. They'd found a box of them in one of the cabinets. It meant they'd be able to save the lantern batteries for a while longer.

The stairs creaked beneath them but seemed to be safe. Their passage stirred up ruffles of dust and mouse droppings that crumbled under their feet. The upper hallway was dark but not long, with several rooms opening off it.

"This looks like the bathroom," Tobin said.

Elanna peeked inside. A tub, a sink and a toilet. She longed for a bath suddenly. Everything about her felt soiled.

She stepped inside the room and pulled back the curtain around the tub. The material came apart in her hands, falling into a thousand crumbling pieces. With a wince of distaste she wiped her hands and looked inside the tub. There were several bottles there, the contents glimmering in her candlelight.

"Shampoo," she said with a sigh. "I need a bath. You do too. Let's see if the pump up here works too."

"Those towels don't look like they're in very good shape," Tobin said, tugging one. It held together.

"Then we'll find something else. I'm filthy!"

"The water's going to be cold."

She poked him gently. "You've been spoiled."

He rolled his eyes. "You've probably never had a cold bath in your life. Are you sure?"

She laughed but nodded. "It's been a long time, true. But I need a bath, Tobin. And to brush my teeth! And to find clean clothes."

"That's a pretty tall order. But I think we can manage."

She hugged him. "You'll feel much better. I promise."

A quick search of the bathroom yielded two toothbrushes still in their original packages. Some toothpaste, still good once they squeezed out the first inch or so, and some soap. Along with the shampoo and the towels, they were set.

"You can go first," he told her gallantly. "You need it more than I do."

His words made her blush until she realized that he was teasing her. She was so relieved that he hadn't suggested they share the bath, she couldn't even pretend to be mad at his comment. "All right."

The thought of being naked in front of him had suddenly intimidated her. She'd undressed in front of hundreds of men, but somehow this would seem different. Just as everything about him was different, she thought as she wiped the dust out of the tub with one of the towels.

The water she coaxed from the hand pump was cold, but once she got past the shivering, it felt marvelous. The soap was smooth against her skin and the shampoo left her hair gloriously soft. She combed through the tangles with a brush she found in a drawer. She wrapped herself in the towel. It was long enough to cover her to her thighs. Rapidly, Elanna soaped her other clothes in the water and wrung them out. It would have to do.

"You done yet?" Tobin called, and she told him she was.

"You smell so good," he said when she opened the door.

"You're just saying that because of how bad I must have smelled before," she replied.

"No," Tobin replied. "I was really only joking about that."

She held the door open for him. "Your turn. I'll wait downstairs. I want to hang these things up by the fire."

He was swifter in the bath than she'd been. When he came downstairs, the towel hung low on his lean hips, her cheeks got hot again. It was so strange to feel this way about him. She'd never had to wonder before if a man she found attractive would be interested in sleeping with her.

"Ready to check out the rooms upstairs?" he asked.

She nodded, not trusting herself to speak. The towel tucked around her all at once felt no more substantial than air. She clutched it and wished he'd taken longer in the bath to give her clothes time to dry.

Tobin didn't seem to notice her sudden shyness. Nor did he seem self-conscious about the way his towel rode so low on his hips. She followed him up the stairs, waiting for his towel to slip off entirely. What would she do then? Laugh, blush, or jump on top of him?

Fortunately, she didn't have to find out. He'd left the lantern at the head of the stairs, and it lit the upstairs hallway. Tobin pushed open the door on the left.

"Not much in here."

Her cheeks were still warm, but she was calming down as she followed him into the room. "It's a sewing machine. Battery run. We had them at home, for taking apart clothes the Gatherers found and making new. "

Aside from the machine and several bookcases, the room was empty. Some bolts of material, thread and other sewing supplies took up space on the shelves. The room didn't even have a curtain on the window.

The next room was just as devoid of personality, though it did have more furniture. A double bed, a dresser and a chair. Some faded pictures hung on the wall, but the closet was empty. Nobody had lived in this room.

Across the hall was the third door. It opened into the largest room. A massive bed dominated the room, but it was the bed's contents that made her gasp and step back.

"It's all right," Tobin said, holding her. "They've been gone a long time."

Two skeletons slept in the bed. Whatever clothes they'd worn had long ago rotted away, leaving only the clean bones behind. Their heads rested together on the same pillow; their hands were next to each other between them.

"This was their room," Elanna said. She wasn't really frightened, just startled. Now she felt as though she were intruding. She spotted a photograph in a frame on the dresser, and knew it was of the couple in the bed. They both smiled into the camera. "They looked nice."

Tobin opened up the closet to show the rows of clothes inside. "I think we'll be able to find something to fit us in here."

She took him by the hand and pulled him into the hallway. "Later, Tobin."

"But, Elanna…"

"Later," she said firmly, pointing him toward the other bedroom. "They're sleeping now."

"They're dead," he told her in a tone that clearly said he hoped she knew that.

"Obviously," she replied with a roll of her eyes. Men could be so dull-witted. She shut the door behind them. "But this was their house. We're guests here. Whatever we take from them will still be here in the morning."

Tobin shrugged. "But we could find something to wear…."

She stopped him with a finger pressed to his lips. "Tomorrow."

"All right," he said, clearly not understanding her reluctance but willing to play along. "But it seems pretty silly to me."

This time she stopped his words with a kiss. "Tobin. Quiet. Come to bed with me."

Suddenly, understanding dawned in his eyes, and he looked at the bed. His tongue snaked out to lick his lips, and the sight made her shiver, and all the more because she knew he wasn't doing it to be seductive.

"All right," Tobin said, a little breathless. "Let's go to bed."

Chapter 24

She knew she should take the lead. She didn't. Tobin's mouth against hers was achingly sweet, and when his hands left hers to wind in her hair, she caught her breath at the sensation.

"I want..." she began, though she wasn't quite sure what she wanted, after all.

"Shhh."

He put the lantern on top of the dresser and gathered her up, moving her toward the bed and pushing her gently down. He didn't lie on top of her, and she was glad. He was much taller and heavier, and she didn't want to feel crushed. Instead, he moved onto the bed beside her and simply cradled her in his arms, her head tucked under his chin.

She was thankful he no longer wore his shirt. It was one of the Tribe's. She didn't want anything of the Tribe on him, not now.

His skin was smooth, his chest hairless except for the twin circles around his nipples and the thin line leading from his navel downward. The sun had browned him in the past, like it did the garden workers, and his muscles were taut and well-defined.

"You've used your body before," she said, knowing it wasn't what she meant but hoping he'd understand.

"Not for this," he replied, voice thick.

She tilted her head to look at his face. "Are you shaking?"

He managed a smile. "I'm sorry."

She shook her head. "Don't be."

Then he was kissing her again, opening her lips with his. His tongue stroked hers softly, without force, and she shivered. Her fingers traced patterns on his chest and stomach, and when she reached the knot he'd tied in the towel around his waist she didn't hesitate.

For a moment she thought he was going to stop her. His hand pressed hers, and she let go of the knot. He sighed against her, and moved his hand away. She tugged fabric apart slowly, all at once aware that he was far more nervous than she.

She pushed on the light material of the towel until it slid down his hips. He kissed her. They leaned back on the bed, pressed against each other. She took his hand, no longer able to wait, and brought it to her breast.

He moaned. She bit her lip to hold hers back. Tobin rubbed his fingers over her nipple, which had slipped from beneath the towel. When the cool air finally hit her bare skin, her shudder was not from the chill.

He put his mouth on her, teasing her nipple with his tongue. She arched into the embrace, running her fingers through his hair, wanting him to take his mouth away to kiss her but never wanting him to stop. He moved with unpracticed urgency, tugging her flesh with his lips until she felt a familiar release building inside her.

He sat up suddenly, as though someone had slapped him. "What?"

She looked down to her chest. A thin white stream had dribbled from the breast he'd been lavishing his attentions on. She wiped it away, and no more came to take its place.

"It's milk," she said. "I only stopped nursing my last baby three months ago. Sometimes…sometimes I still leak a little."

He touched her breast, wonder clear on his face, and then touched her cheek. "I just didn't expect it, that's all."

He traced the silvery white lines on her abdomen, turning her toward the light to see them better. "Scars?"

"Stretch marks," she said. The light touch was beginning to drive her crazy.

He bent to kiss each line. "They're beautiful."

She had never thought of them that way before. They were just a part of her. Now, with Tobin, she saw them as he did. Marks of motherhood. They *were* beautiful.

His breath was heavy. "Is this all right?"

"Why wouldn't it be?"

He rested his hand on her stomach again, tracing the silver lines. "Because of the baby."

She hadn't thought of that. A pregnant hopemother was excused from keeping appointments. A brief flash of unease filled her, but she shook it off.

"I've made love while pregnant before. Once a hopemother learns she's pregnant she doesn't have to keep appointments any more, but it can take a couple weeks, even months to know you've caught."

With a sigh he pulled away from her. "Maybe we shouldn't, then."

No! That wasn't what she wanted! She needed him, needed to be in his arms and not as just friends. Not traveling companions. Lovers.

She put her hands on his shoulders, bringing him close to her body. "It's all right, Tobin."

"Are you sure?"

She could tell he wanted her to be right. He wanted to make love to her as much as she needed him to. And yet, he was willing to push away the obvious desire of his body because he was concerned for her, and for the baby swimming inside her. She'd never known a man to care for her in that way. She didn't know joy could hurt almost as much as grief.

"I'm not sure, no," she said, because she couldn't lie to him. "Hopemothers were excused, yes, but not for any definite health reasons. It was just a precaution, Tobin. We weren't forbidden from keeping appointments, just excused. Most of us looked forward to that excuse."

He nodded, resting his chin on her head. His hands toyed in her hair some more, then down her shoulders and back in a soothing rhythm that could have put her to sleep. She snuggled closer to him, her arms around his back and her thigh pressed between his. She was starting to get cold.

"I just don't want to risk hurting you, or the child," he said roughly. He reached down to touch the long, still healing cut on her leg. "This was bad enough. Elanna, I'd hate myself if anything happened to you because of something I did."

"We'll be doing it together," she said.

"I don't know if I can."

She reached between them to touch him. "This says you can."

"Maybe we'd better just go to sleep."

Now tears threatened. Her hormones were raging, she knew that. But she also felt terribly, horribly disappointed.

"If you don't want to make love to me," she said with as much dignity as she could, "then just say so."

He clutched at her, kissing her forehead. "Please don't say that."

"What should I think?" She asked him angrily. "We're in bed together, we're naked, and you won't make love to me!"

She knew she was being unreasonable. His reasons were strong, and noble. That didn't change the fact that she wanted him, and it didn't make her happy about his refusal.

"Is it a risk you're willing to take?" He asked her gently, pulling her chin up so she could look at his face.

She thought about the months ahead, never knowing for sure if the life she carried would survive. Pregnancy was always filled with anxiety. Would she lose the baby this month? Or perhaps the next? Would the child be safely delivered, and if it lived through that, was it healthy? Would it live? Would it die? Would it nurse and would it grow?

"No," she said finally. Hot and bitter tears stung her nose and throat. "No, I guess not."

Tobin pushed her gently until she turned, then spooned against her. He tugged the covers over them. His hand found hers, and clasped it tightly.

"Sleep well," he whispered in her ear.

She wouldn't have thought she could, but she did.

Chapter 25

Sleeping naked next to Elanna was a sweet torture he couldn't believe he'd put himself through. His entire body ached everywhere it touched hers, but he didn't want to move away. Her breathing was slow and regular, and he knew she slept. He couldn't.

She had a child growing in her, a miracle he'd never seen. True, he'd always dreamed of fathering a child of his own, but as she'd so wisely pointed out to him, did it matter? It was a baby.

But who would care for Elanna during her pregnancy? Who would help her when the time came for the baby to be born? They had to find other people, women, and soon.

How long could they travel? The thought sobered him. How much physical activity could she handle? How long could she walk the grueling miles they'd have to go?

She needed proper food, water. Rest. She needed good shoes. She needed too many things.

Feeling helpless, he buried his face in her hair, breathing in the scent of her. He wasn't ready for this responsibility. He didn't know what he was doing, and she relied on him.

It took a long time for the sun to rise. His eyes grew heavy, but even when he closed them, sleep eluded him. Thoughts ran like rats through his mind, over and over. Nothing he'd ever read had prepared him for this challenge. All he knew about labor was that it made the women scream and needed lots of boiling water.

Oh, God. Sometimes the women died. Could he bear it? Anxiety gripped him, shortening his breath until he had to force himself to relax, to breathe. In. Out. In. Out. Calming himself.

She stirred beside him, stretching. She rolled to face him, her hair a glorious tangle. Her eyes were puffy. Had she been crying, even in her sleep? How could he not have heard?

"Good morning," Elanna said quietly. Did she look a little pale?

"Morning. Did you sleep well?"

She nodded, brushing her tangled curls away from her face. "I guess so. You?"

He nodded a lie. "Hungry?"

Her mouth pursed, and she swallowed heavily. "Ack."

He hadn't heard her right. "What?"

She swallowed again, twice. Her face grew paler. Slowly, slowly, she pushed herself up from the bed and swung her legs over the side.

"Are you all right?" He asked, alarmed.

Her back to him, she held up one hand but didn't speak. Her shoulders shook momentarily. Again, slowly, she stood and with measured footsteps left the room.

A minute later he heard the awful sound of her heaving. Tobin leapt from the bed faster than he thought he could have. He flung open the door so hard it hit the wall and made a hole.

"Elanna!"

She came out of the bathroom. He was relieved to see some color back in her cheeks. He went to her and held her, taking her by the hand back to the bedroom.

"What's wrong?" He asked, close to panic. "Are you sick? Are you all right?"

He didn't understand why she was looking at him with such amusement. She let him sit her down on the bed. When he knelt in front of her, she stroked his cheek.

"Toby. I'm fine. It's called morning sickness."

He sat back, not knowing what to say. "Oh."

She giggled a little. "It's not pretty, but it doesn't last. I usually don't get it at all. I'm sorry if I scared you."

He let out a great gust of relief. "How will I make it through the next nine months?"

She patted his shoulder. "You'll be fine."

He ran his fingers through his hair and scratched the stubble on his chin. "I have no idea what to expect."

"I do."

"Yeah," he said. "I guess you do."

She looked around the room, at him kneeling naked in front of her, and then down at herself. "Shall we find something to wear? And something to eat? I'm starving."

And just like that, she was fine. Did all women go through this? He hated being sick, vomiting. The few times he'd had to throw up he'd wanted to die. Women must be stronger than men, Tobin thought, watching her leave the room to go across the hall. Unbelievably stronger.

"Come on, Toby!"

He followed her to the bedroom. She'd pulled a blanket over the remains of their hosts, tucking it around the bones with obvious care. Now she stood in front of the closet, naked but for a ridiculously large hat. It had a huge drooping and bedraggled feather. She grinned at him, shaking her head to make the feather dance.

"What do you think about this?"

He laughed. "Mmm."

"That is not an answer." She tossed the hat onto a nearby chair and rifled through the clothes on the rod. "But I think I can find some things that will fit us in here."

Though some of the clothes had not weathered the years intact, most were still in good shape. Whoever had worn them had taken good care of them; most things were even covered with thin plastic bags that had kept the dust away. Elanna laid items on the bed, pairing shirts with pants and skirts, shaking out dresses and jackets. The dressers were full, too, though much of the clothing in the drawers had suffered more than those in the closet.

"Underwear!" Tobin said with a flourish, showing her the drawer. "And socks!"

Elanna laughed, pulling a shirt over her head. "Great. That will make a great outfit."

He pulled out a neatly folded pair of briefs and tugged them on. It should have felt strange to be wearing a dead man's underwear, but did he have a choice? The only time he'd ever worn anything right from the package was what he'd found in the warehouse.

Another drawer yielded several pairs of faded jeans. A little too big, but a belt would fix that. He pulled them on, and then a t-shirt from the third drawer. Elanna tossed him a zippered sweatshirt. Everything smelled a little musty, but that would pass in time. It just felt good to be wearing clean clothes after three weeks in the same things.

"What size are your feet?" Elanna asked, her voice muffled as she dug around in the bottom of the closet. She pulled out a couple pairs of sneakers. "Will these do?"

They didn't. Also too big. He'd have to be satisfied with his old pair. "Sorry."

"I guess I'm the lucky one," she said, waving a pair of smaller shoes. "These are just right. The clothes will be all right for awhile, too."

He thought of her belly growing. Something else to think about. What would she wear? He watched her dress, anxiety setting in again. This place had so much to offer them: shelter, food, clothes. Maybe they should stay here until the baby was born.

"What's wrong?" She bumped him from his thoughts.

"Nothing," Tobin said, trying to shake off his nervousness. "You look pretty."

She laughed, rolling her eyes. "Sure I do."

She was wearing a pair of purple sweatpants and a matching shirt with a scooped neck. The sleeves and the legs were too long, and she'd rolled them to fit. Her sneakers were purple and white, with sparkly laces.

"Someone liked purple," Tobin remarked.

"They're soft." She smoothed her shirt. Looking at the bed, she said softly, "Thank you."

Downstairs, he rekindled the fire in the oven again, glad he'd remembered to bank the coals. Water quickly boiled in a kettle from the cupboard. Elanna brought some tea bags, stale but still useable, from the pantry, and some cans of fruit. Breakfast was simple, but good.

"I wish I had some bread," she said wistfully as she drained the last of the peach juice. "Amnon made great sourdough rolls. He showed me how once. It's tricky. Yeast is so precious and so hard to find that using starter is just about the only way to make bread. You have to let it rise just the right amount, or else it won't be as good."

"Maybe you could make some," Tobin said, because she seemed so sad.

Elanna shrugged. "If we could find some live yeast, some flour, some water...I guess I could make some starter."

"We'll have to learn to do a lot of things," Tobin said. He cleared his throat. "I've been thinking."

She looked at him expectantly. "Yes?"

He tapped his fingers on the tabletop, reluctant to admit that he was afraid. "Maybe we ought to just stay here. Until the baby comes."

"What? Why?"

"I think it might be safer," he said.

"I see."

God, was he so transparent? Tobin cursed himself, remembering what Luz had called him. Puny, pathetic. In books, the hero always knew what to do. So, damn it, why didn't he?

She was looking at him without expression. She must be angry. Her face was a smooth blank mask, and he would rather have seen her frowning. At least it was a reaction.

"With the baby coming, I mean," he said, knowing he sounded lame.

"I see."

There, she'd said it again. Still not a quiver of expression on her face. Even her eyes were stony.

"Don't…don't you think so?"

She looked around the kitchen as though assessing it. "This is a nice house."

"And…?" He knew there had to be more.

She shrugged. "It's not exactly California, is it? I mean, I don't know what California will be like, but certainly this isn't it."

"That's just it," Tobin said, relieved to hear that she understood. "I don't know what California will be like, either. If there is a California. What if we get there and it's worse? What if it's like New Jersey?"

"And what if it's better?" Elanna said calmly. She began tidying up the remains of breakfast.

She didn't understand. "But what if it isn't?"

"What if it is?" She stopped messing with the cans and looked at him, hard. "Tobin. I didn't cross that Gehenna of a wasteland with you to hole up in some house just because it's safe. I didn't leave my friends and my life behind to live in a house with no one else around. I enjoy your company, Tobin, but don't you think we'll get lonely? Who will our children play with?"

She turned away from him, bundling up the trash and taking it into the pantry. He heard her bustling around in there, though he couldn't see what she was doing. That was all right. It would be easier to talk to her this way, when she couldn't see his face.

"I'm afraid," he said simply. "I worry that traveling will be too much for you. I'm worried that we won't be able to carry enough supplies with us, and we won't find enough along the way. I'm scared that too much walking will hurt the baby. I don't know anything about women, Elanna, and I know even less about pregnant women. Or babies. I'm afraid I won't be able to do right by you. At least if we stay here, we can manage for awhile, until after the baby comes."

"Tobin?"

Had she even heard him? He didn't want to have to say it again. He heard her shifting things in the pantry, and went to see what she wanted.

She'd found a door. It opened into a garage, dark for the most part but with several shafts of light coming in through two small windows along the back wall. Something was in there.

"I think this might solve some of those worries," she said, turning to him.

As she did, his eyes focused in the dark. He saw what had gotten her so excited. It was a car.

Chapter 26

"Let's see if we can get the garage door open," Tobin said. He didn't want to inch his way through the darkness to do it. That would earn him a barked shin, or worse. "Go around front."

They ducked out the back kitchen door and followed the overgrown sidewalk around to the front of the house. The door screeched but lifted easily enough, once he gave it a hard tug.

With the door open, the garage filled with light. Tobin stepped inside, Elanna right behind him. Dust motes danced in the sunshine. She sneezed.

"Phew," she said, waving her hand in front of her face. "Nobody's been in here for a really long time."

Tobin moved alongside the car, reaching out to touch it. His hands were shaking. It seemed unreal. He'd hoped they might find some bicycles somewhere, but he'd never dreamed about finding a car. Though he'd passed dozens of them on his way to the city, it hadn't occurred to him that the people who'd owned this house might have had one.

The vehicle was small, much smaller than the gatherer's trucks. Its rounded roof and hood made it seem vaguely insectile. It had a door on each side and a small trunk. Dust coated the windows, obscuring the interior. It was probably destroyed inside, he thought, not daring to hope for more. They could sit on bare metal if they had to. More important was if the engine still worked.

"It probably won't run," he said, not wanting to raise her hopes. Or his.

Elanna blew out an exasperated gust of air. "You never know until you try."

"You always look for the best, don't you?"

A shadow crossed her face as she leaned forward to kiss him lightly. "Toby, there's really nothing else to look for."

"You know I have no idea how to work this. Or to drive it."

"I know," she said, and kissed him again.

The kiss grew deeper. When he found himself pushing her up against the car, he pulled away. Elanna didn't protest, but her eyes flickered with disappointment.

"Let's look under the hood," he said.

It took him several minutes to figure out how to release the catch. Once he triggered it, the hood popped up so suddenly it whacked him in the face. Bright pain flared and he stumbled back, muttering curses.

"Are you all right?" Elanna asked, her voice concerned. She sighed when he nodded, holding his nose. He moved his hand so she could look at the injury. "Let me see. Not even bleeding. Be more careful, honey."

His heart thudded at the endearment. The pain in his nose and cheek faded as he watched her poke around underneath the hood. She called him "honey." He felt the goofy grin spreading across his face and didn't even try to stop it.

"Here's the battery," Elanna said, pointing. "It doesn't look too good."

The battery cables were green and crusted. Tobin found a rag on one of the shelves along the wall and cleaned away the crud from the terminals, but it was clear that this battery was dead. All the fluid had leaked out through a huge crack in the casing.

He shrugged away his disappointment. "It was a good try, anyway."

Elanna wasn't satisfied. "There have to be more batteries."

"Think so?" He sounded more skeptical than he'd intended.

She looked at him strangely. "Well, yeah. If these people had a car, they'd certainly have extra batteries to run it. Something like a car takes a lot of juice. Even to go on a short trip would use up a lot of power. I'm sure they have extras here somewhere, and if they haven't been activated yet they'll still work."

He stared at her. She was right, of course. He might have thought of it, but then again, probably not. She knew a lot more about batteries and things than he did. "You're so smart."

She seemed surprised. "Me? No."

He gestured around the garage. "Yes, you. You're right. I bet they do have more batteries. You thought of it, not me."

"Nobody ever called me smart before," Elanna said. "I've had a lot of compliments, but not about that."

He went to her and took her hands. He wanted to kiss away the calluses that had sprouted there, when once her hands had been smooth and fine. "Well, I'm saying it now."

She hugged him, hard. "Thank you, Toby."

They stayed that way for a while. He knew they should get moving, but for now just holding her and smelling her hair was enough. Her head came to just under his chin and she fit perfectly into the circle of his arms.

"Should we look?" she said finally, tilting her face to look at him. "We'll need time to pack before we go."

The garage was dirty with age, but well-organized. It only took a few minutes to find the boxes labeled "car batteries." Elanna let out a squeal of delight when he pulled them off the shelf. They tore open the brittle cardboard and found two rows of five batteries each. Those, along with the other, half-filled box, made fifteen batteries all together.

"I don't know how far they'll get us," Tobin said. "But it's better than walking!"

Elanna whooped, doing a little dance that stirred up the dust until they both began sneezing like maniacs. Laughing, they fled the dirty garage to the sunshine outside, holding hands. Her kisses were so sweet, Tobin thought as she gave him one and then sneezed, still laughing. Dirt had smudged her cheeks.

"You're so beautiful," he told her, and meant it.

"Beautiful, smart," she said with a low curtsey. "Aren't you lucky to have found me?"

"Modest, too," Tobin said, teasing her. She swatted at him, and he caught her hand. "Yes, Elanna. I'd say I'm lucky."

"Me too," she said, becoming serious. "Thanks for taking me away, Tobin. Thank you for being my friend."

He couldn't find the words to say what she made him feel. He didn't have enough experience talking. He'd spent too much time alone. He struggled, trying to force his mouth and tongue to shape the words he knew would come, if only he tried hard enough.

She watched his silence for a moment, disappointment flickering in her lovely gray eyes. "I'll go inside and start gathering some things to take."

He watched her go, his stomach sinking. She'd called him a friend. Was that all she was to him? He was an imbecile. The library in Eastport had an entire section of books with muscled, bare-chested men and half-naked women with flowing hair on the covers. People in those books fought a lot, and they pretended they didn't love each other when they really did, but they never were just "friends."

"I'll work on the car!" he called after her. Fists clenched, he knew his words meant nothing. They were too late. And not right.

She disappeared into the house. He wanted to run after her, take her to the bedroom, and…and what? Jeopardize the baby she carried just to ease his own lust? Tobin slammed his fist into his thigh. With nothing else to do, he went into the garage to try and figure how to start the car.

BY MIDAFTERNOON, Tobin had figured out how to start the car, and Elanna had finished packing up them. Boxes and bags and suitcases bulging with items littered the front lawn, waiting to be shoved into the trunk and back seat.

"Did you leave anything here at all?" Tobin asked her, drinking some of the water she'd poured for him.

He looked good sweaty, she thought as she answered. "Not much."

He cast a skeptical eye at the piles she'd made. "Do you think we can fit all this in the car with us?"

"All we can do is try. It would be silly to leave it behind. We don't know if we'll find more. I packed clothes, food, some utensils and pots and pans. Some jugs of water from the cistern. Candles and matches, and I hope they still light because the lantern batteries won't last forever. Blankets and pillows, because I'm not sleeping on the hard ground without them."

Now his skepticism turned to admiration. "You've thought of everything, haven't you?"

"I tried." She thought of all the things still in drawers and closets and cabinets. She didn't want to leave any of it behind. They represented a wealth she'd never really known, despite the Tribe's storerooms. Practically, though, she knew their space was limited. Not all of it could come with them.

She didn't tell him what she'd found in the back hall closet, though she'd already tucked a box full of her discoveries in the car. She thought of the people on the bed, and the photos of them around the house. Pictures of just the two of them. In some they were younger and in many they were older, but in every photo there was still only the two. No third, no child. They'd never had a baby to wear the tiny dresses and socks she'd found tucked away so carefully. No baby to play with the stuffed toys that had been wrapped in plastic to prevent mold.

Elanna rubbed her stomach. Hope had made the people of that house save and protect those things, and hope was something she knew about. Her baby would wear the clothes and play with the toys, and when she held it in her arms for the first time, she'd send thanks to the people of this house for leaving behind what her baby needed.

Tobin looked at the sun, which had already moved more than

halfway across the sky, then wiped his face with the edge of his t-shirt. "It's getting warmer."

She looked at the sun too, squinting against the brightness. The sun hadn't seemed to shine so brightly in the city, where almost every view was blocked by buildings. "I'm glad. I hate the cold."

"I always liked the winter," Tobin said. "We didn't have to work so hard. Old Pa would light the fires in the stove, and that kept the little house warm. At night I'd dive down under the pile of quilts Old Ma made, and I'd listen to them talk until I fell asleep. Everything seemed clearer in the winter. The stars seemed brighter. The water seemed fresher. It was cold, but inside, together, we were warm."

She thought of the times smoke from the furnaces belched through the heating ducts, making everything stink and everyone's eyes burn. Depending on what the Gatherers had found to burn, sometimes the smoke would reek for days, or even weeks. Heat was precious in the Tribe, and blankets few. Meals in the winter were sparse. Tempers were high. She made appointments just to have a warm body to lie next to, at least for a few hours.

"You were lucky," she said.

He looked at her with surprise. "I guess I was. I'd never really thought about it before. We didn't have much, you know. Not like you did."

"But you had each other," Elanna said. It was more than she'd ever had. She envied him. "Candy and pretty things aren't family, Toby."

"No," he said, touching her cheek gently. "They're not."

Tears in the bright sunlight seemed stupid, and she fought them back. "Are you hungry? I made lunch."

To her surprise, he pulled her into his arms. His kiss was long and sweet, but she sensed an undercurrent of passion in it. Although she wanted to, she didn't respond to it. It would only make him draw away. She took the kiss for what it was, letting him hold her against him. It was better than no kiss at all.

"Thank you," Tobin said, squeezing her. "For coming with me."

"You're welcome," Elanna replied, glad to be here, standing

with him in the sun. It felt good on her face and arms, though she'd have to go in soon. Her skin wasn't brown like Tobin's. She would burn.

"And I *am* hungry," he said, rubbing his stomach. "Let's eat some lunch. And then we can get on the road?"

She nodded, excitement twanging her at the thought of setting off again, this time in luxury. She'd never been in a car before, and though she'd seen the Gatherer's trucks several times, she'd never ridden in one.

Lunch was hurried. Pasta from a plastic package and some canned fruit they couldn't really identify, since the label had faded away. Sitting at the small kitchen table both of them ate quickly, eager to fill their bellies and get on the road.

Now that the car was running and they had supplies, the trip seemed more like an adventure than a nightmare. Elanna forced herself to eat a few more bites of undercooked noodles and drink a full glass of water. She had to start making sure she got enough nutrition, no matter how unappetizing the meal may be. She needed her strength.

"I just want to wash up and change my clothes," she said. "These are pretty filthy. Yours are too."

Tobin looked down at the dirt smudged into his clothes, then turned his hands over to look at the grime crusting his knuckles. "I guess you're right. Who knows the next time we'll get to take a bath?"

She snorted. "It's better than nothing, but I don't really consider it taking a bath. Cold water and that tiny tub…"

He grinned, and her stomach flip-flopped. "You're spoiled."

"And that's a bad thing?"

His smiled broadened. For one delirious moment she thought he might kiss her, but at the last minute he pulled away. She ducked her head, not wanting him to see how badly she'd wanted his kiss.

"You want to go first?" Tobin asked.

She looked around the kitchen, at the dishes and the pot they'd used to cook the pasta. She couldn't leave it like this. Even though they'd never be back, and even though nobody else might ever come through, the house was clean when they found it. The people in the bed upstairs had kept it that way, right up until the time they died. It wouldn't be right to leave things a mess.

"You go ahead," she said. "I'll clean up here. And I want to make one last run through the house, just to make sure --"

"That you got everything?" Tobin reached out to push the hank of her braid over her shoulder. "Sure. I'll go. Can you grab me some clean clothes, or did you pack them all?"

She twisted her mouth at him, and he backed away in mock fear. "No, Mr. Smarty. I didn't pack everything. I'll get you some things from upstairs."

He went into the bathroom and she heard him turning the pump wheel, then the sound of water gushing. It only took her a few minutes to clean the kitchen, since all she did was throw the leftover food into the yard outside and put the dishes into the sink. The water from the bathroom stopped, and she heard splashing.

Like a little boy, she thought with a smile as she went upstairs. She wondered if they'd ever find a place where she could have a hot bath again. Then she thought that she didn't really care, because having a baby to raise as her own more than made up for cold water.

She pulled some clean clothes from the dresser, guessing at the sizes. She tugged a fresh pair of pants off a hanger for herself and fingered the waistband. Time had eaten away the elastic so that the waist no longer sprang back when tugged. She'd have to use a belt, but in just a few months she'd be grateful for the looseness.

She was lucky that the woman who'd lived here was bigger than she was. All the clothes in the closet and drawer would fit her well enough as she grew. Until the very end, she thought with a smile, remembering how big she'd grown with most of her babies. She'd deal with that when the time came.

As she pulled a t-shirt for herself from one of the drawers, Elanna caught sight of herself in the mirror over the dresser. Putting down the clothes she planned to take for Tobin and herself, she studied her image. Mirrors weren't common in the Tribe. Vanity wasn't encouraged. Besides, she knew what she looked like. Now, though, seeing herself in the spangled light coming through the window, Elanna thought about the changes her body would go through over the next few months.

She pulled her shirt over her head and cupped her breasts in her hands for one moment. The nipples peaked against her palms with a familiar ache that she knew would go away in a few weeks. Smoothing her hands down over her stomach, she touched the lines Tobin had said were beautiful. She pulled her pants off, stepping out of them to see the rest of her. Her hips were wide, and that was fine, because hopemothers with narrow hips had a terrible time giving birth. Her legs were strong from all the walking she'd done over the past three weeks, and the wound on her calf had healed.

But was she beautiful? She studied the length of her dark auburn hair in its thick braid. Her face was not thin or fat; her nose not large or small. Her eyes, she was surprised to see as she peered closer, were not blue, as she'd been so often told. They were gray. Her skin was beginning to freckle from the sun.

Was that beauty? She'd never cared before. It hadn't ever mattered before. Even the ugliest hopemothers got appointments.

Now, though, she wanted to be lovely. For Tobin. Elanna turned sideways to look at her stomach. It was still relatively flat, but not for long. She'd start to show soon, as she always did. Earlier and earlier with each pregnancy, it seemed, though taking the weight off after the baby came had never been as hard for her as it had been for some.

She couldn't stop the smile that curved her lips. This pregnancy would be different. She could tell already. Aching breasts, growing belly, swollen feet and ankles and having to pee every five minutes… she would relish each and every moment that she carried this child. Even the labor pains would be more joy than hurt, because they'd be bringing her child into the world.

She hugged herself briefly, trying to force away the worries about the upcoming months. Nothing would be the same this time. She'd always been in a safe place before, with enough food and drink, enough time to rest and care for herself. She'd always been pampered before. She'd had the other hopemothers to attend her when her time came, just as she was there for the others when it was their turn.

Who would help her this time? Her throat closed tight, hurting. She rubbed her belly, fingertips moving over her skin in a pattern that had become so familiar to her over the years. Her child swam inside her, growing. It would be born with an effort of sweat and blood, and she'd hold it warm from her womb, loving it even before she saw its face. But who would help her through the labor, through the pain? Who would catch the child, and who would cut the cord that tied it to her?

Fear, huge and relentless, pushed her to the bed. She sat, trembling, fist pressed to her mouth to stop from crying out loud. The hand not at her lips caressed her belly, soothing the baby even as she fought to calm herself.

She would get through this, she thought fiercely, shaking. Her knuckles broke against her teeth, and the taste of blood made her choke. She looked at her hand, seeing the wounds she'd caused herself. Blood. When the baby came, there'd be a lot more of it.

She would not think about it now. She could not. It would be too easy to let herself wallow in fear for the length of her pregnancy. She'd seen it happen, even to hopemothers who'd caught many times before.

She wiped the blood away with determined strokes. Tobin called her name from the hall, and she rose from the bed. She pulled the oversized t-shirt on and gathered the clothes she was taking for Tobin and herself.

"Coming!" Barefoot, she went to take her turn in the bath.

Chapter 27

There were only three other houses along the road. They went to each of them; Elanna checked the kitchen and Tobin checked the garage. None of the other houses had cars, batteries, or much of anything else.

"That's about it," Tobin said after they'd searched the third house and found nothing they wanted or needed to take along.

Elanna paused on the doorstep, mumbling. Her eyes were closed, her head bent. He leaned closer to hear her words, but didn't understand them.

"Ah-mayn," she concluded and opened her eyes.

"What were you doing?"

"It's Hebrew. I was saying the Shehechyanu," she said, her voice puzzled. "Why?"

"I couldn't understand you."

"You're not one of us."

He didn't like the way that sounded. He didn't want to remember that they'd come from places so different. She had a past and a history, now a language, that he could never experience.

He scowled. "You make that sound so bad."

Elanna looked at him, her lovely eyes showing surprise. "It's not bad. It's not good. It just is."

"Tell me what you said," he asked.

He could tell she was just humoring him, but she spoke anyway. "Baruch ata adonai, eloheynu melech l'olam, shehechyanu, vechiamanu, vehigianu, lazman hazeh."

"That sounds like a mouthful."

He'd offended her. She turned and began to walk away, shoulders stiff and her head high. She moved fast, much faster than he'd expected. He almost had to run to catch up to her.

"Elanna, I'm sorry."

"Didn't you ever pray?" she demanded, turning. "I know you don't have the same customs as we did, but didn't you pray? Didn't you ever give thanks to God?"

His experience with God was Old Pa saying "God damn it." He'd read about God, and religion, and he knew that people had worshipped in churches and synagogues and mosques and temples, but he had no idea what any of those places were. The churches in Eastport hadn't had a congregation since well before his grandparents' birth.

"No," he said humbly. "I guess I never did."

She stared at him blankly. "Why not?"

"I don't know. Nobody ever told me I should."

That seemed to concern her. "Have you ever felt like something was leading you, or helping you, even though you couldn't see it? Or have you ever wanted something, terribly, but you didn't think you'd ever have it? And then you found it?"

He thought of his longing, fueled by the heroines in all his novels, to find someone with whom he could share his life. He thought about his dreams of finding other people. Having children. He looked at her face, so earnest.

"Yes. I have."

"That was Adonai, watching over you," she said. "That was HaShem. God. Whatever you want to call it."

He shook his head slowly. "I don't know if I believe that."

She sighed. "Then what do you think brought you to me?"

"We got lucky," Tobin said

Elanna shook her head. "No. It wasn't luck. It was Ha-Shem, watching out for us."

He wanted to believe her, even though what she said sounded to him like the most fantastic of fairy tales. "All right."

Her smile was worth his agreement.

ELANNA WAS useless when it came to driving. Watching the Gatherers drive by in a parade was no help when it came to actually doing it herself. She gladly gave over the duty to Tobin, who at least could figure out how to ignite the engine.

He was so proud of himself, she thought fondly, as he lectured her on just how far to turn the wheel so the car would go in the direction they wanted it to. She couldn't really care less about the logistics. As long as he knew what he was doing, that was fine with her. But she humored him, because it made her happy to see him act so proud.

"That's great, honey," she said, and was surprised to see his cheeks flush. He was blushing? She'd made him blush, just by calling him a pet name?

Elanna looked out the window, watching the world flash by. He confused her. She'd never been with a man who wanted her but didn't take her. She'd never met a man she wanted so badly.

"We're going so fast!" Elanna marveled, rolling down the window to let the breeze in. Her hair flew back and she stuck her head out, laughing. "I never thought you could go so fast!"

"Twenty miles an hour isn't so fast," Tobin said, laughing with her. He pointed out the window to a battered and rusting metal sign as they passed it. *Speed Limit. 65 Miles An Hour.* "People used to go much faster."

"People used to do a lot of things," she told him. "That was once upon a time."

He glanced at her, then quickly back to the road. She could tell he still wasn't quite sure about driving. He never took his hands off the wheel. His knuckles were white. She wondered how long it would take for his hands to start hurting. She thought that probably he wouldn't tell her if they did.

"Lots of stories start Once Upon A Time," he told her.

"And they all end Happily Ever After," Elanna said. "Do you think we will?"

He was quiet so long she thought he wasn't going to answer. She began to wish she hadn't asked, though she'd tried to make her voice sound light. She plucked at the oversized tee-shirt, not sure what to do.

"I hope so," he said, finally. "I guess it's why I started out on this trip."

"Me too," she said.

EACH BATTERY, they discovered, was good for twenty miles. Less, if they tried to push the little car into going too fast, but never more. They were meant to last a lot longer, but time had depleted them somehow. Tobin quickly learned to turn the car off whenever they made a stop to help conserve the power. They stopped often.

The roads were clear of vehicles, mostly, but they weren't in good repair. Holes that they could've walked or ridden bikes around nearly junked the car. Several times he'd had to ride the shoulder to avoid huge potholes.

When they did come across another car or truck, they stopped to check its battery. They were usually dead. Some had extras in the trunk, and they took them. Once they came across a spot where three cars had collided. The driver of one had gone through the windshield. The elements had worn his bones away to nearly nothing, at least on the half that was exposed outside. The inside half was still there, preserved like leather. Tobin drove even more carefully after that.

They drove, off and on, for a hundred miles. By the time the sun began to set, Tobin's stomach was growling. He didn't want to use more power by turning the headlights on, either. It was a good time to stop.

"How about we call it a night?" he asked, turning to look at Elanna.

She was staring at the road ahead, eyes wide in shock. "Look out!"

Turning back, he swerved to avoid hitting something massive. The tires squealed and the steering wheel rattled in his hands as, heart pounding, he twisted it. With stones and gravel pinging against the windshield, the little car came to a shuddering stop along the shoulder.

Breathing hard, Tobin looked back at what he'd nearly hit. It had loomed up out of the growing darkness like some fairytale beast. It was something else entirely.

He opened the car door to get out, but Elanna stopped him with a hand on his arm.

"Wait," she whispered. She bent her head to peer out through the driver's side window. "Maybe we should just turn around. Go back another way. I saw an exit a mile or so back."

He looked out again at the huge pile blocking all four lanes of traffic. Nothing moved in it, not even a breeze. Everything was quiet.

"I think it's okay," he told her, squeezing her fingers.

Elanna bit her lip, then nodded. "You're probably right. But you're not going out there alone. If you go, I go."

He knew better than to argue with her, but he did make her stand behind him. Dark was falling quickly, especially once the sun passed behind the hulking fortress of wood and debris. The moon hadn't risen yet, but the stars were bright and clear. Tobin searched the length and height of the pile, but without proper light he couldn't see much.

Elanna slipped her arm around his waist. "What is it?"

"Some kind of road block," Tobin said. "I see some trees. Some posts. Lots of junk."

She pointed a blob of white amongst the rest. "A mattress!"

For some reason, that made her laugh. Tobin chuckled with her, and they began pointing out other bits and pieces they could see sticking out from the pile, which not only stretched across the road but as far as they could see on either side. More than a roadblock… a wall. When Elanna spotted a toilet, still intact, resting under a group of metal street signs, neither one could control themselves.

"Stop!" she cried after a few minutes, holding her sides. "It hurts!"

He saw her wiping tears and clutching her stomach. His throat slammed shut. Tobin grabbed her, holding her close and forcing her to sit on the driver's seat. He knelt before her, knees grinding into the gravel.

"What are you doing?" she asked him, puzzled as he chafed her wrists.

"You said it hurts," he said. "And you were crying."

She smiled and touched his face. "Toby, I'm fine."

"But you said --"

"Didn't you ever laugh so hard you cried?" Elanna asked him gently. "Or until your sides hurt?"

He sat back, too relieved that she was all right to be embarrassed at how he'd overreacted. Again.

"No," he said. "I never have. Not until now."

Elanna gathered two fistfuls of his shirt and bent down to press her forehead to his. They were nose to nose, her eyes searching his and her mouth so damned close he knew she wanted to kiss him.

"I'm sorry," she said. "But things will be different for you from now on."

"And for you, I hope," he told her. With every word their lips brushed against each other. She tasted sweet.

Then she did kiss him, and her hands weren't wrapped in his shirt any more. They were wrapped in his hair. She opened her mouth beneath his. He knew he should stop. Didn't want to. Couldn't try to. Every stroke of her fingers along his scalp, every touch of her tongue against his, sent waves of sensation rippling through his body. Straight down to his groin. Heat flooded him there, and pressure. He groaned, giving in to the demands of her mouth and her hands, and he clutched her like a drowning man.

"Elanna," he heard himself say, but the voice didn't sound like his.

"Yes," she said.

He was touching her, holding her, and the kisses were going on and on. The sting of the gravel against his knees seemed far away and unimportant. He drew in her breath as she exhaled it. She was inside him, all over him, all around him. And then she was pushing him away.

He sprawled back on the gravel, feeling it bite his palms. He couldn't think straight, not with the scent of her still in his nostrils and her taste swimming on his tongue. Elanna knelt next to him, helping him up. He shook his head to clear it.

"I'm sorry," she said. "I shouldn't have pushed you."

His pants had grown suddenly too tight. The night air was chilly against his skin, where moments before hot sweat had coated him. A low, dull ache began to grow in the pit of his stomach.

"Damn it, Elanna!"

She shrank from him, just a glimmer in the dark. "I'm sorry."

He ran his hands through his hair and scrubbed his face. He tried to shake off the effect she had on him. It didn't work, not really.

"Do you think I'm made of stone?" Tobin asked her.

Without waiting for an answer, he stalked to the back of the car and opened the trunk. He pulled out one of the lanterns and flipped the switch. Light glared from it immediately, a strong hot blast of it that dimmed quickly. He hooked it to the trunk lid and began pulling out what they'd need for the night. If he kept his hands busy he wouldn't be able to think about touching her.

"No, I don't." She followed him. "I said I was sorry!"

Ignoring her, he went back to unpacking. Blankets. The pillows she'd insisted on. A small box of canned goods and the jugs of water. Matches. Every item he tossed to the ground should have helped calm him. They didn't.

"Don't ignore me when I'm talking to you." Elanna deliberately stepped in front of him, forcing him to look at her. "I'm sorry I pushed you. I guess I just wanted to be the one to break it off. Before you could."

"What do you want me to say?" He bent to the pile of gear he'd thrown on the ground. Anything to not have to see how the lantern light painted shadows on her cheeks.

"I don't know," Elanna said. "But I want you to say something."

"You don't want to hear what I have to say," Tobin said. He took a box of matches into the grass, just inside the ring of lantern light.

"If it's the truth, I do."

"No." He shook his head, pulling up a patch of grass so he could build a fire there.

"Why not?"

"Because I'm angry," Tobin replied, though his anger was fading now. He didn't know why she'd kissed him the way she did, but his response was something he'd have to deal with on his own.

"Don't you know how to fight?" The anger had gone out of her voice, too. She came next to where he was pulling the grass. "Sometimes people fight, Toby. Even people who like each other."

She hadn't said love. His heart twisted in his chest, defeated. "See if you can find some sticks for this fire. Please."

She sighed. Her hand came out to touch his shoulder, but then she seemed to think better of it and pulled away. "All right. I can only say I'm sorry so many times."

"Accepted," he said and concentrated on his task.

It was another long night with her curled beside him. He managed sleep, if only because exhaustion overtook him, but the feel of her against him haunted his dreams. When the sun broke over them in the morning, he was all too happy to roll out of the blankets to stretch away his aches.

Elanna stirred but didn't wake immediately. Watching her in the rosy light of early morning, Tobin couldn't stay angry with her. They would need to talk, though, and soon. They had a long, long journey ahead of them. If they couldn't come to terms with each other, it would be hell.

He stretched some more, wincing. The nights were still chilly, and the ground had been hard. They'd have to figure out some other arrangement, because she wouldn't be able to sleep on the ground much longer. He wouldn't let her.

In the sunshine the roadblock looked even more ridiculous.

Whoever had put it together, and for whatever reason, hadn't cared about making it neat and presentable. It was an overgrown jumble of wood, metal and household odds and ends.

He glanced back at Elanna, who was incredibly still asleep. Maybe being pregnant tired women out. Anyway, the hard ground and the rising sun didn't seem to bother her, and he didn't want to wake her just yet. He wanted to see what lay on the other side of the barrier.

Climbing it wasn't too hard. There were plenty of gaps to use as hand and footholds. He was afraid at first that the structure would shift under him, but he relaxed as he moved higher and not so much as a twig snapped under his weight. Whoever had built it made it strong.

He climbed higher. Sweat ran stinging into his eyes and he turned to look at Elanna. His stomach did a slow roll as he realized how high he really was. It hadn't seemed so high from the ground. Now it seemed as though he could almost reach out and touch the tops of the trees set back from the road, if they were only a little closer.

Just a few more steps and he'd reach the top. Even as he climbed the last few steps he knew it didn't matter much if they were rerouted. They had no time line other than the one he'd created in his mind. That and the seasons would determine how fast they traveled. He didn't want to be on the road when the weather turned cold again. When Elanna's baby would be born.

He stopped, thoughts of Elanna and the baby gone. Deleted. What was on the other side of the barrier left no room for thought other than horror.

With numb fingers he grabbed, hard, to keep from falling. The road below him was an abattoir; the carnage that had occurred there was no less horrific because it had obviously happened long ago. Bodies, piles of bones with shreds of flesh hanging from them, were strewn as far as he could see. Several of them were impaled on pieces of the roadblock.

The corpses wore identical outfits of green, though most of the cloth was faded and torn. Some gripped long barreled things in their hands. Guns? Were they guns? Old Pa had an ancient shotgun that had belonged to his great-granddaddy. It didn't look anything like the weapons these people had carried. What had happened here? What had they been fighting to defend?

A sound like thunder broke the morning silence. Far away it rumbled, but he imagined he felt the barrier shake beneath him. His palms grew sweaty as he gripped a metal street sign that jutted from the pile. Again, silence. His ears strained.

It came again, a low rumble brought on the breeze. His heart began to pound. He looked at the bodies again, the bones in clothes who carried guns. He noticed something he'd overlooked in his initial shock.

All of them were facing away from the barrier. They hadn't been defending it. They'd been crawling over it.

Whatever had killed them was on this side of the roadblock. And judging by the rumble that came again to twist his guts, it was coming back.

Chapter 28

She wasn't sleeping, just lying there with her eyes closed, but when Tobin shouted it startled her. Elanna sat up, heart pounding. She squinted against the bright sun and raised her hand to shield her eyes.

"Get up!"

Tobin was scrambling down the jumbled pile of wood and junk. Her heart leaped into her throat as he lost his footing and nearly fell. Images of Tobin splattering onto the road, breaking bones and maybe worse, flashed into her head. He caught himself at the last moment but didn't slow his frantic pace.

He yelled her name, slipping again, catching himself again, and her stomach jumped. The blankets tangled around her feet and she cursed them because they wouldn't let her up.

"Get up! Get in the car!"

"What's wrong?" she managed to say, thrusting herself free of the tangle.

One more time he lost his footing, and this time he didn't find a handhold. Tobin slid the last few feet to the earth, skidding along the jutting wood and metal. She heard the sound of cloth ripping.

"Be careful!" Elanna reached for him though she knew she was too far away.

He was up and on his feet before she had the chance to get to him. His hands were bloody, and he'd scratched his cheek. A strip of fabric from his shirt flapped as he ran toward her. He didn't seem to notice any of these things. Fear contorted his face, and seeing it made her own heart thud in alarm. What had he seen?

"What's wrong?" she asked again, but he was pulling her by the arm, back toward the car.

"No time," Tobin said through gritted teeth. His hands were cold and wet on her elbow. He propelled her ruthlessly into the passenger side and slammed the door, almost catching her foot.

He slipped into the driver's seat, fumbling with the ignition. His forehead was pale and sheened with sweat. He swiped at his eyes, fingers shaking as he reached again for the keys.

"Tobin? You're scaring me!"

He looked at her then, his mouth set into a grim line she didn't like at all. "We have to get out of here. How far back was that exit?"

"I'm not sure."

He reached over and pulled the seat belt across her shoulder and over her lap. "Put this on."

His face had scared her, but that simple act of putting on her seatbelt terrified her. "Please tell me what's happening!"

He didn't have time. Thunder suddenly filled the world, shaking the road and the car, and them. Elanna gripped the dashboard, watching the roadblock. She expected it to tumble down in front of them, over top of them, any second.

Tobin twisted the keys in the ignition, cursing impatiently and slapping the steering wheel with his free hand when the car didn't start right away. He tried again, harder this time. Still, the engine buzzed but didn't catch.

"The button!" The roar of thunder ebbed and grew incredibly louder, pulsing. She thought she heard voices, too, yelling beneath the noise. She couldn't be sure. "You have to push that little button!"

"Got it!" Tobin pushed the small red button on the control

panel and waited until it turned green. Then he twisted the keys. The car buzzed into life.

He slammed it into reverse and the little car revved, then flew backwards. Gravel shot from beneath the tires, spanging against the windows. The car bumped, hard, as they passed over the shoulder. Elanna thanked Ha-Shem she'd put the seatbelt on. Tobin had not, and he hit his head on the ceiling when the car jolted.

Tobin heaved the wheel as far as he could, and the car turned. Now they were facing away from the barrier. Elanna twisted around to look out the back window, but she could see nothing. Their packages and baggage blocked the view.

"What is it?" she asked.

"Something bad."

The car leapt forward as he pushed down on the accelerator. A high-pitched whining came from the engine. He was pushing the car too hard, too fast. Looking at his face, she dared not ask him to slow down.

Now she heard more yelling over the thunderous roar. She looked into the side mirror, trying to see what was behind them. The car bounced so much her vision blurred, but she saw figures on top of the pile blocking the road. Some of them had already climbed down to the street. They waved their arms and yelled, and they all held strange, long poles.

The end of one of the poles exploded, and the figure holding it fell back. In the next instant, her side mirror disappeared. Pieces of it clattered against the window. Elanna shrieked without breath, and though the sound echoed in her head nothing came out of her mouth.

Tobin pushed the accelerator harder. The whining grew louder, more strained. The car bucked and jumped, but responded, and in the next moment they'd left the roadblock far behind.

Elanna sat back in the seat, helpless. Tobin drove like a madman, hunched over the wheel. The exit was coming up sharp on the right. He wasn't looking at it. He didn't see it. They were going to go right by.

And yet, she couldn't speak. Whatever had destroyed the mirror seemed to have stolen her voice, too. She moved her lips but nothing came out. She'd never been so terrified.

Now the side road was just in front of them. Elanna raised her hand, pointing. Tobin didn't see. His hands gripped the wheel so hard she thought he might leave marks. She pointed, waving her hand, trying desperately to say something. Anything, just to get him to look.

"Go right!" The words exploded from her mouth.

Tobin heard her. Without looking, without hesitating, he twisted the wheel to the right and stomped harder on the accelerator. She didn't see how they could go much faster.

The car squealed as it made the turn, and the engine's whine grew to an ear-splitting wail. The tires slid in the rocks and dirt along side the road. The car shuddered. For one sickening moment the car tilted, and she looked out her window to see the earth rushing up at her. Then the car settled back on four wheels, and they were following the curving road that led away from the one they'd been on. Without stopping the car shot out through an intersection and toward a small stream.

She screamed again, this time with breath. The car flew toward the bridge, where all that remained was two concrete slabs with nothing spanning them. The bottom had rotted away. She couldn't tell how deep it was, but did it matter? They were going in!

Like a pigeon hunching itself into flight, the little car seemed to gather itself and leap. They left the stream bank and cleared the bridge, landing on the other side with a rattling thump that threw Elanna against the restriction of her seatbelt so hard it cut her neck and shoulder. Tobin didn't fare so luckily. He flew forward and cracked the windshield with his head before falling back.

"Tobin!" She screamed his name, frightened by the blood pouring from a cut above his eye.

Without Tobin's hands on the wheel, the little car spun out of control. They left the smoothness of the road and landed in the growth of the field next to it. The car shuddered, and the engine's whine cut off.

He groaned. Elanna blinked at him, trying to think what had

happened. The pain in her neck and shoulder made her put her fingers to the spot, and they came away red. Tobin winced, holding his head. Blood seeped through his fingers, staining the front of his shirt.

She cried his name, reaching for him, but the seatbelt that had saved her from greater injury now held her back. She slapped at it, forgetting in her distress how to work the catch that would release the buckle. He leaned over, fit his fingers into the slot and released the belt with a click. It slapped against her as it slid back into place. Ignoring it, she slid across the seat to him, wiping at the blood on his head.

He reached up and grabbed her hands to stop her. "Don't!"

"Let me see," she demanded. She needed to know how bad his wound was.

His eyes began to roll back in his head. His mouth fell open. Elanna watched him fall back against his seat, frightened by his sudden limpness. She ripped the bottom of her shirt and pressed the cloth to the cut on his forehead. Within moments the white fabric began to turn red. He groaned. Elanna let out a sob of relief. He was alive.

Though there was a lot of blood, the wound didn't look deep. Carefully she eased the cloth away and wiped his face clean. The cut still oozed, but it looked much better. She tossed the bloody material it to the floor and looked for something else to use before he woke up and began to fight her off.

Reaching into the back seat, she pulled out a towel. It was a little dusty, but she didn't have time to worry about that now. Elanna folded the cloth into a thick square and pressed it back onto Tobin's head.

They were still sitting like that when the little boy appeared at Tobin's window.

Chapter 29

His head hurt. His hands hurt. His neck and back and all his limbs hurt. A groan built in his throat but his mouth was so dry nothing came out. He cracked one eye open and shut it instantly against the light that was a sliver of glass in his head.

The next instant he sat straight up, the groan turning into a cry that forced its way out of his parched mouth. They had to keep moving! Get away from whoever had built the barrier.

He looked to the passenger seat. Elanna was gone. The door hung open. He looked down to his lap, at the towel, covered with blood. Whose blood? Hers? His? Frantically, Tobin searched for her but could see nothing.

His door, bent in the crash, wouldn't open. He punched it, cursing, and felt the bones in his hand protest. The skin over his knuckles split. More blood. He climbed over the gearbox and slid across her seat. Out the door, falling into the earth where the dirt had been slashed and churned by their arrival.

He would find her. If it meant fighting every one of those soldiers, whatever they were, he would find her. Tobin rolled himself to his knees, and then his feet. Waves of nausea and dizziness assailed him; he went back down to one knee. He sank his head onto the knee, fighting the sick sensation in his head and stomach. He had to find Elanna.

"Tobin?"

He whirled, and dizziness nearly overtook him again. He fought it, struggling to his feet to find her. She stood at the back of the car, but in the next moment she was there beside him. Holding him. His arms went around her and he felt a relief so great it was almost like passing out.

Maybe he was passing out again. Tobin shook his head, jarring it, until the pain woke him up again. Elanna was talking to him, but he couldn't understand what she was saying. They didn't have time to talk. They had to move. Go. Get away.

"Shhh," she said, smoothing her fingers over his brow, and he realized he'd been muttering. "It's all right, Toby. He says it's all right."

"Who?" Her touch didn't take away the pain, was in fact making it worse, but he didn't tell her to stop. It was enough that she was there, and that she was all right. That she hadn't been taken from him.

"Amos," Elanna said.

Tobin forced his eyes open to see a small boy standing next to Elanna. His face was solemn beneath a large straw hat. He wore a plain blue shirt and black pants with suspenders. His feet were bare.

"Ich bin Amos," the little boy said. "Ihr sint English?"

Tobin looked at Elanna. "What's he saying?"

Elanna shifted a little, sitting on the ground to cradle Tobin on her lap. "I'm not sure. But I think…I think he's speaking Yiddish."

It was all too much for him. Tobin felt himself graying out again. He clutched at Elanna. His eyes didn't want to stay open.

Amos grabbed his nose and twisted it sharply. Tobin sat upright with a yell, consciousness rushing back to him with instant, painful clarity. The boy ducked back behind Elanna, who held Tobin's arm against hitting him.

"Toby! He was only trying to help."

Tobin felt his nose carefully. It wasn't bleeding. His fingers explored the gash high up on his forehead. Wincing, he saw blood on them when he looked, but not too much of it. It hurt like hell, though, even when he blinked.

"You hit the windshield with your head," Elanna said.

"Are you all right?" Tobin put his hands on her shoulders and looked her over. Aside from the red weal on the tender flesh of her neck, he could see no injuries.

"I'm fine, thanks to my seatbelt," Elanna said. "Thanks to you."

Now his breath came easier and his heart began to slow. He saw Amos peeking from behind Elanna, and he gestured at the boy.

"C'mere," Tobin said. "I'm not mad, Amos. I won't hurt you."

The little boy shook his head and stayed where he was. Elanna murmured something to him that Tobin couldn't decipher, and Amos stepped forward. Tobin held out his hand and the boy shook it twice, quickly, before stepping back out of reach.

"What did you say to him?" Tobin asked.

"I said that you weren't mad at him, and that he was a brave boy to stop and help us."

"And he understood you?"

She looked perplexed. "I think so. My Yiddish isn't so great, I'm afraid. And some of his words are different. And the accent. It's almost like he's speaking Yiddish, but not quite. I think we understand each other, though, don't we, Amos?"

Watching her reach out to ruffle the boy's hair, Tobin felt unreality wash over him. "What about those people at the barrier? The ones with the guns?"

Amos didn't answer. Instead, the boy looked past them, over Elanna's shoulder, and jumped to his feet. "Papa!"

Tobin forced himself to sit, though every movement made his head throb and his stomach twist. Elanna shifted, too, looking to see where Amos had gone. She held onto him, and he felt her shiver. She was afraid, too.

"Amos!"

The man calling out wore the same sort of straw hat as Amos. It shaded his face from the morning sun, but Tobin could see he wore a full beard, brown shot through with gray. His dark pants rose just to his ankles, showing dark socks and black, heavy shoes that looked as though they could walk through anything. His white shirtsleeves were rolled up to expose muscled forearms, brown from the sun.

The boy ran to his father, who clutched him to his side and stared at Tobin and Elanna. Apprehension was clear on his face, even with the beard and the hat shielding his expression. He spoke sharply to the boy, who nodded and pointed at them.

"He's afraid of us," Elanna murmured. "We should get up and talk to him."

Get up. Tobin hoped he could. He took a deep breath and gathered what little strength he could find. Even then, he had to lean heavily on Elanna just to stand.

Once on his feet, he felt a bit better. His legs, at least, didn't seem to hurt much, and if he concentrated hard enough he could stand without shaking. Walking, though, was another matter altogether.

"Can you make it?" Elanna asked softly.

Tobin gritted his teeth. "I can try."

As they stepped toward the man with Amos, the man moved back. He pulled Amos with him, though he never took his eyes from Tobin and Elanna. The boy struggled briefly, pointing and jabbering some more in the language Tobin couldn't understand.

"He's telling his daddy that we're all right," Elanna said. "That we aren't…something…I couldn't quite catch it."

Tobin paused, not wanting to scare away the man or the child. He raised his hands into the air, hoping the man would see he was harmless. Unfortunately, he had to let go of Elanna to do that, and his head began to spin dizzily again.

"Don't you faint on me," she whispered, knuckling him sharply in the ribs. "You'll take me down with you if you fall."

"English!" The man shouted.

Tobin looked at Elanna. "Is he talking to us or asking us a question?"

"I don't know," she said.

"English you are?" the man shouted.

A question, then. But how to answer. They weren't English, at least not in the way Tobin thought of the word.

"We…we're American!"

"Ve all Americans are, naw vunst," the man said back. Tobin was relieved to see the twitch of a smile cross his mouth. "But you English are? Yankees?"

Tobin realized he could understand the words, if not the content. He remembered reading Mark Twain, long ago. "I guess you could say I'm a Yankee. Sure. I'm not from Connecticut, but --"

The sound of thunder rent the air again. It was still far away, but coming closer. Not from the direction they'd come, but from the side.

Tobin saw the man look toward the side road just on the other side of the creek. He clutched the boy to him harder. Amos squeaked, growing pale-faced under his hat.

The man turned and began to run, holding Amos up so the boy wouldn't fall. He did anyway, going to his knees on the road and letting out a shrill cry of pain. When his father yanked him up, Tobin saw the boy's pants had shredded.

"Wait!" Elanna left Tobin to run a few steps after the man and the boy. "Please! What's that noise? Help us!"

The man didn't slow, and she tried again. "Helfn mir, bitte!"

The man stopped and turned. The thunder grew louder. Tobin imagined that the earth trembled under his feet. Maybe it did, or perhaps he was still having trouble standing. Either way, he didn't like the feeling.

"What is that noise?" Elanna cried.

There seemed to be no distance now between Tobin and the man. Their eyes met, both unwavering. Tobin thought the man meant to come back, to help them. Instead, he turned and picked up the boy, then continued to run. They passed out of sight just around a corner, and were gone.

"They left us," Elanna said.

He was alarmed to see that her face had grown pale and sweaty. She licked her lips nervously, eyes gone wide in fear and shock. She was, he saw with a start, going to faint.

As if in slow motion, Elanna began to sink. Tobin grabbed her by the arms, hard enough to sink his fingers into her skin. She groaned, head sagging and knees buckling. He couldn't hold her up, not in his condition. Instead of him knocking her down, she was going to do it to him.

Now the air was definitely trembling. He stared in wide-eyed horror at the side road that twisted sharply away, out of sight. They were coming, those people from the barrier. He knew it. They were coming with their guns and their trucks, or whatever it was that made that ear-wrenching noise.

Elanna slipped from his grasp and puddled to the ground. He tore his gaze away from the horizon long enough to look at her. Her eyes fluttered, not quite closing. Her hands batted at the air, trying to grab him. She wasn't quite out.

Tobin didn't know what to do, or where to turn. He saw the thick gouged marks in the earth that showed exactly where they'd left the road and where the car had stopped. The car would be no protection.

"Tobin?" He knelt beside her, and she clutched his shirt. "I can't get up."

"You have to get up."

Now he could hear whoops and cries along with the sound of the roaring. With numb fingers he pulled on her until she could stand along with him. He didn't dare look back now. He didn't want to see their deaths, and he was afraid that's exactly what was coming for them.

He'd had nightmares like this, ones in which something was chasing him and he couldn't move fast enough to get away. Only this time it was no dream, it was real, and it would appear around the corner any minute.

"Run!" Even as he spat the words, he knew they'd do no good. Neither one of them could move any faster than they were.

Elanna tripped and fell, sprawling. Tobin went with her. It was his pants that shredded on the blacktop this time, but if his skinned knees hurt he didn't notice. He rested his cheek against the gravelly surface, surprised at how warm it was. If he could lay here and sleep, maybe it would be over soon. Maybe he wouldn't have to wake up.

Thunder of a different sort roared out from the road ahead. Elanna screamed from beside him, and he lifted his head. The beast bearing down on them was the largest he'd ever seen. Its four legs pumped up and down, straining to pull the large wooden wagon to which it was harnessed. Its hooves clattered on the road with a sound like pottery breaking.

Small Amos clung to the wagon seat beside his father, whose expression was fierce and determined. The man pulled hard on the straps attached to the animal's mouth. Its hooves slid on the road, spraying up gravel. Some of it hit Tobin in the face, and the dust stung his eyes.

"A horse!" Elanna said from the dirt beside him.

Reading about them was not like seeing one in real life. He wondered briefly if he had, indeed, passed out again, and was dreaming. Or maybe, he'd died. But he'd never remembered smelling anything in dreams before, and if he was dead, surely he wouldn't smell anything either.

The horse had lifted its tale and dropped a pile onto the ground. No, he had to be alive and awake to see and smell that. Hysterical laughter bubbled in his chest.

"Kummen zie, bitte," the man said. "Hurry, Yankee. They soon will here be."

Tobin looked up at the high wagon bed, and down at himself. "No way. There's no way."

"I'll help you," Elanna said. "You can lean on me."

"In the wagon not." The man looked to where the sound of the hooting and rumbling was almost upon them. "Under it you will go! And hurry!"

Tobin looked at the champing, stamping beast, and then at the high wagon. Plenty of room under there, but what would hide them? Elanna hadn't hesitated, though, and was squirming underneath.

"Into the grass," the man said, clucking to the horse. Obligingly, it moved a few feet closer to the edge of the road, where the weeds and grass grew thick. "Hide there."

Tobin didn't hesitate again. The rumbling and yelling was so loud now that he could make out the individual words, even over the sound of the engine or whatever it was that was making the racket. Whoever was coming wasn't crying out warm welcomes, either. He scooted under the wagon, following Elanna to where the grass was thick. He rolled in, and the man clucked to the horse again. The huge beast bent to chew at the grass, its massive teeth grinding and chomping mere inches from Tobin's face.

He'd gone just in time. Around the bend roared a vehicle twice the size of one of the Gatherers' largest trucks. Clinging to it on every side were men in green uniforms. Just like the bodies on the other side of the barrier.

Chapter 30

Made of some greenish gray metal, the huge vehicle rolled not on wheels but on two gigantic metal treads. It had no windshield, only a tiny, shuttered opening on top of what looked, absurdly enough, like a turret. The long, thick cylinder jutting out from the turret was anything but absurd.

The men hung off every side of the massive vehicle. As they whooped and waved their guns around, Elanna shuddered. They acted like children, really, playing at a game. This was no game.

Though they all wore green, she could see that their uniforms were not identical. They looked like they'd been pieced together from several different styles. In some cases, they didn't fit very well, either. Pants legs dragged and jackets flapped. All of them wore helmets and masks of black netting that made their faces disappear. And they all had guns.

As the big vehicle pulled to a stop on the other side of the creek, they jumped off it one by one, and began shouting at the man.

"Hey, old man!"

"Enoch Stolzfus!"

"Hey!"

Their other comments were far less polite. They jeered and

taunted him, some of them making obscene gestures to go along with their insults. Through it all, Enoch said nothing. Elanna couldn't see him from his hiding place in the grass, but she imagined him as stony-faced.

Let them stay on the other side of the creek, Elanna prayed. Tobin's breath puffed hot on her cheek as she leaned closer to him. He settled his arm around her shoulders, both of them wriggling into the dirt. She buried her face in his shoulder for a moment, glad for the strength of him next to her.

The horse bent his head to pull up another mouthful of grass, right from above her head. She swallowed heavily to stifle her yelp of surprise. She'd seen a horse before, a long time ago, but not from this close, and not one this healthy.

"The Gatherers caught one, once," Elanna whispered to Tobin. "A horse, I mean. From the Park. There's a herd there, but it's wild."

"What did you do with it?"

He looking out through the grass, not at her. She knew it was stupid to be talking, but the words had blurted out before she could stop them.

"We ate it," she whispered. She shot a sideways glance at the horse, and then up to the wagon. "It was a cold winter, Tobin."

He looked at her then, and smiled. She could've kissed him for the grin, which somehow made her feel that everything was going to be all right. She did kiss him, lightly on the cheek, and his grip around her shoulders tightened.

"They're coming across," Tobin whispered grimly.

Elanna bit her lip. The fear that had settled in her stomach when he'd shouted at her to get in the car was still there, but she'd grown numb now.

The first man jumped across the creek easily enough, but the one to follow him had no such luck. His foot slipped in the mud, and he fell, splashing into the shallow water. Spluttering, he flailed his arms as he got to his feet, dripping.

He didn't seem so scary now, Elanna thought. Apparently, his friends felt the same way. Judging by the catcalls and insults ringing in the air, these men were merciless even to their own.

"Shut up!" The wet man said, making threatening gestures at the others. He had the high, whiney voice of an adolescent girl. "Just shut the fuck up!"

The harsh language coming from the high-pitched voice shocked her and made her want to giggle, too. Elanna pressed her face further into Tobin's shoulder. If she laughed, they were dead. No matter how ridiculous the man who'd fallen into the creek looked or acted, these men were dangerous.

She counted quickly. Ten, and who knew how many inside their vehicle. Four of them had crossed the creek. Two stopped to examine the rough gouges the car had made when it crashed, but the other two kept coming.

"Ruich," she heard Enoch say, as though to the boy.

Quiet, still. She knew he was actually talking to them. They didn't need to be told.

They both pulled back into the grass. Now she could see nothing but shadows and the occasional movement of the horse's head as it cropped at the weeds. A sharp pain stung her eyes, and she realized she'd forgotten to blink.

"Hey, Stolzfus!" Not the voice of the one who'd fallen into the water. This one was deeper and more authoritative. "You got our fucking stuff?"

"Yes," Enoch said calmly. "In the back of the wagon, it is."

"Walsh, check the wagon."

Elanna heard a snort and some thumping. Someone, Walsh, she guessed, was searching the wagon.

"Where's the red-beet eggs? And didn't I tell you no more freakin' chow-chow? Where's the apple butter? Didn't I tell you to send more apple butter next time?

"We the one small crock of apple butter have there," Enoch replied. "The rest is all. No more will there be until autumn."

Not being able to see what was happening was worse than having to watch. Elanna moved, but Tobin's arm held her down. He slowly, slowly, turned his head to face her. His cheek pressed into the dirt and stones, but he didn't move again.

"No," he mouthed. "Stay still."

A cramp was working its way into the tender muscles of her calves, both of them. If she didn't shift her position soon, the pain would get worse. She didn't move, though her eyes had begun watering at the pain. Instead, Elanna dug her fingernails into the dirt, not caring that small stones and grass got shoved beneath her nails.

"You see anybody in a car?" asked the second voice. "Two people. They came this way."

"No, no," Enoch said. "Nothing like that we have seen today."

Two shouts from farther away, near the car. They'd found it. Elanna heard boots thudding on the road, but she couldn't tell if both men had moved away from the wagon. If she didn't stretch her legs she was going to scream. Biting her lip didn't help, and neither did clenching her fists. The cramps had locked the muscles into a throbbing spasm.

Just as the horse let out a loud, whinnying cry, she straightened her legs. The pain relaxed instantly, and tears filled her eyes from the relief. Tobin's expression twisted at her movement. Had they heard her?

A moment passed, and then another, without the green uniforms parting the grass to discover them. Still, whatever numbness had crept over her was gone now. She was back to being terrified.

"We found the car!" came a shout.

"And it's full of all kinds of shit!"

She was confused for a minute, then realized what they meant. Stuff. The car was full of stuff.

"Report, Private Lovett," said the husky voice.

This one was another high voice, though not of the one who'd fallen in the creek. "One vehicle, Lieutenant. No occupants. Blood on the steering wheel and seats, though, so they're wounded."

"Is the vehicle operable?" asked husky voice.

"No, Lieutenant, Sir," said the voice of the one who'd gotten wet. "The front axle's been snapped."

"Shit and piss on a brick!" Lieutenant, Sir shouted.

"But the car is full of all kinds of shit," Private Lovett said. "Maranian dripped on most of it, though."

"Fuck you!" Maranian squealed.

Elanna heard the sounds of scuffling.

"Enough!" It was the fourth voice, as yet unidentified. "I don't have time to stand around here all day listening to you bitch. Stolzfus, take that wagon over to the crick and start unloading it. Lovett, Maranian, you get back to that car and start unloading whatever's in there. Lieutenant, check the perimeter and see if there's any sign of the intruders."

"Yes, Sir, Major Kodak, Sir," said Lieutenant.

Elanna heard the sound of boots stamping on the pavement, and then they moved away. Enoch clucked to the horse. The wagon began to move, the wheels creaking.

Her breath stuck in her throat and her mouth felt as though it were filled with dirt. She couldn't move, couldn't breathe, couldn't think for the terror that filled her as the wagon started to pull away from their hiding place.

Only Tobin's grip on her shoulder kept her here. Without his touch to tether her to the earth, she would have flown away. He trembled beside her and she turned to him, loving him for trying to comfort her even through his own fear.

Then the wagon had passed, heading toward the creek and the soldiers. Without its shadow to protect them, Elanna felt horribly exposed. Surely the men in green could see right through their sad hiding place! In any moment, they'd reach in and pull them out, maybe shoot them with the guns, or maybe worse. Her eyes, wide and staring, burned, and yet she was too afraid to close them.

Minutes passed, slow and dragging. Each strangled breath, an eternity. Waiting. She had to blink and didn't want to, knowing that in the second she was blind they would be there.

Nothing happened. She heard shouting. Tobin seemed to relax beside her. Could they be safe?

"Hey, Maranian! Shift your skinny ass and get this shit over to the tank!"

"Fuck you!" Maranian yelled back. The high voice broke into a cough, then a sneeze. "I think I'm getting fucking sick!"

"Serves you the fuck right," Lovett yelled back. "Dumb ass!"

Elanna pressed her hands to her ears, wanting to block out the language. She'd heard the words before, though never so frequently. Strangely, though, the more they said them, the less offensive the language became. She was struck again at how childish their behavior was, with the posturing and name-calling.

"No sign of the intruders anywhere, Major." This was the one they called Lieutenant. He'd moved away from their hiding place, but Elanna knew that one small sound or movement from her or Tobin and they'd be discovered. "I checked the tree row, and there's nothing. A piece of material that might have been theirs. Maybe they went that way."

Major Kodak snorted. Sickly, Elanna realized the man had not moved away from them, but instead had been standing so silently as to make her think he had. At the thought she might have moved, or breathed, while thinking nobody was near, her stomach lurched.

"They won't get far. Not if they're wounded."

Kodak snorted again. "I want to know who they were. Where'd they get a car and the batteries to run it? What about all the stuff in it? They're too valuable to forget, Lieutenant. Search again."

"Yes, Sir."

"Lovett! Maranian! Shift your asses!"

Elanna heard the thump, thump, thump of boot steps again, this time returning. A breeze kicked up, swaying the grass that hid them. Several of the strands parted and stayed open.

She could see out. And if she could see out, they could see in. Tobin's hand stopped her from reaching out to rearrange the grass. A quick glance told her that he didn't see the opening. He didn't know they were in danger.

"Major, you should see all the shit we found!"

This was Maranian, then, the wet one. Water puddled from his dripping pants and around his boots. A tiny rivulet formed, moving along the pavement to the roadside. It entered the dirt in front of

Elanna. She watched in silent horror as it moved toward her, a thin silver line against the brown earth. It touched her arm, cold.

"Clothes! Food! Cans and stuff, you won't believe it!" Lovett squealed.

"Jesus, Lovett, calm down," Major Kodak said. "We don't need a hissy fit."

The breeze tickled the grass again and Elanna prayed it would close the gap. It didn't. The men didn't seem to notice, perhaps because they stood so close. Elanna could have reached out and touched their boots, had she been insane enough to want to.

Maranian broke into another sneezing fit. Coughing followed, short, barking gasps that nearly doubled him over. Then some more sneezes, until Major Kodak muttered in disgust.

"Jee-sus H., Maranian! What the fuck's the matter with you?"

"Permission to de-mask, Sir," Maranian responded in a voice clearly filled with phlegm.

"Yeah, yeah," Major said. "Desnot yourself for Christ's sake, so we can get out of here. The rest of you might as well de-mask, too."

With another quick sneeze, Maranian reached up and pulled off the helmet. With it came the black netting that had covered his face from view. As he did so, Elanna bit back a gasp of shock.

He wasn't a man at all. Maranian was a young woman, no more than a teener really. And so were all the others.

Chapter 31

Elanna stiffened beside him, but Tobin didn't know why. The tall weeds that hid them from view still blocked his sight. Without moving anything but his eyes, Tobin strained to see what had startled her.

That's when he noticed the break in the undergrowth right in front of her. He tried to measure quickly by sight, but couldn't convince himself they were too far back to be seen. Then he realized that whatever had caused Elanna's reaction was not fear of being caught. Something else had caught her attention.

With his cheek mashed into the ground, he couldn't do more than roll his eyes. And if he moved....Thankfully, he didn't have to. The breeze that had parted the grass in front of Elanna now closed it, opening a gap in front of him. It was small, too small to expose him. He thought. He didn't know. His stomach swooped like a gull. He wanted to inch backward, into the brush, but didn't dare.

He rolled his eyes up as far as they would go, though he expected to see little more than boots and legs. Fate had blessed him with more than that. And then he saw what had made Elanna go rigid beside him.

The one they called Maranian, the one still dripping, had long blonde hair and the face of a cherub. They were all sweet-faced, even the tall one he guessed was the one they called Major Kodak. His mouth dropped open until he made a conscious effort to close it. These foul-mouthed soldiers were girls?

And young girls, he noted, as the one he guessed was Lovett again giggled and teased Maranian for falling in the water. Now, upon closer inspection, he could spot the tell-tale bumps on their chests that marked their womanhood, but bumps were all they were. How old could they be, really?

Well, no matter how old they were, or what their gender, they still had guns. And they weren't afraid to use them, he remembered, thinking of the crazy ride away from the roadblock. They were just as dangerous now as they'd been before, even if his mind wanted to refuse to believe it.

"C'mon. Let's get the fuck outta here." This was Lieutenant, a tall girl with black hair that fell past her shoulders. Bits of dirt and leaves clung among the dark strands, and the hair gleamed with grease. Sweet-faced, maybe, but not too clean. "Hey, Stolzfus! You and that brat done loading that shit into the tank?"

Incredibly, within a few seconds, they'd gone. Marched away in their heavy boots. Tobin's entire body seemed to relax at once; he was a boneless and limp as a rag doll. He hadn't realized how tensely he'd been holding himself until that moment.

He risked discovery by scooting forward to watch the girls head back across the creek. This time, none of them fell. The six or so who'd stayed behind had not all taken off their helmets and masks, but the ones who had looked as feminine as the four who'd just rejoined them. He couldn't see so clearly from this distance, but they all looked just as young and unkempt.

With a shout, Lieutenant jumped back up on the side of the tank. Pulling her helmet and mask back over her face, she pounded on the vehicle's metal side. With a roar that didn't sound half so frightening now, the huge tank lurched into motion.

It sputtered and jerked, heaving forward and grinding up the creek side dirt into a thick mud that splattered upward, hitting many of the riders. He heard hoots and whoops, but no cries of disgust.

Once it got started, the tank moved pretty quickly. It swung back onto the cracked road and soon was out of sight, though the sound of it lingered in the air long after it had disappeared.

"They're girls," Elanna said in a strangled voice. She cleared her throat and tried again. "Girls, Tobin!"

"I saw."

Elanna started to laugh. He turned to look at her, sprawling on the ground and shaking with hysterical laughter. Tears began pouring from her eyes, and she didn't even pause to wipe them away.

A few nervous chuckles escaped from his mouth too. He recognized her reaction as relief, because he was feeling the same thing. After a couple minutes, though, she showed no signs of stopping. Her face grew red and her chest heaved for breath, and still she laughed.

"Elanna, calm down."

She laughed harder. Clutching her sides, her face a grimacing mask of pain and hilarity, Elanna writhed on the ground. The pitch of her laughing grew higher, almost painful.

"Oh, oh," she moaned between spurts of relentless hooting. "It hurts! It hurts!"

Alarmed, he shook her. "Elanna! Please, calm down!"

She bit her fist as if trying to stop the chortling coming from her mouth. It didn't help much. Small snorts and whoops still leaked out, though the intensity of them was dying down.

Her eyes rimmed with red, Elanna finally managed to stem the flow to a trickle. Her shoulders shook as she let out another spare giggle, then one more. At last, her breathing slowed and she smiled at him wearily.

"I'm done."

He gathered her into his arms, pulled her over onto his lap and rested his face in the weed-infested snarls of her hair. "You scared me."

"I'm sorry," she said, her voice muffled against him. "I couldn't help it."

"I know." Tobin suddenly felt like laughing himself. "Girls?"

"Ja, maidlen," said a voice from the road. Enoch Stolzfus had crossed from his wagon back to them. His face was drawn and solemn beneath the straw hat. "Gappers, they are. Ferricked und ferroonstzled."

"Crazy and dirty," Elanna elaborated, and let out another chortle. She wiped her eyes again. "Crazy and dirty girls."

"Bischt du Deutch?" Enoch asked her now, staring at her closely. "Was iss dei naame?"

She looked startled. "Elanna. And no, I'm not Deutch, whatever that is."

"You an English are, like him?" Enoch asked, clearly puzzled now. "But speak the Dutch, do you?"

Elanna looked at Tobin as though she wasn't sure how to answer. "Dutch? No. I thought…ir farshteyt Yiddish? Do you understand Yiddish?"

The older man shook his head. "No."

But they did understand each other, Tobin knew that. Enoch spoke and Elanna answered. He had no idea what either one of them was saying at all.

"No matter," Enoch said with a shrug. "Gappers you are not."

"No." Tobin gently pushed Elanna from his lap. His legs were beginning to cramp, and he wanted to stand. She did the same, rubbing her calves briskly as though they hurt.

"Papa!"

Enoch turned and said something sharply in that other language. "Amos. My boy. The horse he brings. To town we will take you."

"But our stuff," Tobin began.

Elanna laid her hand on his arm. "You need a healer, Tobin. And we can always get more stuff."

He looked back at the man who had saved them. His face was kind. Enoch put his arm around the boy, drawing him closer, and the child looked up at his father with unmasked adoration.

"At least, can't we check to see if they left anything?" Tobin said quietly. "If it's safe, I mean."

"Safe?" Enoch said. He looked back to where the tank had gone over the hill.

Elanna nodded. "Ok. But let's hurry. I want someone to take a look at your head."

They walked back to where the car had skidded off the road. Or limped, rather, both of them moving a lot more slowly as what seemed like a million aches and pains began to set in. Before leaving Eastport he could have counted on one hand the times he'd been seriously injured. Now he'd be hard-pressed to even remember them all.

The car was as they left it, doors hanging open and trunk ajar. Most of what had been inside, however, was gone. The bags, the boxes, the carefully packed bundles, all had been torn apart.

The ground, already gouged when the car slid from the road, was trampled and muddy. Bits and pieces of what the Gappers hadn't wanted littered the area around the car. They'd left behind some clothes, which now were dirty and torn probably beyond repair.

"Damn them," Elanna said quietly. Though no tears sparkled in her eyes, they were thick in her voice. He squeezed her hand. She gestured at the mess, and looked at him helplessly. "Why did they have to ruin all of it? Why couldn't they just take what they wanted and leave the rest? Why waste it?"

He could tell it was the waste that bothered her more than anything else, and he understood why. In the Tribe, nothing could be wasted. Everything had to be used to its fullest potential, because the safety and prosperity of two thousand people rested on it.

The waste bothered him, too, more because of the random violence of it than anything else. "Let's see what's left," he said with a sigh. "See if we can save any of it."

There wasn't much to save. The food was gone. So were the candles and matches. The girl soldiers had spilled the water jugs out onto the ground, which explained the mud, and then crushed the jugs until they were useless. The towels and bedding was gone, and most of the clothing.

He heard Elanna gasp, and she broke from his side to run

toward a small piece of cloth that had been crushed into the dirt. She clutched it to her chest. Her shoulders shook with sobs, but she was smiling. "It's here!"

He couldn't see it. "What is it, Elanna?"

She held it out to him. A tiny gown, white now, though it might long ago have been yellow or pale blue. The material was thin from many washings. He'd never seen one, but he recognized it as a baby's dress.

"It's mine," she said, and let her fingers drift lightly over the faded pattern of ducks and teddy bears. "I've dressed every child of mine in it. I brought it with me when we left the Tribe."

She looked at him nakedly. "It's all I have left of my babies, Tobin, and I thought it was gone."

She wept then, her body wracked with sobs. He couldn't do anything except hold her against him while she cried. His own throat grew tight at her grief, and he rocked her as she had done for him before.

When she'd quieted against him, he pushed her hair away from her flushed cheeks and kissed her. "Let's get back to the wagon before Enoch and Amos decide to leave us here."

Her smile was wobbly but genuine, and she kissed him back. Her hug was so fierce it hurt him, but he didn't push her away. She sagged against him for a moment. To help her, Tobin put his arms under her legs and lifted. His hand came away wet.

He looked down at his fingers, stained crimson. "You're bleeding."

Chapter 32

Hopemothers weren't supposed to grieve. The loss of a child was something to be forgotten, not sympathized with. When a pregnancy ended, sometimes just weeks or even days after the celebration that marked its beginning, nobody ever said anything about it.

The other hopemothers might take your hand, or smile to show they shared the pain, but that was all. If you talked about it, someone else might lose her child too. Superstition, perhaps, but one that was widely believed.

A full-term labor was celebrated and attended by all the hopemothers, who gathered around the mother and helped her bring her child into the world as safely as they knew how. Those whose bodies rejected the blessing of their wombs were not given the same honor. Elanna had lost half as many babies as she'd born. She'd endured the bleeding and the cramping, the gripping pains in her uterus so much like those that heralded the birth of a live child. She'd always done it alone, as dictated, with no one to hear her crying.

Here, though, in the town Enoch had brought them to, the women took care of her as though she were one of her own. They all had strong, firm hands, calloused from work. Those hands held her head over the basin when the nausea overtook her, and placed cold cloths on her brow to ease the pain as her body labored to rid itself of what it had decided was a burden rather than a blessing. Elanna was grateful for the women. Grateful she didn't have to go through this sad journey alone.

They wouldn't let Tobin in to see her until it the worst of it had passed, and she was grateful for that, too. She didn't want to see his face as he watched her pain. And she didn't want to have to comfort him even as she herself sought comfort.

When he did finally come to her bed, though, his eyes were dry and his hands steady. He placed a gentle kiss on her forehead and held her hands. He said nothing.

She'd never had someone to comfort her. Elanna didn't think she had any tears left, but when he touched her she discovered more. They streamed from her eyes in soundless rivers, coating her cheeks and dripping from her chin. She didn't sob. It wasn't violent, this grief that had torn her heart into bleeding strips, and when the tears finally dried she felt cleaned out.

"I'm all right," she told him.

"What can I do," he asked, "to help you?"

The question surprised her and warmed her heart. "You've done it, Toby. Just by being with me. That's all."

He frowned. "It doesn't feel like enough."

She took his hands and looked into his eyes. "I know you want to fix things for me, honey, but you can't. There are no magic words to say, and you can't get out a hammer and pound it straight. You can't fix me."

"I don't know what to do," he said gruffly. "I'm not good at this."

He was better at it than he realized. "Nothing will make this go away but time."

Grudgingly, he nodded. "Okay."

She sighed and hugged him, then sat back against the pillows. "Do you think we could go downstairs and get something to eat? I'm starving."

"Do you think you should get out of bed?" He looked alarmed.

Elanna thought longingly of sinking back into the soft pillows and pulling the blanket over her head. The idea was tempting, but she knew she had to move. It was useless to linger, letting herself dwell on what she couldn't change.

"You're too protective," she teased, just to watch his expression.

"Am I?"

"No," she said softly, and touched his cheek. "I like it. I'm just not used to it."

"Doesn't this get any easier?"

Elanna laughed. "I don't know, honey."

He grinned. "I like when you call me that."

"Honey," she said again. "Help me out of this bed."

She hadn't realized that they were on the second floor until he led her out into the hallway. Three closed doors faced them, ringed around a narrow landing. A steep flight of stairs greeted her as she stepped out of the room, and just looking down them made her feel wobbly. She took his arm to steady herself.

"Why don't you get back into bed?"

"Why don't you let me get some food?" She retorted. She blinked and the world swam back into focus. "I'll be fine then. Come on."

With a long-suffering sigh that made her want to laugh, Tobin moved in front of her. "Let me walk in front in case you fall."

The stairs were narrow and uneven, posing even more of a walking hazard. The handrail, though, was mounted firmly to the wall. With each step, she felt better.

They came out into a sparsely furnished but spotless kitchen. The main piece of furniture was a long table and two long benches. Faded vinyl covered the floor. A massive stove, radiating a delicious, bread-scented heat, dominated one wall of the room. A small sink, complete with pump and bucket, was along one wall.

Elanna didn't know the name of the woman bent over the large stove in front of them, but she recognized her as one of those who'd held her hand during the miscarriage. As they entered the room, the woman stood, her cheeks pink from the heat and her eyes sparkling. Her hair, more gray than blonde, was tucked up beneath a white cap made of netting.

"Rachel Stolzfus," Tobin said by way of introduction. "Enoch's wife. This is their house."

"My goodness!" Rachel cried, wiping her hands on the white apron that covered her dark dress. "Out of bed? Sit, sit!"

Elanna did as ordered, sinking gratefully into one of the wooden benches. Her legs still felt a little wobbly. The woman bustled about the kitchen, opening drawers and stirring a pot on the stove.

"Fress, fress." She plopped a full bowl of soup on the table and followed it quickly with another for Tobin. "Sit down and eat yourself, vunst. Careful, the soup is burny."

Elanna didn't need to be told twice. Her stomach grumbled so loudly it was almost embarrassing. She spooned some soup into her mouth and almost groaned at how good it was. The clear yellow broth brimmed with thick, soft noodles and chunks of meat. It didn't taste like pigeon, but it was good. Small yellow bits floated in the broth too, popping between her teeth as she chewed.

"Chicken corn noodle soup makes a body nice and full," the woman said. She whirled to look at Amos, who stood fidgeting in the doorway. "Stop your rutching and go outside!"

The small boy fled, his mother looking fondly after him. She shook her head, chuckling softly, and wiped her hands on a cloth. "Ach, don't eat yourself full, already! There's cake back yet."

She poured some white fluid into Elanna's glass from a tall pitcher. "Drink!"

Elanna took a sip and nearly choked. "It's milk!"

"Ja, of course it millich is," said Rachel. Now she looked at Elanna with concern. "Iss der millich sauer?"

Is the milk sour? The words weren't quite the ones she was used to, but she understood. "No," Elanna stammered. "It's not sour. It's… it's milk. And it's cold."

Rachel laughed. "From the icehouse I brought it. Milk should be cold, ain't?"

The only time Elanna had ever had anything cold was in the wintertime. And milk….

"Who's milk is it?" She asked warily, putting the glass down.

Rachel frowned. "Whose milk? Well, whoever wants to drink it, I suppose."

"I mean, where did it come from?" Elanna asked.

"Bessie," Rachel said. She put one plump hand on Elanna's forehead. "Bischt du aarem?"

Are you poor? "No, I'm fine," Elanna said. "I just don't want any milk, thank you."

"Ach, and after I to the icehouse went for you?" Rachel scolded kindly. "Drink up. Healthy."

Elanna thought of holding her baby in her arms, its mouth to her breast. Though nursing her babies had always been a joy, the thought of actually drinking milk herself made her shiver in distaste. "Maybe for the baby it's healthy, but not for me. No, thanks."

Rachel looked at her, clearly puzzled. Then she began to laugh. Her plump cheeks grew rosier as she chuckled, then patted Elanna on the arm.

"From the cow! Not from a mother!"

Elanna's blank look made Rachel stop laughing. She looked curiously at Elanna. "Cows you don't know?"

Even Tobin was laughing at her, but she could hardly be angry. Of course she'd heard of cows. But she'd never seen one.

"I've never had cow's milk, either," Tobin said. "Only from a goat."

Rachel smiled and poured him a glass, too. "Bessie, she good milk gives. Better than a goat. Drink!"

Elanna tried another sip, letting the flavor rest on her tongue before swallowing. Maybe it was because it was cold, or maybe just because it came from a cow and not her own body, but it didn't taste so bad. It didn't have the sweet undertone she'd tasted on her babies kisses, but it was good.

"The only milk I've ever tasted was what my babies gave back to me," Elanna said with a smile. "And I don't recommend baby burp as a delicacy."

Rachel paused in her pouring and serving, looking confused. "Babies?"

"Yes," Elanna replied, thinking the woman hadn't heard her.

Rachel looked at Tobin and then at her, a question clear in her eyes. "You other kinder have?"

"I have had other babies, yes," Elanna explained. She took another bite of the delicious broth. "Tobin has never had any."

"He's not your husband?"

"No," Elanna said with a glance at Tobin. "I'm not allowed… I've never been married."

"Gott in Himmel," the woman murmured. "How many kinder?"

"Thirteen," Elanna said quietly. "Eleven lived."

"And no husband?"

"No," Elanna said, lifting her chin. The soup she'd eaten settled in her stomach like a stone. She glanced at Tobin, who had the good grace to look down. "I am a hopemother. We aren't allowed to marry."

"Hopemother?" Rachel asked. "Not allowed to marry? I'm all discumbumperated."

Elanna stirred the soup to occupy her hands, which she wanted to clench. "Where I come from, that's the way things were. Maybe they're different here."

"Ja," Rachel said slowly. "I think very different, ain't?"

The two women stared at each other over the table for a long time. Elanna waited to see what Rachel would do or say. She'd never been ashamed of what and who she was. Tobin had seemed to find her life shocking, even reprehensible, at first. Would Rachel react in the same way? Would the kindness the older woman granted be taken back because Elanna was a hopemother?

"How could your kinder you leave behind?" Rachel finally asked.

Elanna could see the other woman's struggle, and was grateful she'd asked her question without accusing. "My babies were raised by women who couldn't have their own," Elanna said with as much dignity as she could.

Rachel still didn't seem to be getting it. "But…eleven kinder? Eleven times away you gave your babies?"

"Yes."

"How hard for you," Rachel said, her face creased in sympathy. She clucked her tongue again. "The tears you must have shed."

"Their mothers loved them as much as I could have," Elanna said. "Maybe more, because they couldn't have any of their own."

"Let me some bread give you to dop up that soup awhile," Rachel said, as though she could think of no other response. "Your strength you need."

When had she not needed strength? Elanna thought, but turned her attention back to the soup. It was cold now, and she wasn't very hungry any more, but she ate it anyway.

Chapter 33

It wasn't until after he saw Rachel's reaction to Elanna's story of being a hopemother that Tobin truly realized how badly he'd hurt her. He thought back to how he'd reacted, overreacted, when he'd found out her place in the Tribe, and hot shame flooded him. No matter how the rest of the world lived and survived, Elanna had only ever done what she thought was right. Maybe not fair, but right. What was expected of her.

She was very quiet. Although her eyes were closed and her head rested on the back of the chair, he knew she wasn't sleeping. Rachel had urged them to go into the living room and relax after they'd eaten. The room was furnished with comfortable, overstuffed furniture, faded but clean and in good repair.

He shifted a little on the couch, stretching his legs. His whole body still ached, but he was sure that was nothing compared to how Elanna felt. Yet, she'd refused to lay down, insisting she'd feel better if she sat.

"Stop rutching." Her eyes stayed closed, but a smile turned her lips.

Tobin got up from the couch and went to her. Her hands were cold. She kept her eyes closed even when he bent to kiss her lips.

"Don't you want to go upstairs to bed?" He rubbed her fingers to warm them.

"No."

"Are you sure?"

"Please stop hovering over me," she said gently. "I'm fine. I just want to sit here with my eyes closed for a while. That's all. I don't need to lie down."

He still felt so helpless. She said he couldn't do anything for her, and he couldn't just sit here and watch her. He was saved from finding something to do when the door from the kitchen opened.

Tobin didn't recognize the old man who came into the room, but he noticed that his eyes were the same bright blue as Rachel's. They shared the same plump cheeks as well, though on the old man they seemed out of place compared to the rest of his thin, almost gaunt features. His sparse gray beard reached to his chest, resting on the black vest and deep blue shirt. He wore no hat inside the house, but his hair was creased along his forehead, showing he was more often with it than without.

"I am Samuel Lapp," he said formally by way of introduction.

"Tobin Winter," Tobin said, rising. "And this is Elanna."

"I know who you are, English," the old man said. His accent was thicker than that of Rachel or Enoch, but the way he spoke seemed clearer. "What I want to know is when you will leaving be."

Tobin looked at Elanna, who at last had opened her eyes. She sat straighter in the chair. Though her face was calm, her hands betrayed her dismay. She'd clenched them into fists, balling the fabric of her borrowed nightgown in her fingers.

Tobin didn't quite know how to respond. "I'm sorry."

"And sorry we will all be, if soon you do not leave," Samuel said. His voice wasn't harsh, even if the words were. "The Gappers will come for you looking. You should here not be when they do."

"Papa?" Rachel stood in the doorway, her rosy cheeks creased by a frown. "Vass is das?"

The old man said something sharp to her that Tobin didn't understand, in that language Elanna knew. Whatever it was, it made her blink furiously, as though to hold back tears. A slow rise of anger burned in his gut. Nothing should make Elanna cry. Especially not now.

Now Enoch had entered the room behind Rachel, putting his arm around her. She bent her head to his shoulder briefly, then spoke to him in that language. She pointed at her father, then at Tobin. Finally, at Elanna.

"Vatter?" Enoch asked respectfully. "What are you saying to our guests?"

Samuel snorted. "Guests, Enoch Stolzfus? Guests that will our homes bring down?"

Enoch shook his head slowly. "They needed help."

"And help you gave them," Samuel said. "And now, they go. Before the Gappers vit their thundermakers come."

"What are these Gappers?" Tobin was tired of being discussed as though he weren't there. If they were going to throw him and Elanna to the wolves, at least he wanted to know what kind of wolves they were.

Enoch and Samuel turned surprised faces toward him. Maybe they'd forgotten he was there. The younger man spoke first.

"You don't know the Gappers, ain't?"

"No. Who are they? What's a thundermaker? What's the barrier?"

Samuel sighed heavily. He looked around briefly, finally settling his eyes on the couch. He made his painful way from the doorway to it and sat slowly, wincing. "Questions you have plenty, ain't?"

Before Tobin could answer, Samuel found himself with a lapful of wriggling young boy. Amos had come in from outside and launched himself toward the man, squealing.

"Grossvatter!"

The old man held the boy for a moment, smiling. Seeing them together, Tobin could see how much they looked alike. Samuel said something to Amos that Elanna didn't translate, but the boy clearly understood. Without a frown and only a brief backward glance, he went back into the kitchen.

"I did not want him to hear," Samuel said. "The story is for a boy's ears not."

Rachel sat in the rocking chair next to Elanna. "He must sometime learn, Papa."

The old man scowled. "Not naw! He chust a baby is!"

"Please tell us," said Elanna quietly. She'd stopped twisting her hands in the cloth. "I think we need to know."

Samuel sighed again and rested his head on his hands for a moment before speaking. "We Plain People are. We have for generations worked and lived on this land. We followed the old ways, always. We modern things forsook. The automobiles, the electric lights, the devices. We used them not. We lived as our vatters and mudders lived. Plain."

He gave them a long look. "Passed, the years did, and moved on, did the world. But the same we stayed. Our farms, working. Our children, raising. Our Savior, worshipping. And around us, moving on the world."

Samuel's words took on a droning tone, like that of a story told many times before. Tobin sat, his legs suddenly too tired to hold him up. It was easier to sit, to listen to the man's story, told in that droning, numbing voice.

"When my great, great, great grossvatter was the earth tilling, the world ran out of fuel. Men made batteries their cars to run, their houses to light. And still, we Plain People the old ways kept. Nothing fancy for us. Candles we used for light. Horses we used for the plow pulling and for travel. Farming we did for food. And around us, moving on the world."

The hypnotic drone of the old man's words was putting Tobin to sleep. And yet he didn't feel asleep, just that he was dreaming. Though he'd never seen it, he imagined families on their farms, tilling the earth with a horse at the plow. Wearing their plain, old-fashioned clothes while people drove by them in their fancy cars, talking on their fancy telephones. He saw the families gathered in prayer around the dinner table, lit only by the glow of candlelight.

"The batteries that gave the power to the cars and the lights and the telephones killed the babies. Made barren the mudders and the vatters. Stole avay the future. But for the Plain Folk, not. We the batteries did not use. And born our babies were, and lived they did.

And around us, no more moving on the world. No Rapture there was. No end of days. Chust a slowing down."

"What?" Tobin cried, sitting straight up like he'd been stabbed. "What did you say?"

But Samuel had no time to answer him, because the floor came up to smack Tobin in the face.

Chapter 34

"You're awake."

Was he awake? Tobin squinted one eye open.

"How do you feel?" Elanna's weight sank the bed next to him.

"I've never spent more time in bed, feeling like crap, than I have the past two months," Tobin said sourly.

The room was plainly furnished, but the bed was comfortable. Sunshine streamed through lace curtains. Elanna brushed the hair away from his forehead, and he reached up to grab her hand. He kissed it, then held it to his cheek for a long moment.

Then he noticed her clothes. "Don't tell me they're turning you into one of them."

She looked down and laughed self-consciously. "My others were dirty. This was all they had. Don't laugh. You're wearing a nightgown."

Tobin felt the thick material with his fingers, and peeked under the covers. He was, indeed. His legs looked spindly and weak sticking out from the bottom of the hem, and he quickly dropped the blanket.

The look didn't exactly suit her, either. The severe cut of the dress and the white apron overtop hid the feminine attributes he'd grown used to noticing. And yet, with her auburn curls pinned up in a tidy bun, her face had a shining luminosity he'd never seen before.

She touched her hair, as though noticing that he noticed. "I didn't put on the head covering. At home, only married women cover their heads, and then only when they pray. They seemed to find that strange."

He thought covering your head at all for any reason other than to keep the sun or rain off seemed strange. He didn't say that, though. He'd learned not to laugh at faith.

He sat up, expecting his head to roar with pain. It didn't. "I feel better."

"I should hope so," Elanna said. "You've slept a day away."

"Not much of an superhero, am I?"

She frowned at him. "What?"

"Never mind." He had to remember that she'd probably never read a comic book. "I'm starving."

"I can bring you something to eat. Rachel is a wonderful cook. And they have such great food, here, Tobin, you won't believe it! And it's all new, and fresh! If they don't grow it, raise it, or trade for it, they don't have it."

"Something to eat would be great, but in a minute." He knew all about the food. He curled his fingers around hers. "We need to think about getting out of here."

Her expression closed against him. "We can talk about it later."

"No," he said stubbornly. "Not later, now. We don't want to be here when the Gappers come. Whoever they are. Whatever they are. They sound like bad news, them and their thundermakers."

"Tobin, we can't just run away," Elanna protested. She cast a quick glance toward the closed door. "These people have helped us."

"And you heard Samuel! He wants us gone!" he said harshly, not caring who heard him.

She pressed a finger against his lips. "Nobody's going to chase us out until we're both well enough to travel. Enoch told me that, no matter what Rachel's father said. It should only be a few days. And...Tobin..." she sighed. "I like it here."

That answer didn't satisfy him. If anything, it frightened him a little. "This isn't where we're supposed to end up, anyway. As soon as we can get someone to drive us back to the car --"

All at once he remembered what Samuel had told them. "No," he said with a mouth gone suddenly dry. "Not the car. We can't use the car!"

Now she looked puzzled again, and tried to soothe him by rubbing his head. He pushed her hand away, gripping her fingers hard enough to make her wince. He released the pressure, sorry to have caused her pain but too excited to stop now.

"He said it was the batteries that made people stop being able to have children," Tobin said.

A look of understanding rose in her eyes. She pressed her hands to her stomach, tears welling in her eyes. "That's why we...that's why the Tribe survived. The Reb and the one before him, probably the one before him too, they said the same thing. That we survived, had children when the others didn't, because we kept the sabbath and they didn't. It was when we didn't use batteries, didn't use power. That's why we lasted when they didn't, and still...all this time," she whispered. "We could have just stopped using them completely. We could have stopped killing the babies?"

"You didn't know," he said, and could see that his words didn't soothe her.

"These are good people, Toby. Please don't judge them so harshly."

He thought of the roar of thunder, and the men who weren't men spilling over the barrier. He thought about the guns. "Samuel was right. I want to get out of here before those Gappers, whatever they are, get back. It can't be good."

"We have no car. And neither one of us is in the best condition to start walking across the country again, Toby. I haven't forgotten those damned weeks after we left the city. I don't think I can face something like that again." She paused, seeming almost embarrassed. "Not until I've stopped bleeding, anyway. A few more days. That's all."

"You heard what Samuel said," he told her as calmly as he

could. "And I know you remember those girls, those Gappers, looking for us. They wanted to kill us, Elanna. Whatever arrangement they have with these people won't help us. They have guns!"

A discreet knock on the door interrupted them. He couldn't pretend he wasn't grateful for the disruption. "Come in!"

A white-capped and dark-skirted figure entered the room under the burden of a heavily laden tray. The girl was followed by another carrying a pile of folded clothes. Yet a third girl entered, carrying a basin and pitcher. A fourth, giggling, came behind the others carrying a small square of something white and a towel.

The small room was suddenly filled with overpowering femininity. Tobin didn't know where to look or how to act. The girls, all except Elanna, were busy putting down their burdens. And giggling.

Elanna looked annoyed. "Thanks, but I can take care of him."

"Mudder Stolzfus these things sent," said a pretty dark-haired girl. She stole a look at Tobin, and her cheeks colored. She giggled again.

"You can leave them here," Elanna said coldly. "And you can leave us alone, too."

"We came to help redd up the room," another girl said. She giggled too.

"If you want, we can spread the bed across," the first and seemingly boldest said, which set the others girls into peals of squealing laughter. "Make the sheets smooth for you."

"Thank you, but I think we'll be fine!" Elanna repeated, twisting on the bed to glare at all of them in turn.

They caught the hint. Still giggling, stumbling over each other, the girls left. The room seemed a lot larger after they'd gone.

Elanna got up and pulled the tray, and the small table on which it rested, over next to the bed. Delicious smells made his stomach growl. Tobin's mouth watered.

"Soup," she said. "Bread. Some milk. Something they call butter. You spread it on the bread. And these red things are called red-beet eggs."

Tobin tore into the food with relish, slurping up the hot, salty soup and dunking the thick chunks of bread into it. The butter melted into the broth, yellow globs of sweetness floating on the top. He ate those, too.

As he ate, Elanna fidgeted around the room. She lifted things up and put them down. She arranged the curtains, then put them back they way they'd been. She lifted the pile of clothes and set them down without looking at them.

"What's wrong with you?" Tobin asked with his mouth full.

"Those girls were looking at you like they wanted to eat you," she said sourly.

He had to stare at her for a long, long moment before he could speak. When he did, he nearly choked. He'd forgotten to swallow.

"Are you…jealous?" He asked incredulously.

She whirled to look at him. "Of course not."

Her face told him she was lying. She didn't give him the chance to call her on it, though. She thrust the pile of clothes, the towel and the white square at him.

"Here," she said. "I'll be waiting outside."

Just like that, she was gone. Tobin stared after her thoughtfully, unsure what to make of her outburst. Jealous? A warmth crept into his stomach, and he smiled. He knew he shouldn't be glad, but he was.

The white square turned out to be soap. Though unscented, its lather was rich and foamy. He didn't have enough water to bathe as thoroughly as he wanted to, but the pitcher gave him enough to at least scrub away most of the grime.

When he tried on the clothes, he found them to be a good fit. Well, almost. After struggling for several minutes, he realized the pants had no zipper, just a series of buttons. The hems rose to just above his ankles, and the waistband was a little tight. Other than that, though, he looked all right. He looked Plain. All he needed was a beard, he thought, and rubbed his chin. Give him a few more days, and he'd have that, too.

He went downstairs feeling refreshed. His head still ached a little, but not too badly. His other aches and pains had faded too. The sleep had done him good.

"Ah, Tobin Vinter!" Enoch said when he came into the kitchen. "Better you are feeling?"

"Much, thanks," Tobin said.

"Better he is looking, too," Rachel said with a chuckle. "Not so strubbly!"

Elanna wasn't there. Tobin was about to ask where she was when he saw Samuel sitting in the corner next to the stove. The old man saw him, too.

"To the rest of my story you can listen now?" The old man said, with a twinkle in his eyes. "Not falling asleep you will be this time?"

"No, I don't think so," Tobin said. He sat on one of the straight-backed chairs. "I'm ready."

"About the Gappers you want to know," Samuel said, the traces of his good humor gone. "Men and women living together, not married. Shameful. Soldiers from Indiantown Gap. A military base it was, a long time ago. When the world began to slow down, not everything so smoothly died. War there was, sometimes. People who thought what they wanted they could take, without caring. Babies there were few, but soldiers we had in plenty.

But the government who wanted them there couldn't last forever. Soon food they stopped shipping. Clothes and supplies, and weapons, too. The soldiers, the Gappers, down to Annville they came to trade for what they needed. In their thundermakers, their tanks, riding. And for awhile all right that was."

"Why did they go back?" Tobin asked curiously. "Why didn't they stay here? Join you?"

Samuel snorted. "Soldiers they were. What else did they know but war and for war preparing? Young men, foolish men. And their women, not so foolish, ain't?"

Samuel laughed a little. "But soon, not so young. But babies they had, that we know. Why? What protected them? Some government something or other, ain't?"

He laughed again, more bitterly this time. "A few only at first, then more as passed the years. Whatever gave them children blessed them vit girl babies more than boys. So the parents trained them as they had been trained. But soldiers, waiting always without orders, crazy become. And the longer there they stayed, the crazier they got."

"How do they survive up there?" Tobin asked.

"Supplies we send to them, every new moon time," the old man explained. "And then alone they leave us. Until now."

"Until us, you mean."

The old man didn't say anything, just nodded.

"Why'd they build the barrier?"

Samuel shrugged. "Who knows what they fight for? Somevun not liking what the other says, or wanting what the other has. Some following vun, some the other. So some leave, and the ones who stay behind, they are not wanting them to come back. The barrier they build to keep them from getting through."

"But I saw people." Tobin paused and shuddered, remembering the sight of so much death. "They fought, didn't they?"

"Ja." Samuel leaned forward over the table, his blue eyes piercing. "And those girls, those kinder, the fight they vun. Ten years ago, only. Some of them only five, six years old. Against men, they fought. And they killed. And to our town they will come to find you, if looking for you they still are, and if here they find you, us they will kill like those men at the barrier."

"Haven't you ever tried to fight back?" Tobin asked, even as he thought about the carnage at the barrier. These people couldn't stand against guns.

"We Plain People are," Samuel said with affronted dignity. "We fight not."

Tobin swallowed heavily. "What makes you think they'll come here looking?"

"Because something they vant, you have," Samuel said. "Enoch told me that in a car you came. A car stuffed with goods."

Again, what he had made people want to hurt him. Tobin spat out a curse, feeling filthy even as he did so. The old man barely flinched.

"They look for you, will," Samuel said. "Track you, they will. And they will track you here, I do not doubt. They must not find you here."

"No." Tobin wiped palms damp with chill sweat on his trousers. "No, I don't think that would be very good for me or Elanna."

Samuel sighed, his eyes sad. "Selfish Yankee. Not good for you? Or for your woman? My family I am worried for. My home."

"We'll go as soon as we can," Tobin said.

"Go now," Samuel said.

Chapter 35

Elanna didn't know what had passed between Tobin and Samuel Lapp. She was afraid to ask. Tobin flew out of the kitchen into the yard like he was on fire. His eyes were terrible, haunted.

When she saw him stumble and nearly fall, she ran to him although it made the ache in her womb flare into a stabbing pain. "Toby!"

"I'm all right." He shook off her hand when she tried to steady him.

He leaned against a tidy fence post, head down. He wasn't breathing hard, and he didn't seem to be in pain. Elanna waited, quietly. She was used to waiting.

"We need to leave," he told her. "Before those Gappers come here."

She ran her fingers along his arm, down to where his fist clutched the wooden post. He trembled, and she realized he was using every effort to hold himself upright. She put her hand on his, trying to offer him strength without insulting the tender ego all men had.

"They frighten you," was all she said.

"Hell, yes, they scare the shit out of me!" He turned on her.

"Enoch says --"

"Samuel says they want us because of the car, and our stuff," Tobin broke in grimly. "Just like the Tribe."

"No." She shook her head. "Not like the Tribe."

He softened, letting her fold her palm into his. "I'm sorry, Elanna. Worse than the Tribe, maybe, but still the same. They want us because of what we had. They'll probably want to know where we got it, and where they can get it."

"So we'll tell them!" she said angrily. "Big deal Toby, so we point them in the right direction! They won't find much. Not like what you knew about when you came to the Tribe."

The resentment filtered through her tone before she realized it. He heard it and flinched. He turned away, face stony beneath the rim of the straw hat like Enoch's.

"I left a map for them," was all he said.

She didn't speak for a moment, just stood next to him and watched the children playing in the dirt. In the distance, beyond the houses and the street, were the fields. Still mostly brown, even now, she knew that the green would soon begin breaking through. She'd like to see that.

"If you think we should go," she said, "then we'll go."

"It's not just for us. Even if we tell them where we got the car and the food and the clothes, do you think that will be enough for them? Samuel told me they're soldiers, Elanna."

"They're just girls," she said, remembering the fresh faces beneath the dirt. "Teeners!"

"They kill people. And they'll kill us, they'll kill the people here, if they find out we're here. We need to go."

A chill skittered down her spine. She nodded, crossing her arms across her chest and hugging her elbows to warm herself. "All right. Tomorrow morning. We'll go."

Tobin looked over her shoulder, back toward the Stolzfus house. His face was grim, his mouth set in a thin line. He pointed.

"We may not make it to tomorrow morning."

She turned, dreading what she knew she'd see. Gappers, five of them, dressed in green and wearing their helmets with the face masks. They all carried guns.

Chapter 36

Elanna hadn't seen much of the town or met many people other than Samuel and the Stolzfus family. She was surprised to see the number of women running out from their homes. She was even more surprised by the number of children.

Even as her heart thudded in her chest at the sight of the Gappers, her throat closed with emotion at the sight of the little ones. Many looked to be between six and ten years old, but she saw a few toddlers. Their chubby legs and sturdy bodies took her breath away, and when she saw one of the women clutching a blanket covered bundle to her chest, Elanna put both hands on her empty womb. But she did not allow herself to cry. She had no time for grief.

"Move your fucking asses!" Came the cry from one of the Gappers. The high voice sounded familiar. Lovett? Or Maranian? Or maybe just another teener girl.

Tobin held her hand so tightly she winced. "Toby," she murmured, twisting it in his. "Let go."

He didn't take his eyes off the group in front of them. "They're lining everyone up."

"Where are the men?" Elanna asked. Tobin still didn't move,

and she stayed with him. Together, they watched the Gappers parading up and down the street, poking their guns at the women and bending down to frighten the children.

"Out in the fields?" Tobin replied, his answer just another question. "Working?"

One of the taller Gappers barked a series of orders, and two of the others ran off down the street. To find the men? She didn't know, but watching the children crying as their mothers tried to shield them, Elanna was no longer afraid.

She was furious.

"Who do they think they are?" She watched as one of the Gappers, shoulders shaking with laughter, knocked a little boy no more than a toddler into the dirt. "He's only a baby!"

"Elanna," Tobin said warningly, but she shrugged him off.

"They're hurting children!"

Just then, the lead Gapper looked over to where they stood. "Hey you! Chakey and Emma! Get your Plain asses over here!"

"She thinks we're someone else," Tobin said, but Elanna didn't think that was the case. The Gapper'd spoken with a forced, sarcastic accent. She was mocking the Plain People, calling Tobin and Elanna by common names.

"No," she said. "She's just being an asshole."

Tobin looked at her, an odd smile twisting his mouth. "Now you sound just like them."

"We'd better go over there."

He nodded. She could still see the fear in his eyes, but it was further away now. Like hers. Anger could do that.

Together, they walked across the grass to the street. The tallest Gapper motioned with the gun, and Tobin and Elanna got in line. The Gapper strolled over to them, ignoring the others who still taunted and teased the women and children.

With one quick movement, she tugged off her helmet and mask. The young woman with the gun couldn't have been more than twenty years old, though her eyes looked much older than that. Her skin was pale and unmarked by blemishes, though a thin layer of grime coated her fine, even features.

Deep blue eyes, clear as water, glittered beneath heavy brows the same golden shade as her hair. She shook her head to clear her face of some errant strands, turned her face to one side, and spit an amazingly huge glob of spittle onto the ground. Elanna recognized her. Major Kodak.

"You should know the fucking drill by now, Emma," Kodak said. "Were you and Chakey too busy getting it on over there to notice we were here?"

Without waiting for an answer, she turned to smirk at Tobin. "Not out plowing and sowing with the other losers?"

Tobin opened his mouth to say something but shut it quickly. Watching him, Elanna guessed he had thought the same thing she had; his accent, or lack of it, would give him away immediately. So far Kodak hadn't seemed to guess they were the prey. The clothes had helped disguise them. Their voices wouldn't be so easy to hide.

Rachel Stolzfus, arms wrapped protectively around Amos and her youngest daughter Levina, muttered something that Elanna didn't catch. Apparently Kodak heard it. The woman turned quick as a rat, eyes narrowed, to glare at Rachel.

"Speak in English, dumbass!"

Rachel lifted her chin. "I said, we what you wanted sent already."

The Gapper laughed and spit again, narrowly missing Rachel's shoe. "Well, maybe we want something else this time."

Nobody else had time to say anything more, because the other Gappers came back with the men. Elanna saw Enoch, head held high and his face calm. All of the men looked calm, in fact. They all looked alike, dressed the same and most of them with beards.

"Line 'em up!" Kodak called, pointing with her gun. "Two lines, across from the runts and the bitches. You," she said, pointing to Tobin. "Get your ass over in the line with the men. Unless you're a pussy."

She waited to see if he'd react but didn't seem surprised when he didn't. Tobin's jaw clenched, but he wisely kept silent as he moved across into the other line to stand between two men Elanna hadn't met.

"You're all pussies," Kodak snapped, looking them up and down. She bent in to spit again, this time at Tobin's feet. Again, he didn't react, though his face was not as smooth and calm as the other men's. "Never lift a finger to defend yourselves." She made a low sound of disgust in her throat.

"Sir, Major Kodak, Sir!"

The head Gapper turned to the young girl, no more than twelve, who'd called her name. "The fuck is it this time, Dallas?"

Dallas gulped but continued bravely. "Permission to use the latrine, Sir!"

Kodak rolled her eyes but nodded. "God damnit, Dallas, didn't you go before we left headquarters?"

"Sir, no, Sir!"

"Get out of here!" Kodak snapped, and watched as Dallas scurried away. The younger girl tripped as she ran, dropping her gun. The weapon landed in the dirt, clanging against a rock. "Damnit, Dallas!"

"Sorry, Sir!"

Kodak shook her head and rubbed at a spot between her eyes, as though she had pain there. "Tayler! Winslow! Front and center!"

Two of the older girls jogged up, holding their guns firmly. Each snapped her hand against her forehead, then out and down. "Sir! Yes, Sir!"

"Tayler, you start down there with the women and the brats. Winslow, you start with the men. You know what I want to know."

"Sir! Yes, Sir!"

With another of those hand snaps, each Gapper went to her assigned spot and began talking. Kodak walked up and down the rows, watching. Blinking. Spitting every so often, and sometimes scratching, too. Elanna itched just watching her.

It was going to take forever for Tayler to get to her. The Gapper was slow, taking her time with each woman. She even bent down to talk to the children. She asked them all the same question, over and over, even to the littlest ones who couldn't be expected to answer.

"Where are the man and the woman who came in the car?"

One after another, the women shook their heads or mumbled

something in the language that sounded like Yiddish but wasn't quite. The children hid their faces, not speaking. At least Tayler didn't poke them or make them cry.

Elanna shifted her feet. The ache in her womb flared again, and when she moved blood gushed hot between her legs. The thick pad of rags they'd given her to stanch the flow would be soaked through by now. She was starting to feel faint. She needed to sit, to have a cool drink.

Winslow was much faster than her cohort. She'd already worked her way down the line, stopping at each man and looking him in the eye while she asked her question. She could do that because she was exceptionally tall for a girl, standing nose to nose with all but the tallest men. When she reached Tobin, she'd have to look at his chin, Elanna thought woozily. Her legs started to tremble. She folded her hands in the depths of her skirt, clenching the fabric like that would help her to stand.

Now Winslow had reached Enoch, who met her gaze steadily, without flinching. "The others I told," he said firmly. "No man or woman we saw. Avay they ran, into the trees."

Winslow seemed satisfied with the answer and moved to the next man. Tayler had finally reached Rachel, who gave the same answer as the other women had. Next the Gapper would come to Elanna. What would she say? She had a bit of Yiddish that might pass for their speech, but it wouldn't help her if they demanded she speak in English. And it wouldn't help Tobin at all.

The blood was running down her legs now. It was sticky. A rivulet slid over her ankle to drip into her shoe. She thanked Adonai for the heavy skirts hiding this embarrassment.

"What about you?" Tayler looked over Elanna without seeing her as anything but Plain. "See anything?"

Taking a chance, Elanna didn't speak. She hoped a mere shake of the head would satisfy Tayler, whose tender treatment of the children made her seem a little less cruel than her fellow soldiers. The movement made her woozy, though, so that she had to shift her feet again just to keep her balance.

"What's that?" Tayler asked snidely. "I couldn't hear you, Emma. Speak up. See anything?"

"N…no," Elanna ventured. Her voice almost refused to come. Her tongue felt glued to the roof of her mouth.

"S'matter, cat got your tongue?" Tayler asked. She reached out and poked Elanna in the chest, just over the bib of her apron. "Huh, you dumb bitch?"

Over Tayler's shoulder, Elanna saw Tobin take a step forward. She wanted to warn him back, but again her voice wouldn't come. Truth be told, she felt so lightheaded and sick she was almost afraid to speak in case she threw up all over Tayler. That wouldn't go over very well at all.

"Get back in line, asshole," Winslow ordered.

Kodak, who'd been down at the other end of the men's line, whipped her head around. "What's going on?"

"This asshole didn't like the way I talked to his bitch, I guess," Tayler said. She poked Elanna again, harder, and watched Tobin's face.

"'Zat so?" Kodak asked. She stopped in front of Tobin, who'd had the good sense not to step forward again. Elanna saw rage in his eyes, and prayed he'd control it. "So, Chakey. Don't like us messing with your woman, huh?"

Tobin said nothing. Kodak laughed, turning to the other two who joined her. She stopped laughing suddenly as if somebody had slapped a hand over her mouth. Reaching out her gun, she used the tip of it to toss Tobin's hat off his head.

With his face exposed to the sun, the bruising and cuts he'd earned during the past few weeks were glaring. Kodak leaned forward until she was almost nose to nose with him. Tobin didn't move, his eyes looking over her shoulder to catch Elanna's.

"How'd you hurt your face, Chakey?" Kodak asked softly. She reached up one hand and pressed her thumb against the deep purple bruise on his forehead. "Huh, douchebag?"

"Maybe it was a plowing accident," Tayler offered with a smirk that Elanna wanted to slap off her face.

"Maybe he tripped going to the outhouse in the middle of the night," Winslow said. "He sure smells like shit."

The pair of them laughed meanly, not joined by Kodak this time. The head Gapper looked over at Elanna, then back to Tobin. Considering.

She put her hands on his shoulders, ran them down the length of his arms and then settled them at his waist. "I think that maybe Emma over there just likes a little kink in the bedroom. 'Zat right, Chakey?"

Tobin still said nothing, though Elanna guessed it was probably killing him to stay quiet. Kodak, getting no response, put her hand on his crotch. Tobin jumped a little, but her hand at his waist kept him in place.

"Oooh," Kodak breathed in a feminine voice completely at odds with her appearance. "Chakey's sporting quite a package. C'mere girls, and feel this!"

Tayler and Winslow each took a turn, rubbing and giggling. Kodak ordered them away, stepping back in front of him. His face was red as fire, Elanna thought, and her own cheeks burned with fury.

"I can be rough too, honey," Kodak cooed mockingly.

At the endearment, Tobin slapped her hand away. His face had become dangerous, something Kodak didn't seem to see or recognize. And though Elanna wanted him to stay quiet, she couldn't stop the pride she felt when he turned his face and spat on Kodak's boot.

"You can't call me that," he said, wiping his chin.

Tayler and Winslow seemed stunned. They looked at each other, mouths open and eyes goggling. If Elanna didn't feel so terrible, she'd have laughed. Kodak wasn't laughing.

"You punk-ass jerkoff," she hissed. She looked down at her boot. "You asswipe!"

"Sir!"

It was Dallas, back from the latrine. She'd come up behind Elanna, nudging through the line and nearly knocking her over. Now she stared at Elanna, eyes round with surprise.

"Not now, Dallas." Kodak was toe-to-toe with Tobin, gun held in her two hands like she was going to hit him over the head with it.

"But Sir!" Dallas squealed.

The girl peeked around Elanna, looking behind her. Elanna felt another slow, hot burst between her thighs and clamped them together. It was no use. She'd been on her feet too long when she should have been sitting.

"The fuck is it?" Kodak screamed, turning from Tobin to confront the young girl.

"It's her!" Dallas cried, pointing. "She's bleeding!"

"What the fuck?" Tayler said, looking behind Elanna. "Oh, fuck!"

The dismay in her voice brought Winslow, who grabbed Elanna's arms and turned her around. As she did, Elanna shuddered at the wetness of her skirts against her skin. The blood must have stained through. The flow was even heavier than she'd thought.

"Shit on a brick!" Kodak grabbed Elanna by the arms, and suddenly Elanna was glad to be grabbed. Without Kodak holding her up, she thought she might fall.

Kodak ripped the bonnet from Elanna's head and looked at her face. Elanna saw sudden recognition in Kodak's eyes. The head Gapper let go of her arms, and Elanna stumbled back, barely managing to keep her feet.

"Holy shit," Kodak said. "It's her. The bitch from the car, I'm sure of it. And that asshole is the guy!"

She whirled around, gun in the air. "And you all lied to us!"

She couldn't seem to believe it. She shrieked the accusation again, throwing in a few more curses. Even Tayler and Winslow backed off, and little Dallas burst into terrified tears.

"Get them in the truck!" Kodak ordered, poking Elanna in the upper arm with her gun. "Get moving!"

Tayler and Winslow did as ordered, grabbing Elanna by the arms and dragging her away. Kodak grabbed Tobin, who wasn't struggling to get away. He pushed Kodak's hands off him, then ran to catch up to Elanna.

"Let go of her," he said. "We'll go with you, but you leave her alone. Don't touch her."

Something in his voice made Tayler and Winslow do as he said. Dallas looked at him with wide, wet eyes, her cheeks painted with tears. She was just a child, Elanna thought.

"And for the rest of you dumbfucks," Kodak screeched, "We'll deal with you later!"

She pushed her way through the women's line, following them. When she got to Tobin, she shoved him apart from Elanna. Caught off guard, he fell back a few steps.

"And you'd better learn to obey orders, asshole," Kodak said.

Tobin steadied himself, his dark eyes grown darker with anger. Elanna wondered how he could speak so clearly through jaws so tightly clenched, but every word stood out. "Keep your hands off me, and keep them off her, you bitch."

Kodak's eyes widened and her mouth opened in a scream of fury so loud it hurt Elanna's ears. Dallas wailed louder, clapped her hands over her eyes and shrank toward Elanna.

"Shh." Elanna put her arms around the girl. "Shh, sweetheart, it's okay."

The comforting came as second nature to her; the irony that she was soothing the enemy did not escape her. But what else could she do? The girl was crying, and she was just a child, really. Not a soldier, not like those others. Certainly not like Kodak, who had thrown her gun to the ground and was now trying to throttle Tobin.

The girl was large, and she was obviously strong, but pitted against a man as tall as Tobin, she had to stand on her tiptoes to get a good grip. Tobin managed to get his hands up around hers, and began pulling. The other two soldiers stood stunned, seemingly unable to respond.

Now Tobin had Kodak's wrists pinned with his, wrenching her hands away from his throat. She was still screaming, sharp short bursts of angry barking that sounded like they had to be shredding her throat. A word slipped through here and there, a "fuck" or a "shit", and once even a "goddamn tits on fire" that Elanna couldn't make sense of in her muddled state.

Tayler and Winslow were still standing goggle-eyed, weapons dropped at their sides. Little Dallas huddled against Elanna, squeezing her hard around the waist. The girl buried her face in Elanna's stomach, her shoulders thin and bony beneath Elanna's soothing fingers.

With one final heave, Tobin threw Kodak away from him. She went down heavily, landing in the dirt with a thump that nearly buckled Elanna's legs. The Gapper was on her feet in an instant, blue eyes raging and her blonde hair matted with dirt and sweat. With fists clenched, she spat on the ground again.

"Come on, you fuck." Her mouth stretched in a frightening grin. She gestured with her hands before closing them into fists again. "Come on, then. Show me what you got."

Elanna saw the hesitation in Tobin's eyes. He didn't know how to fight. Whatever had gotten him this far was anger and instinct. He was no match for a soldier, trained in combat, even if he was a man and she no more than a girl.

"All right." Tobin opened his arms wide, as though he were going to embrace Kodak instead of fight her. "Give it to me."

With a roar of rage, Kodak launched herself at Tobin. He stepped aside at the final moment. Kodak nearly went sprawling in the dust. She whirled around, expression crafty.

"I knew you were a pussy," she said with a laugh that left Elanna cold. "Just like them."

Tobin didn't say anything. Though Elanna couldn't see his face, his body was tense, his knees bent a little and his hands outstretched. Distractedly, Elanna realized she was seeing him through a fine red haze. She was going to pass out, and soon.

"Gonna have to let you go," she murmured to Dallas in a slurred voice she almost didn't recognize as her own.

"No! No!" Dallas wailed and clutched her harder.

Kodak flung herself at Tobin again, and this time he wasn't able to move out of her way. She wrapped her arms around him, almost like a lover, and used her legs to kick at his. She was too close for Tobin to really get in any blows, so he sunk his fingers into the dirty length of her hair and pulled.

"God damn dirty fighter!" Tayler shrieked, finally coming to life.

Kodak let go, twisting around suddenly. Tobin still had hold of her hair, but now she faced away from him. Elanna could see a look of madness on her face. She was still grinning.

Kodak bent at the waist as though she'd been shot. At the same time, she snapped her head downward, despite the grip Tobin had in her hair. He didn't have time to let go. Her forward motion threw him off balance and he fell at her side, fingers still tangled in her hair.

Kodak ripped her head upright, leaving a chunk of blonde strands still in Tobin's hands. She fell on him, using her hands and feet, and, Elanna saw with horror, even her teeth. She sat on Tobin's chest, knees locked on his ears and hit his face.

Winslow ran toward Kodak and Tobin. "Sir! Let go, Sir!"

"You're killing him, Sir!" Tayler cried, running too.

"Damn fucking straight I'm killing him!" Kodak yelled. With sick terror Elanna saw her lips were wet, glistening red with Tobin's blood. "I'm going to fucking murderize this fuck!"

"Sir, no, Sir!" Tayler cried. "The General says he wants both of them, Sir!"

"Fuck the General!" Kodak screamed, fists still flailing on Tobin's face. "This fuckwad called me a bitch!"

"Sir! You are a bitch, Sir!" Winslow yelled.

Both Tayler and Winslow had their hands on Kodak, who writhed like a rabid animal. Tobin wasn't moving. Tayler and Winslow pulled Kodak off him, both of them using all their strength.

"If you kill him the General will kill you!" Winslow cried in Kodak's ear.

"Get her in the truck!" Tayler yelled to Winslow. "Leave the asshole here! He's not going anywhere. We'll get them back to base and come back for him later!"

"But the General said --" Winslow began and ducked out of the way as Kodak let out another scream of fury and tried to bite her.

"We'll get him later!" Tayler dodged Kodak's feet as she kicked. "We don't have a choice! Maybe the bitch will be enough!"

Winslow didn't have time to protest. "Let's move!"

She began shoving Kodak toward the truck. Tayler followed, barking orders to the other two Gappers who'd been watching the entire ordeal. Those two began moving toward Elanna.

"No!" Elanna cried, trying her best to peel Dallas away from her. The girl clung like a leech, wailing. Elanna's legs wouldn't move. Her ears filled with a heavy buzzing and the fine red haze grew thick in her eyes. She managed one step, but that was all.

Her stomach lurched and her legs buckled. Tobin's face, his eyes rolled back in his head and his cheeks pale, was the last thing she saw before the red haze overtook her. And then she was lost in it, the buzzing blocking all the noise around her except for a new voice in her ear.

"Fuck," said the voice. "This one's out, too.

Chapter 37

Every part of him was in agony, particularly the spot just below his ear, where that bitch had nearly taken a chunk out of him with her teeth. But he wasn't unconscious. Just waiting.

It wouldn't do Elanna any good if he got killed, which is what Kodak wanted to do to him. It wouldn't do either of them any good if they both were taken back to the Gapper's base. So, though it hurt his heart a million times worse than his body's pains to let her go, Tobin lay in the dirt and pretended to be dead. Or close to dead, it didn't matter. They were taking Elanna and not him.

He heard the rumble of the truck as it started and sped away. Now he stayed on the ground because he didn't think he could get up. He didn't want to feel the damage Kodak's fists, feet and teeth had done to him, not on top of what he'd already sustained from the car crash and everything else he'd gone through over the past few months.

"Into the haus take him," a voice said.

"Careful!" That was Rachel. He felt the brush of her skirts as she knelt beside him. She smiled at him and brushed the hair from his forehead. "Be still."

"I have to follow them." Nothing moved but Tobin's mouth and his eyes as he blinked.

"Shh." Rachel's gaze was troubled. She glanced away from him, looking far away. To where the truck had gone, maybe? "Later, you will go. Now, you will rest."

"No," Tobin said. He still didn't get up. His arms and legs felt removed from him, but not numb. No, he hadn't been granted that relief.

"Yes," Rachel said firmly. Two men he didn't know appeared beside her. "Daniel, David. Lift him and to the haus carry him. Sadie! Mary!"

Like magic, Sadie and Mary appeared next to Rachel. Their faces were nearly identical beneath the white caps, though Mary looked a few years older. They both looked like Rachel. Daughters, then.

"Some water, boil," Rachel said, and rattled off a list of other chores. The girls nodded in unison, their brown eyes wide as they stared at Tobin. "Go!"

He wanted to protest more, but suddenly, he was too tired.

THEY PUT Elanna in a small room by herself and locked the door from the outside. They gave her a small lantern with a burning candle in it, a pile of clothes, a basin of water, some rags, and miraculously, an entire package of super sized maxi pads. The kind with wings. She hadn't seen any of those in years. Experience told her the self-stick adhesive on the back would have long ago lost its stick, but they'd included a few safety pins, too.

Dallas didn't want to leave her, but they pulled her away with taunts and jeers. Elanna watched her go, wishing she could help but unable to do anything except sink down on the low cot. Too late, she realized that she'd stain the covers, but she couldn't care. She needed to lie down or else she'd pass out again.

She didn't know how much time passed before she finally opened her eyes again. She shifted on the bed, wincing at the way her thighs stuck together. She swallowed in disgust, then remembered the basin of water and the rags.

They were on the floor where she'd left them. Elanna managed to sit up, waiting for a gush of blood. When it didn't come, she breathed in relief and swung her legs over the bed.

Standing was more of a challenge, but she felt all right. It had never taken her so long to recover after losing a baby before, but then she'd never been subjected to the same stresses, either.

The apron and small cape were no problem to untie, but she fumbled with the unfamiliar snaps at the skirt's waist. She was used to buttons and zippers, not these odd little metal clasps that hooked into each other. She finally figured it out, and the heavy skirt, made heavier from the weight of her blood, dropped to the floor.

She stepped out of it, not wanting to look at her thighs and legs, but unable to avoid seeing. Blood had caked and dried in great maroon splashes from hips to ankles. She closed her eyes for a minute against the sight, though blood never made her feel dizzy. Blood, especially blood like this, was as much a part of a hopemother's life as breathing. Still, she needed to gather her courage before looking again.

The water in the basin turned a dark murky brown before she half finished the job, but she managed to clean herself. The skirt and the underclothes were ruined. She felt worse about that than anything else, because she knew how hard Rachel and her daughters, nieces and sisters had worked to make even these simple garments. It was a waste, the worst sort of sin, but she could do nothing about it.

She took off her shirt and tossed it to the floor as well. It could be saved, at least, though not without a good scrubbing. She found a pair of underwear in the pile of clothes they'd given her. She pulled the bulky material over her legs and up around her waist, fingering the slit in the front with confusion. Men's underwear?

She slipped one of the thick pads in place, then used the safety pins to hold it. She sorted through the rest of the clothes. White socks and a sleeveless shirt. She pulled it over her head. It was too big. Another shirt and a pair of pants, both of the same green as the Gappers uniforms. It looked like someone had splashed dirt or paint or something all over the clothes. There were green, black and brown splotches all over it. As she pulled them on, Elanna thought about the trees she'd seen from the roadside. Clothes like this would blend in perfectly.

Now that she was dressed and clean, she looked at the bed. It wasn't too bad. Only the top cover, a rough, shabby blanket the same shade of green as the clothes, had been spotted. She scrubbed at the stains with one of the rags, but it wasn't much help. She stripped the cover back to expose the plain white sheet beneath.

There wasn't much else to do except sit back down. The room wasn't large enough even to pace in, should she have wished to walk. She didn't. Lying down felt fine to her, though the bed was hard and the sheets smelled vaguely of must. They hadn't even given her a pillow for her head.

Mold marked the damp ceiling. Several cracks ran along it, zigging and zagging in patterns so random she couldn't even force her mind to find a picture in them. The flickering light from the candle should have helped, but didn't. She didn't need cracks in the ceiling to have pictures in her head. Elanna thought about Tobin, pale on the ground, and she wanted to cry.

He'll be fine, she told herself, fighting away the tears. She had to think that, or go as crazy as Kodak. He'd be fine, and she'd get out of here, away from this place with its mold and its cracks.

She must have slept, but without dreams. She woke without opening her eyes, sensing it would be just as dark either way. The candle had burned out. How long ago, she couldn't tell. How long had she been here? Her bladder, uncomfortably full, told her it had been too long.

The door had no knob on her side, and no window either. She had no warning that it would fly open, sending a shaft of blinding light inward, and when it did, Elanna sat up on the bed so fast she thought she was going to fall on the floor. The door banged against the wall and swung halfway shut. Someone kicked it open again.

"Back against the wall!" A voice ordered.

Elanna didn't move. She had no place to go. The door didn't hit the wall so hard this time, and so it didn't close so much either. One of the Gappers appeared in it, one she'd never seen before. A teener girl, carrying a tray of food.

"Eat this," said the girl. "And then you're coming with me."

"Where?" Elanna asked the only question that made sense.

"To see the General," said the Gapper. "He wants to meet you."

Chapter 38

He healed faster this time. Maybe his body was getting so used to being beaten up that it reacted quicker, Tobin thought with as much humor as he could muster under the circumstances. Or maybe it was the vile tea Rachel had forced him to drink, telling him it "make you feel better vill."

Whatever it was, he could sit up in bed without feeling the world spin. If he touched one of the many bruises dotting his skin, it hurt, but if he left them alone he was mostly okay. Leaving them alone seemed like a pretty smart thing to do.

He itched to be on the move. Every second he lay in bed was one more eternity away from Elanna. What were they doing to her? She had to still be alive. Had to be. Wouldn't he know it if she were dead? Surely he'd feel it, somehow. The way he'd feel it if someone cut off one of his arms or legs. She had become that much a part of him.

He'd read about it in hundreds of books, but he'd never actually felt it before. Love. The word tasted bitter on his tongue when he mumbled it to himself. He loved Elanna, and he cursed himself for all the time he'd wasted without telling her. For not making love to her when she'd wanted him to. For bringing her with him at all.

Infuriatingly, nobody seemed to be as worried as he was. Rachel tried to mother him, patting his head and tucking the covers around him. Enoch just lifted his hands in a gesture of innocence when Tobin asked where they'd taken her and what they might do to her. Samuel, the old man, was the worst.

"Worry not about your woman," he said sourly. "Gone, she is. And gone should you be, too! Before back they come for you!"

"Papa," Rachel scolded gently, herding the old man out of Tobin's room. And then something in the language he didn't know, but he could guess what she meant. "Leave him alone."

Just yesterday the Gappers had taken Elanna, but it might as well have been last year, or ten years ago, for as much as it seemed to have changed these people's lives. They rose with the dawn, worked hard all day just to eke out a daily survival, and went to sleep with the evening.

He hadn't been asked to work. He knew nothing of shoeing horses, or mending harnesses. He couldn't plow a field, and he couldn't milk a cow. He was worthless here as a man, and he hated it.

As soon as Rachel let him out of bed, he went out to the Stolzfus back yard, a tidy fenced area that looked out to the fields. The first spikes of green were pushing their way up from the rich brown earth. Some of the younger children were out there, feet bare and heads covered, plucking weeds and stones from the ground. The men were fixing one of the barns, high up on the roof. A hole as large as a man's waist marred the shingles, but they worked quickly. They would fix it by lunchtime.

He looked around the yard, bright in the spring sunshine. He didn't belong here. He could learn to plow and sow, hammer and fix and work, and milk the cows he heard mooing in the barn but hadn't yet seen. He scuffled about in the dooryard, kicking stones with the heavy, clunky shoes that had been Enoch's. Everyone seemed to have jobs. Even the youngest children picked up sticks and swept the yard clean of leaves. Elanna fit in. He didn't.

He could learn, but he'd never fit in. Elanna might, because she'd lived so long with the Tribe, but Tobin had been on his own for such a long time. He might not fit in anywhere, he thought grimly, listening to the men shout back and forth as they worked together.

Rachel's niece Rebecca King tended her infant son even as she stirred a huge, steaming vat of boiling water. Every so often she'd punch down a shirt or pair of pants as they floated to the top with her long stick, and once in awhile, when she'd judged the clothes had soaked long enough, she used the same stick to pull out a piece and slop it into a smaller vat filled with cool water. The work looked hard, and though a nice spring breeze had kicked up, Rebecca's face was red and covered with sweat.

"Can I help you?" Tobin asked.

"This women's work is," Rebecca said, shocked.

So he couldn't even do that, Tobin thought dispiritedly. He sat next to the baby, instead, letting the sight of the infant's toothless grin take away the sting of Rebecca's reproach. The boy waved his arms and gurgled contentedly, sometimes letting out a yell to let his mother know he was still there.

"Ach, listen to him grex, naw," said the young mother fondly of the baby. She paused in her stirring long enough to come over and adjust blankets that didn't need adjusting. "And he rutches around so bad! I can't hardly keep him covered."

"He's wonderful." Tobin reached out to touch the baby's hand. The tiny fingers closed around his thumb with surprising strength. "Strong."

"Ja," Rebecca said proudly. "A fine boy he is. My fourth."

Tobin looked at Rebecca, her work-worn hands and her red face. Her sturdy body covered in plain clothes, and her homely face made beautiful by the love she had for her child. She'd experienced the joys of pregnancy and the pains of childbirth, just like Elanna had, but Rebecca's children were hers to keep and raise.

Elanna would have the chance, too, he vowed. He looked again at the baby, now sleeping peacefully under his mother's watching eyes. As many babies as she wanted.

"Grossvatter!" Rebecca said in surprise, as Samuel came out of the house. "I thought you resting were."

Samuel scowled. "A man ven he's dead can rest."

He nodded curtly at Tobin, and took a seat beside him. The old man looked down at the child, allowing a ghost of a smile to curve his lips before scowling again. Rebecca fussed with the baby a minute more, then went back across the yard to her vat of boiling clothes.

"Ach, my back ouches me something fierce." Samuel stretched, cracking his spine. He sighed heavily and looked at Tobin from beneath furrowed brows. "To the Gappers you wish to go."

"I have to help Elanna. And you don't want us here anyway."

Samuel shook his head, saying nothing for a few minutes. He bent to tuck the already tucked covers around the child, who smiled in his sleep. When the old man did look back at Tobin, his expression was almost apologetic.

"My children I love wery much," he said.

"I wouldn't expect anything else," Tobin said. "You're lucky to have them."

"Blessed by God," the old man corrected, but his face smoothed as he again looked down at the baby. "Blessed by God, Tobin Vinter, these children to have. I chust want them safe to be."

"I know that," Tobin said, feeling a little sorry for the old man. "Believe me, we never meant to bring trouble."

"Ach, trouble brings itself," Samuel said with a wave of his hand. "Those Gappers trouble are. Alvays were."

"As long as you keep giving them what they want," Tobin said, "They'll keep coming back."

Samuel looked at him with surprise. "And give them what they want we should not? Let them to our homes come and destroy, as ten years ago they did during their battles?"

Tobin thought of the barrier, and the girl-children who'd killed grown men and women to defend themselves. The girl-children were on their way to becoming women now. But without men, their numbers would have to dwindle.

"They won't be around forever, not if they're all just girls," Tobin said. "And they've got to run out of ammunition for those guns. I wouldn't be surprised if they've already run out for most of them."

"And the risk you want I should take?" Samuel asked shrewdly. "The lives of these children I should risk for your maybes?"

"Have you ever tried to fight them?"

"Plain People fight not," Samuel said firmly.

That explained the way Kodak and her crew acted. They weren't afraid of retaliation, because there had never been any. These people didn't fight.

"I'm not Plain," Tobin said.

Samuel chuckled, poking Tobin's vest and pointing at his hat. "A Plain man we will you make, ain't?"

"I don't think so. I have to get Elanna back. If that means I have to fight them, I'll do it."

"You afraid are not," Samuel said, not asking the question but making the statement.

Tobin thought about that. "I am afraid. But that won't stop me from going. I have to. Tonight. When it's safer to travel."

Samuel rested his hand on Tobin's shoulder. "God go with you, then, Tobin Vinter."

Tobin stood. "I think I'd rather go by myself, thanks. God doesn't seem to be on my side."

He left the old man in the yard, and went inside to make his plans.

Chapter 39

"I have to pee," Elanna repeated, resisting as much as she dared. The Gapper who'd come to get her tugged on her arm, hard, but the girl stood half a head shorter than Elanna. "And I'd like to do it soon, before I do it on the floor."

"Damn it," the teener grumbled. "I'm just supposed to take you to the General, not any place else."

"Listen," Elanna said reasonably. "I'll only be a few minutes. I have to go really bad. You don't want me making a mess in front of the General, do you?"

Whoever this teener girl was, she wasn't too bright. "Yeah, right. But I'm supposed to take you straight there."

The corridor was dirty and dim, lit only by the sunlight that managed to get in through a series of high, filth-covered windows up near the ceiling. Elanna held back again, despite the girl's tugging.

"Come on," she wheedled. "What's your name, again?"

The girl hadn't given it to her before, but she didn't seem to remember that. Not the lightest matzoh ball in the soup, Elanna thought. The Gapper was still trying to tug her down the corridor.

"Golden," the girl said. "Sergeant Tina Golden."

"Well, listen, Tina," Elanna began, but broke off when the girl began to laugh.

"Tina?" The girl snorted, letting go of Elanna's arm long enough to hold her sides. "Nobody calls me Tina. The name's Golden. Or Sergeant, sometimes, but not Tina. You really are a dumbass."

Elanna mentally rolled her eyes. She wasn't about to argue with the girl over who, exactly, was the dumbass. "Golden, then. Or Sergeant Sometimes. Whatever. I have to pee."

"Yeah, yeah, I heard you," Golden said. "And I told you, I'm supposed to take you right to the General's office."

"Sergeant!"

Golden turned, laughter gone, and snapped her hand up to her head and down. "Sir, yes, Sir!"

An older girl, dressed in the same green clothes as all the others, had appeared from around the bend. "Get your asses up here! He's waiting!"

"Sir, Lieutenant Dowd, Sir!"

"Yes, Sergeant?" the older girl said wearily. Apparently, Elanna wasn't the only one who thought Sergeant Golden might be a little tarnished.

"Prisoner says she has to piss, Sir!"

Dowd sighed. "Release her to me, Golden. I'll take care of it."

"Sir, yes, Sir!"

Golden dropped Elanna's arm and pushed her toward Lieutenant Dowd. "Go with her. She'll take you to piss."

"Thanks." Elanna walked toward the girl, who looked about her own age. Lieutenant Dowd waited until Golden had scurried away before sighing and shaking her head.

"Dumbass," she said under her breath.

Elanna thought it might be wiser not to agree. Dowd took her by the upper arm and hurried her down the corridor again. She didn't look at her, and didn't speak to her.

"How much longer?" Elanna didn't have to fake the desperation in her voice. Her bladder was close to bursting.

"Shut up," Dowd said matter-of-factly. "Prisoners don't speak unless asked."

For some reason, the same words coming from Kodak, or even Tayler or Winslow, would have made her more afraid.

"I really need to go," Elanna said, not sure why she was tempting fate. Maybe she was just tired of being pushed around. Maybe she didn't have anything left to lose?

Dowd stopped, staring at her. Even in the dim light Elanna could see the look of incredulity in the Gapper's eyes.

"Didn't you hear me?" Dowd asked. "I said shut up?"

Elanna smiled. "And didn't you hear me? I said I really have to go. So unless you want me to wet my pants, I'd say let's quit yapping and start walking."

"Do you think I give a shit if you piss yourself?" Dowd asked.

"You might not," Elanna said. "But what about the General?"

Her statement had been nothing more than a guess, a taunt, but it worked. Dowd's expression changed to something like fear. She grabbed Elanna again and began pulling her.

"It's right up here," she said. "We're almost there."

"Baruch Ha-Shem," Elanna murmured, truly grateful.

The facilities were crude, but effective. She didn't know where the water came from to flush the toilet, but at least it did flush. She'd been expecting something more like a hole in the floor.

"Are you done?" Dowd asked, somewhat unnecessarily, since Elanna had pulled up her underwear and pants again.

"Done," Elanna replied.

"Then let's move it," Dowd said grimly, pushing Elanna out the door. "He doesn't like being kept waiting."

"Not a patient man?" Elanna asked more lightly than she felt. Now that she was that much closer to seeing this General, her bravery was fading.

"I wouldn't say that," Dowd said with a smile Elanna didn't like. "He can be patient about a lot of things. Mostly things you wouldn't like."

Elanna swallowed heavily. "I see."

"You might," Dowd said, with something like sympathy in her voice. "Here we are. You go alone."

She opened a door. Elanna had no choice. She took a deep breath, and then she stepped through.

Chapter 40

"This idea crazy is!" Rachel fretted, even as she wrapped hot, fresh bread in a clean towel and put it in the knapsack. She put in a small crock of butter, and one of jam, and some thick slices of cheese. She handed the filled sack to Tobin, her face lined with worry.

"Nobody to the Gappers has ever gone," she said, wringing her hands now they were no longer occupied. "Enoch, make the door shut! I want not the children to hear!"

Enoch did as she asked, closing the kitchen off from the rest of the house. "To the Gappers some have gone," he corrected. "Back here, none have come."

This didn't seem to make Rachel feel any better. She let out a wail and sat suddenly, covering her face with her apron. It didn't make Tobin feel too great, either, but at least he didn't start to cry.

Samuel huffed from the corner, where he sat in his chair by the stove. "No sense does grexing make, Rachel," he said. "The boy will to his woman go."

"I have to go. I have to find her, Rachel."

She nodded, wiping her eyes with the apron. "Ach, I know. But afraid for you I am, Tobin Vinter. Those Gappers are not nice."

That certainly was an understatement. "That's why I have to go tonight. Before they hurt Elanna. And before they come back here, looking for me."

Enoch clapped his hand on Tobin's shoulder. "Welcome to return you are," he said, with a quick look at the scowling Samuel. "To our people, join. With the Gappers we will deal, if we must."

"I'm not your problem," Tobin said, but Enoch's words moved him. Reb Ephraim had asked him to stay with the Tribe because of what he could bring them. These people just wanted him to stay. "We brought trouble with us, and I'm sorry about that. I'll do what I can to keep them from coming here, Enoch. But I don't know if I can stop them."

"We will ready be," Enoch said grimly.

Samuel rose from his corner. "Plain People do not fight!"

"And that is for years why these Gappers take what is ours, and nothing in return give us!" Enoch snapped.

Rachel gasped, her eyes flicking back and forth from her husband to her father. Tobin's heart twisted at the sight. He'd brought dissention to the Plain People. They'd taken him in with open arms, risking their own lives, and what had he given them in return? What Samuel insisted they did not do: a fight.

"And for years they have left us in peace," Samuel said, his old man's voice trembling. He sank back down in his chair. "You don't remember, Enoch Stolzfus, the times before."

"I know," Enoch interrupted, but more gently. "The times before. When the Gappers took by force, and the People suffered for it. But Vatter," Enoch sighed. "That before was. And ten years ago, the Gappers fought themselves, and now who is left? Girls. Only young girls. And still we stand silent when insult us they do, when our women and children they make cry. When their trucks they drive through the fields chust for so, to scare the horses and make the cows' milk sour run. When the crops they tear up, then demand their usual share. Ten years since their big battle, and still we give them food from our own babes' mouths. How much longer, Vatter Lapp? Until dead we all are? Until dead *they* all are? How much longer do we stand without fighting for what ours is?"

"Forever," said Samuel with conviction. "By order of our Holy Savior, who preached the other cheek to turn."

"He also said to thine own self be true, and if thine eye offend thee, pluck it out," Enoch said.

Rachel gasped again. "Enoch! Why you doing this are?"

Enoch turned to his wife. "For the babe this winter you will birth," he said. "For all the kinder."

Tobin stood awkwardly, wishing he hadn't been here to watch the family tearing itself apart. It was all his fault, he thought. But he couldn't change things.

"I need to go now," he told them, hating to interrupt. "It's dark."

"Directions I will give you," Enoch said. "Let me show you."

As he followed Enoch from the kitchen, Tobin paused to take Rachel's hands. "Thank you for everything," he said.

"Come to us back," Rachel told him, "and that will thanks enough be."

Chapter 41

The cavernous room was windowless, damp and cold. Lit by a few guttering candles, it was also mostly dark. Elanna stumbled inward, hearing the door slam behind her. Though her eyes were used to the dim light of the corridor outside, this room was even darker. She blinked, trying to see.

"Step up!" A voice demanded from the room's far side. "Closer!"

She squinted, searching the room while her eyes grew accustomed. "I can't see what's in front of me. I might fall."

A short, sharp laugh, more a bark than a sound of humor, reverberated through the room. "You are a smart little bitch, aren't you? And sassy, too. That's good. I like sassy."

Elanna risked a step toward the voice. Although the corners of the room would always remain in shadow, she could make out the outline of a large chair to her right. She turned toward it, praying the slickness she felt underfoot was just water seepage and not something more disgusting.

"You could use a little more light in here," she said, taking another step.

"Think so, do you?"

Elanna looked around at the candles, most no more than stubs. They not only provided a scant and wavering light, but they smelled bad, too. After learning from Samuel about the batteries, though, she found even these poor candles preferable to the battery powered lanterns the Tribe used.

"I do." Another cautious step, sliding her feet to make sure she didn't trip.

The voice from the throne was unmistakably male, though nothing else about the dark and hulking figure was clear. It shifted, one arm lifting and a hand pointing, but at what Elanna couldn't tell. At once, blinding light filled the room and burned her eyes.

With a sharp cry, Elanna threw up her hands to shield her face. The light was pure white, so bright and harsh it seemed tinged with purple around the edges. Beneath it her hands looked sickly green. With tearing eyes Elanna looked for the source, and saw it came from a series of long, rectangular boxes set into the ceiling.

"How's that?" Came the cold voice. "All the better to see you with, and all that shit?"

Blinking painfully, Elanna looked around her. The room was the largest she'd ever seen, even larger than the storerooms at home. Floor-to-ceiling shelving units divided it roughly in half. Boxes filled every shelf, so that she could see nothing that might be on the other side. Her side of the room was empty except for a raised platform of sort. On it was a chair unlike any she'd ever seen, and on the throne sat the man she thought must be the General.

"My, my," he said. "You are a pretty thing, aren't you?"

Elanna's eyes no longer hurt, but the light was still too bright. It outlined everything in sharp detail, down to the dirty cracks on the floor and the frayed laces in the General's boots. Even from this distance she could see the lines around his eyes.

"Cat got your tongue?" He looked bored. He beckoned her with one finger. "Come here."

She didn't have a choice, not really. Elanna did as he asked, glad to see that though the floor glittered damply in places there was nothing but water there. She stood in front of him, not daring to step up on the platform.

The General looked down at her from the throne. It had a high back, higher even than his head, and was covered in a smooth and gleaming sort of fabric that looked to her like the hide of some animal. Bright bullets of metal speckled the material, maybe to tack it to the wooden frame underneath. The arms were high, and the entire chair was on a circular base that rocked and swiveled as the General moved.

The chair was impressive, but the man sitting on it was even more so. Tobin had been the tallest man she'd seen, but this man, even seated, looked even taller. He sat with one long leg crossed nonchalantly over the other, leaning back in the chair, one arm crossed over his chest and the opposite hand supporting his chin. His finger, also long and finely formed, tapped a mouth that seemed made for smiling.

He wasn't smiling. He was staring, eyes narrowed and brow furrowed. She couldn't see the color of his eyes, but they glittered in the harsh light from above. His hair was the same color as the delicious stuff the Plain People called butter.

He could have been any age from eighteen to sixty, but Elanna guessed he was probably closer to forty. He wore the same green uniform as the other Gappers, but his was pressed and clean, and it fit him perfectly. A shiny row of medals marched across his broad chest, stopping at the gap in his jacket that showed a tight fitting tee shirt underneath.

He wasn't handsome; his skin was too lined and his face too grim for that. But he was compelling, she thought with a shiver of distaste. Power oozed from him like a dank cloud.

"Like what you see?"

The question startled her. Elanna realized she'd been gaping. "I'm not sure."

He quirked his eyebrow at her, leaning forward. "Really."

Elanna swallowed, aware that any move she made and anything she said might go horribly wrong. She was walking on chipped concrete. Any step could be false, and she wouldn't know it until she fell.

"Why did you bring me here?" She ventured, bravely she thought.

"Ah." The General sat back in his chair and crossed his arms again. His finger tap-tapped on his mouth as he continued staring at her. "Well. Let's see. Because you tried to breech our lines?"

"We didn't!" Elanna protested.

He held up a hand, silencing her. "Because you came in a car loaded with stuff I'd like more of?"

"You can have it," Elanna said. "You already do. Those teener girls took all of it."

The General favored her with a smirk. "But there must be more."

Tobin had told her this was what they wanted. For the first time, Elanna understood how he must have felt when Reb Ephraim asked him how to get to the warehouse. It hadn't seemed wrong or bad when it benefited the Tribe, but it did now.

"I can tell you how to get there," Elanna said. "And you can let me go. And Tobin, too."

"Tobin? Is that his name?"

Elanna nodded. The General snorted. He uncrossed his legs and began to rock the chair slowly, back and forth. The motion began to annoy her.

"Pansy ass name, I'd say," the General said, as though speaking to himself. "Pansy ass man, too. Though I must say our Kodak is quite a bruiser."

A bloodcurdling scream interrupted his words. Elanna jumped, heart pounding. The General's rich mouth thinned and he slammed both feet solidly to the floor, stopping the rocking.

"Shitdamnpissfucktits," he swore softly. His hands clenched the arms of the chair.

Elanna noticed that his not-handsome face had gone white. "What's that?"

"Nothing," he said.

The scream came again, punctuated this time by short, sobbing breaths. Elanna wanted to cover her ears against the pain in the sound. She looked behind the chair, along the wall, and saw a door. The screaming was coming from in there.

"It doesn't sound like nothing," she said.

The screams continued, rising into a seemingly impossible crescendo. Elanna thought whoever was making the noise would surely have to stop, but the sound went on and on until she thought she might scream herself.

And yet, wasn't there something familiar about the sound? She'd heard it before, hadn't she? She'd made that same sound herself, many times.

"Get it out!" Came the cry, and Elanna knew what was happening.

"Someone's having a baby," she said, pointing to the door. "In there."

The General put his head in his hands. "Shit. Yeah. I guess she is."

"You guess?" Elanna asked, wincing each time one of the screams leaked out from the door. "You don't know?"

"How could I know?" The General asked her, looking up with wet and weary eyes. "She didn't tell me she was pregnant."

Chapter 42

Samuel looked up at the sky, which had finally grown dark. "Time for you to go, naw vunst, ain't?"

Tobin nodded. "Yeah. It's time."

"Directions, you have?"

"Yes."

"Food? Water?"

"Yeah, thanks."

Samuel sighed heavily. "Ill luck I never wished you, Tobin Vinter."

"I know that, Samuel," Tobin said, though until the old man said it he would have guessed otherwise. "I'm sorry we brought trouble to your people."

Samuel snorted and waved his hand. "Go, naw. Get going. Elanna to save you must."

Tobin bent and picked up the knapsack Rachel had packed for him and the lightweight water jug. He slung both over his back, waiting for the weight to cause him pain and pleased when it didn't. At least not too much.

He'd changed back into his own jeans and shirt and the sneakers he'd found what seemed like years ago in the warehouse. Enoch had found an old baseball cap for him in the basement, instead of the straw one, and Tobin pulled it on his head. He turned back once as he left the yard, seeing the house behind him that had sheltered him for a while. The windows in the kitchen were alight, and several dark silhouettes stood shadowed there. Rachel and Enoch, with Samuel outlined in the doorway.

He raised a hand at them, and they returned the wave. Tobin stepped out through the neatly trimmed grass and in a few minutes reached the cracked and pitted pavement of the road. He didn't turn back again.

The directions were easy enough to follow. The road, though worn and sprung with weeds, took him back to the creek they'd jumped in the car. He didn't stop to look and see if the car still crouched in the high weeds. He had to get to Elanna.

He crossed the creek, remembering how Maranian had tumbled in. He was more careful. He took off his shoes and socks and rolled his pants legs up. The short delay gnawed at him and he forced the anxiety away. He'd get there, and if he took the time to do things right it would be better in the long run.

Once past the creek he stopped to remember what Enoch had told him.

"Road on the left," Tobin said aloud. Darkness swallowed his voice. "Past the burned building with the sign that says Harper's Tavern."

That was easy to see. There weren't any other buildings, burned or standing, on this side of the creek. Tobin put on his socks and tied his shoes. He noticed his fingers trembling and he forced them to stop. When they were still, he stood again and started walking.

This road would take him all the way to the fence surrounding the Gapper's territory. From there, Enoch had said, he'd be on his own. Tobin walked with only the night for company.

Chapter 43

The girl on the dirty pallet was young. Disgust rose in Elanna's throat at the sight of the filthy floor and the grimy, bloodstained sheets. The girl was beyond caring, her face contorted with pain and sheened with sweat.

The scream that had been loud enough to make Elanna want to cover her ears in the outside room was deafening in this small space. The scream trailed off into a strangled cry and a whimper, and the girl appeared to pass out. Her eyes fluttered and her hands, which had been clutching at the dirty sheet covering the impossibly small mound of her belly, fell open.

Four, no five, other girls hovered around the low bed not doing much of anything, but when the girl screamed Elanna saw her pain reflected in their faces. One of them covered her eyes and moved away from the bed. One of them held the girl's hand, her fingers turning red and then white as the screaming girl's grip kept the blood from flowing. One of them, stationed at the foot of the bed, fussed with a basin half-filled with water gone pinkish from blood and a ragged, sopping rag. The other two stood one each side of the door like sentries, staring, their faces slack with shock.

"How long has she been like this?" Elanna asked, shouldering her way past the sentries and into the room. She moved to the girl's side, touched her forehead and pulled back her hand at the heat there.

"Since last night," the girl with the basin said. Dark circles shadowed her red and irritated eyes. "The pains started yesterday afternoon."

"Since last night?" Elanna cried, shocked at the brutality of it. "And you've done nothing for her besides let her scream?"

The one holding the basin grew defensive. "What could we do?"

"Move out of the way," said Elanna without preamble, moving to take the other girl's place.

"Who the hell are you?" Said the Gapper she was replacing, refusing to move. "Who…?"

"Move your fucking ass!" Elanna roared and shoved the Gapper girl's shoulder. The girl fell backward, spilling the dirty water all over the floor.

Elanna didn't take the time to see what the other girl would do. She knelt at the foot of the bed and pulled away the sheet that had dropped down. What she saw encouraged her even as it enraged her. Between the laboring girl's parted legs, Elanna glimpsed the pulsing skin of a newborn's head.

"She's crowning!" She yelled, just as the girl screamed again. Elanna watched as the girl's muscles contracted, rippling, and the baby's head grew more visible. The contraction ended along with the girl's agonized scream, but the baby's head had not moved any further. Blood trickled from a tear in the girl's perineum, and Elanna used a corner of the sheet to blot it away.

She turned to the other girls, who were just standing there. "I need fresh water, boiled. And some clean sheets! Or towels, something to wrap the baby in! And something sharp and clean to cut the cord with!"

None of them had moved. Elanna's throat convulsed with fear and rage. Their incompetence, their laziness, could kill this child and its mother. She'd seen too many births that had gone like this one, the mother too tired from hours of labor to push the child free of the womb. If she didn't help, and soon, they both would likely die.

"Hummer, Smith, Brown! Do as she says," came a male voice. The General. He'd entered the door behind her. His face looked pale and strained. He wiped fitfully at his mouth, as though trying to wipe away the taste of something bad. "Go! Now! Thomas and Charles! Go with them!"

The girls moved, scattering like leaves in the wind, leaving Elanna alone with the General and the girl on the bed. The man moved to the girl's side, looking down on her with an expression Elanna couldn't fathom. It was like he was watching with someone else's eyes.

"Don't just stand there," Elanna ordered, as the girl's body began another assault. "Help her!"

He looked at her blankly. "What?"

"Hold her hand," Elanna said impatiently. "And help me prop her up. Put your hand under her knee and hold it up. She needs to push this baby out or it's going to die."

"Die!" The General's mouth bent into a grimace.

"That's what I said," Elanna said cruelly, not sparing him. "Unless we help her. Now, move!"

The man crouched down beside the girl, who had become lucid after her last contraction. She looked up at him, eyes clearing as she recognized his face. The girl reached out and clutched his hand with a desperation Elanna remembered feeling herself.

"Adam!"

"C'mon now, soldier," the General said sternly. "Get through this. Buck up."

Elanna was busy pressing her fingers against the girl's bulging flesh to prevent more tearing, but she glanced up anyway. "Use her name, for the sake of Ha-Shem."

"What?"

His stupidity infuriated her. "Her name! She's not a soldier, she's a girl, and I'd bet she has a name! Use it!"

"Lansing," the General said as the girl began to gasp with the onset of another contraction. "Come on, now, Lansing."

"Is that the name you call her when you fuck her?" Elanna spat, focusing on the contraction ripping through Lansing's uterus. "General?"

"Amy!" He cried, and she heard in his voice that he hated her. He turned back to the girl struggling below him, and his voice was more tender. "Amy, come on girl! You can do this, sweetheart!"

The baby's head throbbed beneath Elanna's fingers as it struggled to be born. The contraction was strong, but not strong enough. She felt the flutter of the baby's pulse in its soft spot, and prayed she was only imagining that it was growing weaker.

"When the next contraction comes you have to push!"

The girl didn't, or couldn't hear. Or perhaps couldn't understand. She lay back weakly, panting, though her grip on the General's hand didn't let go.

The next one started with no more than a few seconds rest. They were coming almost on top of each other now, pushing the baby out from the uterus and through the birth canal, but slowly. Too slowly.

"Push!" Elanna ordered.

"Push, Amy! That's an order!" The General thundered.

Elanna risked another glance at him. His face was white. He looked terrified.

"I can't!" Amy wailed.

"You have to!" Elanna watched the mound of the girl's belly swell again. She stood up, moving to Amy's side and placed both hands on her belly, feeling the outline of a small rump, legs and feet. "Now!"

"Fuck you!" Amy screamed, nearly lifting herself off the bed as the contraction tore through her.

"Fuck me if you have to," Elanna said, bending down to the girl's face. "But if you don't push this baby out you're both going to die. Now push!"

Amy screamed again but bore down. She'd been in labor too long and was too tired. Even with Elanna and the General each holding up a knee the pushing didn't help. The baby was still stuck.

"I don't know how!" Amy sobbed in exhaustion.

Elanna didn't like the pallor of her skin or the deep, bruised half-moons under her eyes. Amy's hair hung in lank, sweaty strands over her forehead. Elanna wished for a cloth to wipe the girl's face, and cursed the slow moving soldiers who still hadn't returned with what she needed.

"From your bottom," she told the girl, telling her the same thing she'd been told herself. "Push from your bottom."

"What? What the hell does that mean?" Amy gasped. "Ah, fuck, here comes another one!"

Elanna didn't know what to tell her. Amy needed to push, and hard, and do it now. Inspiration struck. "Like you have to take a shit!"

Amy nodded suddenly and bore down, pushing. A gush of blood and birth fluid splattered from between her legs and the baby's head popped free at last.

"Again!"

Amy pushed again, face purpling with the effort, too intent even to scream. As Amy pushed, Elanna pressed down on her belly, using her full weight. The baby slid a little further.

"Fuck, that hurts!" Amy gasped.

"You're doing it, Amy," Elanna told her. "Just a few more pushes."

"You can do it," The General said. He was watching the bottom of the bed with shocked intensity. "Push, Amy. Push hard, sweetheart."

With a guttural moan, Amy did. Elanna left her side and knelt back between her legs. She reached up to cradle the infant's head, easing it to the side and squeezing the nostrils to clear some of the birth fluid. As Amy pushed, Elanna tilted the shoulder, bringing it smoothly out. Once the shoulder passed, the rest of the child slid into her hands with amazing speed.

"God! God! God!" Amy cried as the child slipped out of her.

Elanna cradled the bloody infant with practiced hands, turning it onto its belly and clearing its mouth and throat with her finger. It coughed and then began to cry. "Where's the stuff I need?"

It came none too soon. The other girls burst through the door, one tripping. The towels, a dingy white, fell on the floor.

"Pick them up!" Elanna cried, clutching the slippery baby to her chest as it wriggled and wailed. "And I need the water."

They didn't spill it, Baruch Ha-Shem. And it was clean, or fairly so, and still steaming. She jerked her head toward the closest girl.

"Get a towel. A clean one."

The baby squirmed, its tiny fists flailing. The umbilical cord trailed from its belly back inside the mother.

"The knife!"

They handed her a knife as large as her hand, but it would do. Tucking the infant under one arm, she sliced the cord and clamped it with her fingers, rolling the edges in the way the other hope-mothers had taught her to stop the bleeding.

"It's a boy," she said to Amy reverently and placed the naked child on the clean towel draped over her chest.

Amy reached up to hold the child, her face streaked by tears and sweat. The General looked stunned. The girls crowded around, silently. Elanna had never been to a birth so unheralded.

"You're not done yet, Amy," she said. "You need to push again."

A few last contractions forced the placenta out, and Elanna caught it deftly in one of the towels that had fallen on the floor. She set it aside, uncertain what rituals these people might have for its disposal and prepared to clean Amy and the child.

She pressed a folded towel, soaked in the hot water, between Amy's legs and stood to take the child and wipe it. She stopped, frightened, as the dingy white towel bloomed red with blood almost immediately.

"She's hemorrhaging." Elanna grabbed the rest of the towels and pressed them down. They, too, became wet with blood within seconds.

"Take the baby," she ordered one of the girls, who did so fumblingly. "I need more towels. More water. Help me!"

Amy's arm fell limply off the bed, hanging down toward the floor. Lifeless. No, Elanna thought. No, not now. Not this.

But she couldn't stop the bleeding. It gushed out of the girl on the table, more blood than Elanna would have thought one person could have inside her. It covered the sheets, the bed, the towels, the floor. It covered Elanna herself as she worked to stanch it, rich and earthy smelling, the smell of birth and womanhood.

And finally, the smell of death.

Chapter 44

Once there'd been a high fence of metal links here, but time had done to it what it did to everything else. Now the fence sagged in more places than not, and Tobin had no trouble finding a place to crawl over. The moon gave him enough dim light to see by, but his dark clothes would make him a difficult target to spot. He kept walking, refusing to think about what might happen if he was going in the wrong direction.

He'd ache all over in the morning, but for now the constant movement kept him muscles warm and working. He'd gone beyond the pain, urging each foot forward with thoughts of finding Elanna.

The building loomed up before him almost before he realized it was there. His feet crunched on the rocks and he froze, waiting. Nothing. The windows, many of them glassless and gaping, were dark. At least here. The building itself was a huge, flat-walled box, marked only by the empty spaces of its windows. Not even a door.

Squinting, Tobin looked to left and right. More of the same buildings, so far as he could see. In the distance to his right was a line of smaller ones, whiter in the darkness. They looked more like houses than anything else. What had Enoch called them? Barracks.

He had no idea where he was going to find Elanna, but he didn't have time to waste. He'd start with this building, the one in front of him, but first he'd have to find the door. One direction looked as good or bad as the other, but he chose to go right.

As he turned the corner, a smaller building loomed ahead. Though most of it was as dark as the others, in one or two of the windows he spotted faint, flickering glows. This is where the people were.

Not for the first time, he wished he had a weapon. Even a hoe or a stick with a spike on the end of it would make him feel better than walking into certain danger completely unarmed. Going up against a known enemy, Kodak and her troops, was better than going blind, but they had guns and he didn't. Not a good match.

Not that he could have shot a gun, should he find one. His skills of derring-do were limited to what he'd read about James Bond. He'd have to rely on what he knew he had in abundance, his wits. He was counting on them being a weapon the Gappers didn't know how to use.

Finding his way into the building was easy. The massive metal double doors both hung open, one off its hinges. Even in the dim light he could see deep scratches in the peeling paint where the silver metal glimmered through. Both doors were battered, dented and flaking with rust. More than just the passage of time had done this. Someone, sometime, had beaten these doors with something big and heavy.

Whoever it was had gotten in, too, he thought as he stepped through. And been met with a welcoming committee. He couldn't see too far ahead into the dark hallway, but the floor just inside the doorway was stained dark with splatters of what he assumed was blood. Old blood that had never been cleaned up.

With a shudder, Tobin moved further into the darkness and paused. Without light, he had no chance of proceeding silently. Or seeing where he was going without being seen himself. The corridor stretched far in front of him, but he had no idea how long it was, or even if there were other doors and halls branching from it. It was just too damn dark.

Waiting for daylight would take too long and be too risky.

Damnit, he had to act now! But what to do? He had no candles, no lantern, not even a match.

He didn't have the chance to curse his indecision. A door he hadn't seen directly behind him opened, and light poured out.

"NO! NO!" The General fell to his knees beside Amy's unresponsive body and gathered her into his arms. She lolled against him, arms flailing and head bending on her neck.

Elanna stood covered in blood, helpless to do anything but watch the man cradle the dead girl. She was wiped out, exhausted and close to tears herself, but she hadn't known the girl. The General had not only known her, but it seemed he also might have loved her. Elanna's heart went out to him.

"I'm sorry," she ventured.

He turned on her, face contorted in pain and rage. He let Amy's body slip to the bed with a thud that made Elanna jump. In a flash he was in front of her, gripping her upper arms with fists like iron.

"Sorry?" He asked in a low, dangerous voice. His face was so close to hers she could see the broken blood vessels in his eyes and smell the sharpness of his sweat. "You're more than sorry, bitch. You're dead."

The fear Elanna had dodged in the throne room hit her now. The man in front of her was dangerous, and he was nasty, but as she searched his eyes Elanna discovered one more thing. He was sane. Madness might have excused him, but no trace of it flickered in his eyes. Whatever he planned for her, it sprang from cold and calculating anger and not insanity.

"Why?" Was all she could ask, hating the whining sound in her own voice. She dared not struggle, even though his fingers were digging into her flesh.

"Because you killed her," the General said.

"I didn't kill her." Elanna heard the baby crying, a sound that made her breasts tingle in memory. "I tried to help her."

"You let her die," the General said. "It's the same thing."

"Then you killed her just as much as I did," Elanna hissed. "Because you're the one who got her pregnant!"

He threw her to the ground. Elanna slid in the blood-mucked floor, scrambling to get away from him before he kicked her, or worse. The General didn't come after her. He only stood, staring, fists clenched and stone-faced.

Elanna got to her feet. The baby was still wailing and she risked a glance at the girl who held it. She looked terrified, holding the squirming, red-faced infant out from her body as though it might scald her. Elanna hadn't had time to properly swaddle the child, and its towel was sliding off. Soon, she could see, the girl would drop it.

Elanna didn't care if the man grabbed her. She couldn't let the baby hit the floor. She turned her back to the General, expecting to feel his hands on her again at any minute, and took the squalling infant out of the other girl's hands. She wrapped the baby snugly again and held it to her chest. It quieted, rooting. Elanna looked at the dead girl and bent to press her cheek to the baby's still-moist head.

"I didn't kill her," she repeated quietly. "And I didn't let her die. I couldn't stop it. Maybe if I'd been able to help her sooner--"

"Brown! Smith!" He was no longer looking at Amy's corpse. In fact it was as though she'd disappeared, the way his eyes slid over her without seeing.

The two Gappers who'd brought the water and towels snapped to attention with identical cries of "Sir!" The General stood tall. His face was no longer so pale.

"Take the prisoner to the interrogation room," he said flatly.

"Sir!"

"Yes, Brown?"

"What about the…the…thing, Sir? The baby?"

The General focused for a moment on the bundle in Elanna's arms. "Throw it out the window."

Elanna's grip tightened on the now-quiet child. She'd made it through the blood and death without wavering, but at the General's harsh words her gorge rose. She took a step back, bumping against the wall. She had no place else to go.

"You will not touch this baby," she said.

The soldiers who'd been moving toward her hesitated, perhaps moved by something in her tone. Elanna shuddered but stood her ground. She locked eyes with the General, who looked at her without expression. He swallowed once, then twice and she watched the movement of his throat each time.

"Let her keep it, then, if she wants it," he said. "For now, anyway."

He jerked his head to the doorway and turned his back, dismissing them. Brown and Smith each took one of Elanna's elbows. She let them lead her to the doorway, if only to protect the baby by not resisting them.

Before she let them push her through the door, she hung back. The entire night seemed like a dream, something she couldn't quite comprehend. She spoke to the General's back, unaware until she spoke that she would sound so pleading.

"This is your son," she said. "Your *son*!"

"Get her out of here," he replied, and Brown and Smith followed his orders.

Chapter 45

"What the fuck?" The girl who'd opened the door cried in regular Gapper style.

Tobin turned as she spoke, locking his arm around her neck and covering her mouth with his hand. Keeping her pressed against him, her arms held to her sides by his arms, he pulled her out into the hallway. She struggled against his chest, but without use of her arms she couldn't do much more. She kicked out, but facing away from him her flailing legs connected only with the air. The lantern she'd been carrying fell to the ground but thankfully didn't break.

He waited for someone to follow her, but she was alone. Without letting go of her, Tobin bent and hooked the lantern with one finger. She kicked out again as he straightened, but he managed to keep hold of it. Without its light, the place would be pitch black again.

He pushed the door open and pulled her through. The room was too vast for the lantern to fully illuminate, but from what he could see, it was filled with long shelving units laden with boxes and packages.

The girl, so far as he could tell, was unarmed. She wore the same dull green as all the others he'd seen, but this time a thin short-sleeved shirt and a pair of pants cut off at the leg. In the lantern light, her hair gleamed like silver. Because she was facing away from him, he couldn't see her face.

He couldn't risk her screaming. "I have a knife," he said into her ear. "I'll stick it in your head the second you open your mouth to do more than breathe. Got it?"

The girl, nodded. Tobin kept his grip on her arm and slowly turned her to face him as he let his hand slide away from her mouth. He tensed, waiting for the yell, but she must have believed him about the knife. As he saw her face, he realized with a pang of guilt how young she really was. Then he saw who she was.

"Dallas?"

The girl, eyes bright with tears, nodded. "You're the man from town!"

"My name's Tobin. Dallas, I need you to take me to Elanna."

She coughed, as though she'd swallowed the wrong way. "I don't know."

But he'd seen the truth in her eyes and he stepped in before she could finish the lie. "Don't waste my time. Where is she?"

He saw with another flash of guilt that his grip had begun to bruise her thin arms. Her head only came up to the top of his chest, if that, and she seemed to weigh no more than a feather pillow. He was using his strength against someone so much smaller than himself…and that was shameful.

Smaller, but not defenseless, he thought, thinking of Kodak and her crew. Even this young girl, whose eyes he now could see were deep, dark blue, was trained for combat. She had no gun, but that didn't mean she couldn't fight.

"Major Kodak brought her in," Dallas said. "The General wanted to see her."

"Is that where Elanna is now? With her?"

Dallas looked at him strangely. "The General isn't a chick."

Her sentence made no sense. Chicks were fuzzy yellow birds hatched from eggs. "What?"

"A chick," Dallas said. "You know. A woman. He's a dude. A man. He's the General. Didn't you know that?"

He didn't bother to answer that. "And Elanna is with him?"

Dallas looked wary. “They took her and the baby to the interrogation room after she let Lansing die.”

Her words made a cold sweat break out on his skin. “What’s the interrogation room?”

But Dallas seemed to regret the information she’d already given him. She shook her head. “I’ve told you too much already. If Kodak found out -- ”

“If you tell me how to get to Elanna and promise not to alert anyone that I’m here,” Tobin said, “I’ll make sure Kodak never finds out who told me.”

Dallas shook her head again. “She’ll find out. She always knows.”

He felt sorry for this girl-child, who’d grown up with guns and curses rather than love. She didn’t have much future, he thought. She was destined to become another Kodak.

“Dallas,” he said gently. “If you take me to Elanna, you can come with us when we leave.”

She wanted to believe him. He saw it in her eyes. But then she shook her head again, fiercely. “No! Why would I want to leave?”

“Take me to her,” Tobin urged. “Before it’s too late.”

“If she’s in the interrogation room with The General,” Dallas whispered with a shudder, “it’s already too late.”

Chapter 46

"Again," ordered the General, his voice bored. "Until she's clean, I said."

Elanna crouched, cringing, waiting for the blast of icy water. In a second it came, full force, stinging like a thousand needles piercing her skin. She gasped, helpless, the frigid water shocking the breath from her lungs.

"Stand up!" Kodak, who held the hose, turned the nozzle again, and again the water blasted forth.

Elanna turned, letting the water strip away Lansing's blood and praying they'd finish soon. Even over the roar from the hose, she could hear the tiny boy crying from his place on the floor. He would be getting wet, too, she thought as she pushed her hair off her face with numbed fingers. She had to get him off the floor, and dry.

"Enough," said the General.

Kodak, chuckling with evil glee, continued to spray the water. She aimed for Elanna's softest parts, her breasts, belly and the juncture between her legs, and also her eyes. Elanna raised her hands to block the sting from her face.

Abruptly the blast of water stopped. Elanna opened her eyes to see Kodak kneeling in front of the General, who had both hands knitted into her hair.

"I gave you an order," The General said, staring down at Kodak without expression. "Isn't that right, you little bitch?"

"Sir, yes Sir!" Kodak said in a strangled voice.

"And you ignored my order, didn't you, bitch?"

"Sir, yes Sir!"

The General pushed her away from him so that she sprawled in a puddle of icy, dirty water. "And what punishment do you think is appropriate for such a misdemeanor, soldier?"

Kodak shook her head, seemingly without words. Elanna began to shiver. She found the towel-wrapped child along the wall and gathered it to her chest. Its tiny lips were blue, and it shivered. It had stopped crying.

"I can think of a lot of things," the General said in a mild voice. He sounded like he was talking about the weather. "But I think I'll just send you away for now, Kodak. You're denied the privilege of helping me with this interrogation."

"No!" Kodak cried, standing. "No, Sir, I --"

"Shut the fuck up," the General said in the same mild tone. "And get out. Before you make me angry."

Kodak scuttled away, out the door. The General turned, looking at Elanna with a bored face. She stared back at him defiantly.

"This baby needs dry clothes. And food."

"Why do you care so much about that thing? It isn't even yours."

Elanna looked down at the sweet face, sunk into exhausted sleep. "How can you not care? It's *yours*."

In reply, he tossed her a soft, dry blanket from the table next to his chair. Both table and chair were on a small raised platform, above the water that swirled only sluggishly down the drain in the center of the room. Elanna managed to catch the blanket, and she let the child's dirty, sodden towel fall on the floor.

As the blanket warmed it, the little boy began to root again, nuzzling instinctively at her breast. The familiar sensation tugged her nipples. Elanna let him suckle, though she wasn't certain he'd bring anything forth. The suckling soothed the baby, anyway, even as the unforgettable feeling of it clenched her womb. She felt a fine trickle of blood on her thigh but had nothing with which to wipe it away.

She glanced up to find the General looking at her with amazed disgust plain on his face. He shuddered and seemed to force back a gag.

"God," he muttered. "That's how they eat?"

Elanna didn't answer. She was shivering too violently. She looked longingly at the pile of clothes on the table.

He saw her looking. "Cold?"

The General flicked a switch and overhead lights the color of fire came on, bathing everything in a hot glow. She felt the heat from them and raised her face to it, grateful. So intense was the heat that it dried her in minutes, and a few minutes more made the room start to become unbearably hot.

"I don't mind the heat myself." The General smiled thinly, avoiding looking at her chest. "I'm always cool."

The infant had fallen slack-lipped from her breast. It slept, tiny fists curled and cheeks pink. His tuft of pale hair had dried, sticking up from his pulsing skull. He was beautiful.

"If it's done," the General said, "put it down and stand in front of me."

He gestured to a basket she hadn't seen before. They could have put the baby in it before, she thought furiously as she placed the sleeping boy in it. Instead they'd tossed him to the floor like garbage. She shot a livid glance at the General. He saw her looking, and smiled.

"Here, in front of me," he repeated, gesturing.

She did, lifting her chin and refusing to show her fear.

"Not afraid to show your tits, huh?"

Elanna frowned. She looked down at herself, cleaned of blood and grime. Her nipple, where the baby had suckled, was red and rigid, though the color was fading back to its normal pale pink.

"Why would I be?" He couldn't know, she reflected, that she'd stood naked before men so many times it meant nothing to her.

He looked at her speculatively. "You're not one of them. Those Plain assholes."

"No."

His eyes flicked down to her leg. She expected more disgust, but the sight of her blood didn't seem to offend him. "You on the rag?"

"What?"

He pointed. "That. You're bleeding."

"I…I had a miscarriage a few days ago," she said with dignity.

He tossed her a towel. "Wipe it off."

She did, but more came to take its place. She tucked the towel between her legs, knowing she looked awkward and embarrassed. He didn't seem to notice.

"Christ, you're stacked," the General said. "Turn around."

She hesitated a second before complying, and he was on his feet and in her face in a second. He didn't touch her, didn't grab her, but his look was so menacing it made her stumble back a step. The towel fell off. Her feet sloshed in the last remnants of the water.

"When I give an order, I expect it to be done. Immediately."

"I'm not one of your soldiers," she said.

He stared at her. "You think I give a fuck? You do what you're told."

She lifted her chin. "Or what?"

He cocked his head like a curious bird. "Or I hurt you."

She would have been less frightened if he'd yelled. She thought again that if he were crazy she'd know how to react, how to watch him and expect him to behave. But this soft voice, this calm exterior, scared her more than rolling eyes and ranting would have.

"Is that how you get them to do what you want?" She asked, quaking inside. "Is that how you got Amy into your bed?"

Now his eyes flickered. She saw his fists clench and release, so fast she might have imagined it. She'd struck him in a vulnerable spot.

"Don't even let her name get dirty on your lips," he said in a low voice. "Sit down. There, on my chair. Put a fucking towel down first so you don't get blood all over it."

"And if I don't?"

He looked at her naked body, blood trickling down her thighs, and then met her eyes. "You can't stand against me, bitch. My soldiers can't, and you sure as hell can't. Don't even try."

She didn't think he was joking, but something inside her made her resist.

"Az men ken nit beissen, zol men nit veizen di tsain," she muttered in Yiddish. *Those who can't bite should not show their teeth.*

"A hunt on tsain varft zich oich oif a bain," he answered, shocking her. "A dog without teeth also attacks a bone."

"You understood?"

"Of course I do," he replied. "How do you expect to know your enemy if you can't speak their language?"

He was talking about the Plain People. "They don't have to be your enemy," she said.

"We were sent here to keep peace and order," he muttered.

"That was a long time ago. Things have changed. And they *are* peaceful --"

"Shut the fuck up. You don't know anything."

"So is that all you are?" she asked. "A dog?"

"Sit down in that chair," the General told her in that same calm voice, "Or I slice that lump of shit in that basket into a hundred different pieces and feed him to my troops."

She looked at the baby, who still made no peep. "You can't!"

"I can," the General said, and Elanna knew he'd just discovered her weak spot. He wouldn't hesitate to use it. "Don't think I won't."

Elanna sat, her brief resistance gone. "Don't hurt the baby."

"Put your arms on the arms of the chair."

When she did, he reached deftly beneath them and pulled up the straps she hadn't noticed. He fastened them in mere seconds, pulling them tight enough to cut into her flesh. He tied one more over each wrist, rendering her hands immobile. More straps came out to pinion her legs and feet to the chair legs. She couldn't move. The seat was hard and unforgiving, especially against her bare skin. She'd forgotten to put down the towel.

Elanna winced but said nothing. She thought about the baby. Thought that soon it would wake on its own, hungry again, and that soon she'd have to find something better for it to wear. Cloths for diapers, and a softer blanket…

When the General ripped off the fingernail from her right forefinger, Elanna threw back her head at the agony of it. She wanted to scream, tried to scream, but sheer pain had knocked her breathless. She writhed in her bonds, barely even able to squirm.

"Shhh," said the General soothingly. "Don't wake the baby."

The baby. The baby. She had to think of the child whose life she'd saved. The unwanted infant whose mother died to bring it life. The baby.

Her chin slumped to her chest, and she saw the bloody ruin of her finger. He'd used a pliers, and now he tapped them gently into the palm of his hand. And smiled at her. Hateful, hateful smile.

"On second thought," the General said, leaning close to her so his cheek pressed against hers, "who gives a shit about that baby? Scream for me, pretty lady. Scream real loud."

Elanna found she had no choice.

Chapter 47

General Adam Townsend waited until the bitch's screams died away on their own rather than plug her mouth with one of the dirty cloths he usually saved for that purpose. He watched her dispassionately as she sagged in the torture chair. There was much, much more he could do here, but suddenly he didn't feel like it anymore.

He realized he was bored. And tired. And jeezly Christ, his eyes stung with a sensation he remembered from when he was a child, though it had been more than thirty years since the last time he'd actually wept.

Amy was dead, killed by the brat he'd got on her. He glanced over at the thing in its basket. Like the woman before him, it had screamed itself silent too. Adam repressed a shudder as the basket moved a little when the creature inside it waved its arms.

"Why?" The woman asked him. Elanna. He remembered them saying her name was Elanna, and now she looked up at him from red-rimmed eyes.

Unbroken, he thought with amazement. She was still able to talk, still able to question him. He looked at his pliers, a trusty and well-used tool, but didn't feel like using them. He didn't feel, Adam realized as he tossed them to the ground, like hurting her anymore.

"Why what?" He asked her, more from surprise that she'd asked him then any desire to actually talk to her.

"Why…do this to me?" She wheezed. Snot and tears dripped from her face. Her tits and thighs and belly bore the marks of his hands.

With something like shock, he realized he didn't even feel like fucking her. The stinging in his eyes grew worse. Could it be, he thought, that he was grieving for Amy?

"Because I can," he replied. "Because you took something away from me that I…."

He stopped, stunned. "That I loved."

"…didn't…." Elanna breathed. Her eyes drooped, and then her head fell back down.

Adam tried to find the anger that simmered beneath the surface of his emotions for as long as he could remember. The anger had helped him rise through the admittedly sorry ranks of what remained of this poor excuse for an army. It had let him demand, and receive, the power which had forced the few remaining oldsters, those who didn't agree with his policies, to back down and obey his orders. It was even the anger that fueled the charms that had wooed the growing army of girl-soldiers into abandoning their parents and making him their leader.

Their lover, their father, their God. The one who commanded them to force the rest of the adults, those who wanted to defy him, out of the barracks and away. He was the man who'd ordered the barrier, who'd overseen the teams of girls, none older than twelve then, as they'd ransacked the countryside looking for things to use in building the wall. And when their parents, the oldsters, the ones who thought it might be time to put down the guns and stop the war, had tried to cross and reclaim their children, he'd been the man who'd led those girls into the fray. They'd slaughtered that off-shoot army, and left their sad, tired bodies to rot as a lesson to anyone else who thought to cross him.

For ten years he'd fucked and bullied his way through the battalion of young girls and women he'd inherited. Trained them to be strong and hard, and unforgiving, just as he'd been trained.

Trained them to be soldiers. None had ever died. And he'd never loved any of them until Amy.

"Agh, Christ," he muttered. "Jumped up fucking Jesus on a crutch."

Elanna didn't say anything. He thought she might have passed out, finally. The thought of rousing her for more punishment didn't even get his cock to twitch, much less make him hard. He was tired, dammit.

The baby in the basket let out a peep. Then the anger came back, not full force but a taste of it was enough. Adam leapt up on the platform and stood over the basket in three swift steps. Fists clenched, he looked inside at the thing that had grown inside Amy Lansing and killed her by being born.

It had been twelve years since he'd even seen a baby. Sophie Dallas was the last one born here, and he guessed she was a big part of why the oldsters had finally turned against him. They'd called him a monster and a pervert, and why? Because he took a taste of what had been practically shoved in his face?

So what if Sophie's mother had only been twelve years old? Old enough to bleed, old enough to breed. He didn't stop taking what he wanted just because they ordered him to. Little Sophie'd still been pissing in her diapers when the great barrier war had gone down. She hadn't even been there. Probably why she was no good as a soldier, either.

This baby didn't look anything like he remembered. This one was plump and rosy cheeked, batting its tiny fists in the air and squirming in its blanket. It had golden fuzz on its head. As he watched, it kicked off its blanket and pissed, sending a surprisingly strong stream of urine into the air.

Adam jumped back, grunting with disgust. This thing had grown for nine months inside Amy's womb, then torn itself out of her. It had killed her.

He glanced back at Elanna, still slumped in her chair. He'd taken no pleasure in her screams or her blood. Hadn't even managed to get it up enough to fuck her like she deserved to be fucked. And why? Because this little ankle-biter in the basket had killed Amy.

For the first time in ten years he didn't want to be in charge any more. He didn't want to make the orders, or run the drills. He wanted to crawl into the bed he and Amy had shared, and put his face in her hair that always smelled like springtime, and feel her arms around him.

When had she turned from just another of the girl soldiers he'd taken to bed, to the girl who could make him laugh just by crossing her eyes? He'd told himself it was just because she was so great in the sack that he'd stopped fucking anyone else. How could he not have known that he loved her?

Christ, this was fucked up. He scrubbed his face, feeling the stubble there. Everything was shit. He didn't care about the bitch in the chair. He didn't even care about the car she'd come in, or the all the stuff in it.

In his whole miserable fucking life he'd only really cared about one thing, and now Amy Lansing was dead. What else really mattered? Commanding a bunch of women in an army that hadn't been any good in over a hundred years? Harassing those Plain morons down in the valley?

The baby yawned and whimpered, but Adam only looked at it with loathing. He didn't want a kid. Not even a boy child he could train to be just like him. He'd kill the brat and kill the bitch, and then maybe he'd kill the rest of them, too. Better yet, he'd order Kodak to do it. She was one cold bitch, and she'd get more pleasure from doing it than he would anymore. He'd toss her that bone. He guessed, after all these years, he might owe her that much.

"Don't you move or I'll blow your goddamn head off!"

When the door flew open and the man burst through it, Adam figured it was as good a way to go out as any.

"Welcome to Hell," he said to the intruder, and he took a step forward.

Chapter 48

Tobin held the gun as Dallas had shown him, using two hands and spreading his legs wide. The gun had no bullets in it. He wasn't sure he'd be able to hit his target even if it did. Dallas had told him the General wouldn't know for sure the gun wasn't loaded unless Tobin pulled the trigger.

"Welcome to Hell," the man in green said. He raised his hands as though to show he had no weapons, but instead of staying where he was, he moved toward Tobin.

"I said don't move!" Tobin shouted, re-aiming the gun.

The General kept moving, crossing the concrete floor with swift, relentless strides. He stopped just out of arm's reach, as though taunting him. Tobin kept his hands steady. Holding up the weapon made his arms ache.

"The fuck are you?" the General asked with a sneer.

Tobin was really tired of that question. "I'm here for Elanna."

"Ah. Tobin. The man with the pussy name."

Tobin knew an insult when he heard one. "Give me Elanna, and I won't kill you."

The General jerked his head backward. "There she is, champ. Be my guest."

Tobin followed the General's gesture and saw her. Naked and strapped to the chair, her head hanging down so that her auburn hair fell in limp strands to obscure her face. Dark splatters of what he sickly realized was blood covered her hands and arms.

He forced himself to look away from her. He couldn't help her now, not until he took care of the General. Ice coated his throat and made his eyes burn with cold fury.

"If you've hurt her," he spat, "I will kill you."

For one brief moment the General's expression turned bleak and tired before shifting back to antagonistic scorn. "Go ahead, bright boy," he said. "It's as good a way to go as any."

The man stepped toward him, into Tobin's reach, and grabbed for the gun. Tobin gripped it hard, refusing to let go despite being taken unawares. The General drove his fist into Tobin's stomach, and wrenched the gun away. In the time it took to blink, the soldier reversed the situation.

Tobin stared at the barrel of the gun, unafraid. Dallas had said it was unloaded. Everything seemed to slow, even the beating of his heart. He would not be beaten. Not this time. Not ever again.

"Let her go, and I won't kill you."

The General laughed, waving the gun. "Seems to me you lost your chance at that, champ. I've got the gun. I have to admit, I'd hoped for a challenge. You couldn't even give me that."

Tobin stepped forward, bringing his fist up toward the other man's jaw and taking him by surprise. The General took the hit full on the chin, stumbling back a few steps. He didn't let go of the gun.

Before the soldier could get his balance back, Tobin leaped on him. Violence had never felt so good. His fists slammed into the other man wherever they landed. With each blow he heard himself yelling out, wordless grunts and cries that ripped their way from his throat without effort.

The General hooked his leg over Tobin's and rolled, ending up on top of him. The hand holding the gun was pinned beneath Tobin, and though the other man struggled to pull it free, he couldn't. Tobin grinned, feeling his lips pull back from his teeth in something fearsome.

"Your lady is a real nice piece of ass," whispered the General in Tobin's ear. "A real good lay."

The insult gave him strength. Tobin bucked, tossing the man off him. He rolled quickly, shoving his knee into the other man's ribs and slamming his wrist to the ground. Still the General gripped the weapon, refusing to let go even as Tobin began hammering his fingers. The General still hadn't pulled the trigger.

The gun was empty, but Tobin didn't trust the guy not to hit him with the butt. The General used his free hand to gather a handful of Tobin's shirt and pull him to the side. The men rolled, grappling, along the floor.

Tobin still had no idea what he was doing, only that he wanted to kill the man. Smash in his face. Batter him senseless. Hurt him for hurting Elanna.

With a mighty heave, the General shoved Tobin off him and managed to get to his feet. He aimed the gun almost casually, then let it hang from one finger. With satisfaction Tobin saw the stream of blood coming from the other man's nose. He'd made that happen.

"Not bad for a pussy," said the General. He wasn't even out of breath. To Tobin's shock, he put the gun to his own head. "But I don't have all night to wait for you to finish the job."

"It's not loaded."

The man looked startled and then admiring. "Maybe you do have balls, after all."

"Just let her go," Tobin said. "And we'll leave. We'll tell you where we found the stuff, and we'll go."

"The stuff?" For a minute it looked like the General didn't know what Tobin was talking about. "Oh, yeah. Frankly, champ, I don't give a fuck about that."

He slipped his finger onto the trigger. He aged suddenly, becoming old before Tobin's eyes. He swallowed heavily.

"It's not loaded," Tobin repeated.

Elanna began to stir, lifting her head. "Toby?"

The General's gaze flicked to her. "How sweet."

"You," Tobin said fiercely, "don't even look at her. You've done enough!"

"Boo fucking hoo," said the General. "What love can do."

He pulled the trigger. The roar of the gun filled the tiny room, thundering in Tobin's ears. Elanna cried out, her mouth opening but her scream lost in the echoes from the shot. The General's head disintegrated into a spray of bone and blood, and his body sprawled to the ground.

The gun wasn't empty. Ice coated Tobin's stomach, making him shake. He could have shot the man. The man could have shot him. But instead the soldier had shot himself, and why? Tobin didn't know. He also discovered he didn't care. He'd take his luck how it came.

"Toby?"

He heard crying and turned to comfort her before he realized that although her face was dirty and streaked with blood and sweat, her eyes were dry. But still he heard the wailing. Tobin looked to the floor, and saw the basket there.

"The baby," Elanna whispered. "Untie me, please, Tobin."

He did, fumbling with the straps in his eagerness to set her free. As he unbuckled the last one, Elanna fell forward into his arms. He caught her gratefully, rocking with her on the dirty floor. She clutched at him, pushing her face into the side of his neck and squeezing him hard enough to hurt.

He didn't care. She could claw him to shreds and that would be all right, as long as she was safe. She gave him one last squeeze and pushed herself away. She went to the basket and knelt there, reaching inside to pull out the bundle.

The infant had wriggled free of its blankets, and Elanna wrapped it again. She sang as she comforted the child, a tune without words. She rocked the baby against her chest, letting it root against her breast and latch on, tenderly touching the baby's head as it quieted.

She looked up at Tobin. "They were going to kill it."

He watched her with the child, watched her mothering it. She looked right with a baby in her arms. She winced as the child sucked, holding her stomach with one hand.

He was at her side instantly. "Are you all right? Did that bastard hurt you?"

She smiled and shook her head. "It's not from him. It's the baby's sucking. It's making my uterus contract. It hurts, but it's normal."

She must have seen the confusion on his face, because she smiled at him and reached out to touch his cheek. "The mother died. They wanted to kill the baby."

He thought of the child she'd lost. "I'd say he has a mother now."

Her face crumpled as she rubbed the top of the baby's head. "Everything happens for a reason. Maybe this is why I lost my baby. So I could care for this one."

He wasn't sure he believed that, but if it made her feel better than he'd agree. He realized that although the room's red lights made it almost unbearably hot, she was shivering. The baby had stopped its suckling, apparently satisfied for now.

"We need to find you some clothes," Tobin said. "Get you out of here. Both of you. Before --"

He didn't have time to finish. The door flew open, and a wild-eyed Dallas leaped into the room. "You have to go! Kodak's coming!"

She tripped over the General's body, skidding in the blood and brains, and fell to one knee. For one second she was so focused on Tobin and Elanna that she didn't notice the man on the floor. She looked again, though, her mouth working in disgust as she backed away from the corpse. She scrubbed her hands against her shirt, shaking her head.

"No, no, no, no, no…." the litany went on. She wasn't screaming, wasn't crying.

"Dallas!" Tobin said sharply. He got up and went to the girl, forcibly turning her away from the gruesome sight. "Calm down! You have to show us how to get out of her!"

She stared at him with horrified eyes. "The General's dead! You killed him!"

"He killed himself," Tobin said harshly, then softened. She was just a girl, not much more than a child, really. "He shot himself in the head with the gun, Dallas."

"But…why?" The girl asked. "Suicide is only for when you're captured, to prevent the enemy using torture to get their information..." She paused. "Were you torturing him?"

"No," Tobin said patiently, wishing he could help her work through this. He didn't understand the Gappers, but he knew the General had some hold over them.

"Then why?" Dallas asked again, voice breaking. "You mean he just…left us? He left us?"

"Yes," Tobin said firmly, holding onto the idea, though he had no idea what she meant. "He left you. Abandoned you. You don't have to be loyal to him any more."

"He left us," she repeated slowly, voice shaking. She looked up at Tobin with wet eyes that were no longer so horrified. "He said he'd never do that. Not like our moms and dads. He said he'd never leave us, and he did! He did!"

"He did," Tobin said, holding her by the shoulders. "And now we need your help, Dallas."

"My name is Sophie," the girl said. She threw one more swift glance at the body on the floor. "And I'll help you."

KODAK PACED the floor of her quarters, fuming. He'd sent her away, the old bastard. Away, when she could have been torturing that bitch Elanna!

She stopped, catching sight of herself in the cracked mirror that hung on the wall. Her hair was a straggly mess, and dirt painted both her cheeks. She reached up to touch her face, wishing the light were better and then grateful that it wasn't. She didn't want to see.

No wonder he'd sent her away, she thought, running her hands over her body, checking it over. She was sloppy. Dirty. Not like Lansing, who's always taken the time and effort to bathe regularly, even when it meant using icy, frigid water. Lansing was perfect, Kodak thought with more than a touch of malice. But now, Lansing was dead, and Kodak would make sure she'd be the General's favorite again. Like she used to be, before Lansing started growing tits and flaunting her tight and perfect ass in Adam's face.

"I'm glad she's dead," Kodak said aloud, spitefully. "Her and the brat."

She'd never get pregnant again, Kodak thought and patted her flat stomach. She'd never let something grow inside her, sucking her energy, making her bloated and unable to perform as a good soldier. And if something did catch inside her, she'd rip it out before it could get hold.

Kodak heard a single shot from the direction of the interrogation room, and froze. Something was not right. The General didn't allow weapons in the room, preferring to use more intimate methods in his questioning. A gun could fall into the wrong hands. The wrong people could get hurt.

Kodak left her room and headed for the interrogation chamber. She'd risk his anger at disobeying his orders. She'd risk his fury at her assumption that he might need her help. She just wanted to make sure nothing had gone wrong.

The door stood open, which was very wrong. When she stepped inside, things got worse. Even though he was face down and covered in blood and other matter, Kodak recognized him.

Stunned, she stood there without moving. He was dead? He couldn't be dead. Not Adam. Not their leader, the man who'd made her a woman and a soldier.

But he was dead. She nudged him with her foot and his only movement was from her pushing. Nobody could survive a massive head wound like that.

Reality hit her, and Kodak dropped to her knees beside the man who'd given her her first gun and her first orgasm on the same day. Her vision blurred and she batted at her face, terrified. What was wrong with her eyes? Chemical warfare? What had happened?

It wasn't until the hot tears welled from her eyes and slipped down her cheeks that she realized she was crying.

. . .

ELANNA QUICKLY PULLED on the clothes Sophie had brought her. Nothing quite fit, of course, but she had no time to be choosy. Sophie'd even managed to find her some thick rags to help catch the final remnants of blood.

Wrapping her fingers in bandages hurt, but Tobin helped her and they managed a decent job in a short time. The baby boy was sleeping again, his color waxen but his breathing even. Elanna felt a tug of worry about the baby's welfare, but she'd done all she could. Either her milk would come in or it wouldn't. Either they'd get out of here alive, or they wouldn't. It was out of her hands. All she could do was try.

The girl had aged in the past twenty minutes, Elanna thought sadly as she watched Sophie burrow in a box of clothing to find some things for the baby. She wasn't a child any more. Sophie pulled out a thick wad of handkerchiefs, all in the same green and brown splattered pattern that was so common here.

"Will these work?"

"They'll be fine," Elanna said, taking them. She smiled at the girl, who hesitantly smiled back. "Thank you, Sophie."

Tobin paced, looking up and down the rows of tall shelves constantly. "We need to go. Can you help us find a back way out?"

The girl nodded, putting the box back onto the shelf with the automatic movements of someone who's been conditioned to do an action without thinking about it. "Most everyone's still asleep. Some of the others are taking care of Lansing…of Amy. But most are sleeping. Except Kodak, she's --"

A shriek rent the air, muffled through the thick walls. It came again, then again, a furious, frenzied wailing that made Elanna's stomach turn. The baby in her arms startled awake, flinging its tiny arms apart and arching its back. It began to cry, but breathlessly, as though it had little energy.

"We need to go *now*!" Tobin said. "Before whatever the hell that is gets closer."

Sophie shuddered. "It sounds like Kodak."

"We need to go, Sophie," Elanna said gently.

She rocked the baby, soothing it. Its makeshift diapers were wet and the t-shirt she'd pulled over its tiny head nearly swallowed it up, but they didn't have time for better dressing. She bent to tuck the baby into the backpack Sophie'd pulled from one of the boxes. It wriggled for a moment, screwing up its little face, but when she tucked some more soft t-shirts around it, the baby quieted and stared at her. It had light eyes. Elanna kissed the top of its sweet baby head. She helped Tobin slip the straps over his shoulders. He'd carry the infant because he was stronger, and so that she could get to it quickly if she needed to.

"We go out the back," Sophie said. "There's a door back here that I don't think anyone else knows about. I only know about it because they send me in here all the time to look for stuff. I know it's just to get me out of the way because I'm a bad soldier."

The girl's voice broke a little but she shook it off. She looked up at Elanna and gave her a wobbly smile. "I suck as a soldier. I'm a fucking horrible soldier."

Elanna pulled the girl into her arms and hugged her tightly. "Maybe you're a bad soldier, Sophie Dallas, but you're a very good girl."

The three of them froze as they heard pounding footsteps from the corridor outside. The frenzied shrieking had stopped, replaced by the sound of many voices yelling. Doors slammed.

Sophie led them through the maze of dusty, sagging shelves. The thin light from the lanterns didn't reach back here, but she led them confidently. The aisles were wide and free of debris, so they had no fear of tripping. Within moments they'd reached a small door set so inconspicuously into the wall that Elanna had to strain to see it.

"Here," Sophie said. "I used to use this to sneak out of training."

She pushed open the door and they stepped out into the night. Not night for so much longer, Elanna noted, seeing the first pink touches of light in the sky. The sun would be up soon.

The night was not silent. Tobin pulled them back against the wall as several doors slammed and a group of Gappers ran across the yard. They moved with purpose, already dressed in their uniforms.

"They're dressed for drill," Sophie said, puzzeled. "But it's not drill day."

Her confusion cleared in a moment. Kodak's voice, strained but still recognizable, rang through the yard.

"Move, you cunts! I want you ready to fly before the sunrise! I want to slaughter those Plain fucks in their beds! We'll find those strangers, and I want to pull them apart piece by motherfucking piece with my teeth, goddammit! They killed the General, those fucking dicklickers, and I want them *dead*!"

"No," Elanna breathed. She turned to Tobin. "Toby, she found the General. She's going after our friends!"

"We have to get there first," Tobin said grimly, watching the flurry of activity. "We have to warn them. We have to get them to fight."

Chapter 49

Kodak had to physically restrain herself to keep from leaping over the hood of the truck and strangling that dumb fuck Wilson. The other girl fiddled with the electrical line, trying to get the truck to fire up, but she was taking too damn long. Kodak snapped her fingers rapidly, first one hand and then the other, and rocked on the balls of her feet. Finally she couldn't stand it any more.

"What the fuck is wrong with it?" She pushed Wilson aside to stare into the guts of the machine.

"It's old," Wilson said flatly. Her eyes were dry but haunted. She'd been in the room with Lansing until she died. Wilson jerked her hand toward the row of dark garages. "Like the rest of them. I might not be able to get it started."

Kodak didn't lose her temper. Well, not much. "You get it started," she said and fixed Wilson with a look that made her step back. "Or I fuck you up. Bad. Worse than the General ever did."

Kodak didn't give a flying fuck about how the rest of them grumbled. She was in charge now, because she was the best. The strongest and the best, and she'd take over where the General had left off. But better, she thought. He'd gotten sloppy lately, even lazy.

"A new order," she said aloud, just to hear the words. "A new fucking order!"

"Sir!"

"Yes, Thomas, go ahead."

"We only have three working weapons, Sir!"

Kodak sighed, reigning in the desire to slap Thomas to the dirt and make her eat it, just because she didn't like the way she looked today. Instead, she forced a smile to her face, noticing that the other girl recoiled from the expression as though she'd bared her teeth to bite instead of grin. Good. That was just fine. She didn't need friends, she needed soldiers.

"What's wrong with the others?" She meant the ones that had been working for the past few months, not the ones that had been sent to the junk pile already.

"Sir, they're just jammed up."

"Clean them!" Kodak barked, turning back to the truck to talk to Wilson. Thomas, however, didn't leave. She stood there, shifting stupidly from foot to foot with an embarrassed, shifty look on her face that made Kodak's blood boil. "What? What's fucking wrong with you? Didn't you hear me?"

"Sir, they're clean."

"Fuck!" Kodak screamed, wishing there were something else she could say. Something stronger. Fuck just didn't do it for her anymore. "Jesus motherlicking humped up dicksucker!"

Thomas winced against the onslaught of obscenity but stood her ground. "They're jammed up, Sir. I'm sorry."

"Sorry!" Kodak yelled. "Sorry won't buy a twat rag to wipe your sorry cunt with! Sorry doesn't do diddlyfuck for me! You go clean those fathersucking weapons and get them working or else I'll wipe my ass with your face!"

And still Thomas didn't flee before her. "Sir, I beg your pardon Sir, but we've cleaned them all. And even if we got them working again, we don't have enough ammo --"

For one horrid moment Kodak thought she might have burst a vein in her head. Her eyes actually pulsed in time with her heartbeat, throbbing, while red bursts clouded her vision. She stumbled forward, leaning against the truck.

"Sir! Are you all right?" That was Wilson, putting her hand on Kodak's shoulder.

"Wilson," Kodak gritted out, "if you ever fucking touch me again without permission I'll cut your hand off and make you eat it."

"Yes, Sir!"

She shook her head until she could see again, and straightened. She didn't miss the look Thomas and Wilson exchanged, but she'd deal with that later. Right now she just wanted to get this bitchly buttreaming mission into gear. She wanted blood.

"Find Dallas," Kodak said. "She knows where all that shit is. Then load the weapons, get this fucking truck running and let's load it up, for Christ's sake!"

Thomas snapped off a salute that would have made the General choke, but Kodak let it go. The other girl ran back toward the barracks. There'd be time to whip these pansies back into shape, after they slaughtered those fucks in town. After she fucked up that pussy Tobin and made his bitch watch.

"Get back to work, Wilson!"

"Yes, Sir," Wilson said without enthusiasm.

"You don't even care, do you," Kodak stated. She watched Wilson's face carefully. "Why don't you care, Wilson?"

"I care, Sir," Wilson said, turning back to the truck.

"No, you don't," Kodak said. "They killed the General, Wilson. Doesn't that make you mad?"

Wilson turned, her fingertips dark with smoke and soil from the stubborn engine. "No, Kodak. It doesn't."

Kodak couldn't believe what she heard. "They killed him, Wilson. Blew his head to bits with his own gun! And that doesn't piss you off?"

Wilson shook her head silently. Then she bent back to work under the hood, twisting the scraps and strands of wire that connected the battery packs to the starter cables. One fell, slipping through her fingers and getting lost.

"Well, that about fucks that up," she said.

Kodak was still in shock over Wilson's total lack of anger. "What, you're done? You can't do any more?"

"What do you want me to do?" Wilson flared. "I've got shit to work with! All this shit is falling apart, Kodak! It's all I can do to keep any of it together, much less operating!"

Kodak reached out and grabbed the other girl's throat. "Fix it, Wilson, or I swear on the General's name I will fuck you up. I will fucking kill you."

She let Wilson slide from her grip. The other girl fell heavily against the truck, crying out in pain as she cracked her head. Kodak spit on the ground beside her. Wilson got to her feet and started working with the wires again.

Fear, Kodak thought with satisfaction, was a wonderful motivator.

Chapter 50

"Can you run six miles?" Tobin asked Elanna. "Or more?"

She didn't even know if she could walk that far, but she nodded anyway. She'd try. "Do you think we can get there before them?"

Sophie paused to look back at them. "If we go through the fields and the woods, and if we go fast. We might be able to get there before they do."

The girl grinned. "I dumped the ammo into the dry rations boxes. They'll never look there. At least they won't have a lot of bullets."

Sophie had led them around the back of the building and through a maze of rotting vehicles. Now the four of them had reached the open land beyond the central compound. Elanna looked nervously at the sky.

"Do you think they'll see us?"

Sophie stopped again, looking down at her clothes. She pointed to Elanna's and Tobin's, both in the same brown and green splattered pattern. "Not in these."

Elanna wanted to hug the girl again, but they didn't have time. Instead, she just followed behind Tobin. The baby's head peeped out of the backpack, but she'd tucked him in firmly. He didn't wobble around. Thankfully, he was asleep. The constant rhythm of Tobin's stride must be soothing him.

A gust of breeze brought the sound of curses to them. Sophie looked back again, the wind whipping her fair hair about her thin face. "Kodak. Yelling at Wilson. The truck won't start."

Elanna hadn't heard more than muffled shouting, and she was stunned that Sophie'd been able to pick out what they were saying. "That's good though, isn't it?"

"It's good for now, but Kodak won't settle for that," Sophie said, starting forward again. "She wants the truck because it's faster than the tank. She wants to get there fast. She'll make Wilson fix it, or she'll fuck her up."

Tobin looked up at the pink blush of the rising sun. He shifted the straps on his shoulders. "It's all we have. We just have to hope that it's enough."

They really didn't run, but walked at a pace that soon had Elanna fighting for breath. Her legs ached along with her belly, which still needed recovery from the trauma of losing her baby. Had that only been four days ago? She'd lived an eternity since then. The infant on Tobin's back opened his eyes for a moment and let them slip closed again.

She was worried about the child. He was sleeping so much, even for a newborn. And so tiny! She'd never born a baby that small, not even her first. Elanna kept her eyes on the sweet fuzzy head, concentrating on the baby so she didn't have to think about the pains in her feet and legs and stomach.

Sophie led them slipping through the trees and brush with practiced ease. The girl moved silently, seeking just the right places to put her feet and the right bushes to move aside. Tobin and Elanna weren't so quiet.

None of them spoke. Walking took all their effort, especially at the pace Sophie set. Elanna was determined not to ask for a break, though her throat felt like sand. The sun rose higher overhead, painting the sky with gold now. They'd been walking forever and not long enough.

"Halfway there," Sophie said suddenly. Her words after the

silence were shockingly loud. A bird, startled, flew from the bush in front of her, and Elanna fought back a scream.

Tobin turned to look at her, and the concern in his eyes made her want to cry. He saw she was fine and smiled at her, though it didn't reach his eyes. He looked tired, the dark scruff of his beard standing out against his unusually pale cheeks. And still they walked.

At last they reached a place Elanna recognized. The stream they'd jumped in the car, the one Maranian had fallen in. They were close now, she thought with relief. She stumbled to the water, kneeling in front of it to take huge gulps of the clear cold fluid.

Sophie did the same, though she did that silently and without splashing, too. Tobin slipped the pack from his back before he, too, knelt, and Elanna stopped seeking satisfaction for her own thirst long enough to check the child.

His eyes were open, and he started to cry. Alarmed, Elanna pressed her fingers to the boy's tongue. Dry. No tears, though he wailed and flailed his tiny fists.

"The baby's getting dehydrated," she said. "I have to nurse him. Try to give him some fluid, something, or he will die."

Tobin looked back the way they'd come. He didn't tell her they didn't have much time. He just nodded and helped her pull the baby from its swaddling.

Elanna put the baby to her breast, a motion so familiar she didn't even need to think of it. The infant rooted listlessly, his dry lips scrabbling against her nipple. He latched on, sucked for a moment and then began to cry weakly.

"Come on, sweetheart," Elanna cooed. She willed calmness upon herself. Nursing didn't work if the mother or the child were upset and tense. She took some deep breaths, though every moment that passed screamed that the Gappers were closing in. "Come, sweet baby. See what mama has for you."

She didn't realize she'd called herself mama until she saw Tobin's face contort. He looked away, bending back to the stream and drinking. To hide his reaction, she thought. And what it was, she didn't know.

"There," she said, as the baby tried again. This time he sucked more vigorously, beating his little hands against her until she pressed them between her fingers. "Drink, baby. You need to drink."

It was too hard to know if anything was letting down. Too early for the sharp tingling that would signify she was producing full milk. The baby tried, though, valiantly.

"Water?" Sophie asked shyly. She held out a small metal collapsible cup. "For the baby?"

It might work. Elanna dipped her fingers in the cup and wet the infant's lips with them. He sucked at her fingers eagerly, and protested when she pulled them away. She dipped again and again, letting the baby get as much of the fluid as he could, then putting him back to the breast to suckle again.

Finally he fell asleep again, tiny fingers curled around hers. She slipped one finger into the corner of his mouth to break the suction, and slipped his mouth from her nipple. It didn't take long to bundle him back up and slip him in the backpack again.

"I'm ready," she said.

Crossing the stream took no time at all, and then they were on the move again. Racing, Elanna thought, struggling to keep up with Sophie and Tobin. At least they hadn't heard a truck coming. They were still ahead.

Despite the early hour, when they finally reached the Stolzfus barn they found Enoch inside with his brother-in-law, Abe. Both men looked startled to see them, and Elanna realized that dressed as they were, the men thought they were Gappers. Then Enoch recognized Tobin and strode to meet him.

"Tobin Vinter!"

"Enoch," Tobin greeted. He slung the backpack from his shoulders and handed it to Elanna. "We don't have much time. The Gappers are coming."

Sophie hung back behind Elanna. Enoch saw her and his eyes flickered recognition, but he didn't say anything to her. Elanna put her arm around the girl's thin shoulders, offering her comfort.

"Gappers? Here coming?" Enoch asked. He exchanged a look with Abe. "Why?"

"To kill you, and us," Tobin said grimly. "We…we had a little trouble up there. Kodak wants war. You have to get ready to fight. If you don't fight them, they'll kill you all. She's coming, and she's mad. She's crazy. And she wants blood."

Abe, an older man whose beard had more gray than black, cleared his throat. "We about fighting know nothing. We weapons have none."

"You have lots of weapons," Sophie spoke up, then ducked behind Elanna again. The girl took a deep breath and stepped forward. "You have those."

She pointed to the rows of farming implements. "And those." To the bins filled with carefully salvaged nails and screws. "And you have fire, don't you?"

"It will work not," came a familiar voice from the barn's doorway. Samuel shuffled through it. "Tobin Vinter. Return I knew you would, and with trouble bring."

"It will have to work," Tobin said, ignoring the rest of the old man's comment.

"It can't," Samuel said stubbornly. "For even if away we send them, back again they will come."

Elanna handed Sophie the backpack and baby. The girl took the burden gingerly, then more firmly when the baby didn't protest. Sophie looked at the baby with something like awe.

"Unless kill them all we do," Enoch said.

Everyone turned to look at him. Elanna's heart broke at the fury in Enoch's eyes. It was because of her and Tobin he'd been pushed this far, she thought. Their fault. Sophie crowded against her, shivering, and Elanna wondered what she thought. They talked of killing the girls and young women who were her family as casually as though they spoke of swatting flies. How must she feel?

"There must be another way," Elanna said.

Tobin glanced at Sophie, and Elanna saw her thoughts reflected in his eyes. "I hope so."

Sophie shook her head. "Not with Kodak in charge. She's wanted to come down here and kick ass for years."

"What about the others?" Tobin asked. "Will they follow her?"

Sophie looked at him blankly. "Well, yeah. It's what we're supposed to do."

"You didn't." Elanna spoke the words gently. Sophie continued to hold the backpack steady while Elanna worked the tiny boy free of his blankets. "You helped us."

Sophie blushed. "You were nice to me. Kodak's never nice to me."

So loyalty was as easy as that, Elanna thought. She opened the baby's diaper and began cleaning him. He fussed a little, waving his feet and fists. Sophie watched with big eyes.

"That's Lansing's baby, huh? The one that grew in her belly?"

Elanna nodded. Enoch and Abe exchanged glances again, this time including Samuel. Elanna wrapped the boy in some spare cloths and held him out to Sophie. "You want to hold him?"

"This baby a Gapper's is?" Samuel asked. "And a boy child, at last?"

Elanna nodded again, avoiding their gaze. She settled the infant in Sophie's arms and showed her how to prop the baby's head. Sophie's smile was precious.

"His mother died in birth," Elanna said. "They…they were going to kill him. He's mine now." Now she looked up, determined. "He's mine."

"And a better life with you he will have," Abe said.

Samuel grunted. "And after him they will come."

"No," Elanna said. "They don't want him. I do."

"Other people's bread tastes better," Samuel said. "They will want that child back."

Sophie raised her face. "They don't want him, just like Elanna said. They hate babies. They hate him for killing Lansing. Nobody there likes babies. They don't love them, or play with them, or hold them at night when they're scared! They don't care if they're too little and they fall behind in drill and scrape their knees! They call them mistakes…"

The girl was sobbing. In a few sentences she'd managed to paint a picture of how life had been for her, growing up. Elanna saw that the men had the good grace to look ashamed.

"Shh," Elanna soothed. "It's all right, Sophie. You're with us now."

"The women and children we have to make safe," Samuel said roughly. "Quickly. Before they come."

Tears glistened in the old man's eyes, but whether he was crying for poor abused Sophie or for the terror that was coming, she didn't know. She bent back to the crying girl in her arms, feeling her tears wet the front of Elanna's shirt. The baby, squeezed between them, miraculously was silent. Elanna held them tightly, loving both children as best she could though they weren't her own.

"Faster than that," Tobin said from the barn's doorway. He turned to look back at them, face bleak. "I hear the trucks. They're almost here."

Chapter 51

They didn't have time to hide the women and the children. They didn't have time even to warn them. Kodak led her soldiers with swift and lethal efficiency. The two trucks hadn't even stopped rolling before the Gappers swung down from them, brandishing their weapons and hollering like demons.

"Line 'em up!" Kodak barked out. "Get them out here and line them up!"

The women left their washing and their scrubbing; the children dropped their toys and left them in the dirt to obey. The men who'd already begun the day's work in the fields began making their way back. They all began to form the lines that must have become so familiar after the years of abuse from the Gappers. They didn't know, Tobin thought with sick horror as he watched from the barn, that this time it would be different.

"We can't let them do it," Elanna whispered. "She's going to slaughter them!"

Tobin restrained her from leaping out through the door. "If we take them by surprise we might have a chance."

Elanna leaned against him, trembling, for only a moment before pulling away. Worry lined her face, and he bent to kiss her quickly.

She clutched at him, hard, and he squeezed her in return. He couldn't shake the feeling that this might be the last time he'd ever have the chance to hold her.

The men huddled, muttering, searching the barn for the weapons Sophie had pointed out. Tobin smiled at Elanna, who returned it, before joining Abe, Enoch and Samuel. The old man shook his head slowly from side to side. Not in refusal, Tobin thought. In shame at what they had to do.

"I'm ready," Sophie said, joining them. She'd relinquished the baby to Elanna, who tucked him back into the backpack.

Surprised, Tobin put his hand on her shoulder. "No, Sophie. We can't ask you to do this."

She scowled, her young face becoming old in an instant. "I can fight better than you. I know what to do."

A sharp cry rose from outside the barn, turning his stomach over. They didn't have time for arguing. He couldn't send this girl, this child, out to fight for them. Not against her own people! But what choice did they have? Sophie was right. She'd been trained. They hadn't.

"This is what we'll do." The girl bent to draw a line in the barn's dirt floor. "Their trucks are here. They'll be lining them up, just like they always do, but then Kodak will give the order. They only have three guns that work. I hid the ammunition so they only have what was already in the weapons."

Tobin's blood turned to ice at Sophie's cold description. "They're going to murder them all. Just like that?"

"Once the shooting starts, some may run," Sophie's voice shook, and he was glad to hear it. It meant she was human. "They'll be chased by the others. The ones who don't have guns will use their knives."

"Adonai help us," Elanna said. The color had drained from her cheeks. "What can we do?"

"We don't have much time." Sophie looked up at Elanna. "I'll take you. I'll tell Kodak I chased you here, and the General wounded Tobin, and we left him to die in the field. When Kodak comes over to us, you," she pointed to the four men, "will jump on her and kill her. Without Kodak, the others may stop. But if they don't, you'll have to fight them. Without a leader they probably won't keep on. Kodak's the only one with a taste for blood."

Sophie blinked, her eyes going blank for a moment. "It's been ten years since any of us has been to war. I think Kodak's the only one who really remembers how."

Enoch held up the large pitchfork. "We will behind you be, child."

"What about him?" Elanna asked, holding up the baby.

"Put him the hay into," Samuel said gruffly. He was rubbing his hands as though they pained him. He took the long metal bar Abe held out to him, and hefted its weight. "The cows out in the field are. He safe will be."

Elanna looked stricken but kissed the sleeping baby and went to the back of the barn to tuck him away there. Tobin grabbed a deadly looking farming tool from the hook on the wall. It was time. Before Kodak had a chance to start her slaughter.

"Just one more thing." Sophie paused, her voice wobbling. She swallowed heavily and lifted her chin. "You might get the others to quit, but not Kodak. Don't stop until she's dead."

THOUGH SOPHIE only reached her shoulder, the girl was strong. Sophie shoved Elanna through the door so hard she went to her knees, shredding the skin. She didn't have to fake her cry of pain.

"The fuck is this?" Kodak said, turning. "Dallas? The fuck you doing here?"

"I brought the prisoner, Sir!" Sophie said, snapping her hand against her head in that gesture they used. She forced Elanna to her feet. "Followed her here from base, Sir!"

Elanna didn't imagine the gleam of pleasure in Kodak's eyes. The older girl actually smiled. The grin made Elanna shudder.

"So you're not a total loss after all," Kodak said. "Bring her here."

Elanna let Sophie push her toward Kodak, her resistance real. "Just let me go, Kodak. Let us all go."

Kodak snorted, leaning in close. "Not a chance, bitch. This is my party, now." Her attention snapped back to Sophie. "Where's the dude?"

"He…he died, Sir. The General shot him, and --"

"Shit." Kodak's face darkened with displeasure. "Lovett!"

"Sir, yes, Sir!"

"Dallas, tell Lovett where to find the douchebag's body. Bring it to me. Just because he's dead doesn't mean I can't fuck him up a little."

She turned back to Elanna. "Don't worry, sweets. I'll let you watch."

Elanna spat in the Gapper's face. Kodak's eyes narrowed, but she didn't pull away in disgust. She didn't even bother to wipe away the glob of spittle clinging to her cheek. Instead, she turned to the rows of people standing silently and obediently, waiting for the Gappers to get what they wanted and leave them alone. Even though she knew Kodak's intent, Elanna reeled with shock when the lead Gapper pointed to the end of the women's line. At a child.

"Begin," Kodak said to one of the Gappers Elanna didn't recognize. She didn't yell. If anything, her voice sounded disinterested and casual.

The soldier looked from Kodak to the child, who now clung to his mother's skirts and looked up at the strangers with wide, frightened eyes. "Sir?"

"Didn't you hear me, numbnuts?" Kodak asked, still in the same light conversational tone. "I said begin. Now. With that ankle biter there."

The child's mother looked alarmed and gathered the boy, just a toddler, into her arms. The men and women began murmuring, looking at each other with concern. This wasn't what they were used to.

The soldier faltered, shaking her head. "Sir, I --"

"Didn't I make the object of this mission clear?" Kodak screamed in the other girl's face. "Weren't you paying attention, Hadley? Or did you have your head up your ass?"

"No, Sir!" Hadley shouted. She looked back at the little boy again, biting her lip "Sir, I can't. He's just a kid."

Kodak pulled a knife the length of her forearm from her side sheath and slit Hadley's throat from ear to ear. Gouts of blood gushed forth, splattering the ground. Hadley fell without a sound. Kodak didn't stop. She reached for the screaming child and pried him out of his mother's arms. She gripped him by the hair and held the knife to his small throat.

"I said, 'begin!'" She yelled to the other soldiers, who looked as stunned and sick as the People. "Or you'll get the same as Hadley!"

The knife was huge, and the child small. His mother began to scream, and the blood and the sound of her terror spurred the soldiers into action.

Nobody had to push Elanna to bring her to her knees this time. Her legs buckled beneath her and she went down hard. Tasting dirt, she spat and spat again, imagining it was blood.

Everything was chaos. She couldn't tell who was screaming and who was running. Elanna struggled up on numb legs, unable scream, or to run. Unable to think of anything but stopping Kodak.

"Sir!" Sophie screamed.

Kodak turned from the slaughter, a hot and gleeful grin on her face. Elanna tried to reach her, wanting to rip out the eyes twinkling so madly with good humor. A body fell on her, nearly knocking her over again. It was one of the Gappers, a long knitting needle protruding from one eye. Elanna begged Ha-Shem for forgiveness at her joy.

"Sir!" Sophie said. "You can see much better from up here, Sir!"

The girl gestured up the short ramp leading to the barn doors. Her eyes met Elanna's over Kodak's shoulder, and Elanna instantly knew what the girl was planning. Sophie smiled, a strained grin that only tweaked the corners of her lips, but Kodak didn't seem to notice. She crossed to Sophie, moving closer to the barn doors.

"Dallas, get your sorry little punk rear down there," Kodak said, but without malice.

Sophie had no time to reply. One of the barn doors flew open, knocking her off the ramp and down to the ground. The men leaped from inside. Tobin fell on Kodak first, taking her to the ground with him and smashing her face with his fist. Enoch, Abe and Samuel watched for a moment, then ran to help their families.

"You!" Kodak screamed through a mouthful of teeth and blood. "Dallas said you were dead!"

"I guess I just got lucky," Tobin said, just before Kodak heaved him off herself with a practiced twist of her hips.

Elanna stepped over the body, meaning to head toward Kodak again. The children, a boy and two little girls, stopped her. Screaming and bloodied, they clung to her legs. Without thinking Elanna scooped them into her arms and ran.

Staggering, she nearly dropped them, but desperation drove her on. With every step she waited for a blow to take her down, but miraculously nobody came after her. She hitched the children higher on her hips and felt the one clinging to her chest wrap its arms around her neck nearly to the point of suffocation. Dangerous red spots began blinking in front of her eyes and her breath wheezed in and out of her lungs, and still she ran on.

She misjudged the porch height and hit the first step with her shin instead of her foot. Elanna fell forward, the children falling from her arms to land on the wooden porch. The one she'd been carrying on her front rolled away, crying, but, Baruch Ha-Shem, she hadn't landed on the girl.

"Up, up!" She cried to them, getting up herself and limping up the second stair. The children ran to her and she gathered them in her arms, stumbling toward the front door. The screen door stuck, refused to open. Elanna yanked it so hard it sagged on its hinges. She and the children fell through the doorway and into the small living room.

She hadn't been in this house before, and didn't know where these babies would be safe. Upstairs? They'd have no way of escape up there. She looked back over her shoulder, expecting to see the Gappers hot in pursuit, but again they'd been blessed. Nobody seemed to notice they were gone.

"Through here." She tugged two of the little ones by the hand and managing to lift the littlest one onto her hip again. She pushed them and herself through the kitchen into a small back bedroom, where she found a large wardrobe. "Inside!"

She put the children into the large cupboard and kissed them all. "No more tears," she said, putting on a smile she didn't feel. "You'll be all right here. I promise. Stay quiet, do you understand?"

The boy, the oldest, nodded. His chubby cheeks were streaked with dirt and tears, but he put his arms protectively around the smaller girls. "Ve vill twiet be."

Elanna's throat closed at the child's bravery. "I know you will, honey. And I'll be back for you soon, okay?"

The children nodded, huddling together. Elanna kissed them all again, fighting back tears she didn't want them to see. With another bright smile she closed the wardrobe door and slipped out toward the front door again.

She paused, looking out to the field beyond, where the fighting continued. She couldn't see who was fighting whom, so much dirt and blood had covered all the men and women both. Her heart lurched as she scanned the battle. There were more children out there. One behind a large rock, face down in the grass. Another two huddled beneath one of the large wagons, only inches away from a Gapper who was beating a man with a stick.

She had to help the children. Without another thought, Elanna ran into the fray.

Chapter 52

Kodak's mouth hurt, but not as much as that bastard would hurt when she was through with him. Already she was on her feet, spitting out the teeth the punk had managed to loosen in her mouth. She advanced on him, laughing at the puny little rake he had.

Tobin swung at her, and she ducked. The force of his swing shifted him off balance, and she used that. Kicking up and out, like the General had taught her, Kodak struck the back of one of Tobin's knees. He went down like a stone, grinding into the dirt.

"Come on," she taunted. "You can do better than that."

He got to his feet with a swiftness that surprised her. Maybe this dude wasn't such a punk, after all. The glitter of fury in his eyes made her falter for just one second.

"Anger can make even the weak strong," she whispered to herself. One of the General's teachings. She looked around at the melee, and for the first time began to wonder if she'd made a mistake.

The people were fighting back. Without their guns, the Gappers had little advantage against men and women fighting to save their children. Kodak cursed as she saw Gourley and Chestnut each raise their weapons and pull triggers that did nothing more than click dryly. The women dropped the guns to the ground as two of the Plain men tackled them. Who had the third gun?

"Not what you expected?" Tobin dropped the useless rake.

Kodak bounced on the balls of her feet, flexing her fists. "I can take you in hand-to-hand, jerkoff. You might be bigger than me, but I can still kick your ass from here to Sunday and back. I did it before, and I'll do it again."

Tobin's face was stone. "I don't think so."

With a roar, she launched herself at him. They came together with a thud that jarred her aching jaw, but Kodak ignored the pain. She had her hands on his throat, squeezing, loving the way his skin pulsed beneath her fingers...

And he threw her off. The bastard got his hands up between hers and tossed her off him like he was taking off a coat! Kodak sat stunned for a minute, feeling the pain begin in her back and ass where she'd hit some rocks. Then she was on her feet again, screaming, letting the fury fuel her strength the way it always did.

She hit him in the chest with her shoulder, bringing him down. They both thudded against the edge of the ramp leading to the barn. Tobin shouted as she landed on top of him, grinding her fingers into the tender spot just above his collarbone. His hands came up and found her hair, which had come down from its restraining ties. He pulled it, tugging her head back along with it, and she was forced to let go long enough to try and stop him.

He didn't let go. Her hair was coming out by the fucking roots. Blinking away tears of agony, Kodak brought up her knee. Bingo! She hit the bastard right in the crotch. The move guaranteed to drop a man, she thought, waiting for the pain in her head to stop as he fell away.

Tobin didn't let go. His breath whooshed out of him in a faltering gush, but he still held on.

"Try again," he wheezed.

Kodak's fury rose a notch, something she wouldn't have thought possible. The pain from her tortured hair was making her crazy. She couldn't think. She'd never dealt with someone who wouldn't quit. Someone like her.

They'd rolled down the ramp, grappling. Now he was on top of her, knees digging into her armpits. His weight on her chest was pressing the breath from her. Her head was on fire. She thought he was going to tear her scalp right off her head.

With a shot more luck than skill, Kodak stopped trying to free her hair and clocked Tobin on the side of the neck with one hand. With a grunt, he let go of her hair. Gagging, he moved just enough to let her wriggle free.

Now they faced each other, smeared with dirt and sweat. She wasn't grinning anymore. Kodak risked a glance over her shoulder to see how her soldiers were doing, but couldn't do more than glimpse the fighting before turning back to face the most dogged enemy she'd ever faced.

"What are you waiting for?" Tobin turned his head to the side and spat blood.

Kodak didn't throw herself at him this time. Something was happening to her, something bad. Her scalp and jaw ached fiercely, and so did the small of her back from their most recent fall to the ground. She couldn't seem to make herself move. Something she'd never felt before paralyzed her limbs. With disgust, she realized it was fear.

Kodak spotted Dallas still standing on the ramp. Dallas had a gun, the third gun. Maybe the only one that still worked.

"Dallas!" She yelled. "Shoot the fucker!"

Dallas shook her head, refusing. Kodak was overjoyed to find that her anger came back in an instant, erasing the fear. Tobin stood between her and Dallas, but she'd take care of him and then teach the little bitch a lesson.

Chapter 53

Tobin saw Kodak's attention shift from him to Dallas, so he wasn't prepared for Kodak's full-body attack. This time she hit him with the top of her head, connecting squarely under his chin. They both went down again, but instead of hanging onto him, Kodak scrambled to her feet and ran over him.

Her foot caught him in the throat, and suddenly he couldn't breathe. Choking, Tobin swung out his hands, trying blindly to catch her. He missed. She was over him and onto Sophie.

Tobin rolled over and got to his knees, pushing himself up from the ground while fighting for breath. Kodak held Sophie up against the closed barn door by the throat, using her knee between the younger girls legs to prop her up.

"When I give an order, you will obey it!" Kodak screamed to Sophie. With each word she banged the girl's head against the wood.

Sophie's legs kicked futilely. Her face was slowly turning red as Kodak throttled her. Tobin put his foot on the ramp to get to her, and slipped.

"No," Sophie managed to say. "Not this time, Mama."

Kodak banged Sophie against the door again. "I told you not to call me that! Never call me that!"

"You're…hurting me…." Sophie muttered. Her eyes began to roll back, showing the whites.

"You're damn right I'm hurting you!" Kodak shrieked. She noticed Sophie fading and shook her until the girl opened her eyes again. "You're nothing but a goddamn mistake, Dallas! Nothing but the worst fucking mistake I ever made in my life! I should have used a coat hanger to rip you out of me!"

Tobin had his hands on Kodak's shoulders when the shot rang out from Sophie's gun. The bullet tore through Kodak's back and whizzed past his ear, close enough to burn. Kodak fell against him, but he managed to keep his feet. He let her drop to the ramp, where she fell on her back. Her eyes were wide and staring, and her hands clutched at the air.

Sophie slid to the ramp, too, leaving a thin trail of blood on the door behind her. Ignoring Kodak, Tobin stumbled to the girl and gathered her into his arms.

He cried her name, holding her against him. The trembling he thought was sobs was instead a series of small convulsions. He looked frantically for the source, and found it in the large nail sticking out from the door. Kodak had pounded Sophie's head against it. The girl was dying.

"No, oh no," Tobin whispered, rocking Sophie in his arms.

"She was…my mother…." Sophie spluttered in a moment of coherence. Her red-rimmed eyes blinked up at him. "And the General…."

"Shh," Tobin said. "Just rest, Sophie. You don't have to talk."

"You were nice to me," she said. "I…."

And then she was done. Her body shook a few more times. Her eyes didn't close, but the life went out of them. Uncaring of the battle still going on behind them, Tobin pressed his face against the young girl's cheek, and he wept.

Chapter 54

Rain might come and wash the fields clean of blood, but the memory would never go away. The Plain People had done what was against their nature to do: they'd fought. But had they really won? Elanna closed her eyes against the sight of the Gapper bodies strewn like broken dolls across the grass. There could be no winners in a war like this.

"Shhh, hush now," she soothed the children who clutched at her. Some cried while others bore the shock with stony faces and dry eyes. They were the ones who would dream of this and remember it, Elanna thought, and her heart broke for the innocence lost today.

None of the people had escaped injury. Many had died. Most still wandered among the bodies, searching for their loved ones. Husbands knelt beside their wives, weeping, and mothers called frantically for their children.

"Come along, sweethearts." Elanna stood. She could never take away the tragedy that she and Tobin had brought these people, but she could give them back something they'd thought they'd lost: their children.

She helped the smallest children link hands and the older children to lift up the ones who couldn't walk. The two infants she carried tucked against her chest. She'd managed to shield twelve in all, plucking them from the places in which they'd sought shelter. She could only pray that the others were safe.

They left through the house's front door, stepping onto the wooden front porch in almost total silence. Elanna found she couldn't speak even to cry out to the women and men walking in the battlefield. So she walked with the children, one small step at a time, toward them.

"Sarah!" Cried the first young mother as she caught sight of them. She picked up her skirts and ran, stumbling on the uneven ground.

Elanna couldn't see, couldn't breathe at the sight of the young mother sweeping her daughter into her arms. The woman wept and laughed, rocking the little girl back and forth. She pulled away to look at her face, stroking the girl's hair and then clutching her close again.

"Thank God, thank God," the woman whispered over and over.

One by one, the mothers and the fathers saw that Elanna had brought the children. A man she recognized as Rachel's brother Levi rose from where he'd been kneeling by the body of his wife, and stepped forward hesitantly to meet her. Beneath his beard Levi's face was gray with weariness and shock, and his hands trembled as he reached out for one of the infants Elanna held. She surrendered the baby to him gratefully.

Levi Lapp held the child in his arms and sank to his knees as though his legs were unable to hold him up. The baby, a tiny girl only a few months old, began to wail. He held the child as though he'd never seen her before, his face blank with grief. His hands began to tremble so badly Elanna thought he might drop his daughter to the ground, but instead he brought the baby to his chest and mingled his tears with hers.

One by one Elanna relinquished the children, weeping with the parents as they were reunited with what they'd been certain they'd lost. Only when she'd handed over the last child did she turn toward the barn. She couldn't move forward. She couldn't move her legs.

All around her the sounds of grief and joy became nothing but background noise. Her heart thudded in her ears and still she could not move. She had saved the babies. All but one.

She couldn't, wouldn't think about Tobin. She couldn't think of him dead. He had to be alive. He had to be alive. He had to be alive…

In a daze she at last forced her legs to move, step by solid step toward the barn. The doors hung open. She went up the short ramp, stepping over Kodak's body with nothing more than a glance. Then she was inside, blinking against the dimness.

When her vision cleared, she saw him. He wasn't moving. Tobin sat slumped along the back wall, hunched over next to the straw where she'd hid the baby boy.

The light went out of her life. In that instant Elanna didn't know if she were alive or dead, only that she ceased to feel. Her limbs were stone, the only thing that kept her pinned to the earth so that she didn't fly away, hurtling into the sky and the stars and the great abyss of night.

She managed a step forward, and then another, but the wooden floor came up to meet her and she found herself on her hands and knees. Splinters gouged her hands and brought thin streamers of blood to her flesh, but she didn't feel them. Her hair hung in her face, and she pushed it away. Crawling. And then not even crawling anymore, unable to move, unable to do anything but lay on the floor and wait to die.

"Elanna?"

"Tobin?"

She didn't know how they reached each other but within moments she was in his arms. Was she crying? Was he? She didn't know, couldn't tell, didn't care. He was alive. He was here. He hadn't left her.

"Baruch Ha-Shem," she whispered, echoing the young mother's prayer. "Thank God, thank God."

A thin wail rose from the hay. The infant. Alive. Weakness assailed her and she had to sit. Tobin held her as she sank down next to the backpack, where the squirming child still lay. She lifted the baby from the pack, smelling its sweet baby smell, and held it close against her.

"I thought for sure…." She trailed off, not wanting to even put words to the thoughts that had been so awful.

"I know," Tobin said. He held her shoulders, looking down with her at the baby in her arms. "But Elanna, there is something I have to tell you."

He told her about Sophie Dallas, and how she'd died. They held each other as they cried, rocking the infant between them. And eventually, they got up from the barn and went out to face what had happened.

Chapter 55

"Just go," Samuel told them later, his face aged by dozens of years instead of hours.

So they went. They couldn't stay. They weren't welcome, and Tobin didn't blame the Plain People for wanting them gone. Though they hadn't intended it, he and Elanna had brought violence and change. Worse, they'd brought death.

With nothing more than some food and clothes, Tobin, Elanna and the baby left the small town that would reek of bloodshed and hatred for a long time. They put their feet to the road and walked, without speaking. There didn't seem much to say.

The town fell away behind them as they walked, disappearing into the past like the memories never would. The road was firm and without rocks that might make them stumble. And for that, at least, Tobin was grateful.

"I'm going to call him Eitan," Elanna said at last. She nursed the baby as she walked, and Tobin still marveled at how easy she was with the child. "It means strong. He'll have to be strong."

He heard the catch in her voice and knew she was crying. Tobin stopped to take her by the shoulders pull her close. Eitan whimpered once and then was silent.

"I love you," Tobin said.

"I know you do," Elanna said. "And I love you, Tobin."

They stood together for a long time, saying nothing. There weren't words to help what they'd gone through go away. More than that, they didn't have to speak. It was enough just to feel her next to him, to hear her breathe. Some time they might talk about what had happened with the Gappers and the Plain people, but for now their silence was enough.

They started walking again, not fast and not slow, not even sure where they were going. They had no map. And for now, it was enough just to move.

"There is a story," Elanna said after some time, "in the Torah. Our holy book. It's one of the first stories, actually, and it tells about the beginning of the world."

She told him the tale quickly, of how Adonai had created the beasts and the plants, and how at last he had created man and woman. About the place they'd lived, called Eden. Tobin had read the story in a book, too, though in her telling it gained more clarity to him than it ever had before.

"It was a perfect place," Elanna said. "A place to start fresh."

She stopped again, to look at him. "Do you think California's the place to start again?"

"An Eden, you mean?"

She nodded. Eitan cooed against her and she brought the baby up to nuzzle its soft head. Tobin reached out to touch the fuzzy hair, still in awe that the child had survived.

He thought about her story, and her question. "I don't know. Do you?"

Elanna bit her lip. "I think so. I hope so."

"I hope so too," Tobin told her, and they started walking again.

He'd left home with little more than what he carried now. Somehow, this felt right. When he'd left Eastport he'd had only the vaguest dream of what he wanted to find. A woman to love. Children. Other people. A place where he could be happy.

He'd found them all but the last one. California, if it still existed, beckoned. He strode through the night, Elanna at his side, thinking of the ocean. Would it look different in California? Tobin thought it must. Brighter, somehow, or more alive. A place to start fresh and new. And so they walked, content in their silence, toward the dream.

Seeking Eden.

***

About the Author

photo credit: Whitney Hart Photography

I was born and then I lived a while. Then I did some stuff and other things. Now, I mostly write books. Some of them use a lot of bad words, but most of the other words are okay.

If you liked this book, please tell everyone you love to buy it. If you hated it, please tell everyone you hate to buy it.

Find me here!

www.meganhart.com

readinbed@gmail.com

facebook.com/READINBED

twitter.com/Megan_Hart

instagram.com/readinbed

bookbub.com/authors/megan-hart

goodreads.com/Megan_Hart

CPSIA information can be obtained
at www.ICGtesting.com
Printed in the USA
BVHW031303010321
601396BV00015B/74

9 781951 868277